UNDER
THIS
FORGETFUL
SKY

UNDER THIS FORGETFUL SKY

LAUREN YERO

Atheneum

NEW YORK LONDON TORONTO
SYDNEY NEW DELHI

atheneum

An imprint of Simon & Schuster Children's Publishing Division • 1230 Avenue of the Americas, New York, New York 10020 • This book is a work of fiction. Any references to historical events, real people, or real places are used fictitiously. Other names, characters, places, and events are products of the author's imagination, and any resemblance to actual events or places or persons, living or dead, is entirely coincidental. • Text © 2023 by Lauren Yero • Maps (pp. vi–vii) by Robert Lazzaretti • Jacket illustration © 2023 by Pablo Hurtado de Mendoza • Jacket design © 2023 by Simon & Schuster, Inc. • All rights reserved, including the right of reproduction in whole or in part in any form. • Atheneum logo is a trademark of Simon & Schuster, Inc. • For information about special discounts for bulk purchases, please contact Simon & Schuster Special Sales at 1-866-506-1949 or business@simonandschuster.com. • The Simon & Schuster Speakers Bureau can bring authors to your live event. For more information or to book an event, contact the Simon & Schuster Speakers Bureau at 1-866-248-3049 or visit our website at www.simonspeakers.com. • The text for this book was set in Utopia Std. • Manufactured in the United States of America • First Edition • 10 9 8 7 6 5 4 3 2 1 • Library of Congress Cataloging-in-Publication Data • Names: Yero, Lauren, author. • Title: Under this forgetful sky / Lauren Yero. • Description: First edition. | New York : Atheneum Books for Young Readers, [2023] | Audience: Ages 14 up | Audience: Grades 10–12. | Summary: When rebels infect his father with a fatal virus, sixteen-year-old Rumi ventures beyond his city's protected walls and meets Paz, who offers to guide him on his search for a cure, but may have an agenda of her own. • Identifiers: LCCN 2022024917 (print) | LCCN 2022024918 (ebook) | ISBN 9781665913799 (hardcover) | ISBN 9781665913812 (ebook) • Subjects: CYAC: Survival—Fiction. | Interpersonal relations—Fiction. | Dystopias—Fiction. | LCGFT: Novels. • Classification: LCC PZ7.1.Y494 Un 2023 (print) | LCC PZ7.1.Y494 (ebook) | DDC [Fic]—dc23 • LC record available at https://lccn.loc.gov/2022024917 • LC ebook record available at https://lccn.loc.gov/2022024918

To my parents,
for everything

DESIERTO DE ATACAMA

PROPERTY
OF THE LIBRARY OF
PARAÍSO

OCÉANO PACIFICO

LA CORDILLERA DE LOS ANDES

Serena
Coquimbo
TRASH HILLS

Las Termas
CANYONLANDS

Río 5

Isla de Lobos

Cachagua

The Wastes
Paraíso

Río Autopista

CHEMFIELDS

St. Iago

MAPUCHE NATION

Talca

N
O   E
S

Global Union of Upper Cities
3rd Quadrant, Sector 1B
Elevations listed at pre-Breach sea level

LOWER CITY

 St. Francis
2,850 m

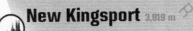 **New Kingsport** 3,819 m

 Cuzco 3,399 m

 New Peace 3,650 m

Brasilia
1,172 m

 Sucre
2,750 m

 Lerma
1,152 m

 St. Iago
1,870 m
Primary industry: **Biotech**

Additional Information:
Lines of Intercity Connection
Threat Level
Evacuation Routes
Attack History

UNDER
THIS
FORGETFUL
SKY

The old ones want these stories to be lies.
The young ones want them to be true . . .

—Gabriela Mistral, "The Storyteller"

Old Woman of Creation, Old Man of Creation!
Young Man of Creation, Young Woman of Creation!
Look down on me and hear my stories.
Look down on me and bless my stories with your
sweet, sweet breathing.
Let me say something true. Let me say something true!

Oh, children. Long ago, when the maiden earth still dressed in her gown of gilded green, there lived two cities: the City of the Sky and the City of the Sea. These cities were full of people and water and ferns, glass and stones, salamanders and crows. Sparkling things and dull, quiet things. Things that birthed and shouted. Things that crumbled and died. Things that moved.

And these two cities, if not always happy, at least were not alone.

But one day the Sky looked down upon the Sea and was afraid—afraid that the Sea would swallow his city and take what was his. So he said to his people: Gather stones and lay them across the horizon. Girdle the orb of the world to keep out the wildness of the Sea! The people of that shining city in the clouds were afraid. Oh, how they were afraid. So they gathered up stones.

Here is where our story begins, dear children. With this fear, our story must always begin . . .

P A Z

When first we met, prisoned together in that cellar room, he was my enemy. He was a smooth-handed boy, a full-belly boy. A boy from Upper City.

Las Oscuras had roughed him plenty. They'd taken his rich-boy clothes and gadgets and tossed him on the bench across from me. His skinny brown chest was tatted and bruised, and his face was swollen. A long drip of spit and blood and tattoo ink dangled from his lip like a slimy spiderweb. He couldn't have been much older than me.

Las Oscuras hadn't beaten me yet—just tied me up in that cellar room and left me to listen while, in the house above, the boy shrieked like a demon cast into the light of God. I wondered when my turn to scream would come.

Las Oscuras.

My city feared their name more than they feared Zabrán or chems or bombs. Insurgents, some called them. Terrorists. Murderers. Their inked-up faces haunted our forests, and their presence hung over our city like a never-lifting fog. Most were too scared to even speak their name. But I wasn't so sure. In the twists of my guts and the holiest corners of my heart, I wondered how

3

it would feel for their badge to burn on my skin—to be part of something big and powerful instead of pushing all alone against the cold, new-moon tides of the world.

Gray light leaked through the floorboards above, and I peered into the cracks to try and catch sight of the tatted guards of Las Oscuras who stood there waiting. But the ropes that bound me made it so I couldn't move without tipping the bench where I sat.

"Hijo de puta," I said into the dark cellar air.

Across from me, the Upper City boy's swollen eyes opened to slits.

"Hello?" he said. "Is someone there . . . ?"

He could scarce see a thing through the dark—couldn't see that I was tied up, same as him. "Shut it, flaco," I said. My voice coiled like a snake. "Shut it, or I'll tat you again. I'll tat your eyes."

The boy flinched. That was all it took. The wobbly bench beneath him pitched sideways, and he fell to the ground. His face rammed into the dirt of the cellar floor.

I laughed. "There you go," I said. "Eat your filthy tears. Taste them, just like you made us taste them. They're bitter, no? Bitter with tiredness and hunger and fear and . . . and . . ." I searched for the words that would break this boy's body, that would mend the gash his people had torn in the world. But there were no words for such things.

"Who are you?" the boy asked.

"My name is Paz," I said, then added, "something you know nothing about."

"I'm Rumi," he said.

I stayed quiet. I didn't want to hear his story. I didn't want him to know mine.

"Paz. That means *peace*, right?"

"It means *peace*."

"Paz, please. Why am I here? Tell me what they want, please . . ."

"You are the worms in my belly, flaco. You are the dirt in my mouth and the boot on my neck. Why should I tell you anything?"

"Please," he said. His face pressed into the floor. "Please . . ." He started to cry and writhe against his bindings, quiet as a snake on fire. And I smiled. This boy's ancestors had built the walls. His kin had told us to eat dirt because they wouldn't give us their bread, to drink the ocean because they'd poisoned the rain. He was a filthy cerdo. A greedy little god. And he deserved to die.

PART I
UPPER CITY

1

R U M I

rubbed my eyes against the brightness of the AutoTram station and ran through the doctor's words again. *This is going to be your year.*

My backpack slumped to the floor between my feet, and I nudged it upright. I straightened my shoulders too. Overhead, pigeons hopped from beam to beam of the station's arched glass ceiling. Their shadows rippled through streams of late-afternoon light.

It's going to be a shining year, the doctor had said. *A coming-out-of-darkness year.*

My hand slid into my jacket pocket and brushed against the pill bottle that lived there. I tapped one blue pill onto my palm, then another, and tossed them both to the back of my throat.

Right, I thought. The world will be fresh and new. The colors bright. My smile honest.

But I still have to make it through today.

The station was full but not crowded. Corporate commuters mostly, heading home from work. The tidy click of shoes on marble tile. A few other students in the green uniforms of my school sat scattered around the station, but I pretended not to see them. Instead, I watched the pigeons. Watched and waited for a repeat in their code. No matter how long I stared, I couldn't find any. It was all perfectly random. Perfectly real.

Except, of course, for the pigeon crap that had once made them such a nuisance. None of that anywhere.

"Are you feeling all right, Mr. Sabzwari?" The voice came through my specs. It was a nurse from the Clinic, the one who always sounded a bit too concerned.

I glanced around the station. I didn't know where the cameras were, but I knew the nurse could see me. Nurses didn't like it when you sat and stared into space for too long. They assumed you must be thinking bad thoughts.

"Fine," I said. "I'm doing fine. Just heading home for dinner with my family."

"I know, Mr. Sabzwari," the nurse said. "Rough day?"

I nodded toward one of the station's spec screens, which had been playing archival footage of terror attacks on a loop for the past half hour. The hantavirus victims of New Stockholm. The wildfires in the oil fields of Alaska. The twisted metal of a BulletRail train smoldering in desert sand. A memorial of sorts for today, the ten-year anniversary of the crash.

"Rough day, yeah," I said.

The nurse was silent for a moment, probably checking my vitals. Or maybe he just didn't know what to say. My mother had been on that BulletRail train ten years ago, called away on an urgent trip for work. But her train had never made its destination. A faction of Las Oscuras had derailed it in the Northern Desert, killing everyone on board.

"Your vitals look good, Mr. Sabzwari," the nurse said. "I know today's not been easy, but you're almost on the other side of it.

Remember what the doctor said this afternoon—this is going to be your year. Right?"

My cheeks flushed. "Right," I said. "Thanks."

My train arrived, and I boarded the half-full car along with a handful of others. A holographic girl stood across from me, smiling, adverts tracing her body like tattoos. Her eyes met mine, and I smiled back. It felt somehow rude not to. But then my specs twitched with a new message, and I looked away. Probably from Wen, I thought. Some manic little note telling me to stop obsessing over stuff I couldn't control and *just live my life goddammit.* But no. It was from a guy at school who'd barely said ten words to me in all my life.

We're all rooting for you, mate, it said. Don't let today get you down!

The train rocked gently, and I closed my eyes. Everyone at school knew what had happened. How I'd taken too many citizen pills—an accident, though not everyone believed me. Now I had a regimen of Clinic appointments and a team of doctors assigned to look after me. I'd returned to school last week from my stay at the Clinic to find that my reputation had changed—from straightforward, straight-A Rumi Sabzwari to something altogether more confusing. All eyes were on me now, all the time. And I hated the attention.

Thanks, I wrote back. That really means a lot.

School that day had been predictably awful, full of special in memoriam activities and teachers pausing in the halls, giving me that smile adults give to let you know they're one of the good ones, that if it were up to them, all the bad things that had happened in your life would melt away. The only normal bit had been at lunch rotation with Wen. I'd seen him sitting alone by the large dining hall windows, a mug of black coffee in front of him, and he'd motioned me over.

"You on a diet or something?" he'd said, nodding at my empty lunch tray as I sat down.

I shrugged. "I could ask the same of you."

Wen smiled and raised his mug. "Breakfast of champions. And lunch of champions. And afternoon snack of . . . you know." From his jacket pocket he took a pill bottle, carefully tapped four pink pills into his palm, and swallowed them with a gulp of coffee. I looked away. I used to give him a hard time for downing pills like candy. But neither of us brought it up anymore.

From across the dining hall, two fourth-years—one big and baby-faced, the other small—made eye contact with Wen and walked to our table. I recognized them but didn't know their names.

"Gentlemen," Wen said as they sat down.

"What a shit show," the shorter guy said. He unwrapped a SoyChewy bar and took a bite. "I can't believe we still do this whole memoriam bullshit every year. You know, they've talked about the crash in *every single one* of my goddam classes. I mean, get over it already."

I looked down.

Wen took a long sip of coffee. "Maybe *you* should get over it. I mean, seriously—it's one lousy day." He shot a glance in my direction, his fingers drumming on his coffee mug. "Oh, by the way," he said. "I'm just about out of dexies. Think you guys could get me some more?"

The two guys looked at each other. "Awfully bold, bringing that up here," the shorter one said. He ate the rest of his SoyChewy bar in two large bites and crumpled the wrapper.

Wen laughed. "I've never been in trouble a day of my life. You think dextroamphetamines are what's gonna nail me?"

The bigger guy shook his head. "Not all of us have famous parents protecting our asses," he said. "You want to keep this thing going, you better learn to be discreet, all right? And don't let your friend here get ahold of them. It's bad press."

My cheeks turned hot.

"Yeah, yeah," Wen said.

The two guys stood to leave. "We're still on for tonight?" the short one said.

Wen looked at me and smiled. "You bet we're on."

The bigger guy tapped two knocks on the table, and then both of them walked away.

Wen glanced over his shoulder as they left. "Man, fuck those guys," he said. "I get that people are tired of all the phoniness. Like, which of these school admins stays up all night crying about their second cousin's boss who died in the crash that day? But seriously. Have some respect."

I nodded, picking at a hangnail on the side of my finger.

"What's happening tonight?" I asked.

Wen took another long sip of coffee and smiled. "Oh, nothing that concerns you. Wouldn't want to pull you away from your evening with Daddy Dearest."

The grass twinkled a soft blue green on my walk home from the AutoTram station. Each house in my neighborhood looked like a painting. Windows glowed warmly. Walkways bloomed. Stately trees arched their limbs over perfect, peaceful gardens. How much of it was real? I had no idea. The last time I'd seen the world without the filter of my specs, I was too young to remember. Were the houses real but the colors fake? Was the grass real but not the trees? Were the people moving through their nightly routines in the lit windows of the houses really there, or was it all part of some algorithm intended to make me feel as safe as possible? The unreality of it all had started getting to me lately. It reeked of nostalgia for life before the Breach. Life before the walls.

The night air had that familiar smell to it, of dust and metal, and it formed a pit in my stomach as I paused in front of a white-trimmed town house with ivy climbing the front portico. My house. I pushed through the front gate and climbed the steps. The front door unbolted at the touch of my fingerprints. In the privacy antechamber, a scanner confirmed my residence and the security latch on my specs unlocked. I hung my specs on my wall hook, next to Baba's thin wire frames. Father's hook was empty.

"Baba?" I called as I stepped from the antechamber into the house. "Father?"

The warm smells of my grandfather's cooking filled the air— ginger, garlic, saffron, mint.

The living room was dark, but light spilled from the kitchen, casting a long beam across the wide Persian rug. On the mantel, the glow illuminated Father's display of artifacts from before the Breach: the wooden chess piece inlaid with ivory, the hand-painted vase, the iron rod twisted from the blaze of a bomb. Beside this collection stood a photograph of my mother, with golden eyes and long black hair.

"Father?" I called again.

A shadow stepped into the beam of light, and I turned to see Baba standing in the kitchen doorway, smiling. His linen shirt hugged the fullness of his belly. His beard was neatly combed.

This past year, his hair seemed to have gotten whiter, and his shoulders seemed more fragile, more sloped. But the deep brown of his eyes still glittered with his smile.

"Rumi, child," he said. "You're home early!"

With a hitch in his steps, he walked toward me and pulled me into a hug. He smelled of spiced tea and camphor, and I held on for longer than usual. His hugs felt like medicine.

"Come, sit," he said. "I'm preparing your favorite."

I followed him to the kitchen and watched from the table as he poured hot water over a pot of Kashmiri chai—the kind his mother used to brew in South Pakistan, where he was born. I'd been taking tea with Baba since I was six years old, when he moved in with us after my mother's death. It was our ritual, our balm against the world.

"Salt or sugar?" Baba asked.

"Sugar, please."

He smiled and poured my tea. "Ah, child, one day I shall convince you of the superiority of our salty Kashmiri chai. . . ." He dropped two sugar cubes and a splash of milk into my cup and brought it to the table. Then he returned to the vegetables frying on the stove.

My hands wrapped around the steaming cup. "Will Father be joining us tonight?" I asked.

"Of course, child!" Baba said. "It's the anniversary. He wouldn't miss it for the world."

I took a sip of warm, milky tea. "It's just . . . I noticed his specs weren't hanging with yours. I thought maybe he needed to work or something."

Baba paused for a moment. He set down his wooden spoon and turned to look at me. "Your father busies himself to hold his feelings at bay. Since he was a boy, he's done this. Do be patient with him tonight. As the good poet says, our grief is still glistening."

I nodded solemnly. Glistening, I thought. Like an open wound.

My first Clinic appointment had been just a few weeks earlier, a memory so vivid it hurt. I remembered sitting silently by Father's side, listening to him tell the doctors the story of how he came home late from work that night, saw the light on in my room, knocked to no answer.

"I lost his mother ten years ago," Father had said. "I can't lose my son, too."

Someone else might have cried as they said this. But not my father.

Baba turned back to the frying vegetables. "You appear to have made it through the school day mostly unscathed," he said. "Was it as bad as you feared?"

I gave my best smile. "Worse," I said. "My lit teacher had this brilliant idea to pair our class with students from other Upper Cities. She said it'd be good for us to have a chance to talk through our memories of the day of the crash." Anchorage, Johannesburg, Murmansk, New Granada—the cities my teacher had chosen weren't random. Each had been the victim of a major terrorist attack within my lifetime. "*An act of remembrance,* my teacher called it."

Baba's smile poorly masked his concern. "And who did you pair with?"

"Some girl from Rotterdam," I said. "She was nice."

I pictured the girl, a holograph in a chair. She was younger than me, short and sturdy with a soft, round face. A heart-shaped necklace lay flat against her red school uniform.

"Hi," I'd said.

"Hey," she'd said.

"This is . . . weird."

The corner of her lip turned up in a smile. "Tell me about it," she said, her palms rubbing her knees. "So . . . Rumi from St. Iago, right? What's it like there—is it nice?"

"It's fine, I guess. Probably a lot like . . . Where'd you say you were from, Rotterdam?"

She nodded. "I bet you have the same boring spec overlays we have here."

I smiled. "Let's see . . . Do you have a Mirror District?"

"Check," she said.

"A central stadium?"

"Check."

"A Clinic?"

She looked away. "You bet." The light caught her hair, like light sometimes did in old photographs. It made me want to reach out and touch her, to know she was real.

"Do you work?" she asked.

I nodded. "At this little all-night diner. It's fine."

"Same," she said. "They've got me working concessions at this multiplex. It's the whole dead-parent thing, I think. Give the sad kid a work assignment, keep her mind off the gaping hole in her life." She took the heart-shaped pendant between her finger and thumb and slid it absently up and down the chain.

"Who'd you lose?" I asked.

"My dad," she said. "What about you?"

"My mom, in the crash ten years ago."

"Mine was last year."

"I'm so sorry," I said.

She looked at me then. "How long until it starts feeling okay?"

17

I'd shrugged. "Ask me in ten more years."

At the kitchen table, I sipped my tea. When I heard Father come into the privacy antechamber, I stood from my chair. He stepped into the kitchen wearing his official blue Governance uniform, the one decorated with many honors and reserved for official appearances. Behind his specs, his eyes looked tired.

He took off his jacket and draped it over the back of his chair. "Your shoes, Rumi," he said.

I looked down at my feet. Of course. I'd forgotten to take off my shoes at the front door. I started to untie them, but across the kitchen, Baba clicked his tongue. "For shame, Arman," he said to Father. "This is the first thing you say to your son, today of all days?"

Father raised his hands. "You're right, you're right. I shouldn't have. The day has me on edge, is all. Dredging up old memories."

Father's day had been as awful as mine, I knew. The press conference a few hours earlier—at which Father had been asked an indecent number of questions about my "incident"—was why he was dressed so formally tonight.

Baba scooped steaming biryani into a serving bowl, and I stood to help him bring it to the table. "Your father always forgets his manners under stress," Baba said conspiratorially.

Father unbuttoned the collar of his shirt and rolled up his shirtsleeves. "Enough whispering, you two," he said. "Consider me duly reprimanded."

As Baba heaped fluffy golden rice onto our plates, I watched the expression on Father's face shift ever so slightly. I knew what was coming next.

"Your appointment today," he said. "Did it go well?"

I nodded and glanced at Baba. "They reduced my meds again.

to Upper City Cuzco. You remember Cuzco? All the Old World cathedrals . . ."

I looked away. This Cuzco bit was almost certainly a lie. But I'd learned a long time ago not to ask too many questions about his work outside our city.

"Don't you care?" I said. "Don't you care about today?"

Father stared at me in disbelief. It was a cruel thing to say, but I didn't take it back.

Baba placed his hand on mine. "Rumi, child," he said. "You mustn't say such things. You cannot imagine the depths of your father's love for you, or for your mother."

I looked down at the gift box still open on the table in front of me. "Funny way of showing it," I said.

Father sighed. "You have a wonderful life, Rumi, full of so much promise. But you need to understand that not everything is about you. The sooner you learn this, the better."

My face felt hot with all the things I knew I couldn't say. "Yes, Father," I said. The gift box stared back at me. The yellow beads felt like an indictment. *Look at the child you once were,* they seemed to say. *What happened to that child?*

Father pushed back his chair and stood. "Thank you for the delicious meal, Baba Joon." He bent down to kiss Baba's cheek, and Baba clutched Father's hand in both of his.

"Travel safely, my son," he said.

Father nodded and pulled his hand away. "I'll see you both tomorrow," he said. Then he walked from the kitchen and out the front door. Somewhere on the street outside our house, a car door opened and closed, and the car drove away.

"I should probably go too," I said to Baba, my throat tight with spoken words. "To work, I mean. The doctors prescribed me

I'm almost back down to a standard citizen's dosage. The doctors say I'm really starting to show progress."

"That is good, child. So good to hear," Baba said.

A message came through Father's specs just then, but he unlatched them and set them down on the table. "Yes, Rumi," he said. "It's wonderful that you're feeling better."

My hands tightened around the warm mug, and I forced a smile.

"Thanks," I said.

Father nodded matter-of-factly, as if to punctuate the conversation. He didn't like talking about my appointments. I sometimes wondered if he wished I didn't have to go to them at all.

We continued eating in silence. Outside the kitchen window, the sky turned purple with the coming night. In the distance, a signal tower blinked yellow, informing us that the borders of our city, St. Iago, were secure. Not secure enough to switch to green, though. I'd never seen the light turn green. Only yellow, orange, red, and ultraviolet. The varied colors of alarm.

When I'd finished my second helping of biryani, Father cleared his throat and pushed his own plate aside. Then he took a small box from his jacket pocket and set it on the table. Written on top in Father's bold handwriting was my name. The strong, careful lettering.

"Now, I know the doctors said not to make a big deal of the anniversary this year," he said. "But I wanted to do something. . . ."

I picked up the little box. It felt light in my hands.

"Open it," Father said. It came out as more of a command than a request.

I unclasped the box and hinged the lid open. Inside were tiny yellow beads—eight, to be exact—forming a single molecule.

"Do you remember when we used to build these together?" Father asked.

I nodded.

For my tenth birthday, Father had given me a model chemistry set. I'd pretended to love the gift because Father had been so sad at the time—even though by then my mother had been gone for years. He and I had spent so many evenings at this very table connecting ceramic beads. I'd shape black beads of carbon into dinosaurs, make long mazes of oxygen chains. And Father would never correct me or tell me what to do. He'd just sit across the table from me building his own molecules. Hydrochloric acid. Penthrite. Propane.

"Your mother was always much better at this," he'd say.

Father took the delicate yellow structure out of the box and turned it over in his fingers. "Do you remember what this molecule is?"

I held out my hand, and Father passed the ring of beads to me. "It's sulfur," I said.

His face creased into a tired smile. "The first molecule we ever built together. I found your old chemistry set in the attic the other day, but the connectors had cracked—and it was an elementary set anyhow. So I got you a new one. I know you're beyond these models in your classes now, but I wanted to replace it anyway. It's in your room, waiting for you."

I set the sulfur molecule back in the box and traced the edge of the box with my finger.

"Thank you, Father," I said.

He shifted forward in his seat and rested his elbows on the table. "You know, I was thinking—it's about time to start visiting universities, no? I thought next month we could plan a trip, just

the two of us." The hint of a smile flashed across his face. He loved to talk about this sort of thing—about everything the future held for me. "Are you still thinking of applying to schools on the continent, or will you be aiming farther afield?"

I took a sip of tea and held the liquid in my mouth for a moment before answering. "Do you think we could hold off till I have a chance to talk it over with my doctors?" I looked down at my plate as I said this. I already knew the Clinic's opinion on the matter. They thought that university visits would be highly beneficial for me, a way to keep my mind focused on the future. But every time I thought about that future, my brain went into a panic. The future claimed to have a place for me, but I knew deep down that I wouldn't fit into it. No matter how I tried to bend and twist myself, I just wouldn't *fit*.

"Of course," Father said. "Whatever your doctors think best."

"Maybe you could pick up some university intel on your travels for work, though," I said, trying to lighten the mood. "Or is th stuff top secret?"

Father wiped his mouth with a napkin and placed his s back over his eyes. "About that. I have some unfortunate I'm needed abroad tomorrow—intercity Governance b I'm scheduled to leave tonight, right after dinner."

My skin tingled as he said this. Our family had alwa point of being together on the evening of the annivers become something of a family tradition. Father and tell stories about my mother—things about her I'd n know for myself. We'd pull out old photo albums,

"Now, I know what you're thinking," Father routine diplomatic visit. Nothing to worry ab goes smoothly, I'll be home by dinner tom

more hours today." This wasn't true, of course. The doctors knew how important it was for me to spend this night at home with Father and Baba. But with Father gone, the thought of staying home suddenly felt pathetic, childish.

Baba nodded. "Your doctors know what is best," he said. "But if you'll spare your grandfather just one more moment . . ." He stood and went to the living room. When he came back, he held in his hands an Old World photo album, its green leather cover worn with use. From the earliest days of my Citizen Training, I'd been taught that any connection to my family's history and traditions was unpatriotic. To be a good citizen of Upper City meant to leave behind the ugly baggage of the world that came before. But this line of thinking never convinced Baba, who stubbornly insisted on sharing stories of his life before the walls.

"Did I ever tell you the story of how our family came to live in Upper City St. Iago?" Baba asked.

I swallowed hard, wanting to leave. Knowing I should stay.

"It was your father, right?"

Baba's eyes twinkled. "I was only a child when our family received the invitation, and I too assumed, at first, that my father had earned us our citizenship. His work to bring peace to our country gave him a high Deservingness Quotient, to be sure." He opened the photo album to a picture of a middle-aged woman with dark, piercing eyes. "But, in fact, it was my mother who'd granted us entry. She'd been a renowned geneticist before the Hot Wars, specializing in crops that could grow in the most austere conditions. With St. Iago seeking to define itself as a post-Breach hub for the biotech industry, our city's Governance had of course eagerly welcomed her into the walls."

He turned the album to another page and suddenly, gazing

back at me, were my own mother's golden, smiling eyes. She wore her medical scrubs and coat, her Governance ID clipped to her lapel. A few dark strands of hair fell around her face. She was stunningly beautiful. "In this way," Baba continued, "my mother was not unlike yours. They both took it as their life's work to breathe beauty into the world's desolation."

I stared at the photograph of my mother. I had so few memories of her, but I knew her legacy well: a brilliant young chemist who'd helped pioneer the cocktail of drugs now prescribed to every citizen of every Upper City. They were the drugs intended to keep us all sane inside the cities' walls, the same tiny blue citizen pills I'd taken the night I almost died.

"Today is the day your mother died," Baba said. "She saw suffering in those around her and used her talents to ease their pain. I see so much of her in you. I think to myself and marvel at what you will do in your life, at who you will become."

My throat tightened. "I'm not sure I see things that way, Baba."

Baba nodded and took a long sip of tea. "Your life is your own, Rumi. Remember that. It is no one's but your own. Now, as the good poet says—go if you must. Move across the night sky with those nameless lights!"

2

P A Z

The boy in the cellar room,
The spit and blood and tattoo ink,
That's not where my story begins.
Not really.
They say you can change the meaning of a story
just by the telling.
When you tell a story, you get to decide who's the dragon
and who's the hero and all that.
You can spin light out of darkness and water out of sand.
Maybe one way you tell it you end up happy,
but another way, you end up dead.
They're tricky things, stories.
Let me try again.

To begin, I am Paz Valenzuela-Valenzuela de Paraíso, daughter
of no man, daughter of the jaguar. There's fire in my blood and
the sea in my eyes. Touch me and you'll see that fire and water
are all that I am. But more like than not, you can't touch me.
Because why?
Because, weón, I'm too damn fast!

No.

That's still the old me.

It's the way I used to talk

Back when the gamest thing I had to outrun

Was a horny piss-covered billy goat.

I know better now.

I need to tell this one true.

Think back

Before the boy and the cellar room.

Before the spit and blood and tattoo ink.

To the anger swelling deep in my guts,

That raging sickness that some people

Call revenge.

Think back . . .

I t was springtime, one of the last days of cold and wet before the heat set in for good.

The waxing moon lit up the hollows of the rafters around me as I crouched beneath a mess of shelves stuffed full of Old World treasures—paintings and mortars and blank-faced screens, dull-colored maps that sketched out the vicious stories of the world. The garrets of the Library looked how I imagined Old World museums must have looked once. And I was a ghost, haunting the treasures of the past.

I wasn't supposed to be up in the garrets at all, of course. That floor was used for two things only: stashing Old World miracles and locking up prisoners, and on that day I was no prisoner. But

I never was much good at following rules. I'd been sneaking up there for months. Early in the morning, before a long day of scouting clouded my spirit with the stink of the city and the weight of its work, I'd climb into the lonesome garrets and study the forbidden maps I'd tacked to the wall. Maps of my city, Paraíso. Maps of the surrounding lands. A mess of black marks dotted the maps like stars. The dots followed the course of the Autopista River, a rushing churn of water that flowed through the gulch formed by the collapse of an Old World highway.

I took a charcoal nub from my satchel and, with my good arm, made another mark just east of Paraíso. *Picaflor,* I wrote next to it. *Hummingbird.*

Months ago, when the dead creatures began to number too many to count, I'd started marking these forbidden maps with the places their stiff little bodies had fallen, looking for a pattern.

My official scouting map went only to the edges of Paraíso—as if that was where the universe ended. As if whatever lay beyond was none of my concern. But up here in the darkness, in piles of maps unremembered in the damp and dust, I learned for certain something I'd always known deep in my guts. The lampblack marks—my constellation of the dead—they all pointed to one place: the walled-in city of St. Iago.

Two floors down, a heavy door echoed open. The world below was waking up. Other scouts were reporting for our morning meeting. I had to get down before anyone caught me.

I slid my charcoal nub into my satchel and cut my way through the dark. Back out on the empty passageway, I locked behind me the door I'd picked and crept toward the staircase that led down to the Library's main Entry Hall.

The air was early-morning dim. Nobody'd come yet to light

the lamps. I leaned over the railing and listened to the quiet. The staircase twisted down in a single curl to the blue-painted tiles on the Entry Hall's floor. The tall windows of the Entry Hall, still black with night, seemed to watch me.

A pair of scouts walked across the giant hall below and disappeared down the North Corridor. Then another group came through. Hiding above in the shadows, I recognized each scout—the slow, solemn ones; the quick, cocky ones; the ones that came in together or all alone. Most all of them were older than me, at least by a little—at fifteen, I was one of the youngest scouts to be employed by the Library. Still, not one of us had seen our eighteenth birthday. The Library elders made sure that scouts were young. Fresh-minded. When a scout got too old, the elders moved them on to other jobs—maintaining old electric lines, ferrying messages north or south. Nobody ever learned much about the things we were scouting or why. Which was why I had to be careful. I didn't want to find myself out of a job.

When the last scout had passed through the hall, I ran down the stairs, slapping garret dust off my shorts as I made my way to the scouts' quarters. Oil lamps flickered on heavy worktables, two scouts sitting at each one. I took a seat in the empty chair next to Maribel, who was busy sorting stones. She shot me a sour look when I sat next to her, and I flashed a smile.

"What?" I said. "Weón, you think I can't wake up ass-crack early too?"

She rolled her eyes and went back to sorting. Maribel was a real mind-the-rules kind of girl. She didn't want a thing to do with the likes of me. Which was fine. I didn't want to talk to her, either. I didn't want to talk to anybody. I just wanted the elders to come in and start the meeting already. The sooner it started, the sooner it'd be over.

I cleared a space at the table in front of me and spread my chart across the worn, dark wood. Next to the chart, I laid out the things I'd collected on my mission the day before: the upriver water samples, the animal scat wrapped in dusty plastic bags, the shiny piece of tech sure to earn me a bonus from the elders. Next to these things, I placed the picaflor. With my sinner's arm I made the cross over his green-velvet body and made a note at the bottom of my chart.

Nine more songbirds dead, I wrote. *City side of the gulch.*

I laid my charcoal nub on the table and squeezed out the aches in my sinner's arm. For months, I'd been turning in findings like these—dead hawks and salamanders, white-whiskered coypu dried out beneath their feather-soft fur. But nothing ever changed. The elders tested the chems in the water and the toxins in the animal scat, cut open the creatures' bodies to see what kinds of poisons had made them die. Then they wrote their findings in that heavy, hide-bound ledger book and told us we all were safe from harm. But this was a lie. None of us had been safe since before the Breach. The chemfields and the minefields, the poisons bleeding their filth into the river—all of them shared the same name. And that name was Upper City.

But there's a saying in Paraíso: sin pega, no vales nada. *Without a job, you're nothing.* I was lucky to have this high-class job as a Library scout. I had a curse hanging over my head—in the eyes of the Library, my right arm was a sinner's arm, shriveled and shameful. Most everybody in my condition picked trash. If I held up the bright green picaflor and told how I'd traced the stiff bodies of a thousand poisoned creatures all the way to St. Iago,

I knew how it would look. It would look ungrateful. It would look like I was courting radical ideas. Everybody knew what they did to traitors.

At the worktable behind me, one of the scouts cleared her throat. "Oye, Paz," she said with a barb to her voice. "I see Cienfuegos still has you patrolling the gulch, huh? Would've thought he'd graduate you from that entry-level stuff by now . . ."

It was Yasmín, looking for a rise. Everyone knew this was a sore spot of mine. The elders never gave me any exciting missions outside the city like they gave most other scouts. They'd taken me for an honest-to-God troublemaker from day one.

I smiled and turned around. Yasmín could be a real bitch. Una weona levantada de raja.

"The pay's the same for you and me both," I shot back. "I don't see much reason to give a shit where I go. Besides, is it my problem if the elders don't fancy me replaceable enough to send out into the fray?"

Yasmín just laughed, and I lost my smile. She knew I was eager as a street dog for a mission that would take me outside the city.

Right then the door to the corridor opened, and Cienfuegos, the Library's chief elder, walked in. The whole room went quiet and stiff. We all faced forward, waited.

Cienfuegos was wearing his wine-red elder's robe that morning, which meant he was in no mood for pleasantries. The lamplight cut a deep shadow into the wrinkle between his eyebrows, making him look not altogether harmless and not altogether sane. He was white-haired and soot-toothed and old, but he was still so tall and so severe that I sometimes wondered if he got to be as powerful as he was just on account of how he looked.

He coughed and set a heavy ledger on his lectern, signaling us all to stand for the pledge. We stood. "For the life of our people," we recited. "For order after the Breach, I pledge my honor to my city and my loyalty to the Library. I pledge to resist Las Oscuras, to reject their lies. On the souls of my mother and father and all I hold most dear, I pledge these things. May our light shine ever more brightly. May we one day recover the world we lost."

The old man coughed again. The sound echoed through the room.

"May we one day recover the world we lost!" he repeated as we all took our seats again. "We take this pledge to help us remember the days before the Library. When life was chaos. We choose to remember because it's death to forget." He looked across our faces, pausing at each one. When his eyes stopped on mine, a shiver ran through me. The elders seemed to know things, things they shouldn't have been able to know. I sometimes wondered if they could read your mind. I tucked my feet under my chair and hoped to God the garret dust on my boots didn't show. But after a moment, he moved on.

"Muy bien," he said to the room. "You may be seated. Now. What have you honorable scouts brought me today?"

He started at the front, and one at a time, each scout gave a report on the findings of their current mission. Juanfe had found a new petrol tank on Ruta F-98, south of the city. Nicanor had found a freshwater spring bubbling in the hills. Maribel had caught sight of Las Oscuras on the trade routes through the mountains. My turn to speak got closer, and my heart set to racing. I wanted to speak the truth of what I'd found—even if I knew there was no use in it—to show Yasmín and the rest of them that my sinner's arm did not make me some helpless girl who scarce could do her job.

Cienfuegos scribbled something in his ledger and then fixed his cold blue eyes on me. "Paz?" he said.

"My mission's going well, señor," I said. "I got water samples and soil and scat samples all the way up to the boulder crossing. Plus, I found one of those mirror screens in a box in a truck. I know the elders've been looking for those. . . ." Yasmín cleared her throat behind me, and I shot her a glance. The way she was smiling . . .

"Also," I said, my voice shaking, "I found a bunch of songbirds dead, just like last month. I made a note of it on my charts last time, but nothing's come of it. I don't want to cause trouble. I just thought that maybe I could run a trace farther upstream, out near the chemfields, so the elders could figure the concentrations. . . ."

"What is this nonsense, mija?" Cienfuegos said. The way he said it—mija, *my child*—caught my ear funny. There was no care in it, only power.

"It seems like neurotoxins. I think they're being leached down from the highlands—from the chem-poisoned desert surrounding St. Iago. If you'd just let me . . ."

"That's quite enough," he said. He smiled and looked at the faces of the other scouts. "You must know, mija, that we run very careful tests here at the Library. We cannot allow ourselves to jump to dangerous conclusions."

My face was burning hot. *But the maps,* I wanted to say. *The constellation of the dead.* "Puta la weá," I mumbled.

"Watch your mouth, child," Cienfuegos boomed. "I could easily suspend you from your duties until you find yourself in a state of mind more fitting of the privileged position you occupy here at the Library. Do you understand?"

"Yes, señor," I said. "It won't happen again."

Maribel's head was tipped down to her chest, but I could tell she was smiling. They all were. I could feel their smiles burn in my throat.

The check-ins kept on, but I didn't hear a word. The sound turned blurry before it reached my ears. At some point, the last scout went quiet and Cienfuegos closed the meeting and left the room. I kept my eyes down as the others filed out. Yasmín bumped my shoulder as she passed me.

"Mira la revolucionaria!" she said. *Look at the little revolutionary.*

I looked up and smiled so they'd see I wasn't angry. Like I was in on the joke too. But nobody met my eyes. "¡Viva la Resistencia!" Yasmín shouted as she shouldered open the heavy door and walked out into the corridor. Everybody laughed.

My chest pinched. I hung behind till the room was empty, packed up my satchel alone. "Puta la weá, weón," I said, louder this time, into the empty air.

3

RUMI

On the front steps of my house, I flipped up the collar of my jacket against the evening chill. My hand dipped absently into my pocket for more pills, but I caught myself. The Clinic would know if I took any more today. Still, I could feel that familiar darkness bleeding through, and I wasn't sure how else to stop it. My skin felt dead, like modeling clay. My lungs were a clogged drain, filling with cold, murky water.

Just then a voice came through my specs. The Clinic nurse again.

"Your cortisol is tracking high, Mr. Sabzwari," the nurse said. "Is everything all right?"

I walked down my front steps and pushed through the gate onto the sidewalk. "Everything's fine," I said. I tried to sound upbeat. "Like you said earlier, it was a rough day. I'm about to head to work, actually. I thought maybe I'd walk."

The nurse sounded unconvinced. "You're also tracking pretty high on your new meds regimen. You need to slow down with the pills if you don't want to end up back at the Clinic. Are you sure you're doing okay?" The concern in his voice was growing.

I smoothed down my hair and cleared my throat. "I said I'm fine."

The nurse paused. "Why don't you wait there? I'll send a car."

"I'd really rather walk," I said. "It'll help me clear my head."

There was another moment of silence. I wondered if the nurse was running this by the doctor on call before giving me an answer. After nearly a month of restrictions on everything from what time I went to bed to how I got to school, the doctors at the Clinic had recently decided to grant me a few freedoms—the freedom to move about the city without asking permission, the freedom to control my own meds. This was all part of my treatment plan. But they were still monitoring the chemical levels in my blood. They were still tracking me everywhere I went. I knew I was walking a fine line. If I wasn't careful, they'd take these freedoms away just as quickly as they'd granted them.

"All right, Mr. Sabzwari," he said at last. "I'll check in again later this evening."

As soon as the call ended, I closed my eyes. My fists clenched and unclenched.

"Mountains," I said into my specs. "I need mountains."

All at once the world around me transformed. The sky turned starry and deep. A blanket of grass shimmered with moonlight. In the distance, snow-mottled mountains rose hazy and godlike into the night. I could almost smell the sweetness of the pines.

This kind of thing used to help whenever I felt myself slipping. I'd whisper words into my specs like spells—*mountains, forest, sea*—and then let myself imagine that somewhere, somehow, these miracles still existed, that life could contain such beauty. The aching promise of these places had always brought me back into myself.

Lately, though, all that had helped were the pills. Since the night that landed me in the Clinic, I'd been trying to find comfort in these images again, but they only made me want to run, to never stop running.

Where could I go, though? I thought. Where *is* there to go?

Grayed-out neighborhoods slid past me as I walked. The neighborhoods turned to shops, then the shops turned to high-rises. By the time I reached the Mirror District, whole caravans of grayed-out people shoved past me, shouting and laughing. I didn't look at them, though. My eyes stayed focused on the distant snowy mountains.

I walked for so long that I almost forgot where I was going. But then a pair of double doors sprung open in front of me, and a group of wasted uni students pushed past. A wave of greasy air and bad synth music eddied into the street behind them, and the smell was unmistakable—the deep-fried smell of the Purgatory Diner.

Right, I thought. I was walking to work.

I took a deep breath and tapped my specs. In an instant, the mountains disappeared and the whole world blazed back at me in one flashing smear. I squinted against the strobing lights in the diner's windows. It all made my head ache—the music; the grease and cologne; the hazy, starless sky. Still, I willed myself to push through the diner's glass doors, and before I knew it, I was elbow-deep in a bucket of raw shoestring fries, salt stinging the corners of my fingernails.

"Don't think for a second that you're getting overtime credits for working today, kid," Federico said, his back to me as he knifed a slab of butter onto the griddle.

"I wouldn't dream of it," I said. "It's worth all the grease burns in the world just to be in the presence of such greatness as yourself."

"And you'd best not forget it," Federico said with a laugh.

"Legendary greatness. Never been a guy who could brown a sandwich quite like old man Rico."

I smiled and settled into the task in front of me. It was easy working the line with Federico. Thirty years separated us. He had a wife and a family, and I had nothing to prove to him. It was simple—do a good job, then go home. Which was the whole point of "meaning therapy," I guess. All of us working menial jobs that could otherwise be automated were there because it was prescribed, because the doctors thought that if we just got out of our houses, busied our hands, saw a few new faces, maybe our minds wouldn't slide into the dark corners that had sent us to the Clinic in the first place.

Federico cleared his throat behind me, and I turned to see him toss a greasy towel over his shoulder. "Gonna hit the walk-in when I'm through with this order," he said. "Care to join?" He slid the corner of a beat-up candy tin from his pocket and tapped it twice with his pointer finger. That familiar rattle. I wondered what was inside. Dexies, benzos, straight-up citizen pills?

"No thanks," I said. "You know I get high on your company alone...."

He slid three perfectly golden Reuben sandwiches onto a plate of fries. "Suit yourself," he said. "But I'm a married man—don't you go and get any ideas. Order up!"

Just then Claire stuck her head through the waitstaff window as three more orders dropped into the lenses of my specs. "Hey, Rumi," she said. "Some little tweaker out here won't stop asking if you're working today. Want me to tell him to fuck off?"

I peered through the window to a table at the far corner of the dining area, and my stomach sank. It was Wen. The turned-up collar of his big green coat hid the bottom half of his face as he flicked a sweaty strand of hair from his eyes and waved at me like a fool.

"No, it's fine. Tell him I'll be out there in a minute."

Claire slid three plates piled high with fries onto one arm and balanced a tray full of drinks in the other. "Tell him yourself," she said. "That guy's a total asshole."

I wiped my hands on my apron. "Offer's still on the table," Federico said, tapping the candy tin in his pocket.

I shrugged. "Maybe later."

Sharp beams of neon light cut through the darkness of the dining area. Electrotribal funk pulsed through the speakers. Groups of uni students squeezed around tables, laughing and nodding as armies of angels and demons on the ceiling overhead waged a holographic battle that no one seemed to be watching.

"Rumi, baby!" Wen shouted, raising both hands over his head and nearly spilling the mug of black coffee on the table in front of him. I slid into the chair across from him.

"What the hell are you doing?" I said, just loud enough to be audible. "You know you're not supposed to come here." This job was part of my recovery plan and, as the Clinic had made clear, Wen—with his own stubborn habit and his fuck-the-world attitude—explicitly was not.

"You've got that right!" he said, flicking hair from his eyes. "But if you think I'm about to let you spend this most hallowed day whoring yourself out in some godforsaken slag heap, then you really are crazy. I mean, honestly, Rumi, this simply will not do!" He spoke—shouted, really—in a steady stream, one word tumbling into the next. Manic, twitchy, barely pausing to breathe. He was clearly blazed out of his mind on whatever black-market amphetamine he'd gotten his hands on that week.

"So, listen—no, no, just listen. I've got a surprise for you. Grab your shit and let's go."

I blinked. "Go? I just got here. There's this thing called a *job*, Wen. Some people have them. . . ."

Wen buttoned his jacket and downed the last of his coffee. "That's your boring problem, Rumi. Not mine. Figure it out. I'll see your ass outside in five." He shoved open the doors and walked out with two middle fingers in the air, not bothering to turn around.

I sat at the table alone for a minute. Imagined myself going back to the kitchen to finish my shift. Imagined the easy back-and-forth of conversation between Federico and me, Claire rolling her eyes at every other thing I said. But my hands were clenched. My heart was racing. Everything in me wanted to run. To run and never stop running.

Ten minutes later, I was back outside.

"My mom always told me you were a bad influence," I said.

"Ha! Good thing she's not around to see just *how* bad—am I right?"

I shook my head. "C'mon, man. You know mom jokes are off-limits. What's this big surprise anyway?"

Wen fumbled in his pocket for a cigarette and lit it. "In all your years of knowing me, what makes you think I'd answer that question?" He pinched the delicate roll of dried tobacco between his fingers and inhaled. "How'd you commemorate the big day? Did you and Daddy finally duke things out?" Wen had been watching my ups and downs with Father play out over the last few years, but he didn't pry. If there was one thing he knew how to do, it was mind his own business.

"Not quite," I said. "He had to duck out early. You know how it is. . . ."

"Sure," Wen said. "I know how it is." From his pocket, he took a small plastic case containing a dozen or so metallic-looking marbles.

"What's that?" I asked.

Wen looked at me in disbelief. "Rumi, my dear boy, you have *got* to get out more!" He took two marbles from the case and swiped one across the sensor in his specs and one across mine. Then he attached them magnetically to our spec transmitters. The marbles glowed electric blue. "It's a simple hack," he said. "It'll loop some SimPlay gaming footage into your account for the next few hours, and the surveillance AI won't know the difference when they study your feed. I've got hundreds—use them all the time. You've seriously never heard of these?"

"I mean, I guess I've *heard* of them," I lied. "I've just never seen one in real life."

"Sure thing," Wen said, smirking. "Now, just send a message to your minders saying you decided to go to your friend's house for some wholesome first-person shooter fun."

Warily, I messaged the Clinic nurse. I expected him to respond with a reprimand, but he didn't. Whatever you need, Rumi, he said. We'll keep an eye on your feed tonight. Be well.

Wen dropped his cigarette, half-smoked, to the ground and stamped it out with his shoe. I followed him to the Benson heliocycle parked curbside across the street. A luxury model, midnight blue. "Dad says he's thinking of getting me a third-issue MonacoSol for my sixteenth," Wen said, gazing at the deep-blue machine. His light eyes turned glassy as he ran his hand over the cycle's silky front fairing. "He doesn't trust me with a new pup like this, even though I know he can afford it."

"That's probably wise," I said. "Your record isn't exactly spotless."

Wen hopped on the Benson and tapped his specs to accept the rental charge. "Rumi, I swear. Sometimes I think you're an old-ass dude trapped inside a young guy's body."

My cheeks flushed. "I just—"

"Kidding!" he said as he snapped on his helmet and adjusted the popped collar of his coat. "Only kidding. Man, you gotta learn to take a joke. Hurry up and nab that one, okay?" He pointed to a red Galyx cycle parked farther up the curb.

I mounted the cycle and the engine shuddered to life.

With the swipe of his thumb, Wen synced his music feed to mine, and a glittering dreampunk soundscape swelled in my ears.

"Now that's more like it!" he shouted. "All right, mon ami. Let's ride!"

I cinched the collar of my jacket tightly around my neck. In the rear mirror, the diner pulsed its strobing light onto the street. But up ahead, Wen raised one hand over his head and pumped his fist into the air with the music. It was enough to make me smile—an honest, real smile. What did I have to lose?

4

RUMI

dverts slithered the streets like iridescent dragons as we left the Mirror District and drove toward the city center. Part of me hoped this was just a little joyride before heading back to Wen's house for some uneventful SimPlay. But another part wondered what mysteries lay ahead. I was feeling empty and reckless again, like I could do anything.

In the distance, the glow of Borlaug Square blazed into the night sky. That was where Wen seemed to be taking us, though I couldn't understand why. At that hour, all the stores would be closed.

As we neared the square, Wen slowed his cycle to a crawl, and I followed his lead, ignoring the dread tingling down my spine. Dread that I was slipping, that I wanted to slip beneath the dark.

"So this is the big surprise?" I said through my specs. "You're taking me shopping?"

"Patience, dear boy," Wen said.

The square was eerily empty. Adverts glittered for no one but us. The manic lights—thin and airy, insubstantial—seemed to swallow everything. Fighter jets made of light circled overhead, their contrails transforming into images: a woman wearing a stethoscope, a child reading a book, a young couple wrapped in each other's arms.

Our fight is for your lives, the images read.

I thought of Father, strapped into the seat of some Governance freight copter. Of the yellow molecule, Father's gift to me. *To my ungrateful son,* the beads had seemed to say. *May you remember what's precious. May you someday find a way to heal the pain you've caused this family.* . . . . I sank into the sting of Father's disappointment. Relished it. Held on to it as the one bright, true feeling left in the blinding sea of the world. Clusters of images, renderings, memories, all of them flat and pale. Digital wind and spinning planets, stardust and the dust of my skin, Father's weary eyes and tsunamis and terrorists knocking trains from their rails, supernovas. Nothing safe, nothing real.

Wen pulled his cycle to the curb, and I did the same. "Well, mon ami," he said, walking over to me. "Are you ready for your surprise?" And just like that, he took off his specs.

I froze. A few weeks ago, some kids from our school had been reckless enough to break off their specs in the middle of the Mirror District. They'd faced interrogations. Public outrage. A violation of the Surveillance Protection Act.

"What the hell are you doing?" I whispered.

"Shit, what was I thinking?" Wen said. "Okay, just stay calm. . . . Maybe I should pour out libations or something. Prove I'm still an honest patriot. Got anything good—any whiskey or dexies or keynos or . . . ?" But he couldn't keep a straight face.

Of course Wen would joke about something as serious as this.

"Kidding!" Wen said. He tapped the blue marble on his specs. "These little devices are killer, man. You can do anything you want with them on. See, watch."

He reached over and swiped the specs from my face.

I blinked, dumbfounded. But nothing happened.

"What about the security latch?"

"Oh my god, you're such a square!" Wen said, grinning now. "Good thing you have me to keep you off the straight and narrow, right?"

I stared into the chasm of the night sky.

The quiet. The stillness. The void.

All was blankness, gray dust.

I waited and listened. Tried to grasp what I saw.

The streets had lost their brightness. The trees were gone. The adverts and streetlamps and brightly lit storefronts—all gone. Even the buildings, which moments before had danced with light, were now nothing more than concrete stacks veiled by massive screens—the vacant eyes of some horrible monster, watching.

And in the distance beyond my city's walls—enormous, snow-capped mountains . . .

For the first time in as long as I could remember, I was seeing the world undisguised.

That's when I noticed it. On the opposite side of the square was a ladder—tall but inconspicuous—scaling the side of a building with a screen covering its entire facade. The ladder climbed a few stories and stopped at an unmarked door. If I'd been wearing my specs, there was no way I would've seen it.

Wen followed my gaze and flashed a look that made my stomach turn. I knew that look.

"Last one to the top is shanty scum!" he called, and started sprinting across the square.

By the time I made it across the square, Wen was already climbing the side of a nearby dumpster to reach the bottom rung of the ladder. I looked up four stories to where the ladder ended: at a landing and a metal door that seemed to lead behind the screen.

A dizzying lightness filled my chest. "What do you think is up there?" I asked.

Wen grabbed the bottom rung and heaved himself onto the ladder.

"I don't think, Rumi. Thinking is *your* problem."

Before I could offer a comeback, he started to climb. When he reached the landing, he slapped three beats at the base of the door—casually, as though he'd done this a million times. There was a slight pause followed by a shuffling sound. Then the door opened, and a hand reached through to pull him inside, into the space behind the screen.

Every nerve in my body tingled.

Hushed voices and laughter floated down from the open door. Soft light flickered inside. I recognized one of the voices instantly. She didn't even have to speak for me to recognize her. I knew her by her laugh. A loose, easy laugh. A laugh that mocked you even as it laughed with you. Laksmi's laugh.

Oh god.

Laksmi Nahali slung daggers when she walked. She held a room captive with the curve of her collarbones. She regarded the whole world and everything in it with scorn. She was the dark-haired poetess of my dreams. Wen knew this, all of this.

Just then Wen peeked his head through the doorway. "Well, are you coming or what?"

The massive screen above thrummed its current into me.

"Coming . . . ," I said.

Damn it, Wen, I thought. What the hell are you thinking?

I tried not to look down as the pavement sank beneath me. When at last I made it to the top, a hand extended through the door. The hand belonged to Tique—a fourth-year at Lyceum who I knew only by reputation. Tique the Freak. No plans for uni, shanty sympathizers for parents. Or, as Father once put it, *the enemy within.*

"Specs in the sack," Tique said. He held out a pillowcase.

I passed him my specs with their glowing marble attachment and noticed that Tique wasn't wearing his either. "No specs, no DigiCloths, no dazzling virtual devices of any kind behind the screen," he said. "It's our only rule." Tique dropped my specs into the pillowcase, and I stepped through the doorway. A latch clicked shut behind me.

It took a moment for my eyes to adjust to the dimness, but slowly a candlelit chamber of steel beams and gratings came into focus. The space was small—only slightly bigger than the living room at my house—but the latticework walls and floor made it feel much larger, as though we were suspended in the night air. Colorful pieces of cloth hung from the scaffolding like curtains with no windows. Cigarette smoke hung thick in the air. I tried not to cough.

Twenty or so people clustered around the room, leaning against steel beams. I recognized many from school: the strung-out son of Lieutenant Governor Paulson, the outspoken twin daughters of the Governance Chief of Security, the grandson of a prominent political philosopher. Every one of them from a family of importance.

Just like Wen, I thought. Just like me.

Someone passed me a flask. I took a sip and tried not to wince as the vapors rose from my throat into my nose. Whiskey,

I guessed, maybe rum. On the other side of the room, Wen motioned to Tique for a lighter. And there she was. Laksmi Nahali. She wore her scholar's vest with the top unbuttoned, nothing underneath. Her head rested on Tique's shoulder, but she looked directly at me. Her charcoal eyes smoldered; her dark skin gave off its own glow.

Wen was busy lecturing Tique and Laksmi by the time I joined them, sitting next to Wen. "And how about Kapital's new one," he said loudly. "Have you heard it? Oh man—it's, like, three fucking hours of this heart-bleeding, snap-your-fingers pop *glory* that's gorgeous and melodic and, like . . . like, approachable, am I right?"

Laksmi glanced at me. Her smile wanted to destroy me.

"I mean, what's so *wrong* with a simple, perfect melody?" Wen continued. He was ranting already. Sweaty. Manic. "Why's it have to be so goddam esoteric and *difficult* to be considered good? I mean, sometimes a guy just wants to smack his gum along to a goddam fucking pretty song, you *know*?"

Tique nodded, humoring Wen but not really listening. He sat with one arm draped around Laksmi, looking like some sort of Old World magician. His long black coat and dark eyeliner were either totally ridiculous or exceedingly cool—I couldn't tell which. When his eyes met mine, he dipped his head theatrically and smiled. He leaned past Wen and Laksmi to offer me a cigarette, but I shook my head.

"I shouldn't," I said, trying to sound casual.

He shrugged and pinched the cigarette between his lips, extending his hand toward me. "I'm Tique, by the way. I don't think we've officially met."

My grip felt cold against the warm confidence of his. "I'm Rumi," I said.

He looked at me, one eyebrow raised. "Yeah, I know," he said.

I waited for him to move back to Laksmi, but instead he got up and sat next to me.

When he didn't say anything, I shifted uncomfortably. "So, what is this place anyway?"

Tique ran a hand through his carefully mussed hair, looking across the room. "I guess you could say it's a peek behind-the-scenes. A break from the spec screens and SimPlay and adverts—from the madness of all that order. A little bit of rust does a body good, you know?"

I nodded, not understanding.

Tique shifted closer to me then, and his voice turned conspiratorial. "I mean, of course *you* know. It's what you were trying to do that night, yes? Escape the madness? Crawl outside the smallness they handed us, telling us it was *life*?"

My stomach clenched. "It was an accident," I said. I didn't want to talk about that night. It was mine and only mine. Something so private it hurt.

"Oh, don't be embarrassed," he said, louder now. "What I mean to say is that it shows you have guts. You have conviction. You've broken free!"

I looked down at my hands folded in my lap. That night, alone in my bedroom, I hadn't broken free of anything. Thinking of that night was like touching an open wound. The edges were safe, but the meaty center was revolting, impossible to touch. How to give words to despair?

"Thanks, I guess," I said.

"Plus, I bet your dad *hated* the whole thing," Tique added. A nearby group of third-years smirked.

Just then a girl sitting near me broke in. "Did you guys hear about the fires?"

"Yes. God, it's awful . . . ," someone else said quietly. "I heard it's the dry season out there. They say it could go on for months. . . ."

A few others chimed in, all of them expressing concern. Invisible needles pricked the back of my neck. This kind of talk, about the world outside the walls, got people called in for interrogation. Such things simply weren't said. Even when I was a child, Father had made sure I kept such thoughts to myself. *It's not your place to comment,* he'd always say. *You should be grateful you don't have to think about such things.*

What am I doing here? I thought.

Then, from the opposite side of the room, a commanding voice broke in.

"Who even cares?" The voice belonged to Marco Arnheim, star of our school's debate team. "If they want to light their forests on fire, kill their own people, burn their goddam livelihoods to the ground, what's it got to do with us?"

The flask made its way back into my hands. The liquid inside tasted awful, but I kept drinking. In a flash of panic, I convinced myself that Wen's hack hadn't worked, that our specs were transmitting all of this, buried away in that sack. What would Father say if he found out?

Somewhere in the shadows, another girl cleared her throat. "Didn't Upper City New Kingsport start the fire, though? Something to do with high-voltage transmission lines?"

"All the better!" Marco said, his voice rising. "Those shanty terrorists deserve it. They gave up the right for us to give a shit about them a long time ago. Before the Breach."

Laksmi laughed at this, and a shock shot through me with the sound. "That's awfully rich, Marco, considering what your daddy does for a living. All that bougie crap you buy for Lydia doesn't pay for itself. You know it comes from—"

But Tique cut her off. "Children, children. Enough of the bickering. Eat, drink, and be merry, for tomorrow's a school day!" Laksmi looked annoyed, but she didn't say anything. Everyone else settled back into their own conversations.

Just then Wen shouted, "Hold up! That's not a record player, is it?"

"Sure is," Tique said. "I found it last week in this little Old World salvage shop. Try it out if you want." Wen slid over to the stack of records piled next to the pre-Breach music player and placed one reverently on the turntable. The *schwick, schwick, schwick* of the spinning record quieted the room. Then, as if from another world, a woman's voice began to sing—something deep and mournful about being a child with no mother, about being such a long way from her home.

I glanced toward the wall where the sack of specs hung and began scripting the best way to get my specs back, slip down the ladder and back into the world. But then Laksmi shifted toward me and took the flask from my hand, and I lost all resolve.

"Hi," she said. Her chin hovered just above my shoulder.

My mouth went dry. My bones went hollow.

"Hey," I said. Her black hair brushed against my cheek, filling my head with its dark, sweet spice. "Have you—I mean, do you come here a lot?"

She tapped the flask with her first and middle fingers and looked around. "I guess. When everything else gets boring."

I nodded a bit too emphatically. "Yeah," I said. I opened my mouth to say more but came up with nothing.

I followed the walkway to my platform, lost in the rhythm of my own steps. At the bottom of the stairs, a clock blinked four fifteen in the morning. I'd slept only a few hours, but in that brief interval, my life had transformed into the stuff of dreams.

Just then my specs twitched with a new message. Here it comes, I thought, bracing myself for some frantic note from the Clinic, demanding to know where I'd been. But the message wasn't from the Clinic. It was from Baba.

Come home, Rumi, the message said. Come quickly.

"Has anyone ever told you that you have a real way with words?"

I cringed. There was that smile. Laksmi, destroyer of worlds.

"No, it's fine. I mean, most people don't have anything interesting to say. Take your friend Wen, for example . . ."

I smiled. "No comment."

"Listen," she said, shifting closer to me. "Don't worry about Tique. He doesn't know what he's talking about. I mean, it's not all that strange, what you did. The fact that we have no control over what happens to us is just—sometimes it's too much to take." Her eyes held mine, and she rested her hand on top of my hand like it was the most natural thing in the world. "I just wanted you to know that I'm really glad you're okay."

My heart raced. A hundred thousand words spun galactically slow in the silence between us. Her cool, soft hand felt like a lifeline—the only thing in the world that was real. I let my fingers close around hers, and she didn't pull away.

"Do you ever think about what it's like out there?" I asked.

She blinked. "You mean outside the walls? Sure, all the time."

"What kinds of things do you think about?"

"Honestly?"

"Honestly."

She shifted even closer to me, as though we were the only two people in the room. "I think a lot about the ocean," she said. "Like, in the images they show us at school, it looks sick and yellow. Toxic, you know? But I've also heard that it's the deepest blue you've ever seen. That it's full of life. It's just—we have no way of knowing which is true."

She tucked a strand of long black hair behind her ear. Her eyes smoldered. I felt lit up with her. Incandescent. We sat like that for so long that the silence between us became soft and familiar.

"I think it's probably blue," I said at last.

"What is?" she asked.

"The ocean. I think it's probably, you know, the deepest blue you've ever seen."

Her smile was radiant. "Me too," she said.

And then somehow, impossibly, her lips met mine. And in that moment nothing existed. There was no world and no Father. No walls. There was only Laksmi's soft, hungry kiss. . . .

And the night began to dance.

Laksmi twirled her hair to one side and rested her head on my shoulder. Record after record filled the space behind the screen, and I let myself get swept away. I let myself smile. Voices sang about love, true and tender. Voices sang the blues. My head spun with the sounds of a world at once familiar and strange—a world that sang of cars and sweethearts and loss. It was a world known to me through archival footage and history texts, barely remembered because no one at the time knew it was about to be forgotten. In this half-waking state, I thought I heard a freight copter fly overhead. Maybe it was Father's, I thought. But with Laksmi resting against me, I didn't even care. The universe shrank to the size of that candlelit room, to the warm glow radiating between my hand and hers.

And for once I didn't feel so alone.

I woke hours later to the sound of Tique's voice. "All right, comrades. Wakey, wakey."

Laksmi stirred beside me. My head buzzed with broken sleep, but my chest felt light.

Wen stood and stretched. "Well, mon ami, what'd you think of your surprise?"

"It was better than anything I could've imagined. . . ."

Laksmi opened her eyes and smiled. "He doesn't have much of an imagination, does he?"

"Okay, lover boy," Tique said, patting my shoulder. "Let's get moving. The business wanks start their daily slog soon. Don't want to give away our little secret."

In a daze, I blew out the candle beside me, fished my specs from the sack, and climbed down the ladder after the others. The square was still empty, but the sky was smudged gray with the subtle approach of morning.

As we walked toward the AutoTram station, I followed the othe[r] lead and slid my specs back into their security latch. All at once, t[he] digital world rushed back at me. With a little twist, I detached [the] blue marble from my specs. "Mind if I hang on to this?" I asked V[en]

"Sure," he said with a shrug. "Just don't be an idiot and u[se it] all the time. It only has one loop. Surveillance bots catch patt[erns] like that pretty quick."

"Noted," I said.

In front of us, Laksmi slung smooth, dangerous circle[s with] her hips as she walked. My heart beat with her name, he[r eyes,] the brightness of her lips. How could lips look *rebelliou[s]*? [She] terrified me, and I couldn't stop thinking about her. I did[n't want] to stop thinking about her.

Wen nudged my arm and smiled. I swallowed the h[eart] in my throat and tried to smile back.

At the station, we splintered off to our separate [trams.] "See you in a few hours," Wen called over his should[er.] [Laksmi] didn't wave, but she held my gaze long enough for [my heart to] jump. Then she disappeared, her hair twirling down [into] a beautiful tangle.

5

PAZ

You learn to see things in the dark.
It's so dark down here you'd think
You wouldn't be able to see at all,
But your eyes change.

I can see the shape of her, there in the corner.
I can see the stacks of paintings left to rot.
I can see the slope of my own two arms
Resting on my knees,
My left arm straight and strong,
My right arm curled and small.
Like two sides of me:
The good parts twisted,
The evil parts strong.

I can see you,
Your face like the moon's,
And I want you to be real.
Are you real? Are you here?
Is it true that I'm telling you my story?

A s I said, it was springtime.

The city was just waking up after a long night of rain, and a blanket of clouds hung over the cerros, where shanty homes clung to the slopes, piled like a catch of fish ready to leap back into the sea. Campesinos made their way silent toward the port down streets thick with the smells of dog shit and fish and the murky stink of rotting leaves. Most everybody I passed that morning was headed downhill, blank-faced with the day ahead. I was the only one hiking up, away from my city and toward the forest for another day of hauling samples from the river.

Cerro Felicidad, Cerro Cementerio, Cerro Iglesia.

The streets emptied out as I walked higher and higher, into hills that had no names. Only us scouts dared go so high, where the walls of buildings sprouted with vines and the deep shade of the forest swallowed the streets, changing them slow back to dirt.

The rotten smiles of Yasmín and the other scouts burned in my throat as I walked. It wasn't until the cool breath of the Autopista River touched my skin that I felt the ugly memory of the scouts' meeting that morning begin to fall away from me. My heart pounding, I scaled the broken concrete of the long-collapsed highway. I could hear the river. I could smell the chill of its waters. I climbed up one last outcrop of rubble and then stood, arms out-stretched in the slanting morning light, to look out over my city.

My city. Paraíso.

I took a gulp of cool, clean air into my lungs. From that perch, the ugliness of the city—the stink and grime and sweat—disappeared. The ups and downs of the land, the colors of the buildings and the trees, the prairies growing from concrete lots—all of it looked so soft and pretty. Fishing boats docked beside half-drowned buildings to the west where the city met the bright blue ocean. Zip lines flew down to the swim basin near the port. Mazes of rotting boards connected neighbors with roofs close enough to span. I could see the old Mercado where Javi and me and Mami lived. Even the bomb craters and charred towers to the northeast, where the ocean met the Wastes looked somehow beautiful. Up on that pile of rubble, I didn't have to remember the ugliness that caked like road muck on our lives. I could think of it instead as a painting, something pretty and separate. Somebody else's twisted fairy tale.

Ya, basta, I thought. *Enough of that.*

From inside my satchel, I took the cloth-wrapped body of the hummingbird, his eyes closed and his bright-green neck feathers shimmering where his beak tucked under his wing. Cradling the bird in my hands, I sat on the broken concrete, my back to the wind, closed my eyes, and said a prayer.

"Señor, dame tu fortaleza, por favor," I said. "Give me patience and strength to know that one day things will change."

Just then a hand clapped me on the shoulder.

Ice water shot through my veins. My heart slammed against my ribs. My left hand flew to my knife, and I whipped around.

And there was Javi. Grinning like a fool.

"That's two for me, Paz! ¿Me oyes? Two!"

I let out a groan and sheathed my knife. "Por Dios, Javi . . . ," I said, trying to act like my heart wasn't pounding.

"Oye, I got you so good. I got you so *good*!"

I rolled my eyes. "Two tags is nothing, even!" I said. "I still got, like, ten tags on you. Weón, you'd be dead tons more times than me."

"Is that right?" he said, coming closer. "All it takes is one time. Just once and . . ." He slid his finger across my neck, slow like a knife.

"Puta la weá, weón." I elbowed him in the gut so hard that he fell back against the concrete boulder. "Save your bullshit for somebody who cares."

Javi smiled. He shook loose his long dark hair and tied it back again in a smooth ponytail. "Suit yourself," he said. "It's too bad, though. I was just about to give you your surprise. . . ."

He pointed to a hard plastic case tucked into a cleft of the boulder.

"No way . . . ," I said. "No way!"

"Brand-new," he said, all proud. "Not even a speck of corrosion. Found it just this morning in the back of a truck. Big old thing. Must've been for somebody's car or something."

I knelt down to look over the plastic case.

"And everything else?"

"Everything else is already up there," Javi said. I handed him the case, which was heavy as a rock. "You got till tomorrow morning before you have to report back to ol' Hundred Blazes, right? What do you say we give it a try?"

I smiled big. "Hundred Blazes" was what Javi called Cienfuegos. Elders hated shit like that. "Insubordination," they called it.

I thought for a second on Javi's plan. Sneaking off while on duty was risky. But, like Javi said, if I made it back to the Library by the next morning, nobody would know any different. I cast one last look across the city of Paraíso spread out below me—cerros, forest and Wastes, ocean sparkling blue all the way to the horizon—and then I took off running.

"Wait up, weona!" Javi called to me.

We ran upriver, through sapling trees and mounds of concrete rubble, until we reached our zip line crossing. The cool river air blew gentle over my skin as I flew across the gulch. Javi glided across to join me, and then together we ran through the forest, taking turns with the heavy case. It felt good to run with Javi, to forget the map and the elders and all the poisoned creatures. Javi was the only person in the world I knew how to trust. He was the only person I could forget myself with, could run with through the forest holding nothing in my mind but wind and trees.

We ran through the rest of the morning and into afternoon, and when at last we came to the edge of the forest, we stood for a moment, shoulder to shoulder. In front of us, beyond the last fold of trees, were the Wastes. Clouds of dust loomed huge and thirsty above the ruins. The broken spires of lifeless towers cut into the sky, splotched orange and gray with lichen blooms. These were the ruined, forbidden lands where Las Oscuras reigned.

In my left hand, I readied my sling and stones. Javi did the same.

Silent, we slid down the gully and ducked beneath an old highway overpass where yellow water always seemed to pool. I glanced back to be sure we weren't followed. Las Oscuras was tricky that way. They'd trail you in the shadows till they figured out why you'd dared step onto their lands. Then they'd snatch you.

We reached our mark—a rusty street sign buckled with vines—and we both crouched down. Across the street from us stood a dust-brown building, its broken windows dark and empty.

"There it is," Javi whispered. "Hiding our jewel in its pocket."

I smiled. In all my scouting, I'd come across only a single door that hadn't been kicked down or shot through or blasted open by scrappers. And that door was in this building.

Javi crossed the street and slipped out of sight behind the rusted car hood covering our entrance. I scanned the Wastes one last time to be sure we hadn't been trailed and then slunk into the building behind him.

The icy smell of dust and old rot filled my nose. In near darkness, we shuffled down a ransacked passageway and up a crumpled mess of stairs. With my sinner's hand, I felt along the second-story hallway for the one door that wasn't busted. When my fingers touched the knob, I sighed relief. Still locked. Scrappers hadn't found it yet, gracias a Dios. In silence, I picked the lock and pushed open the door. Sunlight spilled out into the rubble-filled hallway, stinging my eyes as we stepped inside, into an apartment forgotten by the whole world.

"Buenas tardes, queridos," I said.

A row of pictures hung in frames on the wall near the entryway: a boy sitting straight as a pine, a girl missing both front teeth, a baby making a fuss of the bow on her head.

"Hope you don't mind us stopping by unannounced," Javi said.

This was part of the game we played. We pretended like we'd been invited over, like the strangers whose pictures hung on the walls were our cousins or something. It was the best way we knew to keep the ghosts of that place at bay. The people in those pictures were long-ago dead.

In the big yellow room at the center of the apartment, I laid out our tools. Javi took the battery from its plastic case and set it on the table. On the floor beside me, a different car battery—one that never would take a charge—was still connected with belts and wires to a bicycle we'd snuck into the apartment over a year ago. This new battery would be our fifth try.

I stripped the casing from a skinny red wire and trimmed off the fray. Javi started disconnecting the old battery from the bicycle.

"You done your chores for this month's Festival?" Javi asked as we worked.

I laughed. "Not even close. I'm thinking about skipping this one. What do you think of that?" On Festival days, our whole city gathered for feasting and stories before parading down to the Lighthouse for the burning. There, all of us with sinner's arms and sinner's legs and sinner's minds would circle at the front of the crowd to let ash from the fire rain benediction down on us. But I didn't want ashes to rain on my face anymore. I didn't need any such benediction.

Javi shook his head. "What do you think the Library elders would say?"

"The elders can suck it, weón. Why do they make things like this forbidden, anyway?" I pointed to the bike and the car battery. "Just think if we had *electricity* and all. Not just an hour here and there when they say we can have it, but whenever we want. All the tech we scouts find—think of what we could do with it if they just let us . . ."

"You know why." Javi tugged at a knotty mess of wire. "For 'The Good of the People.'"

A quiet anger churned in my guts. "Por favor, don't start with that. Why they gotta control every tiny piece of our lives and pretend it's for our own damn good?"

"Don't be such a kid, Paz," Javi said. "Everybody knows that if the Library elders let us do this kind of thing, pretty soon we wouldn't need them at all. And if we didn't need the elders, then why would we have to listen to what they say?

"But you've got to admit that the Library does some good, too. Mami says you scouts are close to mapping the chemfields and minefields all the way to the Cordillera. Hell, the road between

Paraíso and Temuco is almost safe enough for little kids to travel. We're finally starting to feel like a *country* again, Paz—and it's all because of the Library. Just think about it for like half a second."

I knew this was true. But it didn't get to the heart of my question. I was really asking about the picaflor, about the killing of things small and soft and beautiful. I was asking about my sinner's arm and my chem-poisoned mother and the burning that would come in a few days at the Festival de los Santos.

I set down the wire cutters and looked at Javi.

"You know there's another way," I said. "Las Oscuras."

Javi flinched at the name, but I didn't take it back.

"Don't say that kind of thing," he said. "Don't even think it."

"Sometimes I think about joining, you know." My heart raced to speak the words out loud. "Sometimes I think that, if they recruited me, I'd be proud to take their mark."

Javi looked up at me with hurt in his eyes.

"Is that right?" he said. "You'd be proud to wear their mark? Proud to show your tat to Cienfuegos and all the elders and let 'em burn you in the Lighthouse on some Festival day for your treason?"

I laughed off this last bit. "I wouldn't show it to the elders, weón! I'm not *that* crazy. I'd wear it proud for myself. Like, for what it'd mean to me. Remember what Las Oscuras did for my mother? When nobody else would dare even touch her, not the elders, not anybody." My eyes welled with tears, but I didn't let them fall.

Javi sighed. "You've got a right to feel that way. Your mom and your arm and all . . . but if I have to choose between one crooked power and another, I choose the Library." He tightened the bolts and tested the belts for tautness.

"It's not just my mom and my arm. It's *all of this*." I motioned toward the bombed-out buildings and rubble-filled streets out-side the balcony window. My throat burned with words I'd left to smolder for too long. "What're we doing anyway? Scouting the waterways? Mapping the lands? Testing little patches of soil? ¡Una mierda! Upper City chems are still poisoning the land and the water. You know damn well that Las Oscuras isn't really the enemy. The real enemies are those greedy cerdos hiding behind their bombs and their walls. Upper City is still bombing and thieving wherever they can. They have all the power, and what have we got? We've got *nothing*."

My belly shuddered. I could burn in the Lighthouse just for speaking such things.

Javi looked down at his hands. He didn't say anything for a long while.

"The sea," he said at last. "At least we have the sea. And the forest. And fresh fish, and fried-up cochayuyo ... Upper City's got none of that. Las Oscuras has none of that either. All they can offer is revenge. You'd throw your life away if you joined them, Paz. You couldn't ever come home again. You understand that, don't you? Once you join them, you're *marked*. Anybody in Paraíso sees you with a tat, you'd be ashes! I mean, I agree that we've got to do something. I'm just not ready to die to make it happen. . . ."

Javi took one last look over the battery and then hopped on the bike and started pedaling. The wheels spun into a blur. I walked over to the balcony doors to let in the breeze. Things with Javi always seemed to turn into a fight lately, and I hated it. Maybe he was right. Maybe the sea and the fish and the cool forest air could somehow be enough to make me forget the Breach.

I sat back down on the couch in silence. Javi's jaw clenched as he pedaled.

"Las Oscuras wouldn't want me anyway, you know." I held up my twisted arm and gave it a little shake. "What would a girl with a sinner's arm have to offer the most powerful band of revolutionaries this side of the Breach?"

Sweat beaded on Javi's forehead as he kept pedaling. "I hope you're right. For your sake."

Outside, the sun pierced itself on the ruined spires of the Wastes. Javi pedaled till it got so dark I could scarce see his face. And that's when I saw it. I had to crouch to be sure, but it was there. A red light, flickering.

"It's working!" I shouted. "It's taking the charge!"

Javi pedaled faster, and the red light steadied. When at last it changed to green, he jumped off the bike. "Well?" he said. "What should we try first?"

We lit a candle and looked around the room—at lamps, kitchen gadgets, electronic screens. But nothing seemed right. Then Javi crouched beside a table in the corner and unlatched the little brown case sitting on top of it. Inside was a black disc with a thin metal arm.

"That thing plays music, no?" I asked.

"Let's find out."

Javi connected the music player to the battery, and the black disc began to spin with a soft, crackly sound. Magic. Old World magic. Neither of us moved. The pluck of a guitar floated through the air like a ghost. And then a man's voice started to sing. . . .

The voice sang in Spanish, rich and clear. He sang about the pain we all carry around with us, how that pain turns into a black and bitter ocean.

And who but us can make it clean again?

The ghost played three songs, and then the record went quiet. Without a word, Javi stood and played it again. I sat spellbound. The crackling, the guitar, the voice. Magic.

No puedes volver atrás, the ghost sang. *You can't go back to the way things were before.*

We listened until the battery lost its charge. Javi stood to close the case. "We should be heading back now, no?" he said. "Mami will worry."

But I didn't move.

"I'll follow after you," I said. "I'm supposed to be on a scouting mission, not snooping around with my brother. Somebody sees us together, I'll never hear the end of it from the elders." A good enough reason, but not the real one.

Javi looked at me sideways. "You sure?"

I nodded. "Ask Mami to set a plate for me, yeah?"

He kissed my cheek. "All right, niña. But be careful."

I latched the door behind him and then walked with a candle to the bedroom at the end of the hall. From the bedside table, I took a thin red journal and opened to my dog-eared page.

> *November 5*
>
> *If Eva doesn't see a doctor soon, I fear the worst. Bernardo's arm is healing, so that's something cheerful to note. Strange, though. I can hardly stand to write that word—"cheerful."*
>
> *How long before they turn off the lights and the water? They turned off utilities in Valpo last week. Everyone with petrol drove toward the Cordillera in search of snow. Or so I heard. But what happens to those of us with no petrol left?*

I read several more pages until I made it to the last entry. *December 10. Bernardo threw the microwave off the balcony yesterday,* it said. *I don't know what to do.*

I closed my eyes. How many times had I read these pages? Again, I thought of Las Oscuras. How they'd shot down Upper City copters and showered medicine in the streets. How they'd strapped themselves with bombs and blown to pieces the Upper City dozers meant to tear through our lands. Javi was right about a lot of things, I thought. Javi was almost always right. But on this one thing, he seemed dead wrong.

I placed the journal back on the bedside table and blew out the candle, then felt my way down the stairs in the dark till I found the patch of moonlight that marked the way out. All was quiet in the ruins outside. Sling and stones in hand, I stepped into the silver night.

6

RUMI

The windows were dark when I climbed the steps to my house. My head spun with possibilities for why Baba had called me home so urgently. Maybe someone had found out I'd taken off my specs and gone behind the screen. . . .

"Baba?" I called into the darkened house. My voice sounded hollow in the gloom of early morning. "It's me, Rumi."

No answer.

In the kitchen, I noticed a stack of unwashed dishes in the sink. Baba always cleaned his dishes right away. He never left them for later. Upstairs, the door to Father's room stood open a crack. A faint light from inside cast a beam into the hallway.

"Baba?" I called again, pushing the door open.

In the middle of the room, the ladder to the secret emergency annex extended from the ceiling. Harsh light streamed from above. I paused for a moment in the bedroom doorway, composing myself. But nothing could have prepared me for what I found.

The first thing I saw was the medical cot surrounded by plastic walls. Father stared out at me from inside this plastic cell. His brown skin looked thin as wax.

The next thing I saw were Baba's tears. I had never seen my grandfather cry.

My eyes darted between Father and Baba. Father in a plastic room, looking like death. Baba crying, a crumpled handkerchief in his hands.

"You've left your spectacles downstairs, yes?" Baba asked. His voice sounded hollow, like a wooden bowl. I nodded blankly. "Good, good. That at least is good."

The attic's stagnant air smelled sweet, like pine. I sank into the chair next to Baba, facing Father. The plastic sheeting formed a cage around him. "Why is he—?" I said to Baba. Then I turned to Father. "Why are you—?"

"There's been an ambush, child," Baba said softly. "In the shanties of Lower City."

"Lower City?" I said, turning to Father. I was surprised by how steady my voice sounded. "This is bullshit. I knew you weren't going to Cuzco."

Father raised his hand to stop me. "I know what I told you, Rumi," he said, his voice weak. He sounded like some other person, like a voice from a dream. "It happened outside one of the Lower City shanties. A tattooed man grabbed me, forced open my jaw. It wasn't until after I returned to St. Iago that I realized . . ."

The air in the room turned thin.

"Realized what?" I asked. Baba bowed his head. He seemed to be whispering to himself. A curse, maybe. Or a prayer.

"Zabrán, Rumi."

My ears muted with the word, as though I'd been plunged underwater without warning.

"But it can't—you can't be . . ." Images I didn't want to see flashed through my mind, archival footage from before the

Breach. Zabrán hadn't been the first pandemic to sweep the world, but it had been the last and most devastating, because it had been weaponized—an unknown virus in a town called Hastings, just south of London, leading months later to victims of bioterror dying in overcrowded hospitals all over the world. No one knowing what to do.

"What are you even doing here?" I said to Father. "Aren't the Governance labs engineering some kind of . . . of antivirus?"

"No, Rumi. They can't," Father said. Then he corrected himself. "And even if they could, they won't. Their primary mission is to secure Upper City against contaminants. And I am now a contaminant." His voice had turned eerily calm. Official. "My blood scans were fine when I reentered the city—and the cadet working security let me through without the typical forty-eight-hour quarantine. But now the scans are definitive. The vaccines I've gotten weren't effective against this strain. It's only a matter of time before the fever sets in. Then, one by one, my organs will fail, followed by delirium, shock, death."

Baba held Father's DigiCloth out to me in silence. I tugged at the corners, and the cloth went rigid in my hands. The device was offline, but on the screen Father's bloodwork had been mapped onto a graph of every known strain of the virus. At the bottom of the chart were three words: "ZABRÁN. STRAIN UNKNOWN."

"But . . . there has to be a cure."

Father shook his head. "If there is a cure, it's of no use to me. If it exists, it's out *there*."

The images of pre-Breach hospitals came relentlessly now. Contorted postures of grief and death. I'd first seen this footage in primary school as part of my basic citizen tests. Back then I'd been shocked that doctors had tried to keep the infected alive.

Why hadn't they just let them die? Why had they tried to save people who were beyond saving? But this. My father. *This.*

"So, what now?" I demanded. "Now you just . . . *die*?" My voice sounded angry as it echoed in my ears. And I was angry. Angry at the plastic sheets surrounding his bed. Angry at Father's official composure. Angry at myself, at my city's walls.

"Now we wait," Father said. "We don't know yet how bad this strain is. Perhaps it will pass. But in the meantime, you must tell no one. This is of the gravest importance, Rumi. I can only imagine what the Governance would do to you and your grandfather if they found out." For an instant, the resolve in his eyes broke, and I saw his gaping fear. I'd never known Father to break rules, much less break the law. This new recklessness terrified me.

"And there's nothing—" I started. "There's no way anyone could go . . . out there? To look for a cure?"

"Don't be a child, Rumi," Father said. "Out there is chaos. Lower City has lost all sense of what it means to be human. They murder their own brothers to survive another day. They can't even clean their own water. Can you imagine? Drinking the poisoned rain of that *wasteland*?"

I tugged at the corners of the DigiCloth, and it went limp again in my hands.

Father propped himself upright in bed and hooked a bag of clear solution to the intravenous drip that fed into his arm. "I'm inducing a coma-like state now," he said, "which should slow the pathogen's development somewhat—give my immune system a chance to respond."

"Okay," I said, numb.

"Your grandfather will bring me out tomorrow. We can talk more then." His breathing slowed as the liquid trickled into his veins.

"Okay," I repeated. As though the word held the key to the universe.

I followed Baba in silence down the ladder and into the kitchen.

"Take sabz chai with me, Rumi?" he asked.

I took a seat at the table. "Yes, Baba," I said. My voice felt hollow.

Baba poured hot water into a teapot and lowered himself into the chair across from mine. His tidy fingernails tapped the glaze of his mug. I waited for the questions that always followed these silent moments. But no questions came.

At last I couldn't stand it any longer.

"What are we going to do, Baba?" I asked.

"We must be patient, child."

"But Father is . . ." I couldn't bring myself to say it. *Dying. Father is going to die.*

Baba rested his hands on the table. "Do you remember the story of your namesake?"

I nodded. Baba had spoken many times of the poet Rumi. He loved to speak of pre-Breach poetry—he said it was nothing like the poetry composed inside the walls. "You told me Rumi was a Sufi poet. And that almost all of his writings were lost during the Breach."

"Indeed, they were," Baba said. His eyes glittered with the bright mischief that always overtook him when he told this story. "But! My father was a good man, a good man and a scholar, and every night when I was a boy, he'd speak aloud the Molana's poems. I have never forgotten them, not one. Shall I share one with you now?"

"Yes, Baba," I said obediently.

He closed his eyes, and his face relaxed into a smile. "Let me see . . . Yes. There it is." He recited:

> *I once died as a Rock and became Plant.*
> *Then I died as a Plant and became Animal.*
> *I died as an Animal and became Human.*
> *Why should I fear? When was I less by dying?*

He opened his eyes. "Why should I fear!" he repeated. "You have your mother to thank for this namesake, you know. Your father wanted to call you Neils. Neils! Can you imagine?"

I took a sip of tea and looked out the window. In the distance, the western signal tower blinked yellow, assuring us that St. Iago's borders were secure. The irony wasn't lost on me.

Baba drank the last of his tea and yawned. "Well, my child. You must excuse me. I slept not at all last night, and my body is far too old." He stood and kissed my cheek. "You will still go to school today, yes? We must proceed as normal."

I nodded, though my stomach felt sick.

"Don't worry, child! As the good poet says: Why should we fear?"

"Yes, Baba," I said. But I didn't understand.

In a daze, I went upstairs to the bathroom and turned the shower as hot as it would go. The air grew heavy with steam. I wanted to run, to never stop running. But my world was so small, surrounded by walls.

"Out there," I whispered to myself. "Out *there*."

Back in my room, I put on my school uniform and slid my DigiCloth into my backpack. Each movement was slow and deliberate. I was all body and no mind, an exoskeleton with nothing inside. I tapped two pills into my palm and swallowed.

Downstairs I found Baba in the living room, fast asleep in his chair. The thin light from the window made shadows of the wrinkles around his eyes. I unfolded a blanket to drape over his bare legs, and that's when I saw it. On the floor, tucked beneath his chair: a piece of paper.

My breath caught in my throat.

A civilian in possession of paper was considered an enemy of the state. The Governance monitored all information exchange, and paper couldn't be easily monitored. Only once in my life had I touched real paper. When I was nine, the Intercity Intelligence Agency had captured a high-ranking Lower City insurgent. To commemorate this, they'd awarded several declassified documents to the men and women who'd carried out the mission. Father had been among them. He'd brought home the crisp sheet one evening, letting me hold it before hanging it in a frame on the living room wall. He'd seemed so brave to me that day. A true hero.

My heart pounded as I carried the contraband up to my bedroom and unfolded it on my bed. I couldn't believe what I saw. It was a map unlike any I'd ever seen. The Official World Map that we studied in school showed only the Upper Cities and the transit lines connecting them. All else appeared as a blank space labeled "Lower City." But on the map spread in front of me, Lower City was marked with rivers and forests, deserts and towns. With cities . . .

I scanned the map for my own city, St. Iago—a dot boxed in by thick black lines. I traced my finger across the alien landscape surrounding it—mountains to the east, an ocean to the west. As my finger journeyed wider, I came upon more dots: Serena, Arica, Uyuni. Around one of these—a Lower City named Paraíso—a circle had been hand-drawn in red ink. Beside it, in Father's careful handwriting, were four words: *Solomon Cienfuegos, Library Informant.*

I sat on the bed, trying to make sense of it. I felt helpless, crushed beneath the weight of things beyond my control. I began to fold the map, no idea what to do with it, when something on the reverse side caught my eye. A list, scribbled in Baba's fluid cursive:

—Nonstop red-eye to New Kingsport
—Car number seven
— Third stop: front door
—5:28 to departure

I paused for a moment. Had Baba lost his mind? Was he planning to travel north, all the way to the Upper City of New Kingsport, at a time like this?

The realization came in waves. *Why should I fear?*

Oh god, I thought. Baba was planning to *leave*. To leave Upper City in search of a cure for Father.

My head felt light as the pieces clicked together. Perhaps Baba knew something about this Library informant, about the existence of a cure outside Upper City. He'd started his life outside the walls, after all—maybe he had some secret knowledge about the workings of Lower City. Still, leaving the walls now would be complete madness. There was no way he'd survive.

But I knew him well enough to know he'd try.

Without a second thought, I fumbled through my drawers for a lighter. I'd be saving Baba's life by destroying this contraband. But then came a knock on my door.

"Rumi, child?" Baba said.

My skin went cold. I stuffed the map into my backpack and slammed shut the drawer just as Baba peeked into the room. "Shouldn't you be heading to school?"

I forced a smile. How long had I been up in my room? "I was just leaving now," I said.

"You must hurry, hm? Take your father's heliocycle so you'll not be late."

"Yes, Baba," I said.

In a cold sweat, I kissed him goodbye and hurried downstairs.

Old Woman of Suspicion,
  Old Man of Suspicion!
Young Man of Hazard, Young Woman
  of Desperate Opportunity!
Have we wagered wisely?
We storytellers, keepers of forgotten truths—
Have we kept our oath to the future?
These questions pull like thread through our bones.
And who but the young ones can be our judge?

O h, children. Our story tonight is of the shape-shifters, those who move between worlds like frogs. Who come from above, the City of the Sky—to hide, to hunt, to eat. Like you, like me, these in-betweeners know the truth of why the world split in two. The truth of fear. They know they can cross over. They also know they'll never stay.

The first of his kind arrived when our City of the Sea was still shrouded in darkness—no moon and no stars, just the dark of the sky and the dark of the land and sea. He scrabbled down cliffsides, his long limbs reaching; he slunk through trees, with a fist full of shining jewels. When at last he reached the dark streets of our city, he began to knock on doors.

"May I stay for the night?" he'd croak from the darkness. And in the thin candlelight seeping out from the houses, he'd extend his long thin fingers to show off his glittering jewels.

But the people inside were afraid. Oh, how they were afraid.

"Move on, friend," they'd say. "There's no room here." Then they'd close their doors and lock them well and sleep uneasily through the night.

And what did he want, this in-betweener? Some thought him a spy, some a spirit. On door after door he knocked, through this city of endless night. None would let him in.

But a wise elder got word of this stranger with a fist full of jewels. "Come inside," the elder said when at last the shape-shifter arrived at his house. "Tell me, what is it you seek?"

The stranger ducked through the doorway to the wise elder's house, his skin a ghastly green. "I've brought you a gift of peace and friendship," he said, and he spread his jewels on the table. They shone with an otherworldly light, a light not seen in our city for a long, long time.

The wise man's eyes went wide at the sight. "And what do you ask in return?"

"I cannot say," the shape-shifter said. "Only know that you will owe a debt. And when the time comes, that debt must be paid."

The wise man looked at the dark outside his window. And what did he do?

He took the jewels.

When will the shape-shifter collect on his debt? you ask. None among us—not even we storytellers—can say. But it is the shape-shifter's jewels that light our world. Who can fault that wise old elder for accepting the shape-shifter's gift? Where would we be without it? Who among us would choose to go back to the way things were before?

7

R U M I

The school day passed in a blur. I shuffled from class to class, trying to make myself invisible. At lunch rotation, Tique told me that Laksmi hadn't shown up for first period and asked me if I knew why. I shook my head and shrugged. I hadn't even noticed Laksmi was absent. My mind was fixed on Father, on Baba, on the contraband stuffed in my bag.

Why should I fear? Baba had said. *When was I less by dying?*

By third rotation, the scheduled rains had begun. Outside my classroom window, kids from the primary school stomped in puddles, their mouths open to the sky. ". . . As I mentioned last class," Professor Xi droned from the front of the room, "this text was published in the year 42 of the New Common Era. The author, Hannah Ganz, was the first to comment on shifts in Upper City self-perception. The walls of our cities, Ganz claims, function as a third body—our physical bodies being the first, and our political bodies the second. Drawing from pre-Breach philosophers such as Foucault and Habermas, Ganz argues that . . ."

Her words formed a slurry of sound. I looked back to the children playing outside in the rain. It wasn't until Wen cleared his throat from the desk beside mine that I snapped back to the present. He slid his Digi to the edge of his desk and tapped it to mine.

Hey, what say we ditch Devi's lecture this PM? Better to be out there, rain or shine, than stuck in here, eh?

Out there, I thought. If there's a cure, it's out there.

OK, I wrote.

Good man! Meet you by the bikes after this snoozefest.

On the top level of the parking lot, I found Wen suiting up next to his bike. Rows of brightly colored heliocycles glinted with droplets of water. A ray of sunlight pierced the clouds.

Why should I fear? I thought.

Wen straddled his bike as I neared him. "Hey . . . ," I started.

"No, no, no," he said. "Don't tell me we should go back. I forbid it!"

"It's not that. I just—I need to ask you something."

He strapped on his helmet. "Anything, mon ami. Tell me your heart's desire."

I scanned the empty lot before taking the metallic marble from my jacket pocket and pressing it to my specs. When it glowed, I took off my specs, and the world turned gray. Wen gave a conspiratorial smile and did the same.

"Listen." I lowered my voice. "I need you to get something. From your mom's lab."

Wen stared back at me. "*Get* something? Like *steal*?"

I nodded.

He smiled, disbelieving. "Straitlaced Rumi, won't even take a puff of smoke into his dainty little lungs, wants me to filch from a Governance lab. You're kidding, right?"

"I'm not." My voice dropped to a whisper. "I need vaccines, Wen. I'm going out."

"Shut up," Wen said.

"I can't tell you why. Just know that it's serious. I don't have a choice."

He tore off his helmet and threw it at me. "Shut the hell up!"

I glanced behind me. The parking lot was still empty.

"Well?" I whispered. "Can you help?"

"What the holy motherfucking kind of question is that?" Wen shouted. "This is perhaps the single most exciting thing that's happened in my entire life! If you think I'm not going to use every bit of my cunning and charm to get what you need, then you don't know Wendell Francisco Mankovich!"

I couldn't help but smile. "The thing is, I need them really soon."

"Say no more. I'll do some sleuthing straightaway. Figure out what unholy plagues we'll need to protect you from." He snatched his helmet from my hands and strapped it on with a flourish. "This really takes the cake, Rumi. The whole goddamned cake!"

My stomach fluttered as I watched him speed out of the parking lot. Plans had been set in motion. Plans that would defy the most inviolable laws in Upper City's constitution.

With my specs still in my hand, I stared at the naked world— the wet, lifeless dust; the engineered clouds overhead, making way for the sun after the rain.

What was I thinking? Who did I think I was?

I expected to find Baba at the kitchen table when I came home, waiting to ask me about the map. But the kitchen was dark. Upstairs, the door to Father's room was closed. By now Baba must've known that I'd taken the map. But how could he say anything? Admitting he knew about it would be to admit that he possessed it in the first place.

I went straight to my room and sat on the bed. As a child I used to dream of what it would be like to leave the walls, to journey into the unknown. But those were just fantasies. The lessons we'd learned in school about the peaceniks of the fifties—the only civilians known to have defected from Upper City—had made this perfectly clear. I'd seen footage of their bodies lying side by side, white sheets blotched with red. Not one had made it back alive. They'd defected sixteen years after the walls were sealed off for good, four years before Father was even born. And no one had tried since.

I beat back the thoughts that dug into me like needles. You have no idea what you're doing. You're going to die out there. Still, how could I live with myself if I didn't try?

Why should I fear?

I was supposed to meet Wen at midnight behind the screen for the vaccines. That didn't give me much time, and evening came quickly as I put together supplies. When I heard Baba knock on my bedroom door, my stomach sank.

"Dinner, Rumi?" he said.

Downstairs, the kitchen smelled of coriander and cinnamon. Two cups of tea waited on the table, and I took a seat behind one of them. Baba brought a bowl of golden rice to the table—leftovers from the previous night. "How was school today?" he asked as he sat down. He was wearing his specs with their full online capabilities enabled—a safety precaution, I guessed, since our family was almost certainly under heightened surveillance after Father's disappearance.

"Fine," I said, nudging a piece of chicken across my bowl.

"That's good, child," he said. But he wasn't smiling. Instead, he looked at me intently—like he wanted me to listen to his eyes, not his voice. "Did I ever tell you the story of my family's escape from South Pakistan?"

I hesitated. This was a story he'd told me many times. It was one of his favorites.

"No, Baba," I said. "I don't think you've told me that story before."

"Ah, how can that be?" he said. "I was a boy of six or seven, but I remember those days vividly. My mother and I would spend the day hidden in our tiny apartment while my father traveled to the hospital to treat those wounded in our country's civil war. Always there were air raids and gunshots in the distance, and I never felt safe until my father returned for the evening.

"Ah, but once he returned, we'd all sit on the rug in the center of the room and take tea, safe from all the world!" He said this with a laugh, but his eyes didn't sparkle. And it was his eyes, I knew, I should be watching.

"I shall never forget the poem my father recited the night before we began the long journey that would lead us here, to St. Iago." Baba closed his eyes, and his face turned serene.

> *If salt water did not travel from the sea to the sky,*
> *How would the garden be watered by rain?*
> *When the drop left its ocean home and returned,*
> *It found an oyster shell and turned into a pearl.*

I stared back at Baba, looking for a clue in his expression. "Don't you see, Rumi?" Baba said, unblinking. "Why should we fear? When were we less by dying?"

+ + + +

An hour before midnight, the lights downstairs went dark, and I heard Baba sink into his chair. Barely breathing, I tiptoed from my room. The door to Father's bedroom was open a crack, and cold light seeped from the annex above. I crept down the hall as quietly as I could, but just as I passed his open door, Father's voice called down from above. "Rumi?" he said.

I froze. Maybe I'd just imagined it.

But then he spoke again. "Rumi, is that you? Come, come up."

I stood for a moment, uncertain. If I told him my plans, he'd do everything he could to convince me not to go. He'd remind me how powerless I was, how little I knew about the world.

Still, how could I leave without saying goodbye?

I climbed the stairs.

In the stale attic air, the clear plastic sheeting surrounding Father's cot sagged slightly. Inside, Father's body looked shrunken and frail.

He smiled weakly. "Do I look all that bad?"

I sat in the chair beside his plastic cell but said nothing.

"Your face is saying many things," he said. "Just like your mother's used to. Her face could carry out entire conversations!" There was no meanness in his voice, only resignation. His brow gathered together, protective. "What's to be done, Rumi? My only child will live his life as an orphan in a house of spirits. And it's my fault."

My face burned. "I'm sixteen," I said, more bitterly than I intended. "You're not allowed to say my life is your fault."

Sweat glistened on his forehead. "That's not what I meant, Rumi. Why must you always twist my words to mean the worst?" His eyes narrowed then, and he pushed himself upright and peered through the plastic. "What on earth are you wearing? And what are you doing with that backpack of yours, at this hour?"

My cheeks flushed. I tried to conjure an easy lie but came up empty. And I realized then that, even if I told the truth, there was nothing Father could do to stop me. Not this time.

"I'm leaving Upper City," I said. "Tonight."

"What are you talking about?" Father said.

My back straightened. I could feel my resolve growing stronger. "I'm going to Lower City to find a man named Solomon Cienfuegos. To find you a cure."

Father's eyes turned feverishly sharp. Evidence of the virus colored his face—the fluid pooling under his eyes, the dark spots on his skin. "You can't," he said. "I won't let you."

I stood from my chair. "I'm going, Father. With or without your blessing."

"Please," he said. "I can't lose you, not like this."

I slid my hands into my pockets and clenched my fingernails into my palms. "This is the first time in my life when I can do something real. I have to try."

Father's pleas followed me into the hallway. But I knew I had no choice. I couldn't live with myself any other way.

In the garage, I secured a large jug of water and a length of rope onto Father's cycle. The rest of my supplies—a canteen; a case of PuriTabs; SoyChewy bars; a compass; a lighter; a first aid valise; a sharp kitchen knife; my specs and DigiCloth, loaded with Father's bloodwork; the map with Baba's note scrawled on the back—were already stuffed into my pack. Then I checked the time.

Twenty minutes to midnight.

Across the dimness of the living room, Baba slept in his chair. I took one last look at the kitchen table, the dirty teacups beside the sink. My life.

Shaking, I walked out the door and closed it behind me.

+ + + +

I was five minutes late for my meeting with Wen, and I raced to the top of the ladder to find him there, ready with the meds from his mother's lab. He seemed almost giddy. He'd nearly been caught, he said, stealing the vaccines, and his "inside guy" hadn't been so lucky.

"They took him for questioning," Wen said, breathless with excitement. "They'll probably come for me next. But don't worry. I've got an alibi. Plus, what would a tweaker like me possibly want with vaccines anyway?" He laughed, unzipping a coldpack case to reveal a tidy row of syringes.

"So, I got you typhoid, yellow jack, and hanta. Zabrán is a little tricky since there's so many strains, but I nabbed the most comprehensive one I could find."

"Thank you, Wen," I said as I rolled up my sleeve. "You don't know what this means."

"Don't mention it," he said. "It was seriously my pleasure." He flicked a sweaty clump of hair from his eyes and shot me with the first two vaccines.

I winced. "And you won't say anything about this? Even though I can't tell you why I—"

Wen cut me off. "You don't have to tell me a thing, mon ami." He swabbed my other bicep and flicked the third needle. "I'll even tell the profs at school that you're abroad visiting Toronto or some shit, interviewing for university. I'll be sure to call you a smart-ass wanker, just to keep it believable." He stuck bandage strips over the dots of blood on my arms, and I rolled down my sleeves. "You are coming back, though. Right?"

"Of course I'm coming back," I said, though I had no idea if this were true.

Wen extended his hand, and we shook. "All right. Godspeed, comrade. Don't trust those Lower City devils. Wily bastards, all of them!"

I strapped on my helmet and mounted Father's heliocycle. "I won't," I said over the hum of the motor. Then he slapped my back, and I sped toward the BulletRail station.

A handful of passengers waited on the platform for the red-eye to New Kingsport. I counted the cars when the train arrived and wheeled my cycle into car number seven—now at the head of the train—like a kid following bread crumbs into a forest, no idea where they'd lead.

Why should I fear? I thought. Why should I fear? And yet I was terrified.

There were two other passengers in car number seven—a man and woman too lost in their specs to notice me running my fingers over the tender lumps where Wen had shot me with vaccines. I leaned my head back against my seat as a soft puff of air closed the doors to our car. A woman's voice announced that the train would make three in-city stops before departing the walls; that a routine spec scan would be performed at the final stop; that passengers should kindly sit back, relax, and enjoy their journey. My heart pounded as the train picked up speed. Beyond the city walls, the train would reach upward of one thousand kilometers per hour as it glided, frictionless, in a magnetized tunnel of steel.

But I'd be gone before then. I'd be outside.

The train slowed to a stop. The doors glided open, and the woman's voice announced that all passengers commuting within St. Iago should clear car number seven at this time.

The skin on my neck tingled. The cars on all BulletRail trains were self-contained, with no doorways to walk between cars due to the train's high speed while it was in motion. What was different about car number seven?

The other two passengers in my car got off, but no one else boarded. A few minutes passed before a puff of air again closed the doors and the woman's voice announced that the train would make two in-city stops before departing for New Kingsport. A spec scan would be performed at the final stop. "Kindly sit back, relax, and enjoy."

At the second stop, no one boarded.

"One in-city stop before departing the walls," the woman said.

A routine spec scan.

"Kindly sit back, relax . . ."

I could hardly breathe as I ran through Baba's instructions. *Third stop. Front door. Five minutes twenty-eight seconds to departure.* "This will be our final stop before departing the city of St. Iago," the singsong voice said. "A routine spec scan will be performed momentarily. Thank you for your cooperation."

As the train slowed to a stop, I set the timer in my specs—five minutes twenty-eight seconds and counting. I wheeled my cycle to the front of the train car and took Wen's marble from my pocket. But as soon as I attached it to my specs, a message dropped down. A security breach has been detected on this account, the message read in large bold letters. Respond immediately to avoid disciplinary measures. My stomach sank as I blinked away these words. It was an official message, from the Governance. They must've detected the loop in my specs.

And that's when I saw them: through the small window above the rear door, two men in Governance blue, waiting on the platform.

Shit, I thought. Shit, shit, shit.

I ducked down and tried not to panic. But they'd already seen me.

"Rumi Sabzwari," said a voice through my specs. One of the Governance men on the platform made eye contact with me through the small window and nodded solemnly before continuing. "You are in violation of the Upper City Surveillance Protection Act. It's within your rights to surrender willingly. Otherwise, you'll be taken by force."

My mind raced for a plan but found none. Once the doors opened, they'd take me away. And I'd hear of Father's death on some gossip thread without ever seeing him again.

I closed my eyes and waited.

But nothing happened. The doors didn't open. Through the window, I could see passengers on the platform entering and exiting the other train cars. But for some reason, the doors to car number seven stayed closed.

Through the train car window, I could just barely make out the words of the Governance men to a BulletRail engineer, who'd rushed over to meet them on the platform. "What do you mean, out of order?" one of the men in blue said, peering into the dimness of my train car.

"Nothing I can do . . . Just have to pick him up on the other side . . . New Kingsport, that's right . . . No, he can't get out."

My face turned hot. Baba's instructions. They had to mean something.

Third stop: front door. Five minutes twenty-eight seconds to departure.

I pushed my cycle away from the window, out of sight of the Governance men, and wheeled it to the front door on the opposite side of the train car. Outside this door, I saw only blackness— not the bright lights of the station. Should I wait the full five minutes and twenty-eight seconds? I wondered. But no, Baba's note seemed to be saying that this was when the train would depart. If I waited that long, I might miss my chance.

In desperation, I yanked the handgrip of the door. But it didn't move. I kicked at the metal latch with all my strength, but it wouldn't even budge.

Damn it.

A full minute passed as I searched for anything that might open the doors. My knife? My rope? Then I remembered the repair compartment at the back of Father's heliocycle. With shaking hands, I crouched beside the rear wheel and fumbled open the latch. Inside were two pairs of pliers, screwdrivers of different sizes, a crowbar, and a set of wrenches.

A crowbar.

I jammed the curved iron rod between the doors and pushed against its shaft as hard as I could. Nothing moved. I tried for better leverage. Still nothing. Two minutes thirty seconds left to departure. My neck was cold with sweat. Desperate, I moved the crowbar lower and began stomping it with my boot, grunting with each stomp. I lunged into it with my whole body, and at last the doors shifted, though only slightly. Light filled my chest. I lunged again with all my strength—once, twice, three times—and finally the front doors shot open all the way.

Cool night wind swirled into the train car from the darkness outside. Sand whipped my face. I understood right away why the engineers had programmed the doors to stay closed here. The train was misaligned at this final stop before leaving the city. Most of the train remained inside the station, but the tip of car number seven, the head of the train, peeked outside the walls. The front doors of my train car opened into the void of night.

I checked the time in my specs. Fifty seconds to departure.

On this section of track, the steel tunnel was only scaffolding. I could see straight to the ground, roughly four meters below. In a blur, I hooked my rope around a metal handrail above the door and secured the other end to my cycle—a makeshift pulley—then leaned all my weight against it to create a counterbalance. The cycle sank to the ground with a thud. Then I waited. For what, I wasn't sure. To change my mind? To get caught? Waiting for someone to tell me I didn't have to go?

No, I thought. I have no choice. Either I jump or Father dies. Just like my mother.

Ten seconds to go, five seconds, and I jumped.

My breath suspended in my chest. My arms hovered over my head. And just as my feet touched the desert sand, the doors on the train above hissed closed, and the train sped away.

No alarm sounded. No searchlights flashed. The Governance men must've assumed I was on my way to New Kingsport. Above me, my city's walls towered into the night, glowing a dull, watch-ful green. Wind howled against them—a low, deadening sound. These walls were astoundingly tall, braced with steel and armed with missiles. They were walls of progress, walls of freedom and civilization. And for the first time in my life, I was on the outside.

I untied the rope from my cycle. In the distance, all was pitch-black. Maybe there were cliffs and boulders out there. Maybe more enormous mountains, like the ones I'd seen when my specs were off in the square. Maybe a jungle. I had no way of knowing. But I'd made my choice. I mounted my cycle and started the igni-tion. Its vibrations felt like home. With a thousand doubts turn-ing my stomach, I pressed my boot to the accelerator and drove toward a foreign horizon.

PART II
PARAÍSO

8

PAZ

Before you came,
I'd speak prayers to the dark.
I'd speak prayers to myself, to no one.
This world is made of shit, I'd say,
It's shit and it has no brightness to it.

But my prayers whispered out into nothing.
The little bird was still full of poison.
The light of day was still lost.

What kind of God, I'd say,
Would show me the truth of the world
Only after it was too late?

From her open-eyed sleep,
She'd laugh at me.
Oye, weona, she'd say,
You're such a fool.

But then you came.

You came and asked for my story.

Think back.
To our family's flat in the old Mercado.
To the black mate gourd.
The wooden bowls.
The baskets of fruit, buzzing with flies.
To the way the waxing moon would beam
Into the bedroom through cracked cobweb windows
As it sank toward the sea.

Think back to Mami,
To the way she kept up with my age.

Most parents didn't know their kids' birthdays. Most parents just made a guess when the hair started growing under their kids' arms—*that means you're twelve,* they'd say. But Mami knew my age to the day. I was born the day the bombs dropped. The day a tattooed man wrapped me in a bloody shirt and carried me seven flights of stairs to Mami's flat at the top of the old Mercado and asked her to care for me as her own. Mami had been a friend to the mother who birthed me, when everyone else had disowned her. They'd been two rebellious girls running barefoot through the streets, letting their hair fly loose behind them—my mother the jaguar and Mami, who wasn't anybody's mami at the time but was instead called Aylen. She and my mother became pregnant at about the same time, which had settled something in Mami's revolutionary heart. But my mother's own heart kept burning until it burned her up, and almost burned me along with it.

"I'll remember that day as long as I live," Mami would say whenever she told me the story. "Javi's teeth were just coming in. The smile he made when he first saw you . . ."

The Upper City boy asked me once,
"How come your English is so good?"

"How come your Spanish is so bad?"
That's what I said to him at the time.

Because I'm lucky,
I think now.
Because Mami pried open the world with her songs.

Think back to that boy.
To the fateful threads
That brought him and me together.

I remember coming home that night from the yellow apartment, my stomach in knots as I pushed open the front door flap to the old Mercado and snuck past Señora Paulina, who was snoring loud in her chair in the commons.

Inside my flat, the smell of pisco and old tobacco welcomed me home. Through the doorway to the back bedroom, I could see the sleeping faces of Javi and Mami and the half dozen others who shared our flat—Fernando and his two daughters, Gloria and Alba; Fernando's brother, Maximiliano, and his novia, Caruca; Caruca's mother. I slid shut the door and crept up the ladder to my bunk. The sound of Javi's sleeping breaths floated from the bunk below.

But I could barely keep my eyes closed.

I was sure Javi had told Mami what I'd said to him in the yellow apartment earlier that day—about Las Oscuras, about wanting to join. Javi was good at keeping secrets, but this secret held a danger he wouldn't want to mess with. I imagined him in our kitchen that night with Mami, a steaming mate gourd passing between them as Javi explained how I'd spoke aloud my traitorous sympathies in the calm of that yellow room.

She told me she's thinking of joining.

And what had Mami said in reply? Had she shaken her head? Whispered a prayer that I'd stop asking so many questions of the world, stop searching for so formless a thing as justice? *Why can't she be more like you, Javi?* I imagined her saying. *Why can't she learn to love what she has?*

The next morning, I woke to the scratchy sound of Señora Paulina's voice coming through the window, shouting at the kids she caught dawdling. Javi was gone from our flat already, along with everybody else. Nobody wanted to be caught sleeping late. Señora Paulina was the one who ran things at the old Mercado. Everybody who lived in our building owed her one kind of favor or another, and she never let us forget it.

I was scarce down the stairs when Señora Paulina grabbed me by the arm. "Paz! What in the Heavenly Virgin's name has gotten into you, sleeping so late? You think the birds of the air are going to pay your keep?"

I squinted against the glare of the morning sun on the ocean's waves.

"No, señora," I said. I tried to keep things short.

"I don't have to remind you of all the things that need doing before Festival, do I? You kids still need to harvest the honey, and somebody's got to crush the nettle and setas for Festival tea. . . ." She shoved hunks of bread into her mouth as she talked. Crumbs fell at her feet, and the hens ran to peck at them. "¡Déjame, gallinas—oi, oi, oi!" she shouted, kicking at the birds. "And you girls still need to wreath your garlands—unless you want to wear a big bunch of *nothing* in your hair at Festival! And what would the elders think of how I treat my tenants then?"

"Yes, señora," I said. "I was just about to go to the Parque de la Conquista for some flowers."

"Don't get smart with me, child," she said.

I bowed my head. "It was just a suggestion. . . ."

She wiped a wisp of sweaty hair from her face and kicked again at the hens. "A stupid suggestion," she said. "You'll go straight to the Library, me oyes? I won't let you get me in trouble for keeping you late. But tomorrow, you'll work the fish. Easy stuff like flower picking goes to early risers, not lazy scouts who think they're better than everybody else." She laughed a little at this. She thought herself mighty clever most of the time. "Well, child? What are you waiting for? Por Dios . . ."

I nodded and hurried away.

Scouting that day was nothing to speak of. I walked the hills alone. All day, my words from the night before spun in my head. *If they recruited me, I'd be proud to take their mark.* It was a stupid thing to say, even if I meant it. Traitorous words like that could lose me my job. Our family could lose our flat. Such things weren't spoken. They were scarce even thought.

I dreaded going home.

As soon as I stepped into my flat that evening, Mami called out to me.

"Paz," she said. "Ven acá." *Come here.*

The faces of a dozen little kids turned to look at me as I came into the kitchen. Mami sat at the kitchen table in her green housedress, her hair tied up in a bright pink cloth. The kids sat on the floor all around her. Once a week, some of the kids who lived in the old Mercado came to our flat so Mami could teach them a thing or two in English.

"This is the way we comb our hair, comb our hair, comb our hair . . . ," Mami sang. She always finished her lessons with a song.

The little kids looked from me to Mami, then they screamed back the words to finish the song. *"This is the way we comb our hair so early in the morning!"*

I leaned against the wooden counter and waited as the kids filed out the door. When the last one had gone, Mami patted the table. "Have a seat, Paz," she said. "Habla conmigo un rato."

She poured hot water into our family's mate gourd and passed it to me. My fingers felt for the familiar grooves in the worn black leather as I clinked the bombilla between my teeth and took a sip. The tea was hot and bitter and it burned my tongue.

"You know what I'm going to say," she said.

"Yes, Mamita," I said.

She took the gourd from me and refilled it for herself. "I'm not your mother, and I never pretended to be. And I know you're getting older. You're responsible for your own self now."

"Yes, Mamita," I said. "I know."

"But it would be wrong for me to pretend all these years that I never noticed the war going on inside of you."

Her copper eyes held steady to mine. I didn't know what to say.

"Escúchame, Paz." She lowered her voice. "When you came into our home fifteen years ago, it was a blessing from God. But there are things you must now learn for yourself." She squeezed

my sinner's arm as she said this. "When I was your age, I had Javi to look after. And then you. Believe me, I hold inside me the same angers as you. Your mother was my friend, after all. How could I not be angry?" Her voice caught on these words. I wondered how much she was leaving unsaid. "But there are monsters on all sides, Paz. And in this world, even words have a terrible weight. You must be careful. You must be so careful."

"Yes, Mamita," I said. "It won't happen again."

I snuck out that night, not to the garrets of the Library but to the apartment in the Wastes. I had to. I needed to step through its doors into a life where the Breach had never happened, where the world was still whole. I went straight to the back bedroom and picked up the journal.

> *February 23*
> *I brought baby Eva home from the hospital yesterday. Ernestino begged to hold her as soon as we walked through the door. Can anything warm a mother's heart so much?*
>
> *Adelita is less sure. She spent all day studying Eva from a distance with those big brown eyes of hers. She just needs time, I think. That child loves deeply, not quickly.*

> *March 6*
> *Bernardo picked up a few extra projects here in Viña this month, so I don't have to return to work just yet. I tell myself this is a good thing—even when he comes home deathly tired and covered in soot.*

I know he wants to protect our little family, to
watch the children grow fat and healthy. I know
his work gives meaning to his days. Still, when
he leaves in the morning, I sit on the balcony and
look across the water and pray that God will
reset the hidden clocks of the world. Some days, it
seems like all I do is pray.

I shut the journal and closed my eyes. What's wrong with me? I thought. My life was good, wasn't it? Good enough at least. Why couldn't I find a way to be more like Javi? Why did I always have to feel things so strong they made me want to scream?

I didn't return the journal to the bedside table that night. Instead, I slid it into my satchel before making my way down the stairs in the dark and back out into the Wastes.

I had almost made it to the zip line at the gulch when it happened. I felt an arm hook me around my shoulders and a firm hand grip a rag across my mouth. A painful smell flooded the world, and my mind went dark. There wasn't a thing I could do.

9

R U M I

For two days, I rode my cycle without sleeping. The sun burned my hands until they blistered. I hadn't thought to bring gloves. I tried not to think of the hugeness of my decision to leave my city with no idea what would meet me on the outside, the insanity of it.

But my ignorance glared all around me.

A rocky desert landscape extended in all directions as I drove my cycle through the maze of barren hills. The massive, snow-capped mountains that had loomed so large over St. Iago now retreated into the distance, taking with them the promise of water. Wisps of sulfuric steam seeped from cracks in the earth. I pictured pools of magma churning beneath my cycle's tires and felt smaller than I'd felt in my entire life. The Earth was a wild, hungry animal, and all I had to protect myself against it were the gears and cylinders sputtering beneath me.

I rode for so long that I began to fear there was no city called Paraíso, only endless rock and steam. But as the sun sank into evening on the second day of my journey, a dark blur rose between barren hills. I stopped my cycle and pulled the map from my pack, blinking away the blindness of two days of sun. According to the map, that dark blur was a forest. Once I reached the forest, Paraíso would be just be a few more kilometers. There I'd find the man whose name Father had scribbled on the map—Solomon Cienfuegos, the man who'd help me find a cure for Father.

Before I knew it, this endless desert would be a distant memory.

I sped toward the trees with warmth in my chest and my head filled with thoughts of a hero's welcome home. But as I neared the trees, my cycle spun on a rock and kicked a cloud of dust from the ground. With the dust cloud came a smell—something rancid and sharp, like burning hair.

No, I thought. No, no, no.

I knew from drills in school what that smell meant. The ground was toxic. Poisoned.

Immediately I stopped my bike, ripped off my shirtsleeve, and tied it over my nose and mouth, just as they'd instructed in the PSA footage. How long did I have before the spasms overtook me? I had to make it to the forest before this happened. I'd have no chance if I fell to my knees in this toxic sand.

I sped toward the forest faster than I'd ever dared to ride before—200 kilometers per hour, 220, 240. News bulletins from past terror attacks flashed through my mind. The attacks on Paris. Istanbul. Manhattan. Images of chaos and wreckage. Of victims. The image of a Governance spokesman in a navy-blue suit delivering a press conference. *Those who seek to destroy our freedoms are growing stronger by the day. The Governance has raised the Warning Level to Ultraviolet. Curfew is set to twenty-one hundred, at which time all citizens' specs will tune to GovNet 3 for the latest on the conflict. . . .*

But these thoughts scattered in a rush of pain. My stomach clenched, like I was drowning on air. I lost my balance, and, in one violent motion, my cycle lurched beneath me and sent me crashing to the ground. The sand scorched my hands and arms. The forest was there—*right there*—but it didn't matter. I coughed and gagged. My vision turned cloudy. On legs almost too shaky to stand, I stumbled toward the trees like a person possessed. The world around me dissolved into a swirl of wind and darkness.

Father was right, I thought. The world outside the walls was a poisoned wasteland.

But all of a sudden, my vision cleared. All around me was a forest taller than any I'd ever seen. At the base of a giant trunk, I fell to my hands and knees and vomited everything inside of me. The universe wrung itself from my body, and all that was left were the trees.

I lay back onto the grass, sweaty and shaking, empty of even my name.

Hours passed as I fell in and out of consciousness. When at last I woke for good, the sky had grown dark. The distant call of a bird rang out across the forest, heartsick. I stared up at the trees— long-armed dancers, suspicious in the presence of a stranger. The moon spied on me through their leaves.

"Water," I whispered to myself. "I need water."

I turned to my side and squinted into the dark. There was my pack, several meters away. My cycle was nowhere to be seen. I pushed myself to hands and knees and then to my feet, but my legs were like strips of wet cloth, and I fell into the paste of my own vomit. My head pulsed with a dull, thick ache.

But I had to keep trying.

On forearms, I crawled to my pack and pulled out my canteen. As I held it in my hands, I almost cried. Not enough. Not nearly enough. I tried to remember how much water had been left on my cycle. I'd packed an entire case of PuriTabs, but not much water.

I'd figured I would find more along the way. Ignorant. Inexcusable.

I opened the canteen and sipped the warm liquid slowly, careful not to spill a drop. Tomorrow I'll look for more, I thought, trying to convince myself of something that seemed increasingly uncertain. Tomorrow I'll feel stronger. I took a SoyChewy bar from my pack and ate it slowly. Its salty sweetness flooded every part of me. I tried to think ahead to the morning: I needed to find my cycle. I needed to find a water source. I needed to determine the distance remaining to Paraíso. . . . And without knowing how or when, I fell deep into sleep.

"Get up," I heard myself saying, far away, from within a dream. "Get up, dammit."

I opened my eyes. Morning had broken. A cold mist crept through the trees like a spirit. The forest smelled dark and sweet— the same smell as Laksmi's hair. But in the slanting light of morning, everything seemed sinister, like some otherworldly filter on my specs had been placed over reality. Instinctively I touched my face. But no, there were no specs. This was no projection, no game.

On aching legs, I retraced my steps to my cycle. It lay on its side, out of reach in the toxic sand, its solar fuel cell cracked beyond repair.

Shit, I thought.

I could make it to Paraíso on foot, but how would I get back to St. Iago? A thick despair churned beneath this question, and I ignored it. I'd find a way. I had to.

With hollow movements, I assessed what I had in my pack— a handful of SoyChewy bars, a case of PuriTabs, my first aid valise, my knife. Then I opened Father's map. If I was reading it correctly, Paraíso was just five kilometers to the west.

Just then I heard something snap behind me—a twitch in

the brush that was more than just wind. I spun around. For the briefest moment, I swore I saw a silvery face peering at me from the underbrush. Panicked, I fumbled for the knife in my pack. But when I looked up again, no one was there.

I let out a nervous laugh. "Have to be more careful," I mumbled to myself, strapping the knife to my belt. The gesture felt absurd. A few days ago, I'd used that knife to slice tomatoes.

Several kilometers toward Paraíso, the forest began to change. The tall trees became scarce, and smaller ones grew in their place. Grasses and shrubs replaced the mosses and ferns. Flecks of sky began to wink through trees, and I broke into a run. The blue of the sky grew wider and wider. I passed one final cluster of trees, then a meadow of flowers. And then the world flung open before me like a curtain.

Spread out below me lay the city of Paraíso.

At first I saw only color—deep greens and pinks, charred blacks and browns. The city below looked like a maze. Streets crisscrossed at strange, sharp angles, narrowing and disappearing, then reappearing out of nowhere. Houses were piled on top of one another in surreal clumps of misshapen squares. Scrap-metal shanties grew like tumors from crumbling buildings. The geometry defied reason. It was unfathomable, chaotic, beautiful. And there in the distance, an endless stretch of perfect blue. The unmistakable expanse of the ocean.

A huge smile spread across my face. "You were right, Laksmi," I said. "It's the deepest blue I've ever seen. . . ."

Another twig snapped behind me. This time I had no chance to react. An iron grip clasped my arms, and a hand pressed firmly over my nose and mouth. In a panic I gasped, and a sharp smell swept me away.

1 0

PAZ

What else do I remember from that day?
The day everything changed.

The sounds of breathing. Light from an open hatch—a line across the dark.

And a man's whisper.

"Look at the two lovebirds," he said. "How precious."

At first I didn't gather the meaning of these words, lying there in the dark. Then I felt the boy shifting behind me, and all at once it came back. The cellar room. Las Oscuras. The Upper City cerdo. We'd been prisoned together in that room, just the two of us, all night. Twice they'd dragged him up the stairs. Twice they'd left me to listen while above the boy screamed for mercy. And now they'd come for me.

"How precious," the voice repeated.

"Sí, poh. Precious," said another.

They were both men's voices. They didn't speak the mix of Spanish and English I was used to in Paraíso. They spoke in Spanish alone.

I pushed myself upright with hands still bound and squinted

through the murky dark. Around the room, silent tatted figures blended into the shadows. With my teeth, I pulled my shirt to cover my bare shoulders. The way these men watched me made me wish I had no body at all.

A man stepped out from the group, a small man with a sinner's arm like mine.

"Buenos días, mija," he said in a low, rough voice.

The man's whole body was tatted—even his face, which was a mess of shapes and lines so thick that the shimmering ink covered almost every inch of his skin. He walked a slow circle around me. I couldn't stop staring at his face as he walked—red gums, silver lips, the wild whites of his eyes. A prowling demon.

"A Library scout, I see," he said, all in Spanish. "Did you think your little scouting badge would keep you safe from us, hm? That you could roam the Wastes any way you pleased?"

"No, señor," I said. Then I added, "I'm careful."

My voice sounded weak and small. I was a plaything, a rat trapped by the tail.

"Not careful enough, mija," the demon-man said. Then he turned to the men behind him. "They must not warn these young ones about us back in Paraíso anymore. Shall we take her outside, cabrones? Make her remember our name?"

The men's voices boomed all together. "Hear, hear, Comandante."

"Lobo, Castro," the man said. "Stay with this Upper City trash. I'll send for him when I'm ready. The rest of you, follow me outside with the girl." And with that, the silver-faced man they'd called Comandante snatched me by my bindings and dragged me up the stairs. The wooden steps slammed my hip bones as he climbed.

Outside, the sky was gray with dawn. Dew wet my back as the comandante hauled me through the grass. I did my best to scan my surroundings: a roadway to the east overgrown with trees, a row of vine-covered electric poles to the south. But I recognized nothing. We were deeper in the Wastes than I'd ever dared to go.

The comandante threw me to the wet ground, and I clenched shut my eyes against the blows I knew would come. Dios, dame fuerza, I thought. Dame valor. But instead I felt something drop into my lap.

My sling and stones.

"We've heard of a Library scout who can work miracles with a sling," the comandante said. "Rumor has it that this scout can hit a big cat between the eyes at seventy paces. Might that young legend be you, mija?"

Through my cold terror, I tried to think clear. So, they weren't going to kill me outright. Was this some kind of test? To see what skills I might offer in exchange for my life? I knew Las Oscuras sometimes recruited through kidnappings. Was that happening now?

I sat up straight and cleared my throat. "Untie me and maybe I'll put on a show," I said.

The comandante smiled his silvery smile and sliced the knots at my hands and feet.

"Here's your theater. Let's see what you can do."

My heart raced. I stood and closed my eyes. I could almost feel the pulse of sun as it rose in the sky. I could hear the breathing of the men standing guard at a distance, men who would strike me down where I stood unless I could prove I had something they wanted.

I opened my eyes. To the north, a bird preened itself in an old jacaranda tree. Not too high, but far enough for it to be a tricky shot. I placed a stone in the cradle of my sling.

En el nombre del Padre, y del Hijo, y del Espíritu Santo . . .

Three circles at my side found the rhythm; one deadly arc over my head got the speed. I shoved all the air from my lungs with the release, and the bird—a dove—fell to the ground.

I turned to the comandante, smiling. Hopeful.

"That's very good, mija," he said. But he sounded bored. "Unfortunately, we are not currently in need of a bird hunter."

My smile disappeared. A shivering panic rose in my throat. Those few seconds of hope were part of the game—a bit of fun with their cornered prey before they strung me up alongside that Upper City cuico and left me for the dogs. It was a trick, and I fell for it.

My fingers twitched. I had to think fast. How many men could I pick off before one of them took me down? There were six total. Impossible to get them all. But I had no choice.

"Shall I retrieve the boy?" one of the men asked the comandante.

"Sí, poh," the comandante said. "Get the boy."

Three of the six men turned to walk toward the house, and I saw my chance.

In one motion, I swooped to snatch one, two, three rocks and slung them quick as I'd slung in all my life. The first two rocks hit one man in the gut and another in the chest. The third rock hit the comandante right below the eye.

"¡Hija de puta!" the comandante screamed behind me as I fled.

I tore through the bramble growing from cracks in the road. My lungs burned. My legs pounded beneath me. And for one single moment, I thought I was free—that I'd escape their death grasp, that I'd make it back to Paraíso alive to tell Javi the tale of my capture. . . .

But then my legs tangled under me, and my face rammed into the broken street. I tried to stand, but my legs wouldn't move. A pair of bolas wrapped tight around them.

I went limp. No escape.

The comandante's bootsteps stomped toward me. He snatched me by my shirt, yanked me from the road, and held me fast against him, our faces close to touching. His eyes clawed at mine. Against his silvery face, they burned bright as copper. But behind his rage, I saw the hint of something else. Something cold and curious.

"Gustavo," he shouted to one of his men, not breaking my gaze. "¡Arriba con la cabrita!"

Bring up the little goat. Me, the little goat.

The comandante tossed me to the road and walked back to the house with his hand clutched to the wound on his face. Then a huge man with the eyes of a shark tatted on his temples came toward me. He grabbed my wrists and pulled me into his arms.

"Make one sly move, preciosa." He flicked his tongue in my ear. "I dare you."

I wanted to scream, but my body only trembled as he hoisted me over his shoulder like a slaughtered animal and carried me back to that rot-hearted house. The floorboards creaked under his steps. But instead of taking me to the cellar again, he brought me upstairs, tossed me to the floor of a dim room, and left me alone, slamming the door behind him.

I couldn't stop shaking.

I don't know how much time passed with me alone in that room. It felt like hours. The dim room watched me. I seemed to be in some kind of stash house, full of Old World treasures stowed away like seeds in a mouse nest. Golden necklaces and scarves in colors I'd seen only in dreams hung from hooks on the wall. Rows of weapons and ammunition stared back at me from the shelves. I shivered and thought of Javi. How worried he must be. Tomorrow at Festival, what would he say about where I'd gone? The thought of Festival brought me near to crying—the deep-sea fishermen's sails on the horizon, the cigarettes rolled with corn husk and honey, the kids with sashes weaved from wildflowers . . .

Somewhere downstairs, a door slammed. The floorboards creaked as somebody climbed the stairs. I pulled my knees to my chest as the steps got closer. Then the door opened, and the comandante himself stepped inside.

The cut I'd given his tattooed cheek was clean now and bandaged, and his animal anger was gone. But still, he watched me with a calculating look. "I do apologize for our inhospitality, mija," he said, all in Spanish. He sat on the floor next to me. With a knife from his belt, he sliced the ropes of the bolas still wrapped round my legs.

I said nothing.

"Relax, child," he said. "If we wanted you dead, you'd be dead. Understood?"

I nodded, unsure. "Sí, Comandante."

"Please. Call me Víctor. After the poet."

He tossed aside the heavy bolas, touching the cuts on my knees with a gentle hand. A sick feeling came over me as he did this—the feeling that this was just another game, that this man was still toying with his prey before it slashed its neck.

"You know the poet, yes?" he asked.

"No, Comandante."

"Ah, mija. How much you have to learn! Víctor Jara was once the voice of this great land—long before the walls went up and the world fell to pieces, he was a voice who fought for the people, who resisted the evils of injustice. So powerful were his songs that those who feared him smashed his fingers so he could no longer play his guitar." The comandante held out his right arm to show me the shriveled hand and twisted fingers of a sinner's arm. Just like mine. "For this, my friends call me Víctor," he said. "It is a badge of honor, this arm of mine, though many have tried to make me ashamed of it. Yours is a badge of honor too. I hope you realize this. I hope we can become friends, mija. We've had such a difficult start."

The comandante stood. He took two cups down from a shelf on the wall and poured from a kettle something dark and thick. "Coffee?" he asked.

"Sí, porfa'," I said. I took the steaming cup from him and gave a little smile as I tried a sip. I'd never tasted coffee before. It smelled like earth but went bitter on my tongue.

The comandante studied my face.

"You think of us as the enemy, don't you, mija? Las Oscuras—the wielders of chaos! Thieves, murderers. Terrorists. What is that little oath they make you take as children? The oath to 'resist the shadows'?"

I didn't answer. I didn't know whether to trust this new bit of kindness.

"Oh, do speak, mija." His eyes turned sharp. "Don't make me make you."

"The pledge," I blurted. "They make us scouts take it every morning. *For the life of our people,* it goes. *For order after the Breach, I pledge my honor to my city and my loyalty to the Library.*

I pledge to resist Las Oscuras, to reject their lies. On the souls of my mother and father and all I hold most dear, I pledge these things. May our light shine ever more brightly. May we one day recover the world we lost."

"Yes, yes. 'One day recover the world we lost' . . . So touching." He sipped his coffee. "And you believe these things, mija? You believe yourself to be a candle against the shadows of Las Oscuras?"

"I believe you are killers," I said, this time in English.

He nodded. "Sí, poh. At times we must kill. But let me ask you this: Is it honorable, sometimes, to kill? To kill for the greater good?"

"Depends," I said. "Which good is the greatest? Yours? The Library's? Upper City's? All of you kill in the name of the greater good."

The comandante smiled. "That's right, mija," he said. His voice was calm, but his words were slippery. "You've identified the flaw in my question. What seems to be good for one person may be the greatest evil for another. The greatest good for the Library is to protect the people of Paraíso, no? To protect them from us, from Las Oscuras. This is why puta madres like Solomon Cienfuegos burn our brave men and women in the Lighthouse when they discover our ink on their skin. Yet the elders do not call this murder, do they?"

"No. They call it execution," I said. "Justice. For the good of Paraíso."

"And what about Upper City?"

I froze, not sure how to answer. We scouts weren't supposed to talk about Upper City. *Keep your opinions to yourselves,* the Library elders always told us.

"Let me tell you a story," the comandante said. "When I was

a boy, not much older than you, an Upper City air fleet raided our town. Amid the smoke and screaming and people running this way and that, I remember one man sitting on a street corner clutching a bottle of milk in his hands, his face splattered with blood. He held the bottle in front of him like an offering to God. 'My wife and child,' he said to everyone passing. 'My child is hungry. See, I have her milk. Please, have you seen my wife, my child . . . ?'"

The comandante sipped from his coffee.

"What of these killings? Of Upper City's chemical bombs and armored walls?"

My heart sped with the thought of my own mother, shaking and pale, choking on her chem-poisoned blood. But I tried not to let it show. I needed to hide from this man the secret rage that lived closest to my heart. I wasn't sure yet if his kindness could be trusted.

"I guess you could say that Upper City commits their killings for the good of Upper City," I said. "They kill to protect their own kind."

The comandante smiled. "To protect their own kind, yes. Just as the Library's killings are justified in the name of protecting their own kind." He drank the rest of his coffee and set the cup on the floor beside him. "Now, tell me, child. What about Las Oscuras?"

My skin tingled. Was this the real test? I wondered. A test of my loyalties? I thought back to the yellow apartment, to the words I'd spoke to Javi. Could those words save my life?

"I guess Las Oscuras kills for the good of everybody."

"How so?"

"Las Oscuras kills without caring for their own kind. They're martyrs, you could say—they kill ready to die. If everybody in their ranks got killed but the walls of Upper City toppled, Las Oscuras would call it a victory."

The heat of the words I'd spoke to Javi kept building inside me. And all of a sudden, I wasn't putting on an act to save my skin. I meant every word. "Folks in Paraíso fall ill to all kinds of sicknesses that had cures before the Breach. Every year, we get hit harder with storms and swallowed deeper by the sea. Every year, kids die from chem-poisoned water and old blast mines. And the Library elders aren't doing a thing about it. Es una mierda."

The comandante nodded. "You're right, mija," he said. "The elders make a false enemy of Las Oscuras. And in doing so they turn a blind eye to the true enemy—Upper City."

The fear that had seized me when I first saw the comandante shifted with these words. This man still frightened me, but it felt like a fear I could trust. I looked the comandante straight in his copper eyes.

"What is it you want from me?" I said.

"Ah, child. I thought you'd never ask!" The comandante's face crinkled into something like a smile. But there was no joy behind it. "I must be honest with you. It was no accident that we found you last night. My men have been following you for quite some time, watching you come and go from the Wastes with such bravery, such disregard for your own well-being. Let's just say it was long overdue that you and I became acquainted."

I thought of the countless nights I'd spent in the Wastes, alone and with Javi, trying to find escape from the world. How much did the comandante know?

"I see your rage, mija," he said. "I know you want the blood of Upper City. And I can give you this. In fact, I can give you the blood of that Upper City kid right now, if that's what you wish. One well-slung stone and he's gone."

The Upper City swank. I'd almost forgotten. To kill this boy. To watch his eyes go cold and blank . . . But something in the comandante's voice made me think there was a better option.

"Or?" I asked.

"Or you can save him. Set him free. Gain his trust. Learn why he's here. A bit of research, if you will. You might even call it your first mission."

So this was it. This was what it felt like to be recruited.

"If you choose this path," the comandante continued, "you'll take the boy to Paraíso. You'll make him feel safe. Then you'll ask him his reasons for coming to Lower City. We could torture him for this information, of course, but as they say—you catch more flies with honey than vinegar. When you and I meet again, you'll tell me what you learn. Then I'll explain to you our mission to upend the orders of the world." With these last words he stood and walked to the door. "The choice is yours, mija."

The comandante's words flowed through me as I followed him downstairs. I could feel his strength in my veins.

Outside, the morning had melted away, and the noonday sun warmed my face. I scanned my surroundings again as I followed the comandante across the field. To the south, the sun glinted bright off the spike of a distant building. It was a building I recognized. If I followed the ruined road in that direction, I could reach the zip wire at the gulch in a half day's walk. So long as the Upper City swank could keep pace . . .

The man with the shark tattoo came from the stash house dragging the Upper City boy behind him. The boy squirmed and cried and begged for mercy, bloody and shirtless. The filthy rag tied round his face hid his eyes.

"Please!" he said. "I'm begging you!"

Pathetic.

The shark-faced man threw the boy to the ground and kicked him in the gut. "Cállate, cuico," he said. "Upper City swine get no requests in these parts."

"Hang him by the arms," the comandante ordered. His gentle tone was gone.

The shark man hung the boy by his wrists from a branch of the jacaranda tree. And for the first time, I got a clear sight of the tattoo they'd given him the night before. Across his jaw, they'd tatted so many lines that, from a distance, the tattoo looked pure silver. From this silver, a single line trickled down his neck, tracing the vein of his life. The line ended in a perfect circle. A target. The spot that would stop his beating heart.

The boy shook with sobs. He wasn't begging with words anymore, just noises—like a cornered animal. The shark man socked the boy hard in the stomach, and the boy groaned.

The comandante came up next to me then and handed me my satchel. I felt inside for my sling and stones, the woman's journal, my knife and scouting notebook. Everything was there.

Next, the comandante placed the boy's pack in my hands and nodded toward the tree where the boy was hanging. "The choice is yours, mija," he whispered, his voice a curled viper, ready to strike. "Sling true, and the boy is dead. Or choose to save him today—to join us!—and learn just how fragile the orders of the world really are. It's a system of strings. Cut one string, and you cut them all. . . ." With a gesture, his men all disappeared into the forest. Only the comandante stayed at my side, waiting to see what I'd do.

I breathed shallow, caught between two dreams. I'd dreamed of a moment like this since I was old enough to understand where the aches in my arm and the hunger in my belly came from. To have one clear shot at an Upper City cuico. To see his life dangle helpless before me . . . Greedy little god, I thought. Human tapeworm. *Sling true, and he's gone.*

I placed a stone in the cradle of my sling and circled it at my side. A steady rhythm. A deadly rhythm. Three circles there, a death-quick arc over my head, then *release*.

The stone sliced through the brush and knocked against the trunk of a tree with a *thwack*.

"Take that, mierdas!" I shouted. I slung another and another into the brush near where the comandante's men had disappeared. "And don't you ever come back!"

I turned to the comandante, and he nodded. "Moonrise tomorrow," he whispered to me. "Wastes side of the gulch." Then he disappeared into the trees.

I was one of them now. Paz de Las Oscuras. My heart raced to think it.

"Hello?" The boy's voice came from behind me. "Is someone there?"

I climbed a limb of the jacaranda tree to cut loose the ropes that held him, and the boy, still blindfolded, cried out as he crumpled to the ground. Never cry out, I thought with a smile. Never show your enemy how easy it is to make you scream.

I jumped down next to him to untie his blindfold, but he jerked his head away.

"Hold still, flaco," I said. "Por el amor de Dios. I'm trying to help you!"

At the sound of my voice, the boy went still.

I untied the bloody rag from around his eyes and then set about freeing his wrists. He stared back at me, disbelieving. "Paz? Why are you . . . ? Where did they . . . ?"

I stood and pretended to scan the trees for the comandante's men. "No time to explain, flaco," I said in a harsh whisper. "They might be nearby still."

"Thank you." The boy was close to sobbing. "If there are words, I don't know what they'd be. . . ."

I pulled him to his feet and tried my best to sound like a friend. "Listen, flaco. Enough crying. We gotta get out of here. I know a place, but we have to move quick, okay?"

He nodded, solemn and serious.

"Good," I said. "Let's move."

11

RUMI

The Lower City girl climbed a chain-link fence and landed without a sound on the other side. Her green eyes blazed wildly against her sun-darkened skin. Standing there, helpless among the ruins, I couldn't help but think of that glittering room full of silks and jewels and weapons, the tattooed men swarming around me, stabbing my skin. How I'd begged for mercy. How they'd shown me none. And then, that man. His arms and neck and the dome of his skull silver with tattoo ink. Something about the way he moved. Something snakelike and inhuman. His vicious smile . . .

On the other side of the fence, Paz shaded her eyes from the afternoon sun. Dried blood from a cut on her forehead flaked into her short, dark hair. Her legs, too, were covered in scrapes. Her right hand and forearm, I noticed, were curled and small, the skin a mottled pink instead of brown. This Lower City girl who'd thrown curses at me the night before had saved me from those men.

Wen had warned me not to trust anyone from Lower City. Devils, he'd called them. But this girl who'd saved my life—what choice did I have but to trust her?

I gripped the fence and pulled myself to join her on the other side.

12

PAZ

We hurtled through the Wastes over bomb-pocked rubble and downed electrical poles and snakes sunning themselves on slabs of concrete. The boy surprised me as we ran. He was swift and strong and didn't fall behind. By the time we reached the entrance to me and Javi's hideout, I was breathing just as hard as he was. Crouched behind an old tramcar, I scanned the Wastes. The afternoon sun lit the shadows. Birds sang; nothing moved.

I slunk across the sunlit rubble and motioned for the boy to follow. Chalky dark swallowed us as we stepped into the building. I put the boy's smooth hand on my shoulder.

"Don't want to get lost in here," I whispered.

His fingers clutched tight to my shirt, and I smiled. Already his trust was growing.

Up the dark stairs, I picked the lock to the apartment. "We're here," I whispered.

"What do you mean *here*?"

I pushed open the door. A line of brightness shot into the corridor. The apartment looked just as it had the night before—photographs on the walls, couch and table and bicycle right where Javi and me had left them. But it all seemed changed.

"Those men—do you think they'll find us?" the boy asked.

I opened the doors to the balcony, and a cool wind swept inside. "I don't think so," I said, stepping onto the balcony to clear space for a cook fire. "I was careful."

The boy followed me out. Sweat and dried blood crusted his dark skin and thick black hair. He wasn't tall, but he had an uprightness to him, a graceful sort of strength that surprised me. His tattered shirt covered some of his fresh tattoo, but I could see the crosshatched lines that crawled up his neck to his jaw.

It's a system of strings, the comandante had said. *Cut one string, and you cut them all. . . .*

Soon I'd wear the mark of Las Oscuras. Soon my skin would bear their beautiful lines.

"Can I help?" the boy asked. He looked at me with wide, dark eyes. Trusting eyes.

"How about you get a fire started?"

"I—I don't think I know how."

I shuffled bits of fallen plaster off the balcony with my boot and pointed to a stand of trees growing nearby. "Can you tell the difference between safe tree nuts and poison ones?"

He looked at me, embarrassed.

I wiped the sweat from my forehead. This kid wasn't a spy or a soldier. What the hell was a smooth-handed swank like him doing in the Wastes anyway?

"How're you with a sling?"

"I've . . . I'm sorry," he said. "I've never used a slingshot before."

I crouched and took my sling from my satchel. "Well, then, flaco, looks like there's not much here you can do." Then I remembered the comandante's words. *Be kind to him. Gain his trust.*

I set the sling on the floor. "I guess you could gather kindling for the fire. Don't get anything built—that stuff's toxic. And nothing green. Old, dry stuff. ¿Cachai?"

"Sure," he said. But I could tell he was nervous.

"Don't worry. Nobody'll see us."

I kept the boy in my sights while I slung a couple of fat chinchillones for our meal, and I had the animals skinned, gutted, and skewered by the time he made it back to the balcony with a bundle of broken limbs. He dumped them on the landing and wiped his face with his sleeve.

"About time," I said, taking a stick from the pile and shaving off some tinder with my knife. The boy sat next to me and watched wide-eyed as I lit the tinder with a precious match. I blew on it till it burned orange, then built kindling around it. The boy, eager to help, handed me sticks from his pile as the sun sank low in the sky.

When the meat crisped up, we moved inside and sat on the floor around the low wooden table. "What is this place, anyway?" the boy asked, sucking grease from a bone.

I smiled. "It's a treasure is what it is. Found it about a year ago. Scrappers've been scouring every bit of Paraíso since the Breach, but they never found this place. Nobody knows about it. Not even Las Oscuras." I said this to make him feel safe, though I now knew it was a lie. "When you find a place like this, you keep it secret."

The boy's eyes rested on the Old World music player in the corner of the room. "There's a place like this back in St. Iago—where I'm from. A secret place, I mean. One that most people don't know about."

"Oh yeah? What dangers you got to hide from in that swank city of yours?"

"Not dangers, exactly," he said. "It's just . . . a place where nobody's watching you. Where you don't have to be anything at all. You can just kind of exist."

I shoved a hunk of gristle in my mouth. "Is that why you came to my city? Just to *exist*?"

"No," he said, picking at a bit of sinew with his fingernail. "I'm here for my father."

I leaned against the chair behind me and stretched out my arms. Now we were getting somewhere. "Your father?" I tried not to sound too curious. "He's here in Paraíso too?"

"No. He's in St. Iago," he said. He closed his eyes, and his face went pale. "I guess there's no reason to keep it from you. My father was infected with a virus. Hastings fever. Zabrán. Black Tie. Whatever you want to call it."

I clenched my teeth. Zabrán. The Death Angel. I was a child when Paraíso last saw an outbreak of Zabrán—the infected left on sheets in an open field to die. I'd heard rumors that the virus was flaring again in the North. Still, how had it jumped to Upper City?

The boy continued. "It's a different strain than the one that caused the original London outbreaks. Father travels to Lower City for work, so he's vaccinated against the known strains. But his vaccines weren't effective against this one. If he's not treated soon . . ." He drew a shaky breath. "I came to Lower City because I had reason to believe I could find a cure. I came looking for a man named Solomon Cienfuegos who works for some kind of library. I don't know what I was thinking, though. It all sounds like nonsense now."

The skin on my neck prickled. "Cienfuegos?" I said. "How do you know Cienfuegos?"

The boy looked up. "His name was written on my father's map. Do you know him?"

"Virgen santísima, flaco," I said. "You *are* far from home! Of course I know him. I work for the Library myself." I sifted through my satchel and pulled out my scouting notebook with its official Library seal. "I'm a scout for them."

The boy ran his fingers over the bloodred wax of the Library's seal.

"I can't believe it," he said. He rubbed his forehead like he was gearing up for some kind of thank-you speech. But I cut him off. I needed more information.

"I guess this means you're going to be some kind of hero when you get home, huh?"

"I don't know about that," he said. "No one knows my father is sick—just me and my grandfather. Father's convinced that the Governance will 'remove' him if they realize he's sick."

"Remove?"

The boy stared out the balcony doors, watching the sky grow dark. "Remove the threat of contamination. Like, kill him." He tried to sound brave, but he looked dizzy with fear. "Do you think this man Cienfuegos knows of a cure for this new strain?"

My stomach fluttered.

"I don't know," I said. "We've not had a case of Zabrán in Paraíso in years. Only way to find out is to ask Cienfuegos himself."

13

RUMI

Below us, the city of Paraíso spread like a black velvet sea, dotted with torch fires. The smell of smoke and dead fish, old urine and burning garbage, threaded the air.

"What's the matter?" Paz said, ahead of me.

"It's just . . . that smell." I tried to breathe through my mouth, but the smell seeped in anyway.

Paz lifted her nose to the sky and inhaled. "What smell?"

I couldn't tell if she was joking.

The city of Paraíso took shape around us as we left the forest and walked downhill, into the growing darkness. Graffitied walls of sheet metal formed a maze of narrow alleyways. Flickering torches cast shadows onto potholes in the pavement. Dogs slept beneath darkened doorways. A man without teeth or legs lay curled on a thin towel. I stared at his face as we passed and realized in horror that I couldn't say for certain whether he was alive or dead.

Out there is chaos, Father had said. *Lower City has lost all sense of what it means to be human.* I held these words like razor blades clenched in my fists.

Paz kept silent as we walked. Behind her, I noticed how small she was. Her black hair, cut short and uneven, left bare her long, thin neck. Her shoulder blades winged beneath a shirt several sizes too big; a pair of frayed shorts hung loosely from her hips. The leather boots that laced halfway up her calves seemed to be the only piece of clothing that actually fit her. Her curled right arm swung a shortened arc as she walked. Had she been burned? I wondered. Had she been born this way?

At a large plaza, Paz paused and glanced around. She seemed nervous, like a spy moving through hostile territory. I followed her along the perimeter of the open square toward a palatial blue building with spires that reached into the night. This building seemed to watch over the plaza through the darkened eyes of its windows.

The Library, I thought. We're here.

Paz scaled the stairs to the building and waited for me at the heavy wooden doors that led inside. But midway up the stairs, I froze. For a fraction of a moment, her expression seemed to hinge open, to reveal something vicious underneath. A roaring panic swelled inside me. This is a trap, I thought. She doesn't know Solomon Cienfuegos at all. She's in league with those tattooed monsters, and this is the end.

But when I reached the top of the stairs, her perceived viciousness vanished. "Took you long enough, eh, flaco?" she said.

I smiled back, uncertain. "You're super fast," I said. "Plus that smell . . ."

She rolled her eyes and unlocked the heavy door. "You're crazy. . . ."

The door creaked open into a vast entrance hall, empty and alert, like an Old World cathedral. Oil lamps flickered on the walls. Above, a vaulted ceiling shimmered with pink and golden clouds.

The arched windows now looked inward, watching as our footsteps echoed across the painted tiles toward a spiral staircase that led to the second story.

The second floor was a dimly lit maze of shelves crammed from floor to ceiling with books and loose papers. Many were scorched along their spines. Eventually the maze of shelves led us to a narrow corridor lined with identical closed doors. At the end of the corridor, light spilled from a cracked-open door.

"He's here," Paz said.

I stood out of view as Paz knocked gently on the door. Sweat beaded on my forehead. Both Father's life and mine hinged on the generosity of the stranger on the other side of that door. And what reason did he have to be generous?

"¿Señor?" Paz said.

An old man's voice came from inside. "Paz!" he said. "Where have you been?"

Paz rubbed her nose and glanced in my direction. "I got a little detained." With a solemn look that failed to hide her own fear, Paz motioned me to follow her inside.

In the cramped office, a candle dripped wax onto a desk strewn with open maps and blueprints. The old man turned from this desk to face us as we stepped through the doorway. His eyes glinted in the candlelight, an icy, piercing blue. A red cloak hung over the back of his chair like a limp, bloody animal.

I bowed my head to hide my tattoo. Still, the old man eyed me suspiciously. "Who is this, Paz? Who have you brought to me at such an hour?"

"The boy asked to see you, señor."

Cienfuegos looked annoyed. "Well, what is it? Chin up, boy. Did no one teach you to look an elder in the eye?"

Slowly I lifted my head. Candlelight spilled over the markings on my neck and jaw. My skin felt like it had burst into flames.

In one impossibly swift motion, the old man stood. He held a knife in his hand. "Explain yourself before I cut you open," he demanded. He was tall, muscular despite his age. "We have no sympathy for terrorists in these parts. None!"

I took a step back. "No, sir. Please. I'm no terrorist. I . . ." I glanced at Paz, and she nodded. "I'm from Upper City."

The old man stepped toward me. With one hand still clasping his knife, he placed the other hand firmly on my chest. I looked back at him, helpless. "Touch the heart of a stranger and search their eyes," he said quietly. The teeth on one side of his mouth were missing, causing his cheek to sink into the hollow of his jaw. "The body betrays things that words will not."

My heartbeat pulsed into his hand. I let my fears and hopes and questions rise to the level of my eyes, sharing everything. When Cienfuegos finally took his hand from my chest, I felt dizzy, but also somehow strangely at ease.

The old man set the knife on his desk. His voice softened. "Tell me," he said. "What is your name?"

"Rumi, sir."

"Rumi. Like the poet?"

"Yes, sir. My grandfather has great admiration for the Sufi mystics."

Cienfuegos took a pouch of dried herbs from his desk, packed a fingerful into his pipe, and lit it. The tiny room filled with sweet-smelling smoke. "Well, Rumi of Upper City," he said, sitting back in his chair. "It's been some time since we've had a defector in Paraíso. I doubt Paz can remember the last time!" He handed the pipe to Paz.

"Not in all my life," Paz said. She inhaled and passed the pipe to me, but I declined.

The old man gestured at the bruises on my face, the tattoos. "You've met a violent welcome here in Lower City, I see. But it hasn't deterred you. What you seek must be of terrible importance. So the question remains. Why are you here?"

The air in the tiny room grew heady with smoke.

"I met a violent welcome, yes. But Paz saved me. And she brought me here to you."

Cienfuegos glared at Paz. "I hope this doesn't mean you've been poking around in places you don't belong again, mija?"

I tried to meet Paz's eyes, but she just stared at the floor. My heart sank to think that this girl, who'd risked her life to save mine, would get in trouble because of me. So I turned back to the old man, my voice shaky. "You asked why I'm here," I said. "I'm here on behalf of my father. He's been infected with a virus—a new strain of Zabrán—and I've come to Lower City in search of a cure."

Solomon Cienfuegos leaned back in his chair. "And what on earth has led you to me?"

I reached into my bag and passed Father's map to Cienfuegos. "My father is Arman Sabzwari, Ambassador and Commander of the Central Security Bureau."

At the mention of my father's name, the old man's face lost its color. "Will you excuse us for a moment?" he said to Paz.

Paz's eyes shifted from the map to Cienfuegos, her brow slightly creased. But she left without objection, and the old man closed the door behind her. "Good God, boy!" he said. His voice was hushed. "Can't you see she doesn't *know*?" He muttered something in Spanish and ran a heavy hand through his white hair.

"Know what?"

"Of my connections, of course. To St. Iago."

My body went stiff. Play along, I thought. Pretend you know what he's talking about.

"Did it happen after my meeting with him that night? In Paraíso?"

"Yes," I said firmly, though I had no idea if this was true.

"Mierda." His hand twitched nervously in his lap. "Una mierda."

I tried not to fidget as the puzzle pieces multiplied. Father had been meeting with this man, perhaps even on the night he was attacked. Had Las Oscuras targeted Father because of these meetings? And why had they met in the first place?

"Who else knows of your father's illness?" Cienfuegos asked.

"Only me, my father, and my grandfather. Father didn't tell any Governance officials. He was afraid they'd kill him."

Cienfuegos relaxed slightly. "Smart man. And the bloodwork— do you have it?"

I nodded and took from my pack my specs and DigiCloth. I pulled the cloth tight, unlocked the passcodes, and handed the specs and rigid cloth to him.

Cienfuegos blinked to adjust the lenses, surprisingly familiar with the device. With his pipe in his teeth, he began to scroll through the bloodwork, mumbling as he read.

"It's just as I feared," he said. "Las Oscuras has been developing a new strain of Zabrán—mostly in compounds in the Altiplano region, far north of Paraíso. The last I heard from the Altiplano Council, there'd been thousands of fatal cases from this new strain."

"And what about a cure?"

The old man shook his head. "I know of no such cure," he said. "I'm very sorry."

My throat constricted. "But—sir, please. There must be something. Somewhere. I left everything. I broke the highest laws of my city to come here. To find you."

Cienfuegos took off my specs and held them in his lap. "Years ago, I met a curandera—a healer—in the North trying to cultivate a treatment for Zabrán." Hope rose in my chest as he folded my DigiCloth and passed it and my specs back to me. "The healer's name is Yesenia. The trouble is, the journey to the town of Serena, where she lives, is a long and dangerous one—seven days at least."

My stomach sank. A seven-day journey would be a death sentence. I had no way of navigating the land, no way of finding food or protecting myself. I'd been outside the walls of Upper City for just a few days, and already I'd been poisoned by chems and kidnapped by terrorists. The thought of attempting such a journey was beyond overwhelming. It was impossible.

Cienfuegos must have read the thoughts creasing my face. "I can see how much this means to you," he said. "You must love your father very much. I can promise you nothing about this healer in the North. But if you choose to risk the journey, might I suggest that we ask Paz to serve as your guide? She's been longing for an important mission like this for some time. If she agrees to accompany you, I would gladly relieve her of her scouting duties for the interim."

"But you said Paz doesn't know about your connections to Upper City."

"That's right," he said, sitting forward in his chair. "And if you choose to make this journey, you must keep it that way. The people of Paraíso have such spite for Upper City. We elders have done our best to explain that you're not our enemies, but many refuse to be persuaded. Paraíso's citizens are simpleminded. If they learned that the Library engages in talks with Upper City, there would be chaos. Everything we've achieved would be lost. Do you understand? You must *never* tell Paz. No matter what."

A prickly feeling ran across the back of my neck like a spider. "Is Paz one of those people? Someone who hates Upper City?"

The old man rubbed the side of his jaw where his missing teeth would have been. His cheek sucked into the cavity of his mouth. "I've had my doubts about her before, I won't lie. But the girl saved your life. It seems you could choose no better person to trust than Paz."

That had been my own reasoning, exactly.

"You must be exhausted," Cienfuegos said. His face softened into a lopsided smile. "You've had quite a journey already. I insist that you sleep here in my quarters tonight. You'll remain in Paraíso through tomorrow's Festival, while we prepare provisions. Your journey north can begin at dawn the following morning." He knocked the embers from his pipe and refilled the bowl with fresh leaves. "Now, call in Paz. We'd best bring her up to speed."

1 4

PAZ

Think back to that boy.
The boy, Rumi.
To the night I left him in the Library
Alone with Cienfuegos.

There was a chill to the air that night. It drizzled its dampness into my bones on the long walk home. I pushed through the door flap to the old Mercado, but even the orange glow of the woodstove in the commons did me no good. Nothing was the same. The sureness of things had gone loose, like the second before a temblor when the ground and the walls don't feel quite right. It meant the awful shaking was about to begin.

That boy. Las Oscuras. Cienfuegos. They were all connected, somehow. Cienfuegos had known the boy's father—an Upper City official—by name. Cienfuegos and the boy had a secret.

But I had secrets too. Tomorrow night I'd meet the comandante by the gulch to get my initiation tattoo. By the time I led the Upper City boy north for Cienfuegos, I'd be wearing the mark of Las Oscuras. I wanted to climb into Javi's bunk and wake him and tell him everything that had happened. But I knew what he'd say.

"Remember," Javi would say. "Remember what they do to traitors."

Tomorrow night was the Festival de los Santos. And on Festival
days, there was always a burning. I'd be careful, I told myself. I
was too sly to get caught.

Still, the thought sent me shuddering into sleep.

The next morning, I joined the other Mercado kids already working the fish down by the wharf, earning their keep. The sun had
just barely crested the cerros to the east, and fierce shards of light
beamed off the sawtooth peaks of the ocean waves.

"Perdóname," I whispered to the fish as I sliced their bodies
open. *Forgive me.*

The wharf hummed around us as we worked, heads down—
the grunts of fishermen, the boot clatter on sea-worn boards, the
cussing of the gulls. When we were little, Javi and me used to sit
on these same wet black rocks, among scar-handed men and
wild slimy things. We'd sit and close our eyes and try to sing back
the songs we'd hear. The rise and fall of the waves. The groaning
of the wind.

When the sun sank low enough for a few bright stars to poke
through the pale blue of the sky, Señora Paulina rang the quitting
bell. My arms were caked with fish scales and guts. The back of my
neck stung with salt. Most everybody else climbed straight into the
water to wash the offal from their arms. But I ducked away alone
to the jetty, where soft waves clapped against the wooden planks.

At least we have the sea, Javi had said. Could that be enough?

At the end of the jetty, I slipped off my clothes and dove
headfirst into the waves. Old World buildings long ago destroyed
pierced the surface of the water like shipwrecks.

I'd been there only a minute when I heard footsteps coming toward me down the jetty.

"¡Oye, Paz!" I heard over the lapping of the waves. It was Javi, his knees dark with dirt. "Mind if I join you?"

"Sure," I said. I didn't have much choice.

He took off his shirt and shorts and jumped in.

"You came back from the Wastes kinda late the other night, no?" he said. "Mami set out a plate for you and everything, but you never came to get it. What, have you been up in that apartment all this time listening to music or something? I bet ol' Hundred Blazes gave you hell."

I smiled. Tried to seem normal. "Weón, ¿me estái webiando? It's not so hard to slip a couple lies past the old man."

Javi laid himself back on the waves, his arms spread out like a cross. "Paz," he said at last. "Did something happen out there?"

My face went hot. "What do you mean?"

"I passed you on your way out here to the jetty and called your name a bunch of times, but you didn't even turn. You got something on your mind?"

He looked at me in that way of his that promised I could tell him anything. And I wanted to tell him—about the Upper City kid and the comandante, about how I'd be getting my mark that night at moonrise. But I knew he'd tear into me, just like he had back in the Wastes.

"Well," I said. "I did meet gazes with a jaguar. That was some kinda rush! It's why I was late coming home, to be honest. I had to hide out for a while till she passed. Nothing too far from normal, though, besides that."

Javi looked sidelong at me. "I know you're lying, Paz."

"Yeah? And what're you gonna do about it?"

"Nothing," he said. "I'm not gonna do a thing. I just want you to be careful, all right?"

"I can take care of myself just fine, weón," I shot back.

Javi dipped his hair into the water and then pulled it into a tidy ponytail. "I better get back to work," he said. "There's still stuff to do before Festival tonight."

He climbed onto the jetty, pulled on his shorts and shirt, and started to walk away. As I listened to his wet footsteps slap down the sea-hard planks, something inside me went soft. What if Javi got swept up in the crowd that night at Festival? Maybe I wouldn't see him before I left for my meeting with the comandante. Maybe I wouldn't see him again for a very long time. . . .

"Hey, Javi!" I called out. "I'll be careful. Honest."

He waved and nodded, and then he walked away.

On Festival nights, they say that the barrier between worlds is pierced. That, as dark comes on, a kind of magic spills over from some other place, a place of dreams and nightmares and miracles that have no names. On Festival nights, they say anything is possible.

The plaza that night was all color and motion. People danced, sloshing around old plastic bottles of homemade wine. Tables spilled with chunchules and pastel de jaiva, locos steamed with potatoes, platters of lengua con palta and pan con pebre. Starlings whirred overhead in chattering clouds, and I watched them with a shiver as they swooped like spirits through the sky.

I walked to one of the serving tables carrying the jars of honey I'd brought from the old Mercado—my contribution to the evening. Two women I'd never seen before sat behind one of the tables, passing out mushroom tea. The shorter, fatter woman gave the girl in front of me her tea and then turned back to the tall woman next to her.

"Oye, did you hear?" she said. "It's Mariana who's going to burn tonight. Qué lástima . . ."

My ears perked at this. Mariana was a scout just a couple years older than me who'd disappeared into the Wastes last winter. Her family claimed she'd been taken by a jaguar.

I stepped up to the table and set down my honey jars, and in exchange the tall woman poured my portion of tea. Then she turned back to the fat one.

"¿Qué lástima?" the tall woman said. She had to shout over the beat of drums. "You're telling me you have pity for her? She knew that the payment for the sins of terrorists was death. She made her choice."

The weather vane on top of the Library spun wild, possessed by wind, and I shivered.

"They said it was Hernán who turned her in," the fat one said. "Her own brother! Tan dura es la vida . . ." She caught me listening then and gave me a little nod to move along.

So it was Mariana who'd die tonight in the Lighthouse. I'd seen plenty of burnings before, but never somebody I knew personally. Never somebody so young.

All of a sudden, the drums in the plaza began to swell. Their rhythms locked tight, racing one another faster and faster. Even the wind, conjured by the drums and the dancing, swirled out of control, sending shivers through the lantern flames. The magic of Festival had at last started to spill over from that other place, from the other side of the sky where Old Man and Old Woman, Young Man and Young Woman lived as kings and queens. And I knew what was coming next. The Storyteller was about to burst from the hole pierced between worlds. She was about to step through from the other side to gift us her stories.

Just when it seemed that the drums would catch fire and the whole plaza would explode with the heat of a thousand souls, the drums hit three final beats and went silent. Darkness fell heavy over top of us. The cracks of the lantern flames were the only sound. I cast a look around the plaza. You never knew where the Storyteller would appear. Sometimes she crept quiet from a darkened corner, sometimes she came down the steps of the Library in a flash of light. My eyes darted through the crowd, searching for her hobbled figure.

Then came a voice, calling from the grove in Mapuzungun. Her voice. It was raspy but strong. It rose and fell in the sacred melody that we heard only on Festival days. She was calling the young ones to come. In a slow procession, those of us who hadn't yet seen our eighteenth birthday made our way to the grove—a circle of ancient evergreen trees at the plaza's edge. I bowed my head, my shoulders brushing the arms of the others. None of us spoke.

The Storyteller sat hunched by the fire at the center of the grove, hands folded in front of her as she finished her song. The dim light from the fire cut wrinkles deep into her cheeks. She came from elsewhere, I knew, from a land of lakes and volcanoes far from Paraíso, a place unpoisoned by Upper City, and she glowed with an otherworld kind of light. Mami told me once not to trust the old Storyteller. She said that the Library elders told the Storyteller what to say in her stories, that her stories were just another way for the Library to soften our people's anger against Upper City. And that even though the Storyteller and her people, the fierce Mapuche Nation, had nothing to do with the Festival burnings, the elders used the Storyteller's voice to make their burnings seem more like justice.

Still, when the Storyteller spoke, I always listened. She spoke in riddles and myths, and I was sure that, underneath the Library's official message, she was trying to teach us her truths. When she spoke, it felt like she was speaking straight to me.

Sparks flew above her head, swallowed by the night. The dark, sweet pines swirled as I found a seat on the ground. The moon had yet to rise over the hills. Soon the comandante would make his way toward the gulch to meet me. Soon his ink would stain my skin.

Javi came up next to me, and I scooted to make room for him without meeting his eyes. "Listen," Javi said in a half whisper. "I'm sorry about earlier. What you do out there is none of my business. I just want you to be safe, is all."

I smiled and nudged him with my elbow. "You got to stop worrying so much, weón."

A toddler plopped himself in Javi's lap, and Javi squeezed his hand.

"It's just that—"

But a sound from behind us interrupted him. I turned to see elders filing into the grove, forming a line behind the Storyteller. The hoods of their wine-red cloaks hid their faces in shadow. When the elders had formed their line, the Storyteller stood. She looked up to the night sky with cloudy eyes, waiting for a story to come down from the stars. The grove fell still with her waiting. That's when I noticed something. Beneath one of the dark red hoods in the line of elders, a face had fixed its eyes onto mine. I squinted hard through the dark, and my skin went cold.

The Upper City boy stared back at me.

Old Man of Forgiveness,
Old Woman of Forgiveness,
Young Man of Justice,
Young Woman of Revenge—
Teach us the key to your cipher,
Show us the path through your maze.
For to us, you are a two-headed coin,
A monster with teeth at both ends—
Each time we turn you over, we find
More of the same!

Oh, children. Tonight I bring to you a story of the days just after the earth split in two, days when the gods of Sky and Sea were locked in unblinking battle, while all around, the world's tender magic fast disappeared.

In these dwindling days of enchantment and ashes, there lived a boy.

Near the sea's rocky shore, the boy lived with his fisherman father and brother in the ruins of the City of the Sea. Each day of his life for as long as he could remember, the boy had watched his brother paddle the current and his father cast nets to the waves. And each night of his life, the three had sat by the fire, sipping sweet honey wine as the men told of their adventures that day. The boy would listen, amazed by these tales, and dream of joining them at sea.

But then one fateful day, the boy saw a shadow creep toward the shore. From the rocky beach, the boy called out. "Father!" he shouted. "Brother!" he cried. But his voice was lost to the wind. The dark thing lurked closer, and the boy watched helpless as Leviathan swallowed his family whole.

From that day forward, the boy was haunted. A single wish gripped his mind: to find and bury the bones of his kin, to bring peace to their wandering souls.

So the boy learned to paddle the waves of the sea and to cast down his nets to the depths. And day after day, tide after tide, he would send down with his nets a wish. "Great Leviathan, please, place the bones of my kin in this net. Let me give rest to their wandering souls."

But all that returned was the sea beast's roar, rolling like thundering waves.

The boy's eyes grew hard with his days on the sea. His skin turned thick and rough. And though he paddled each day, though he cast down his wish, his words now held anger instead of hope. "What can these bones, the bones of my kin, mean to the wild, dark sea?"

Still, the sea beast laughed his thundering laugh and pelted the boy with waves.

Until one day.

One day, the boy's salt-hard eyes saw a streak of light in the waves. In his net he found two gleaming fish—one bright as gold, the other silver as the moon. And as the boy gathered his net to his boat, the golden creature began to speak.

"Tell me," said the fish. "What is it you seek out here on the sea?"

The boy wiped the sweat from his rough cheeks. "To kill the Leviathan is what I seek. Tell me, can you help me?"

"Oh yes," said the fish, "I can."

Oh Mother of Memory, oh Father of Forgetting,
How you both lose your shape when we are alone.
For loneliness scallops our hearts with time,
And turns our remembrances brittle like scabs
That we pick with our fingernails till they scar—
The memory changed, the forgetting impossible.

The golden fish smiled, its lips to the water, and began to drink up the sea. And the silver fish bore a strange, sad look, though this fish spoke nothing at all.

Gone then were the waves. Gone were the waters. Gone was the lightless deep. And there at last in the bone-dry sea lay the beast in a pool of brine.

"Please," cried the beast. "Take pity on me and the bones of your family are yours!"

But the salt-hard boy touched his lips to the pool and drank up the salty brine. And with one final shuddering roar, the beast died at the boy's feet.

Just then the golden fish turned voiceless and pale. It flapped and gasped dead in the boy's arms. And the silver fish bore the same sad look, but this fish spoke nothing at all.

Across the whole world, the boy walked with the silver fish clutched in his arms. But the earth was now a graveyard of bones—of the sturgeon and eel, of the whale and her calf, bleached white in the heat of the sun. And his ruined city, the City of the Sea, looked upon him with fury.

"What have I done?" the boy cried at last. "Tell me. What should I do?"

The silent fish bore the same strange look, and a tear formed in its eye.

"Yes!" said the boy. "That's what we must do—we must cry."

So the boy and the fish cried till the flood of their tears carried them on its waves. The young sun shone down on the boy and his city as he floated across the sea of tears.

And somewhere, down in the deep, the silent fish spread new life to the sea.

1 5

R U M I

I hung in the shadows outside the grove after the old woman finished her story. Cienfuegos stood beside me. I waited for Paz to pass by, but I didn't see her anywhere.

"Who is she—the old woman?" I whispered.

"An asset," Cienfuegos said. "She comes from the Mapuche Nation to the south—a fiercely independent people held in the greatest esteem by all Lower City. In exchange for her stories, she gets to take home some niceties to share with her people. A fruitful exchange. Even though many of her people find what she does shameful, they still accept the medicines she brings when their children fall ill."

"And in return, the Library . . . ?"

Cienfuegos smiled. "The Library elders, of course, determine what lessons these 'authentic' Mapuche stories should teach the youth of Paraíso."

I nodded, piecing together more of the puzzle that was Lower City.

"What now?"

"Now we go to the Lighthouse," Cienfuegos said. His voice had a strange hunger to it.

"What's the Lighthouse?"

The old man smiled. "The Lighthouse is where examples are set," he said. The way his eyes flashed gave me a chill. I followed close behind him, joining the crowd as it wound down the torch-lit street.

It was a long walk to the Lighthouse. Narrow streets of crumbling cobblestone led us past the darkened doorways of buildings so elaborately graffitied that they seemed to come to life all around us. I worried at first that someone would see the tattoos under the hood of my cloak, but no one seemed to notice. Everyone was caught up in the festivities. A group of women with colorful rags in their hair laughed, wild-eyed, elbows linked. A man guzzled dark liquid from an old plastic bottle, gurgling it in his throat. Little kids weaved in and out of the crowd, chasing one another with flaming sticks.

I wondered what would happen at the Lighthouse—maybe more dancing or more stories. But mostly I thought about the journey ahead. Paz, the strange, unpredictable Library scout, would accompany me north to find the healer Yesenia. This jour-ney, which the night before had seemed impossible, now had a shape. In Paz's company, my journey had hope.

As I walked, I began to notice something. Many of the children on the men's shoulders had legs as thin as rails. A boy with legs bent backward walked crookedly on all fours; an old man with unseeing eyes clung to the shoulder of a woman whose bright-pink skin flaked off in sheets. I remembered the toxic chemfield I'd stumbled through at the edge of the forest, the poison dust that had nearly killed me. Paz had called her deformed right arm a "sinner's arm." Is that what they believed? That these were sin-ner's legs and sinner's eyes, sinner's spines and sinner's skin—as though these bodies, poisoned by chems, were a punishment for the sins of humanity?

"Where is Paz?" I asked Cienfuegos, suddenly overwhelmed by her absence.

"That girl is as capricious as the waves," the old man said. "But she never shirks her duties. She'll be at the Library tomorrow at daybreak, you can be certain of that."

Eventually our path brought us within earshot of the ocean. Rounding the corner of a large stone building, I caught my first glimpse of the crowd below. Thousands of people had amassed along the shoreline, pushing their way toward a rocky pier. At the end of the pier stood a tower painted red and white. Its top was singed black.

I followed Cienfuegos onto the pier, and the crowd parted to let us through. The ground underfoot turned from concrete rubble to jagged rock as we walked toward the tower. A cold, salty wind howled above my head. Dark waves broke against the rocks on either side of us.

Cienfuegos led the way to the front of the crowd, and I walked silently beside him, staring up as the red-and-white tower grew closer and closer.

"You asked me about the Lighthouse," he said quietly. "Now you'll see."

At the front of the crowd, we stopped, surrounded by elders in dark-red cloaks like the one Cienfuegos had given me to hide my tattoos. Just then two men came out of a door at the base of the tower. Between them they dragged a young woman, her arms and feet bound, and threw her to the ground.

The crowd roared. Their voices merged with the howling wind, and the hairs on my neck stood at the sound. The people's shouts and laughter on the way to the Lighthouse now took on a much more sinister tone. Even the sharpness of the stars above seemed to warp from something full of hope into a monstrous spectacle.

Another man in an elder's cloak emerged from the same door, and the crowd fell silent. He stood over the woman and looked across the crowd.

"Mariana de los Cachureros," he said in Spanish.

Cienfuegos whispered to me a translation.

"*Mariana of the Scavenger Clan,*" he translated. "*Once, you lived among us. Once, you helped your family salvage materials from the Wastes and beyond, and you sold your scavenge at the market. Once, you were a blessing to your mother and father. Now, you are a disgrace!*"

The young woman began to sob into the dirt at the elder's feet.

"*You have broken your oath to your city,*" Cienfuegos translated. "*You have brought shame upon your family. You are a worm, a traitor. A terrorist.*"

In one fluid motion, the old man grabbed the sobbing woman by her hair. With his knife, he cut the fabric of her shirt down the middle to reveal a mark at the center of her sternum: a tattoo of three silver circles, overlapping.

My heart pounded. I scratched at my own inked skin. But Cienfuegos placed his hand on my shoulder. "You have no need to worry," he said. "You are safe with me."

"¡Por favor!" the woman screamed through her sobs. "¡Tenga piedad, por favor!"

Cienfuegos didn't translate her words. But I knew "por favor" meant *please*. I knew she must have been begging for her life.

"*For your treason,*" Cienfuegos said as the man continued to speak, "*the Library has sentenced you to death by fire.*"

Again, the crowd roared.

I'd always assumed that, for Lower City, terrorist groups like Las Oscuras were seen as freedom fighters. That by waging war against all of Lower City, the Governance was implicitly fighting these terrorist groups. And yet Paz had said that the people of Paraíso were terrified of Las Oscuras. Were Las Oscuras and the people of Lower City actually enemies?

The condemned woman cried out again. "¡Tengan piedad!" she screamed at the crowd. Her voice was fierce but hopeless as she pleaded first in Spanish, then in English. "Have mercy! Please!"

I lowered my head, remembering how I'd screamed the same words as Las Oscuras hung me by my hands. If it hadn't been for Paz, Las Oscuras would have flayed me there at that tree. I stared at the tattoo emblazoned on the woman's chest. She was one of them—one of the merciless. I scratched my own tattooed jaw and spat on the ground.

The men grabbed the woman by her arms and dragged her, screaming and sobbing, back into the Lighthouse. "You must trust no one on your journey," Cienfuegos said to me. "The lands to the north are full of informants for Las Oscuras—desperate and lawless, like the woman sentenced today. You must be vigilant. Trust *no one.*"

I nodded.

The men appeared once more from the door at the base of the Lighthouse, their arms empty now, and the elder at the front of the crowd turned to shout orders to a row of archers standing behind him.

"¡Listos!" the elder shouted. Each of the archers lit an arrow with a torch.

"¡Apunten!" he shouted. They took aim.

"¡Fuego!"

Another word I knew. *Fire.*

Five flaming arrows arced through the sky toward a pyre of tree limbs at the top of the Lighthouse tower. The flaming sticks ignited into a white-hot ball and fell into the glassed-in interior of the Lighthouse. Inside the glass, a warm orange glow began to flicker. The howling wind swallowed the woman's screams as the flames rose around her.

"When you return to Upper City," Cienfuegos said, "you can tell your father that this is how we deal with terrorists in Paraíso. No mercy. No tolerance." The muscles in the old man's jaw clenched and released. His hollow cheek sucked into the cavity of his mouth. "Tell your father that Solomon Cienfuegos sends his regards on the smoke of traitors' ashes."

I looked across the sea of faces lit by the glow of the Lighthouse, searching for Paz's short dark hair and pale green eyes. Amid all this violence, hers would be a face of humanity. My eyes jumped from face to face in the crowd. But I couldn't find Paz anywhere.

16

PAZ

The moon's glow had almost crested the cerros in the east as I headed uphill—away from the city and toward the gulch. Toward the comandante. The smell of woodsmoke led me through the bramble to where the comandante sat in the dim orange glow of a campfire, his back against a tree. His silvery face sparkled in the shadows.

"Buenas noches," he said, not looking up. He prodded the fire with a stick, then tapped the smoldering tip on a rock. Sparks jumped and died.

"Buenas noches, Comandante."

A sheet was spread next to the fire, and a kit of needles and vials of ink sat waiting in an open case by his side. The comandante caught me eyeing these and beckoned me to sit.

"Don't be afraid, mija," he said. "Think of Víctor Jara. Of the saint Mahatma Gandhi. Of our Lord Jesucristo. Each of them sacrificed everything for their people. For justice."

"I'm not scared, señor," I said.

"Do call me Víctor, child," the comandante said. He lit a cigarette on the coals, inhaled, and then held it out to me. "Now tell me, what happened with the Upper City boy?"

My hands felt like stones. It was all I could do to lift my arm and take the cigarette from him. "His father's sick, señor. He's got Zabrán." I sat on the sheet, knees hugged to my chest. "Cienfuegos thinks there's a healer in Serena who's got a cure for the kid's father. I'm to guide the boy north to find this healer so the boy can bring home medicine to his dad."

The comandante sat forward. "And the elders will have you and the boy travel alone?"

"Sí, señor," I said. "Cienfuegos thinks it's best. He says the fewer folks who know about the boy, the better. We're supposed to leave tomorrow with the sun."

The comandante smiled his terrible smile. "Mija—it's even better than we hoped!"

I passed back the cigarette. "I don't understand, señor. Víctor, I mean."

The comandante got a far-off look in his eye, like he was sorting through just how much to explain. "As you know," he said, "Upper City has an arsenal of weaponry—chemicals and bombs, unfathomably powerful technology. Things that allow them to . . . how can I say this . . . to forget that they too have bones and flesh and rivers of blood. For many years, Las Oscuras has tried to correct this misconception, to turn Upper City's bodies against them and make them remember that we are all human beings. A virus is a powerful instrument, in the right hands."

"You mean Las Oscuras is using Zabrán as a weapon?"

The comandante nodded. "Our most recent attack—an attempt to infect an Upper City officer with Zabrán—failed. The officer returned to his city knowing he'd been infected, giving the virus no chance to spread to others."

"The boy's father . . . ," I said.

The comandante's copper eyes locked onto mine with such heat that my insides quivered. "God is speaking to us clearly now, mija."

I hugged my knees tighter. "I still don't understand. What will you have me do?"

He took a deep inhale from his cigarette and placed his hand on my knee. "We too know of this healer in the North. But we've yet to find a way to bring her medicine into our possession. She has many people protecting her, people who see Las Oscuras as the enemy. We cannot allow the healer's cure to fall into Upper City's hands, to neutralize Zabrán, our greatest weapon. Your mission is to steal this medicine."

I blinked. "But why me?"

"The Upper City boy trusts you with his life, hija. Only you can complete this mission."

"If I steal this medicine, what happens to the boy and his father?"

The comandante smiled. "Let us worry about the rest."

"And all I have to do till then is keep his trust?"

"Keep it, yes. Strengthen it. You'll guide the boy along a route I will map for you. Las Oscuras has a stronghold in the trash hills south of Serena. When you arrive, I'll find you there."

"I can do that," I said.

The comandante took my sinner's hand in his, which was shrunken and twisted just like mine. Together they formed a fist. "I know you can, mija. You and I are alike. People look at you, as they once looked at me, and they see someone small and weak. But you have more strength than they could ever imagine. Now, there's just one thing left to do." I glanced down at the sheet. The needles. The vials. "This mark is for your protection. Should you meet another comrade during your mission, this is how you will prove your allegiance."

I nodded. I knew Las Oscuras used their tats as a sign of trust. The shimmering ink was impossible to fake—nobody but the highest in their ranks knew how to make it. The higher you ranked, the more visible your tat—which meant the comandante, with his shimmering face, was more powerful than I could imagine. But for the Library elders, the mark was an act of treason. If anybody in Paraíso saw my mark, I'd be sent to the Lighthouse, just like Mariana.

The comandante looked west through the trees, toward the sound of the crowd at the Lighthouse. "After this, there is no going back, mija. Are you prepared to join yourself to us?"

I cleared my throat to be sure my voice didn't falter. "Sí, Comandante. I am."

He leaned forward and blew the coals into a flame. Then he chose a needle from his case and held the needle to the fire till the tip glowed bright and orange.

"Muy bien," he said. "Now lie back and take off your shirt."

". . . Off, señor?" I said.

"Our revolution knows no such propriety, mija," he said.

My cheeks flushed. "Of course not, Comandante."

I unbuttoned my shirt down the middle and laid myself back on the sheet, which was soft and cool and smelled of old rot. This is the only way, I reminded myself. Still, I was shaking. The wind blew cold across my skin. Somewhere in the forest, la lechuza hooted softly. I pictured her silent flight through the trees as she snatched her prey and carried it, screaming, in her talons.

The comandante touched his rough fingertip, warm from the fire, to my chest and shivers flew through me. The heat of his stare fell over me. It wasn't a wanting look. It was a look of owning. "Look at me as I mark you," he said.

I tried to meet his gaze, but my eyes kept darting away to the trees overhead.

"I said look at me," he growled, pressing his hand into my chest. I let out a gasp, but he didn't ease up. He only pushed harder.

Desperate, I looked up into his oil-slick face and begged mercy with my eyes.

And he let go.

I sat up coughing, my hands clutching my chest. "What the hell was that?" I shouted. But he didn't answer. Just shoved me down again and pinned me to the ground.

"You need to understand something," he said, calm as the water atop an undertow. "You are permitted no resistance. Obedience only. Understood?"

I clenched my teeth as he slid my shirt off my shoulders and bared my chest to the night.

"How small is this pain," he said as his fire-hot needle pierced my skin. I twitched with the sting but made no sound. My eyes stayed fixed on his. "How small is this pain . . ."

He needled the last prick of ink into my skin and then sat back and made the cross over me. "Glory be to our heavenly Father, and to his righteous Son, and to the Holy Spirit of Justice," he said, dabbing the beads of blood from my skin. "As it was in the beginning, is now, and ever shall be. World without end . . . Amen."

I looked down at the shimmering circle that now blazed at the center of my chest and rubbed it with my thumb. A never-ending loop. A snake eating its own tail.

"Now come, mija." The comandante stood and kicked dirt on the coals. "Let us pay tribute to our sister." I buttoned my shirt and followed him to the edge of the gulch. In the distance, through a thicket of vines, I could see it. The burning. Its orange smolder cast a beam over the darkness of the ocean. A girl's life burned away in that glow. I imagined Mariana's soul flying from Paraíso, across the night waters toward the hole pierced in the wax-moon sky.

"Lighthouses once were used to save lives," the comandante said. "Someday, they will again be used to save the lives of sailors instead of burning the bodies of saints. Someday soon."

The streets of Paraíso were empty as I walked home past houses crawling with bindweed, past the old belfry tower where Javi and me used to spy on old ladies praying below. The memory of each place sank deep into me. Not just my memories, though. Mine were built atop the memories of the woman whose journal I carried in my satchel, who had no petrol to drive to the mountains. And that woman's memories were built atop those of a hundred million people before her—traders and earthquake survivors, soldiers and explorers and slaves—of dusty churches and blood-thick battles and the soft, sweet smell of the forest floor. And those were built on even older ones—the memories of forest dwellers and roaming fishermen and stewards of a dozen kinds of corn. It was all one great big circle, a spinning hoop that came back to me, here, now. I touched the swollen circle at the center of my chest.

World without end, I thought, and kept on toward home.

PART III
NORTH

17

RUMI

I dreamed of desert birds the night before I was to leave Paraíso for the North. The birds circled slowly, impossibly high, the sky behind them a chemical yellow that seemed to melt them as they circled. Their feathered bodies dripped down the vault of the sky and pooled in tar-black puddles at the horizon. In my dream, I lay faceup on the ground, unable to move as a figure emerged from the distance and began walking toward me. The figure became a girl, and the girl became Laksmi, her hips like a pendulum—smooth and mesmerizing. She wore her scholar's vest and a skirt rolled dangerously short. Her lips were silver, her skin a plane of shifting shadows—tattoos that crawled over her like spiders, creeping up her legs, into the softness of her chest, in and out of her mouth. She toed at me like I was a dead animal, and then continued toward the horizon. The desert birds dripped streaks down the dome of the sky, and I awoke.

A beam of morning light shone onto my face through the window in Cienfuegos's quarters. I pulled out my specs to check for a signal—to see if Baba had sent word or if the Central Security Bureau had dispatched a search team. But there was nothing, still nothing. The digital world had fallen silent, its absence like a phantom limb.

I sat on the pallet Cienfuegos had laid out for me the night before and touched the tattooed skin on my neck. Cienfuegos had given me a salve to ease the burning, but it didn't do much. I pulled on my shirt and stood.

Cienfuegos's office was covered in books—on history and anthropology, on religion, geography. On one wall hung a series of calendars charting the lunar cycle, the cubic volumes of rainfall, the swells of the tides. There were writings, too, in a shorthand I couldn't decipher. I leaned in to see if I could find a pattern in the text just as the door opened and Cienfuegos walked in. I jumped back, flustered. But he didn't seem to notice.

"Buenos días," he said, tipping his head slightly. "You slept well, I hope?"

I nodded and thanked him, but he brushed off my thanks.

"I know these accommodations must feel like an insult to a person such as yourself, accustomed to certain comforts. But please know that if I could offer anything better, in a heartbeat I would do so." From his desk, he produced a slim envelope with a red wax seal.

"This letter has been sealed with the Library of Paraíso's insignia. Keep it safe and close to you, always. There is great respect in the North for the authority of the Library. God willing, it will be enough to excuse the marks on your skin." Next he handed me a sack of nuts and dried red berries along with a loaf of hearty bread. "Provisions . . . ," he said. "I hope it will suffice."

He sat in his chair and began stuffing his pipe. "As you know, one of our brave scouts has chosen to put her life in danger to assist you on your quest. And the Library itself is risking our relations with other regions to share with you information about the healer in the North. We do this freely, of course, to help your father, whom we consider a friend. But if I may ask one small favor in return . . ." From the maps and ledgers on his desk, he selected a thick roll of papers. "Pass these to your father—once he's well, of course. Tell him we're ready to begin construction, that Solomon Cienfuegos remains loyally in the service of his city. Will you do this, Rumi?"

I took from him the roll, which was bound tightly with twine. "And what if Father . . . What if the healer doesn't have a cure?"

Cienfuegos bowed his head. "Then you would have my deepest condolences. But again—in the event, terrible as it would be, that the healer has no remedy for your father . . . were you to pass these papers to one of your father's colleagues, they would know what to do."

I looked down at the roll of papers in my hands, my head spinning. In the event that the healer has no remedy . . . In the event that Father's life sputters and wheezes into silence . . . Numbly, I opened my pack and nestled the papers deep inside, next to Father's map and the Library's letter. Then I extended my hand to thank Cienfuegos.

He took my hand in his. "No, my child. Thank you. You don't know the distances you're spanning, the lives that will change because of your brief time in our city. Your actions will echo for years, their repercussions weaving through the lives of countless others."

I nodded and shook his hand, understanding nothing.

Cienfuegos looked over my shoulder then, and his expression changed. I turned to see Paz, watching from the open doorway. My heart leapt.

"Buenos días," she said, unsmiling.

"Good morning," I said.

She stepped into the room and closed the door behind her.

"You'll need these," Cienfuegos said, ignoring her greeting as he passed her a stack of maps bound with a leather cord. Paz unbound them and flipped through them quickly, nodding at each one before placing them in her pack.

"And you, Rumi, will need this." From a drawer in his desk, the old man pulled a dark-red scarf. "Whatever you do, be sure no one sees the marks of those savages."

I wrapped the scarf around my neck hesitantly, and he nodded as if to say, *That'll do*. Then he turned to Paz. "As you approach Serena, you'll surely see signs of the virus. You were young when we last had an outbreak here in Paraíso. Do you remember what to look for?"

Paz nodded solemnly. "Rheumy eyes, staggers. Sheets left out in open fields."

I thought of Father—his sunken eyes, his feeble voice. The way he'd struggled to sit upright in that bed caged by plastic . . .

"And black flags in the doorways, yes," Cienfuegos said. "Never enter a town if you see these signs. Understood?"

Paz nodded again. "Well, flaco," she said. "Your things are ready. So, now we go?"

The old man reached out to clasp her skinny arm and looked steadily into her eyes. "To be clear, this is our secret. Rumi, this mission—our secret. You know how swiftly rumor flies."

"Yes, señor."

He released her. "Of course you do. Vayan con Dios, hijos. Be careful. Be very careful."

I followed Paz in silence down the corridor and through the maze of books. She was stony as we walked, and I began to wonder whether our conversation in her apartment hideaway—the smiles, the seeming concern—had all been an act. This question brought with it a tightness in my throat. The feeling only worsened as we curled down the staircase toward the heavy wooden doors that led outside. The whole world seemed to stand at a slant—much as it had the night I'd taken too many citizen pills, alone in my bedroom. But this time the menace had a face. It had a name. *Don't trust those Lower City devils,* Wen had said. And yet my life now lay at the mercy of this unreadable stranger.

But the moment we stepped outside and the morning light struck Paz's face, the spell of silence broke. "Oye, you look worse'n a skinned rabbit!" she said. "Didn't Cienfuegos give you something to hide your face?"

"Something, yeah." I ruffled the scarf to hide the lines climbing my neck to my jaw. She took a deep breath and stretched her arms overhead. Her shirt lifted to show the light brown skin of her stomach, taut like a runner's. "Well, flaco, ¿estás listo?" she asked. "Are you ready?"

I nodded hesitantly, unsure of everything. "What's 'flaco' mean, anyway?"

She poked me in the stomach and laughed. "It means you gotta grow some muscles, weoncito! It also means that you should learn some Spanish. . . ."

A cool, clean breeze blew in from the ocean as I followed Paz uphill. She moved quickly with unbelievable grace, and it was all I could do to keep up. The blues and greens and magentas of shacks and painted staircases streaked past in a blur. A small band of dogs ran behind us, their tongues flopping wildly. At first I was nervous and tried to shoo them away, but Paz just laughed. "Don't pay them any mind, flaco, or they won't ever leave you alone!"

We climbed higher and higher until at last we found ourselves among trees. Paz followed the bend of the river without slowing her pace. Finally, at a swinging rope bridge, she stopped. I was breathing hard, but so was she. "Wanted to see if you could keep pace," she said, smiling. "You're not too bad—for Upper City."

My chest heaved. "Thanks, I guess."

In the distance, a panorama of dark green hills rose and fell as far as I could see. That way was north, I thought. Over those hills was my ticket home.

Only one dog had stayed with us all the way to the bridge, a skinny yellow dog with a bright pink wound on its neck. I crouched and extended my hand toward it. "Hey there, buddy," I said. The dog wagged its tail and nuzzled my hand with its nose.

Paz shoved a handful of nuts and berries into her mouth from the bag Cienfuegos had given us. "I'm warning you, flaco," she said, passing the bag to me. "You give it one kind word and that sorry mutt will be yours *for life.*"

"Even street dogs deserve a little kindness, don't you think?"

"Suit yourself," she said. "Just don't say I didn't warn you. . . ."

I wiped my hands on my pants and popped a piece of shiny red fruit from the bag into my mouth. My lips puckered at the impossibly sour taste.

Paz laughed. "Never had pitanga before, eh?"

"I guess not. . . ." I made a mental note of the SoyChewy bars still stashed in my pack.

Paz put the sack of fruits and nuts in her satchel. "Okay, listen. We're about to go into the forest now—the real forest. We gotta stick close from here on. But first . . ." She loaded a stone into her sling and turned to the dog. "It's time for this regalón to go. . . ."

"No, don't!" I shouted, and grasped her arm.

But Paz tossed me off of her. "I'm not gonna kill it, weón," she said. "Just scare it a little. ¡Ándate, quiltro!" she shouted as she launched a stone an arm's length from the dog. But the dog wouldn't leave. Instead it crouched, ears tipped back and eyes wide, unsure what it had done wrong. Paz lobbed another stone, then another, each getting closer until finally one hit the animal in the leg. The dog let out a yelp and darted into the bramble.

"Perdóname, perrito," Paz said quietly. Then she stepped onto the swinging bridge, and together we crossed into the forest.

I don't know how far we walked that first day or how many hills we climbed. We passed sinkholes and bogs and meadows that once were neighborhoods, sprawling concrete ruins with saplings growing from roofs. We passed rocky fields and farmers who raised their eyes to watch, unsmiling, until we were out of sight. Every so often, I swore I saw a silvery face lurking in shadows—bright teeth in the bark of trees, inky lips in the rocks. But every time I felt myself buckling with fear, I'd look ahead to Paz—the patch of sweat at the small of her back darkening her shirt. She was my unmoving center, my fixed point in a spinning world.

Still, my mind paced through calculations as we walked. Father had been infected with the virus for one full day before I left St. Iago. It took me two days to cross the desert, then I'd spent one night as a prisoner of Las Oscuras and two nights in Paraíso. That made six days. If this strain of the virus were anything like those before the Breach, Father had two weeks at most from the initial infection before the lethal phase set in. The coma would buy him an additional day or two, maybe. Which meant I'd used up almost half of my time already.

At midday, we passed a sunny cemetery with tall grass and ancient headstones. I tried sounding out the Spanish epitaphs to fill the silence. "Para siempre en nuestros corazones," I read. "What does that mean?"

"It means . . . *Forever in our hearts,*" Paz said.

"How about—O Madre Mía, ex . . . extiende . . . sobre mí—"

"Um. It says *Mother, open your wings over me,* like . . . *like the eternal stars.*"

I brushed my hand across a headstone that had fallen on its side and pushed aside the grass. The inscription was hard to make out. "What about this one?"

Paz came up behind me, rubbing the muscles of her deformed hand. "It's too hard. . . ."

I smiled. "That's what it says?"

"No, idiota. Okay, it says that there's something tricking—or, no . . . I think it means *twisting.* There's something twisting, like vines growing up a wall. And that this something is also breaking free—or maybe *sprouting*—like moss growing out of a stone."

I stared at the headstone. "What's twisting?"

"Doesn't say," she said, and kept walking.

Like moss growing out of a stone, I thought. Like vines growing up a wall. A living thing, bursting through . . .

"Hey, how come your English is so good?" I asked, running to catch up.

She let out a sharp laugh. "How come *your* Spanish is so bad?"

I paused. "I don't know. I guess I never had to learn."

"Well, that's where we're different, flaco," she said. "You Upper City swanks learn something only if you feel like it. But down here, we learn stuff to stay alive."

The day wore on. The straps of my pack cut into my shoulders.

My feet throbbed. But Paz seemed unfazed. She never once slowed her pace as we hiked through forests and ruins, past the skeletons of churches and petrol stations and an overgrown playground with a bird's nest in the seat of a swing. How strange to think that Father knew these forests and fields. Cienfuegos said Paz must never know of his connection to Father. What would she do if she knew?

Eventually our path intersected with the cracked pavement of an old highway, and Paz took a tattered map from the inner pocket of her satchel. The map didn't seem to be one that Cienfuegos had given her, but he'd given us so many things that it was difficult to keep track. We continued along this paved road, its cracked asphalt sprouting weeds. The sun beat into our eyes as we walked.

"Oye, flaco," Paz said, breaking the silence. "I've got one for you. I run all the time and never walk. Sometimes I whisper, but I can't talk. I've got a bed but don't need sleep. I've got a mouth, but I can't eat. What am I?"

"Um." I stopped for a moment, watching Paz glide effortlessly in front of me.

"Give up?" she called back.

I ran to catch up. "What, is that like a riddle?"

"Yes, it's *like a riddle*. Haven't you got riddles up there in your great big castles?"

"Okay, just give me a second . . . ," I said, out of breath. She seemed to be *quickening* her pace, not slowing, as the day wore on. "So it runs but doesn't walk. It whispers but doesn't . . . Oh, right. I've heard this one. It's a river."

Paz kept walking. "Your turn," she said.

"Wait. Is it a river?"

"Yes, flaco. It's a river. Good for you. You want a medal or something?"

I smiled. "Okay, I've got one. From the top of my head to the bottom of my foot, all I am is tongue. What am I?"

"Where'd you hear that one?"

"My grandfather likes riddles. Riddles and poems."

The highway was following the ridgeline now, and the hills spread in all directions. The dusty sand at the edges of the pavement sprouted with wildflowers.

"Well? Give up?" I asked.

"Gimme a minute! Por Dios . . ."

The sun had begun to set, and the trees on either side of us cast eerie shadows on the roadway. In my periphery, I swore I saw a silver-faced figure clinging to an overhanging limb, hidden by leaves. But when I turned to face it head-on, nothing was there.

"We should stop soon," Paz said. "Before it gets dark. It says on the map that we're close to a town. I'm hoping something's still standing there. Keep us safe from jaguars."

"Jaguars?"

"That's right. Jaguars," she said. "Pumas, too—those have lived here forever. But all kinds of exotic creatures escaped from zoos after the Breach. In these parts, the ones that stuck around were the jaguars."

A rustle in the bush behind me nearly stopped my heart. Paz fell to a crouch, circling her slingshot by her side. Then, out of the bushes, came the yellow dog from that morning, the one with the wound on its neck. It trotted toward me, head lowered in apology for taking so long.

"Chucha, perrito . . . ," Paz said.

She shook her head as the dog came up to her, wagging its

whole body with joy. Then she muttered something in Spanish and held the dog by the scruff, examining the wound on its neck. From her pack, she took a brown glass vial and dabbed liquid onto a clean cloth. The dog whimpered but licked her shoulder as she pressed the cloth against its wound.

"Okay, Violincito," she said, standing. "I guess this means you're ours now. Let's just hope you're a better guard dog than you look."

"Violincito?" I asked.

Paz smiled. "It means somebody who tries to tag along on a date, when it's supposed to be just the two of you. Isn't that right, Vio?"

The town ahead wasn't much of a town at all, reduced to mounds of concrete and twists of steel. Shards of plastic plumbing and electrical conduit rose from the ground like skeletons clawing from their graves. I wondered whether the town had been bombed before the Breach or if it had been destroyed in the aftermath—after Baba's family and millions like them had taken refuge inside the militarized walls of Upper Cities all over the world. Was it bombed in broad daylight or as its inhabitants slept? Both thoughts overwhelmed me.

"Oye," Paz said. "It's getting dark—about time we got off the road. I don't see any black flags. Seems as safe a place as we're gonna find."

She turned off the highway and began climbing over debris, the dog at her side. In the distance, a few houses were still standing. Paz squinted and pointed to a house sheltered by skinny pines, its walls purple with creamy trim. Purple—against a gray wasteland.

"How's that one look to you?" she asked.

"It looks good," I said, exhausted. "I mean. It looks fine."

I hoped the house would be like the apartment Paz had taken me to in the Wastes, but when we reached it, those hopes dissolved. The house had been looted long ago, with few things remaining—a couch covered in mildew, a rusty kettle on the stove. In one bedroom, plastic stars glowed faintly on the ceiling. I imagined a child pasting them up there, standing tiptoe on a chair.

"No fire tonight," Paz said as she swept broken glass from the floor, clearing a space to sleep. "I don't know what kinds of chems bombed this place. No sense risking it."

"Right," I said, though my body was desperate for a hot meal.

Paz the fleet-footed, I thought. Paz, the girl who knows no hunger.

The dark was almost total when Paz's hand found mine with a handful of dried fruit and nuts. "Thanks," I said, and tossed them into my mouth. Salt and sugar. Great god. Elixir of life. I thought again about the SoyChewy bars in my pack. But I didn't want Paz to think I was weak.

"Water?" she asked.

"Yes, please." I took a huge gulp from her canteen before realizing that it likely wasn't purified, and I spat it out onto the floor.

"What the hell?" Paz shouted. "This is all the water we have!"

"I just . . . It might make me sick," I said.

"Hijo de puta. You think I didn't boil this for you? You think I want to deal with you losing your belly out both ends?"

"I'm sorry," I said. "I just . . ."

Paz took her canteen from me in silence and lay down in the dark. "Vio, perrito, ven acá," she said. The yellow dog nuzzled itself into the space beside her and sighed. She was quiet for so long that I figured she'd fallen asleep.

I lay down, near Paz but not too close, and closed my eyes, trying to commit to memory every detail of my journey so far. The glow-in-the-dark stars, the granite epitaphs, the Library full of books. I wanted to be able to recount it all to Baba if I returned.

When, I thought. Not if. When.

"Is it fire?" Paz asked. Her voice seemed to come from nowhere.

"What?"

"'From head to foot, all I am is tongue.' Is it fire?"

"Yeah," I said. "Yeah, it is."

"Good one, flaco." She curled onto her side, cradling her head in the crook of her arm. "We leave with the sun tomorrow, got it? Try'n get some sleep."

Through a broken window, I could see the moon rising in the sky. Outside, the wasted town looked like a foreign planet. I thought of things I'd tell Wen—how so many Lower City kids had severe deformities, how the smell of the city made you want to vomit. How terrorists had taken needles to my skin—all at once, like a swarm of bees. I could almost hear the thrill in his voice as he told me how badass my tattoo was, the protests he'd shout when I told him I'd be getting it removed. Then I imagined the things I'd tell Laksmi. How the ocean could change from blue to green. How it was blindingly bright. How jaguars stalked the darkness . . .

"Good night," I said to Paz, and I tried to find sleep.

Young Woman of the Morning,
Young Man of the Morning!
Old Woman of the Evening,
Old Man of the Evening!
Quiet is the night,
But fierce is the day that you hold
Like an ordnance undetonated in your arms
In the hope that your stillness will quiet her fury.

But she will never be calmed,
For she is born of the hornet's sting
And of the leaf's exhales.

O h, children. What a tale I have for you tonight, of a girl born with a fever that never went cold. A girl named Nahuela.

In the charred-earth days when the soil boiled hot with fear, Nahuela came into this world. Her mother cried as she held her baby, for the child's skin was hot to touch. Afraid she'd birthed a spirit, her mother carried her down to the sea. But the girl would not be cooled. For within her chest beat the young molten Earth, bright as the unclouded sun.

The infant grew into a fierce young woman whose chest

opened to the sky in reckless possibility. Day after day, Nahuela stepped out, dancing from house to house and man to man.

Then came the day when Nahuela found herself with child. She didn't weep with this news. She was joyful, even. But her mother thought differently. Her mother knew that these were not days for happiness—these blackened, boiling days. She knew that the broken world held for its people only one truth—the truth of fear. And so it was that, with tears in her eyes, the woman told her young daughter she no longer had a place in their home.

Imagine young Nahuela asleep beneath the stars, pulling twigs from her wild black hair in the morning. Listen to her sing to her unborn child, a hand on her steaming belly. And here it was that, alone in the forest with a child curled inside, she realized there truly were things to fear.

Oh, children. How to tell you?

Of the day the boiled and blackened earth cried out for a mercy it would not receive? Of the day Old Woman of the Forest and Old Man of the Trees clawed at their cheeks with their fingernails as judgment rained from the sky? How to tell of the blood young Nahuela coughed, or the sound of her screaming?

It was a sound as unspeakable as those you'll hear tonight, dear children—the screams for mercy, the sound of vengeance exacted. You've been told that this screaming pays the wages of sin. But tell me—who could deserve the fate young Nahuela met? As the ashes rain down tonight, think of Nahuela lying in the forest, surrounded by charred black trees. Picture her body broken and burned, holding against her chest a newborn child whose tiny heart beats with fury. Then picture, if you can, a man with copper eyes running through the forest to find her, a man who wipes the sweat from her brow and holds her head in his hands. Can you picture this mercy, this man as he cradles the dying girl and newborn child?

Can you picture the man as he asks what name he should give the child?

Peace, says Nahuela. *My child will be named Peace.*

18

PAZ

Cool light from the window of the bombed-out house cut across my eyes and woke me early to the sound of the boy's slow, wet breathing. I got up, quiet as I could. I figured I could sling a couple fat vizcachas and cook them before the boy even woke. No way he'd be able to keep pace if he didn't have a bit of meat inside him. I left behind a map and some bread—not the comandante's map, of course. One from Cienfuegos. *Gain his trust,* the comandante said. Little steps seemed the best way. Maps. Riddles. Crispy meat for breakfast.

A kiskadee bird sang his morning call from somewhere in the hills as I stepped into the morning, the pup trotting alongside me. *"¡Bien-te-veo!"* the bird sang. *"¡Bien-te-veo!"*

I see you! I see you!

Mami told me once, years ago, that some Upper City cuicos had brought these birds over the Cordillera because they liked their song. Of course, the birds had escaped the walls of the cities, and now they were everywhere.

"So what if you see me?" I mumbled back. "I'm not doing any wrong."

The distance from the house to the woods went quick without

the boy dragging his feet behind me. A circle of smoking coals at the forest edge let me know somebody had slept there the night before. Scavengers, maybe. I hoped they hadn't scared away all the catch.

A deep cleft in a pair of rocks made for a perfect hide. I stilled my breathing and scanned the ruins in the morning light while the pup sniffed around and marked his scent. A frayed plastic bag blowing in the wind caught my eye. Then I saw them. Up ahead, just beyond the reach of my stones. A pack of chubby vizcachas, eyes closed like they were praying to the sun. Qué buena onda.

The pup wiggled next to me, and I grabbed him by his scruff and forced him down. "Stay," I said, and he seemed to understand.

That one there, I thought. The fattest one. He'd make a juicy breakfast. I snuck within range, placed a stone in my sling, and focused on his twitching whiskers. My heart beat steady into the earth as I whipped the cradle over my head and released.

It was going to be a tasty morning.

With my catch slung over my shoulder, I set about rekindling the coals of the abandoned fire. My kindling had just started to catch when beside me the pup's ears fell back. He let out a low growl. I sensed it too—the unmistakable stillness of somebody watching, the breath held tight in a pair of lungs. I dropped into a crouch, sling in hand.

"¡Bien-te-veo!" called the kiskadee bird. "¡Bien-te-veo!"

The wind slipped its chilly fingers up my spine, turning my skin to gooseflesh. Just then a hot hand wrapped around my neck, and my insides turned cold.

"You'll have to do better than that, mija, if you want to stay alive in these wastelands."

My face went red. I stood and brushed a strand of hair from my forehead.

"Comandante," I said. I tried not to sound surprised.

His shimmering face creased into an awful, red-gummed smile. "A well-slung meal, to be sure. But what good is a meal if some man or beast has his hunt fixed on you?"

"How long you been following me?"

"That's none of your concern," he said. "What *is* your concern are the scavengers who could have camped here last night, and the wild dogs drinking your sweet scent. What *is* your concern, mija, is the helpless worm of a boy you left all alone in this snake pit of a town."

I pulled out my knife and started skinning my catch. My cheeks burned. "I'm sorry, Comandante. I just—"

"You just . . . what? You just *forgot* that he is the entire purpose of your mission? That if you don't transport the boy north safely— and quickly!—then you will have *failed*?"

I shot him a sharp look. "We gotta eat, don't we? You think that kid can swallow a handful of dried pitanga every other day and make any sort of haste? He's *slow*. He's *weak*. You said so yourself. How'm I supposed to gain his trust and all if I treat him like cargo?" I grabbed a plastic bag lodged in the rubble at my feet and shook out the dust.

"Tranquila, hija," the comandante said, softer now. "I only say these things to express my concern. For the success of our mission. You must understand what a vital role you have in all of this." The comandante placed his hand on my back. His fingers felt like snakes twisting around my spine. "We cannot succeed without you."

I wriggled from his touch and shoved the gutted vizcacha

carcass into the bag. Blood formed rivers in the plastic's creases.

"Anything else?" I glanced toward the wasted town where I'd left the boy. I didn't want to admit it, but the comandante was right. I should never have left him alone. He was as helpless as a moth in the rain.

"That's all for now," he said. "We have a small encampment in the ruins near Isla de Lobos, two days' walk from here. Tonight you'll stay on the coast in a fishing village named Cachagua, midway between here and there. I marked both on the map I gave to you. Make peace with the fishing village. Tell them of your work for the Library, but nothing of your mission for us or of the boy's history."

"You gonna be watching?"

The comandante smiled and raised his sinner's arm in a gnarled fist. "Hasta la victoria, siempre."

"Till victory," I echoed.

As soon as he disappeared into the woods, I sprinted across the ruins, the pup by my side, up the rotted stairs and through the bedroom doorway. And there the boy was. Still sleeping.

"Rise and shine, morning glory," I said, tossing the sack of meat next to his sleeping face.

The boy shrieked. "What is *that*?"

"That's breakfast, flaco. Buen provecho."

The boy picked the bag off the ground with two fingers. "Looks . . . bloody," he said, nudging it back toward me. "Have you been awake long?"

"Long, yes," I said. "We can't all afford beauty rest. Get your things."

He winced as he stood and rubbed his legs with his hands.

"You okay?" I asked.

"Okay. Just sore."

Great, I thought. Sore already. But I clenched my teeth. "We'll go slower today," I said.

North of the ruined town, I made a small cook fire, and we feasted on crispy meat that fell from the bone. The boy picked the carcass clean, licking grease from his fingers as the sun rose through the trees. I sat with my back to him and pulled the comandante's map from where I'd hid it in my satchel, under the woman's red journal.

"Nice breakfast?" I asked.

He smiled. "I don't think I've ever tasted anything so good."

I tossed a few scraps to the pup, then grabbed my canteen and shook it. Half-empty. "We need to find someplace to fill our water today. Should be a stream coming off the Cordillera this time of year, not too far out of our way."

"How far?"

"Half day to get there, then another half day to our next camp." I portioned a handful of fruit and nuts from Cienfuegos's sack and passed it to the boy along with a hunk of bread.

The kiskadee called again, closer this time. I scanned the trees for his little yellow body.

There.

"I see you too, chico," I called back.

"What?" the boy asked.

"That bird. See him there?" I took the boy's hand in mine and pointed along the sight line. "We say his song sounds like *bien-te-veo*. It means, *I see you*."

"Is it some kind of mockingbird?"

"It's a kiskadee."

The boy lowered his arm. "I've actually been dreaming about

birds. Horrible birds, not pretty ones like that. We don't have many birds in St. Iago. Not flesh-and-blood ones, I mean."

He looked back at the yellow bird in the tree. The kiskadee sang again—*I see you! I see you!*—and another one answered from deep in the forest.

"It's funny—the first time I saw a real bird, it scared the crap out of me," the boy said. "I was six years old or so, playing in the park with my grandfather when this bird comes swooping above my head. It must've been a sparrow or something—just a little brown thing—but I started screaming, 'Make it go away, Baba! Make it go away!'"

I turned back to my map and tried not to picture it—the boy as a little kid, playing in the grass. I didn't want to think of him with his grandfather. I didn't want to think of his fears.

"My grandfather tried to calm me down," the boy continued. "He said it was just a little bird. But I wouldn't listen. I just kept screaming, 'Make it go away . . .'"

I see you! I see you! I see you!

Three birds now called to one another across the forest. Winged little spies. Tattletales.

"Some people think the kiskadees are saying *bicho-feo*, not *bien-te-veo*," I said. "Bicho feo—it means *ugly bug*." I threw a stone at the tree, and the bird screeched and flew away. "That's right—get out of here, you ugly bug!"

I slung my satchel over my shoulder and kicked dirt into the cook fire. "¿Listo?"

From the ruined town, we walked through bone-dry hills covered in wild agave and golden-haired asters. Spirit houses decorated with candles were wedged into the roadside, honoring the long-ago dead. I could feel the comandante's hot hand on my neck as we walked. He was out there someplace, watching. Making sure I stayed loyal to the mission.

Hand-painted signs saying "*se vende queso de cabra*" or "*se venden huevos*" marked dusty roads leading nowhere. I didn't feel much like talking, but I translated every word the boy asked. Don't just play his friend, *be* his friend, I thought. Fool your own damn self. Was there any other way to make him believe deep down that all of this was real?

Afternoon sank into evening before I saw the sparkle of the ocean peeking through the hills to the west, just as the comandante said I would. We turned off the main road and followed a dusty path downhill toward the shore. Soon, the horizon opened onto a deep-blue stretch of ocean. I squinted into the setting sun as we stepped onto the empty beach. All along the shoreline stood weathered cabañas, their insides wiped clean by tsunamis. In the distance, on the other side of the cove, stood a group of men, shirtless and rusty-skinned, sifting their catch. I raised my hand to wave, but they just stared back, shielding their eyes.

The pup whined at my side, and I snapped at him to stay close as we walked toward them. I'd heard of towns like this—where horses and carts came just once a month with goods from the valley to barter. Honest towns, but untrusting. With the boy in my charge, and with both of us marked, everything felt rimmed with danger.

I raised my sinner's arm again and smiled as we got closer.

"¡Hola! Buenas," I called.

The men didn't answer. Their blue-white eyes flared against copper skin. The pup ran ahead of us, tail wagging, sniffing at the shellfish in their nets. I tried to call him back, but before I could, one of the men kicked him sharp in the ribs and he ran off yelping.

You gotta look out for your own self, pup, I thought. But deep down my insides flinched.

"Disculpen, señores," I said, coming closer to the men. I tried to remember the polite way of speaking that small towns still used— the usted form and the subjunctivo. "My partner and I come to you as scouts from the Library of Paraíso. It's our hope that we might spend a night here on your lands. A little shelter is all we'd need. Any one of these emptied-out cabins would do us just fine. We ask of you nothing except, humbly, for your permission."

The boy stood silent by my side, understanding nothing. I held out the letter Cienfuegos had given me, the one with the Library's seal, and a straight-backed man with sweaty dark hair cracked it open. He mumbled something I couldn't quite hear before turning back to me.

"From Paraíso, ah?"

"Sí, señor," I said.

He squinted unsmiling against the setting sun. "The big city."

"Sí, señor," I said.

"Ever heard of a kid named Muñez? Alfredo Muñez?"

I thought for a second. I didn't know anyone by that name. "Alfredo Muñez?"

"Sí, poh. He's the son of my brother. A good boy. His mother worries."

I smiled. This was my chance. "Ah, Alfredito? Ay, por Dios— of course I know Alfredito! He's the gamest fishmonger at the port!"

The man's face changed with these words. His voice turned quiet. "Qué bueno. His mother will be grateful to know he's safe and well. What shall I say is your name, señorita?"

"Paz," I said. "Paz Valenzuela-Valenzuela de Paraíso."

"Ay, qué linda," he said. "You say you're needing a place to stay, señorita?"

"Sí, señor," I said.

"And maybe you will join us for an asado, ah?"

I smiled and shook my head. "No, no. Don't trouble yourselves on account of us. We'll be fine to sleep—"

"Señorita—hija mía. Please, give us the honor of showing you our humble hospitality."

I looked at each of their faces. They were gentle and decent and tired. The comandante said we'd have no trouble here. And a meal of flame-cooked fish would lift the boy's spirits.

"Por supuesto, señor," I said. "Of course we'll join. Muchísimas gracias."

The straight-backed man whistled to a younger man standing farther up shore.

"¡Oye, Fermín!" he shouted. "¡Échame unos traguitos!"

And so the boy and I and our little dog, Vio, sat in the sand with a bottle of pisco between us, listening to fishing boats knock together in the cove. Woodsmoke mixed with ocean air and the sweet char of shellfish over hot coals. Vio rested his head on my lap and shut his eyes. His fur was warm with sun.

The ocean offered her colors to us like jewels—pearly blue and turquoise green. The slow pull of the waves stilled my heart, asking me to match their rhythm. *Come and go, come and go,* they said. *Stay just a moment, then slip away.* I thought back to the old Storyteller's tales of the Sea and the Sky, of their troubled bond, each by turns selfish and beautiful—a tremoring Earth and a surging sea, the bright beaming ocean, the twinkling jewels of the constellations.

At least we have the sea, Javi had said. At least we have the sea.

The boy sat quiet, his feet tucked into the sand. A pair of glasses covered his eyes. He moved his hands over a stiff piece of fabric in his lap, like he was playing an invisible piano.

"What's that you got there?" I asked after a while.

"It's a computer, kind of. It lets me see the world differently. I mean, not right now. I'm not connected to the—um . . . It's complicated."

I laughed. "Too complicated for a simple Lower City girl like me, huh?"

"That's not what I meant." He took off the glasses and held them out to me, together with the rigid cloth. "Want to see for yourself?"

I tucked the frames behind my ears. All of a sudden, rays of light shot out from the cloth, filling my sight with words and pictures. The brightness hurt my eyes.

"What you're looking at now is a chart of my father's bloodwork and vitals, taken the day before I left. I was just counting the number of days he's been sick, trying to see if he was— You know, if he's still . . ."

"You're trying to figure out if your dad is dead already, is that it?"

The boy dug his feet deeper into the sand. "Yeah."

I looked back down at the magic cloth. "Well? What did you figure?"

"I'm not sure. He's been sick for eight days. If his strain of the virus is anything like those before the Breach, he should still have time left. The dominant strain back then was slow-acting. The terrorists chose it intentionally for that very feature—so their targets would come into contact with as many people as possible before they knew they were sick. Increase the spread."

I passed back the glasses and rubbed my eyeballs till I could see clear again. The *terrorists*. The word jabbed me like a thorn, but I forced my cheeks into a smile.

"I think I'll go for a swim," I said.

I didn't look back as I shimmied off my shorts and waded into the ocean. The sea was clear as ice. With the water up to my chest, I leaned back to float on the waves. The flat blue sky above seemed at once close and unending, and I watched as a single yellow butterfly struggled to fly against the wind. The wind was strong and wet, and the butterfly was tiny. But still it struggled. Somehow, it kept flying.

19

RUMI

There was music and dancing around a bonfire that night. There was laughing and singing in Spanish. I declined the alcohol they offered and accepted the food, pretending I understood the words being spoken as I sat next to the fire. Paz plopped down next to me at one point, smiling and tipsy, and whispered that she'd told the men I was mute. Her face was bright from pisco and her smile was wide as she laughed at the notion that I, Rumi, couldn't talk.

I blushed and made a note to myself not to ask her so many questions.

Outside the circle of light and conversation, hiding my tattoo under my scarf, the whole world seemed at once radiant and slow. Paz stood, her arms raised overhead as she sang along to the chords of a guitar, then leaned toward me and whispered a translation. "It's a song about giving thanks to life," she said, "which has given us so much. . . ." I sat there in silence as she rejoined the others. *Thanks be to life* . . . For the vastness of the ocean. For warm sand to bury my feet beneath. For this girl who'd stepped into the turquoise surf, unbothered by the cold, the stark, dry mountains in the distance behind her. The warm glow in my chest began to swell then into a vague but powerful tenderness for this girl dancing and laughing with the fishermen around the fire, this girl who could climb mountains without hunger, this girl who'd floated in front of me on the waves. . . .

20

PAZ

I set a slower pace the third day. We had a steady climb ahead of us along the route the comandante had set, and I didn't want the boy to feel like the cargo he was. Besides, we'd feasted that morning on machas and crab, so we wouldn't have to stop again till late in the day. We could take our time.

Beneath a clear sky with no sign of rain, I scanned the pines for movement, human or otherwise. But I saw no sign of either. The boy was in high spirits after our night on the beach, and he kept pointing things out, like a little kid—a rusted rifle empty of ammo, a pile of orange vials that he claimed were once used for medicine, an old boot with flowers growing out the top.

He tapped the boot with his shoe and smiled. "What lovely forest décor!" he said.

Even when I stopped to check the map, he wouldn't let up his talking. "Hey! I've got a good one," he said. "What kind of flowers give kisses?"

I glared at him over the edge of the comandante's map with my eyebrow raised.

"Give up?"

"Oye. Can't you see I'm trying to work?"

Just then the pup sensed something. I heard it too. Something faint. Far away. Howling.

"Tulips!" the boy said. "Two. Lips. Get it?"

"¡Cállate, flaco!" I said, sharp as a snakebite. "Shut up. Right. Now." I fell to a crouch. The boy bent down next to me and looked into the trees. The pup lowered his head and growled a soft warning.

But nothing happened. Maybe it had just been the wind.

I stood, and the boy stood too.

"Hear something?"

"I'm not sure," I said. "Let's keep moving."

We found water just where I thought we might—cold snow-melt flowing clear over black river rocks. I filled my canteen and the boy filled his, then he dropped something into it—a tiny pink stone.

"Want a PuriTab?" he asked.

I stared at him, blank.

"It's for cleaning the water."

I shook my head and swallowed a big, cold gulp from my canteen. "You stick to your fancy stones, and I'll stick to mine, flaco," I said. I patted my pouch of slinging stones with a smile. He half smiled and looked away.

A few grasses and mosses sprouted near the stream, but the ground on the surrounding hillside was rock-heavy, scrubby pines as far as I could see. I stashed my canteen and map in my pack and readied to leave. That's when I heard it. The snarling.

I whipped around to see a dog, a wild dog, maybe eighty paces downhill from us. Small. Gray. Vicious. Its curling mouth and shining eyes gave it the look of a demon. Our yellow pup raised his hackles and let out a string of barks that curled up at the end. He backed away, sensing something I couldn't yet see.

I armed my sling and pushed the boy behind me, uphill from the wild dog. I could take the little beast, no problem, so long as the boy stayed out of my way.

The wild dog edged toward me, daring me to make the first move. I circled the stone at my side and took aim—*whoosh, whoosh, whoosh*. But then, farther downhill, another dog slunk from the pines. Then another. Conchasumadre. Quiltros. A whole pack of them. Our yellow pup, Vio, looked back and forth from me to the pack of dogs in front of us and whimpered.

"No quick movements!" I shouted to the boy behind me. "Listen, can you climb a tree?"

He let out a groan.

Shit. I tried to think fast. We could make a run for it, me slinging to buy us time while the boy scrambled up a tree. Not a great plan. But before I could think of a better one, I heard the boy's footfalls sprinting uphill away from me. The dogs went wild with barking. The hair on their backs stood in ridges.

"Chucha la weá . . . ," I muttered. The boy gave me no choice.

Quick as light, I slung three stones and sent three of the snarling muzzles whimpering away. Then I sprinted after the boy. Our poor yellow pup didn't know what to do. He started to run with us, then turned to fight. But he didn't have a chance. They swarmed on top of him, and all I heard were his screams.

I kept turning back to sling at the dogs, but there were more than ten of them now—far too many. "Climb!" I shouted ahead to the boy. "Find a tree and *climb*!"

He ran in frantic zigzags in front of me, no idea where to turn. My heart and lungs burned as I chased after him, like they were trying to claw their way out of my throat. How much longer could the boy keep his sprint at that altitude?

I looked over my shoulder at the dogs. They were running, but not at full stride. Almost like they were herding us.

Up ahead, I spotted a climbing tree—not an easy one, but at least not a pine.

"There!" I yelled, pointing. "That one, see?"

"I see it!"

I sprinted ahead and shoved my sling into my pocket before hooking my good arm around the lowest branch. My feet searched for footholds, and I pulled myself up till I could link my ankles around the limb. Then I reached down for the boy and latched his hand into mine. A sweaty, slippery grip. I tried to yank him up, but something was holding him back.

I looked down. A wild tawny dog had sunk its teeth deep into the boy's calf.

The dogs below went wild with the scent of first blood.

"Kick it!" I screamed. "Kick it in the face, goddammit!"

But the boy's eyes were crazed and out of focus.

Shit. Shit.

Still, my grip held firm. I tried to calm my voice.

"Flaco, hey! Look at me!" But he wasn't hearing my words, only the sound of his muscles tearing. Then I thought for a second. "Rumi," I said, gentler now.

With the sound of his name, his eyes focused on mine.

"Rumi, listen to me," I said. "These dogs will tear you to pieces if you don't get the fuck into this tree. Use your free foot. Kick the dog in the face. Do it. Now."

His hand was slipping. He looked about to cry.

"Do it," I pleaded. "Now."

With his free leg, he kicked the dog again and again. But the dog would not let go.

"Please," he said. His face was pale. His dark eyes looked out of focus again. "Please . . ."

His hand was sliding out of mine. With my sinner's arm, I reached down and grabbed his other hand. But there was little strength in his grip, or in mine. His hand felt cold.

This is it, I thought. The boy will die. The dog's jaws were too strong. I welled up with anger at myself. The dogs snarled and gnashed below us, and I almost let go. I couldn't find the strength to hold on any longer.

Why was I struggling so? I thought. This boy was my enemy. The comandante had given me the chance to end this boy's life earlier in the Wastes. Why should I care if he was eaten by dogs now? There was so much anger inside me—anger at the boy's helplessness, at all the things he didn't understand, at his people and what they'd done to mine. But watching him dangle like that, I realized for the first time that I didn't hate *him*. I didn't hate Rumi.

A wave of cold determination surged through me, and my thoughts came clear. "Listen," I said, no heat in my voice. "Hook your arm around my bad one."

He did.

"I'm gonna let go now, okay? I'm gonna let my other hand go."

He nodded. Pale, bloodless. When I released, his whole weight slunk into the feeble hold of my sinner's arm. I trembled and gripped my legs tighter around the tree branch. The dogs went wild beneath us, sensing my weakness.

"Don't let go of my arm, Rumi. Do not let go, you hear?"

He nodded.

With my good arm, I felt for my sling. I set a stone in the cradle, but the stone fell to the ground. More dogs leapt up, trying to grab hold of Rumi's other leg. Mierda. I reached for another stone. Set it in the cradle as well. This time it held. It would be a clumsy shot, but it was all I had. All we had.

I circled the sling and took aim at the tawny dog gripping Rumi's flesh with its teeth. *Whoosh, whoosh, wh—* But before I could release the stone, the dog let go. All at once, they quit their snarling, stopped still, ears alert, and ran into the forest.

Strange, I thought. What had made them run?

But the pain in my sinner's arm blotted out this question.

I released my grip and Rumi dropped to the ground, eyes wide. I eased myself down next to him. The warmth of his body against mine, the salty smell of his tears and sweat, brought me back to that night in the dark cellar room, both of us prisoners of Las Oscuras. But this time I was the one trembling.

He wrapped his arm around my shoulder and pulled me close. My head rested against his chest. I closed my eyes and felt the ache of tears rising in my throat.

"Your leg . . . ," I said.

He leaned forward to look at it and almost fainted.

"No," I said. "Lie back. Don't move."

Blood had soaked through the fabric of his trousers. Dark blood—the kind you never want to see. With my knife, I cut his pant leg above the knee and pulled away the bloody cloth. His calf looked like shredded meat.

"How bad is it?"

"It's not great," I said. "Do you have anything for cleaning it?"

"In my pack. I've got a first aid valise. Bandages, antiseptic . . ." His voice was weak. "How bad is it, Paz?"

"Bad," I said.

With all the water in my canteen, I flushed out the wound;

then I sliced a long strip from his trouser leg and tied it just above his knee, to try to slow the flow of blood.

Inside his pack I found a whole mess of gadgets and cases and glittery packets of food. "You been holding out on me, flaquito?" I said. "Soy . . . SoyChewy bars—they any good?"

He smiled, weak. "Sure. Try one."

I put the bar aside and held up a white plastic case. "Is this the valise?"

He nodded.

The case was full of bandages and tubes with long words I didn't understand. "Point to the one that'll keep it clean," I said. He pointed to a blue-and-white tube, and I squeezed the creamy medicine onto a piece of gauze, untied the tourniquet above his knee, and pressed the gauze firm against the gash.

"Gonna have to stay like this awhile," I said.

"Okay."

I could feel his heartbeat in the tattered flesh beneath my hands. I listened for the sound of the kiskadee bird, for the sound of anything familiar, but heard only wind. No trace of the dogs either. Where had they gone? I wondered if the comandante was watching from a tree, cursing my blunders. Maybe he was the one who'd scared off the dogs.

"Paz?" Rumi said.

"What is it, flaco?"

"I'm sorry for running away back there. For leaving you alone with all those wolves."

"Dogs," I said. "They were dogs."

He ignored me. "And I'm sorry for not being able to climb a tree by myself. For coming to you so needy with nothing to give in return . . ."

I didn't respond, just propped his leg up onto a stone.

"How's that feel?" I asked.

He nodded. "It's okay."

"Want one of your fancy food bars?"

He shook his head no.

"All right," I said. "Later, though, you should try and eat something."

We were quiet again. The sun began to sink into the horizon. The air turned cool. I brushed dirt from my mouth with my sinner's arm, keeping pressure on his leg with my good one. "How's our little dog?" he asked, his arm across his face. "Did he get away?"

"I don't know." I tried not to think of the sound of his screams. "I think so."

"That's good." His voice sounded so weak. "Hey, can I ask you something?"

"Sure, flaco."

"Why do you call your arm a sinner's arm?"

I looked down at my right arm—at the shrunken muscles, the twisted hand, the curled-up fingers. "I was born this way," I said. I held up my arm, giving Rumi a look at the marbled skin, smooth and pink like a scar. "Lots of kids in Paraíso are born with this kind of thing. The elders say it's God's way of atoning for the sins of our mothers and fathers. But I think it's the chems."

"The chems," he repeated.

That's right, I thought. Your city's filthy poison. The chems that killed my mother.

I tried to choke down these thoughts. I didn't want to share with him the story I kept guarded in the softest, safest corners of my heart. But the words kept rising from my belly—churning, blistering words that wouldn't stay inside.

"Here's the thing, flaco," I said. "I know your daddy's sick. I know he loves you dearly and now you feel guilty—like you've got to repay him for all the stuff he gave you as a kid. But I didn't have the pleasure of knowing my daddy. I don't even know his name. And as far as my mother goes, all I have of her are stories."

His weight shifted beneath me. I could sense his unease—a hitch in his breathing, a faraway look that didn't want answers to the questions circling through his head. But I couldn't keep the answers inside me. They demanded to be let out.

"The folks who raised me tell me that my mother was beautiful and wild. They say she carried me in her belly for eight months with the tenderest care, going deep into the forest for herbs to make me a fat, healthy baby, singing songs while I slept inside her. That's where she was when the chem bombings came—deep in the forest. Mycotoxins, the Library elders call them—like naming them does some kind of good. My mother gave birth to me a whole month early and died the next morning."

Rumi looked like he was about to be sick. "Who dropped the bombs?" he asked.

I stared back at him, unbelieving. "Who do you think?" I said.

He got a distant look about him, like he was reliving some painful memory. "I'm sorry, Paz. I'm so sorry. . . ." He kept whispering these words to me, to nobody, as his eyes drifted closed. He seemed to be losing his hold on the world. I covered his shoulders with Cienfuegos's scarf, but it wasn't any use. He wouldn't stop shaking. I didn't know what to do.

Then I got an idea.

"Hey, listen up," I said. "I got some stuff to read you."

He opened his eyes. They looked hazy and scared. "To . . . read me?"

"Yeah," I said. I tried to hide my worry. "I'm gonna read to you from a journal I found in the Wastes a while back. It's from before the Breach. I figure you could use a lesson or two, since it's pretty clear you don't know your history."

He smiled.

I opened the journal and propped it against his knee. It was getting darker, but I could still make out the shape of the woman's smooth cursive curling across the page.

"Twelfth of March," I read, translating. *"Adelita brought home her first marks today. All sevens. She couldn't stop smiling all through dinner. That girl will move mountains one day.*

"Still no rice at the grocery. Trying to keep my head on straight, but I have to admit I'm painfully afraid. Bernardo's been toying with the idea of heading north—all the way to Texas, if we can make it. He's grown terribly nervous these last few months. I keep telling him the rations and outages will pass. He says not this time."

Rumi's eyes were closed again, but I could tell he was listening. I flipped back a few pages, looking for something more hopeful.

"Fifth of June. I came across a poem last night before bed," I translated. *"It followed me through my dreams, and I awoke this morning with its words on my tongue. 'If salt water did not travel from the sea to the sky,' the poem says, 'how would the garden be watered by rain?'"*

Rumi took my arm then, and I looked up from the journal. "Want me to stop?" I asked.

"No," he said. "Keep going."

"'When the drop left its ocean home and returned, it found—'"

Rumi interrupted. "It found an oyster shell and turned into a pearl," he said.

I closed the journal. "You know it?"

"My grandfather would . . ." he started, but he couldn't quite finish. "We'd sit in the kitchen and have tea. . . ."

I wanted to touch the crinkles in his brow and tell him it was okay if he felt like crying. But I didn't. I couldn't. I reminded myself of my mission, that this was all pretend. Tearing down Upper City's walls was more important than anything.

"Nine days," he muttered to himself. "It's already been nine days. . . ."

The sky turned pink, then purple, then gray. I opened one of his chewy bars and took a bite. My mouth filled with sugar and salt, and before I knew it, I'd eaten the whole thing. I asked Rumi if he wanted one, but he just turned away. His skin was hot and shivery. I flipped through his pack and found another shirt to drape over him, then I rested his head on my leg. Darkness fell. I set my sling and stones beside me, knowing full well they wouldn't do much good if I was sleeping. "Got to stay awake," I said to myself, kneading the aching muscles of my sinner's arm with my thumb.

But before the moon rose in the eastern sky, both me and Rumi had fallen deep asleep.

In the morning, I woke with a start and looked around. The hills were silent and wet with dew. The wind sweeping down the hillside had a bite to it that made me shiver.

Underneath Rumi's bandage the blood had slowed, and I could see for the first time deep inside the wound. The flesh was fiery red and swollen. Infected. I didn't have the skills to mend a wound like that. If I didn't think of something fast, the infection would spread. And the boy would die there beneath that tree.

Rumi stirred in my lap and opened his eyes. They were glassy. Feverish.

"I'm gonna fill our canteens in the stream," I said.

I scanned the surrounding hills as I walked. We'd run far off course while fleeing the dogs. I didn't know where we were. But when I reached the creek bed, something caught my eye. I squinted into the distance, unbelieving. There, across the valley, was some kind of outpost. A thin wisp of smoke rose from a chimney. Somebody was there.

Gracias a Dios, I thought. Maybe they'd have medicine—or at least know where we could find a healer. I dipped our canteens quick into the river and hurried back to Rumi, my chest light. He was leaning back against the tree, one arm over his eyes. His thick black hair was a mess of dirt and pine needles.

"Hey, flaquito," I said. "How about sleeping on a nice bed of hay tonight? A barn, maybe, with something hot to eat?"

"That sounds . . ."

"It sounds ungodly wonderful, no?" I tore open a large bandage, slathered more healing cream onto it, and pressed it over his wound.

He winced. "Ungodly wonderful, yeah." I spun the new gauze around his calf and tied off the cloth with my left hand and my teeth. "You're pretty good at this stuff," he said.

"Not near as good as I should be." I took his hand and helped him up, wrapping my arm around his waist and draping his arm over my shoulder. "All right, give me your weight. Don't worry, I'll go slow."

2 1

RUMI

I stumbled over the hills in waking visions, clinging to the curve of Paz's shoulder. The dry grass crackled like flames beneath my feet.

The wound on my calf pulsed with fire, and each pulse brought a fresh wave of nausea. The neurochems I'd taken while Paz refilled our canteens were strong—I should've taken only one—and now it felt like I was moving through the kaleidoscopic world of a dream. Paz walking next to me transformed into Laksmi, and I cried out Laksmi's name. Then Laksmi became Father, and I became his ten-year-old son as his sturdy arms guided me forward. The hills disappeared, and we were walking instead through crowds of travelers, bright digital letters in the sky pointing the way toward the train.

Platform 7: Sucre City. Departing in 3 minutes.

The city of Sucre had acquired a mated pair of jaguars for their wildlife park when I was ten years old, and I'd begged Father to take me. But we'd never found the time.

"Happy birthday, son," Father said to me now. "Thank you for your sacrifice. . . ."

From some distant realm came a string of Spanish curses and

the sting of a slap across my face. I opened my eyes. I was lying in the dirt, and Paz was gripping my face. Her hands were cold on my cheeks. "C'mon, Rumi. Look at me! Look at me."

I was shaking—I couldn't stop shaking.

I felt myself slipping back into a dream but fought it, tried to focus on what was real—my throbbing leg, Paz's cold hands, how it felt to draw a breath with her pressed against me. At last my eyes focused on Paz's wide, black pupils, and the corners of her mouth turned up in a smile.

"That's it," she said, pressing her hand to my forehead. "Dios mío. You're dripping with fever. You got any pills for that?"

"Those neurochems," I said. "I think I took too many. . . ."

"It's not the medicine that's doing this. But we're real close to somebody who might be able to help. See there? That trickle of smoke?"

I squinted to see a cluster of industrial buildings in the distance tucked among a grove of pines. The sight of the buildings brought back Cienfuegos's words at the Lighthouse.

Be suspicious, he'd said. *Trust no one.*

"But what if they're . . . unfriendly?" I asked.

Paz felt my forehead again, then reached down into the grass to pull up a fuzzy leaf the size of her palm. "We've got no choice, flaco," she said. She tore the leaf into pieces and shoved it into my mouth. But I couldn't chew. My teeth chattered. Bits of leaf fell from my lips and dribbled down my chin. Paz shook her head and plucked another leaf from the ground, chewed it into a bright green paste, and pushed the paste into my mouth. A bitter, grassy tang.

"Swallow," she said.

I gagged but willed myself to swallow the pulp.

"Good. That's real good, Rumi. That should bring your fever

down a little." She looked over her shoulder, listening for things I could only imagine. "Think you can walk?"

I sat up. I was shaky still, but the bitter leaf had lent my mind a new sharpness.

"I can try."

Paz helped me to my feet and steadied me. Her sinner's arm wrapped around my waist, and my throat tightened. This girl was my protector—even though her amniotic fluid had been poisoned by my city. Why was she risking so much to help me?

With Paz guiding me forward, I dragged my feet over anthills and scrub grass, plastic bags and bits of metal. The sun spied on us through the trees. The light it cast was both gentle and sinister. Its beams glinted off the broken windows of the industrial compound as we grew closer. The compound had thirty or so buildings—cold, unfriendly structures that looked like some kind of processing plant. Copper, maybe. Its huge concrete warehouses were covered in vines and streaked with soot and mildew. A dull orange rust had eaten through the pipes and bored holes in the metal roofing. The whole place looked abandoned save for the thin line of smoke that curled up from a single structure—a small clapboard house with walls that molted flakes of white paint.

We walked along the compound's perimeter fence until we came to an arched stone entrance, its gate unhinged. Paz steadied me beside the gate and crouched over a puddle to wash the blood from her hands. My blood.

"Listen," she said quietly. "When we get there, let me do the talking. I'll say you're a mute again, just like I did with those fishermen down on the coast. If whoever's inside sees the tats on your neck, I'll tell them you were captive to Las Oscuras, and that I saved you, and that both of us were on the run from them when we got attacked by those dogs." Paz stood and wiped her hands on her shorts. "Here. Gimme your bag."

I did as she asked.

She took from her own satchel the canvas-bound journal she'd read from the night before, along with a stack of maps, and slid them into my pack. "Your bag's too nice," she said. "Don't want them thinking we've got fancy stuff to steal. And I don't want them finding my maps neither. Better to keep our purposes secret, if we can. Wait here."

She slunk along the fence and stashed my pack in an over-grown pile of rubble about fifty meters from the entry gate. Then she wrapped her arm around my waist once more, and together we entered the compound. Cold, lifeless structures rose above us like titans. The slow, irregular drip of liquid echoed through the space. I peered through the buildings to the small white house, its broken windows patched with sheets of plywood. The front door had been removed from its hinges and, in its place, a mildewed piece of canvas hung across the doorway. In front of the canvas were crisscrosses of barbed wire.

Paz nodded toward the scraggly garden plot stretching along the front wall of the house. "Looks like they're growing potatoes," she whispered. "A couple rows of onions. None of it looks healthy, but at least we know that whoever's here has been staying longer than just the night."

Behind the house, a tall fence made of scrap metal and barbed wire enclosed a plot of dirt. The gate in this fence was open. The hairs on my neck bristled. "What do you think that's for, Paz?"

"What, that pen? Sheep, likely. Or goats. I dunno."

"Doesn't it seem odd, though? A fence that tall for sheep?"

"No, flaco. It doesn't seem *odd*—seems like those materials were all these folks could scavenge." Paz resumed walking, and I hobbled beside her, leaning on her shoulder. "And remember you're mute, yeah? Don't speak from now on."

I nodded.

At the walkway to the house, Paz stopped. The mildewed canvas sheet rippled in the wind. Nothing else moved.

"Disculpen, hermanos," Paz called, one hand to her mouth. The slow drip of water echoed. "Brothers. We come in dire need— please. We don't bring any harm."

We waited.

From inside came the sound of scurrying feet followed by creaking wood as someone pried a piece of plywood from one of the windows. Three corners came loose, and the plywood sheet swung around the remaining nail. Inside the window was total darkness. Then something small and metallic peered over the edge of the windowsill. I squinted, trying to make out what it could be. Round, dull metal, hollow in the center. The muzzle of a gun.

I stopped breathing.

"¡Hermanos!" Paz said, her voice louder than before. "Brothers, sisters! I'm— We're lost. My companion here is hurt something terrible. A pack of dogs attacked us in the foothills. He's got fever chills already from their bite."

The muzzle bobbed in the corner of the window but didn't lower.

Paz stood straighter, her body infused with a hardness, a surety. "If you know the pledge and live by it," she continued, "then please help us. May our light shine ever more brightly. May we one day recover the world we lost. Please!"

The muzzle lowered. A dark face appeared in the corner of

the window, blinking from the dimness of the house. I couldn't tell if it was male or female, young or old. Finally, it spoke.

"What's with the tat?" The voice was low and gruff, but it was unmistakably the voice of a girl, probably no older than me.

Paz turned. My scarf had fallen over one shoulder, and my tattoo was visible just above it.

"Las Oscuras took us in the Wastes not three days' walk from here," she said. "They prisoned us. Tortured us. Tatted this boy's face for their own sick pleasure. They said they were gonna kill us both in the morning. We made our break, only just, but they—"

"Hush, you. Let the tat-faced kid speak for his own self."

"He doesn't speak," Paz said. "Can't. He's mute. Sinner's mind too, I think."

"I see," said the girl. Her voice softened. "We know well those ailments. Come around back and let's get a look at him. This front door's not for comings and goings."

The face disappeared from the window, and together Paz and I hobbled around the house. The back door opened as we approached, and the face of a dark-eyed boy—maybe three years old—peered up at us. Another child, a few years older, pulled the toddler inside. The girl who'd spoken through the window stepped around them and closed the door behind her.

"You come from the city, no?" the girl said.

Her skin was deep brown, even darker than mine, and her black eyes had something dull and weary about them. She wore a greasy canvas jumpsuit with the sleeves cut off, the pant legs rolled up past her knees. The muscles in her bare arms flexed as she folded them across her chest.

"The city of Paraíso, yes," said Paz. "Seaside. My people are fisherfolk."

The girl grunted with a nod. "What about his?"

"He's a refugee. Got no name that I know. No history, neither. My folks found him and took pity on him, is all. I see you've done likewise."

"Sí, poh," said the girl. She glanced over her shoulder toward the closed door. The muscles in her arms clenched again. "What do they call you?"

"Iris del Quisco," Paz said without a flinch. She extended her sinner's hand and placed it over the girl's breastbone in the same gesture that Cienfuegos had shown me in his quarters. The gesture seemed bold, risky. I expected the girl to take it as a threat. But instead, she extended her own hand and placed it over Paz's chest.

"Mine's Auralee."

The two girls stood with their hands on each other's hearts, their gazes unwavering, in a moment of tense intimacy. I looked away. In the sky, black-winged birds traced slow spirals high above some helpless animal, waiting for it to die.

Without a word, both girls lowered their hands.

"Got any weapons between you?" Auralee asked.

"A sling," Paz said. "I'm a fine shot. I'd be happy to trade sanctuary here with you for a bit of game. What's around here for meat? Vizcacha? Deer?"

"Fox. Degú."

"Where'd you get ammo for that gun?"

Auralee ignored the question. "There's fox blood stew an' potatoes on the cook fire," she said, opening the door. "I imagine you'll be wanting a bite to eat?"

The air inside the house was cloudy with particulate. I held my breath. Drips of water plinked into unseen puddles. Parts of the roof had caved in, and blades of light from the gaps in the ceiling sliced across the dim space.

When we reached the innermost room, Auralee stopped. This room had no windows, only a hole in the roof overlaid with a clear sheet of plastic that formed a kind of skylight. A large furnace burned at the center of the room, and two children tended to the kettle above its flames. A wet, salty smell filled the room. It was unmistakably the smell of food, but it smelled awful.

Auralee motioned for me to sit on a heap of burlap stacked near the fire. She sat next to me, and the kids tending the kettle scurried away. "Lemme see your wound, boy," she said in a firm but patient tone.

I hoisted my leg onto her lap, trying to seem simple and oblivious as she peeled back the bandage and examined the gash, then lifted my leg and sniffed at the wound.

She made a sour face. "Infected," she said to Paz. "Good thing you found us. Ancho!" she yelled over her shoulder.

A moon-faced boy, twelve years old or so, peeked his head into the room.

"Tráeme los remedios," she said. "Y las entrañas."

The boy disappeared for a moment, then returned with a bulging rucksack in one hand and a bucket of something horrifically foul-smelling in the other. Auralee set the bucket aside and sifted patiently through the bag, pulling out a vial of clear liquid, a packet of gauze, a pair of tweezers, and an empty glass jar. I wondered where she'd gotten these supplies, but I couldn't ask. And Paz offered no questions.

Auralee spread the gauze on the burlap cloth beside her and poured a small amount of clear liquid from the vial into the jar. Then she reached inside the bucket and pulled out a single wriggling maggot.

My eyes widened. I shook my head violently—*no, no, no, no*—and tried to tear myself away. But I was weak with the wound, and Auralee's grip was unbelievably strong. One by one, she dunked the maggots into the jar before setting them, wriggling, onto the fresh piece of gauze.

"Is this safe?" Paz asked.

"It's the only way," Auralee said. "This infection's not gonna clear on its own. You want the kid to survive, tell him to get over his fear of bugs." She held up the tweezers. "Now, help me hold him still. Won't hurt much if he keeps calm. But if he spooks, I might jab him."

Paz's eyes found mine, full with all the words we couldn't say. She touched my hair tenderly, as though soothing a child. Then she knelt beside me and pressed her hands into my hips. "Keep still now," she said gently.

I closed my eyes. There was a stinging pinch in my leg, then another. I bit my arm to keep from screaming and tried instead to focus on the feel of Paz's small hands pressed firmly against me. No one had ever held me like that. I realized then just how safe I felt in her care—this girl I'd met only five days ago. I trusted her beyond reason.

"There," Auralee said, patting my leg. "All better."

I opened my eyes to see Auralee wrapping the wound with clean gauze. "Give it a couple days," she said to Paz. "The bugs'll eat the sickness, then you can wash 'em out." She cleaned the tweezers, put her supplies back in the rucksack, and passed it to the boy named Ancho, who took everything back outside.

"Quite a squeamish kid you got there," Auralee said to Paz.

Paz nodded and smiled.

We ate fox blood stew and potatoes for dinner. The stew tasted even worse than it smelled, and I thought with a desire bordering on lust of the SoyChewy bars stashed in my pack outside the fence. Someday I'll look back on this and laugh, I thought. Someday, back in St. Iago—after I've found the healer and brought her medicine home to Father—I'll be sitting at some café with Wen and Laksmi, and we'll laugh at the absurdity of it all. First, I stumble into a toxic chemfield, I'll say—like I'm telling some kind of joke. Then a band of terrorists inks me with tattoos. Then a pack of wild dogs tears a hole in my leg, and a strange girl fills the wound with maggots while I pretend to be mute. And then we all eat blood stew. *Blood* stew!

No, I thought. That's not how it will go.

Things I once thought funny won't be funny anymore.

Six children joined us for dinner. None were wearing shoes. They ate in silence, staring at the shimmering ink on my neck as they used their hands to spoon rusty liquid into their mouths straight from the pot. I wondered how many more were lurking somewhere in the house.

"How long you been living here?" Paz asked, breaking the silence. The children turned toward Auralee, expectant.

"Our parents died a few years back," said Auralee. She broke apart a lump of potato with her fingers. Steam swirled from its insides. "They left us with nothing. We had to make do. Been moving place to place while it's dry an' staying put with the rains. Our daddy was a doctor, back when we lived among the civilized. But I was the only one of us kids old enough to learn any medicine before he died."

"Is that so," Paz said. She took another potato from the coals and pressed a hole into it with her thumb to let the heat escape. "Sí, poh."

"Whyn't you stay put after your parents died?"

Auralee looked Paz straight in the face. "I don't suppose that's much of your business."

Paz bit off a hunk of potato without breaking Auralee's gaze. "No, I don't suppose it is."

Just then I heard the creak of a gate and the quiet shuffle of feet near the back of the house. I shot a glance at Paz, and she nodded back almost imperceptibly. She'd heard the same thing. An icy fear swept over me. Fear of what, I couldn't say. Auralee had been kind to us, sharing food and medicine even though there was barely enough to go around. Still, something made me suspicious of her kindness. *Trust no one,* Cienfuegos had said.

I looked down and tried to come up with a plan. But Paz beat me to it. "I think the boy here needs to relieve himself," she said to Auralee. "Mind if he goes out the back?"

If Auralee suspected anything, she didn't let on. She scratched at her messy curls, pulled something from them, and threw whatever it was on the floor and stomped it with her foot. "So long as he can find his way back, it's no business of mine," she said.

Paz touched my arm and spoke slowly, as though speaking to a child. "Run out back and take a piss, boy. And don't wander off. ¿Cachai?"

I nodded and limped out of the room toward the back door. Ancho entered the door just as I was about to open it. He nodded and smiled sweetly to let me pass before going back inside.

The night air was cool, and the wind carried on it the chill of the nearby mountains. I waited, allowing my eyes to adjust to the darkness. The moon hadn't risen yet, and the stars looked too clear and bright to be real, like they'd been digitally enhanced. Wen would've laughed at that, I thought—laughed in his loud, careless way. *The real world: realer than real!*

I sensed movement in the darkness. Heard steps padding over the dirt. And then a single vicious bark.

I froze, waited for teeth to sink into my flesh. But nothing happened—just the sound of padded feet. That's when I remembered the tall pen we'd seen when we first approached. I peered through the darkness and saw that the gate was now shut. The dogs must be locked inside.

Oh god.

My chest seized. I tried to breathe slowly. I didn't want to rush to conclusions. But the longer I thought about it, the more sense it made. It was no coincidence that we'd found this compound in the hills. The dogs had driven us here. That's why the pack had left in such a hurry. They'd been *called off*. This was a trap. Maybe Auralee's partners were hidden in the forest, watching us, waiting. Grown men. Men with weapons. What could we do?

Then I heard a scream from inside the house. A dull thud. Silence.

My heart pounded. We should never have trusted this place. It was too good to be true. My only choice was to flee, to grab my pack and Paz's maps and to try to find Yesenia on my own. What help could I be to Paz if I went inside? I was weak. I was wounded. I knew nothing of this world. I was nothing but a burden. If I went back inside, I'd only make things worse.

And besides, I thought. Paz might already be dead.

I imagined Auralee standing over Paz's body—grinning with a knife in her hand, the silent children beside her—and the thought made me feel sick.

No, I thought. I have to help her. I have to try.

I ticked through my options. I had no weapons. No skills to speak of. But I had my pack. My SoyChewy bars. My PuriTabs. If such things seemed exotic to Auralee, perhaps I could use them to bargain for our lives.

As quickly and silently as possible, I limped through the hulking buildings toward the place where Paz had stashed my pack. I tensed against the sound of water dripping on metal. Every drip sounded like an attacker.

But no one lunged from the ruins. No hand cupped my mouth, and no knife pierced my spine. Out the main entrance, I followed the fence to the heap of rubble and searched the broken slabs of concrete until I felt the sturdy lump of canvas. My pack— just where Paz had left it. Clutching it to my chest, I limped back through the ruins across the broken road.

I opened the back door to the house, and nothing happened. No sound. As I felt my way through the dark corridor, the muscles in my chest relaxed. Maybe everything would be normal. Maybe the dogs were just an unfortunate coincidence. Maybe the scream was just one of the children and everything would be . . .

But as I turned the corner, these thoughts dissolved.

There in the main room, Auralee stood behind Paz. One hand bound Paz's arms; the other held a knife to her neck.

"Let's cut the shit already," Auralee said as I stood in the doorway. "Who are you really, and what're you doing here in my woods?"

2 2

PAZ

The tatted circle on my chest breathed air for the first time since the night the comandante needled it into my skin. Auralee had torn open my shirt and seen it. Seen it and smiled a cruel, bitter smile.

But she'd covered it up just before Rumi came barging in to be a hero—like she didn't want him to see it, like she wanted to figure a few things out for herself first.

Rumi had been gone a long time. He must've heard my scream. He must've been standing out there in the night, pondering whether to save his skin or mine.

And he chose mine.

23

R U M I

"Ancho!" Auralee called.

Before I could look around, the moon-faced boy appeared from the darkness behind me and bound my wrists with wire. Paz swore and kicked against Auralee's grip, but it was no use. Auralee's arms flexed with each of her jolts. Her knife cut a thicket of shallow slashes into Paz's neck.

Paz spat and snarled something in Spanish. "Mátame, si quieres," she said. "¡Vivan los revolucionarios!" I heard the words, but I didn't understand.

"Tranquila," Auralee said, smiling. "I'd have killed you both before you even arrived if it'd so pleased me. And I still could. Now hold still." Auralee bound Paz's hands with the same rusted wire that bound mine. She stuffed a rag into Paz's mouth and tied another around her head to secure it. Then she kicked Paz in the knees, and Paz fell to the ground. "You done enough talking for now, diabla," she said. "Whatever your name really is."

Ancho kicked my feet from under me, and I landed with a slap on the concrete floor. Sharp pain shot down my wounded leg as Auralee tied me back-to-back with Paz. Paz's elbows pressed into my back. I realized then what Auralee was doing. She didn't want me to see Paz's face. She didn't want us to communicate in any way. I was as close as I'd ever been to my only friend in that toxic world, and yet I was completely alone.

Auralee squatted next to me, her head level with mine. Her stare was blank. A vein in her left eye bulged red. Paz must've gotten in at least one good hit before Auralee pinned her down. This gave me a surge of courage, and I spat in her face.

Auralee flinched but smiled. She wiped my saliva from her cheek.

"I know you can speak, boy," she said. "We been watching you since you stepped onto our lands. You think you found our stronghold here by some kinda chance?" She laughed an exaggerated *ha!* and turned to Ancho.

Ancho smiled back shyly. Sweetly, almost.

"Those dogs were my dogs," Auralee said, confirming my suspicions. "*Our* dogs. We been hunting the two of you." In her hand she gripped the knife stained with Paz's blood. "You think you can sally in here and wrangle me back to one of your camps again? No way. I'll open up your bellies right here an' now—string you on the road for all your rebel brothers to see—before I let that happen." Her lips curled over her teeth with canine bloodlust. "Do I lie, Ancho? Do I *lie*?"

Ancho shook his head with a reverence that made me wonder how many bellies he'd seen Auralee split open in his brief life.

I stared back at her face with its deadly resolve and tried to comprehend what she wanted from us. Our valuables, of course. Our lives, perhaps. But what were these camps she was talking about? Who was she calling our rebel brothers?

"Now tell me," Auralee said. "Who are you working for? Pascua? Omar? Víctor? The senderistas in the North? Which tatted pack of puta madres owns the honor of your allegiance?"

With these words, it all clicked into place. My tattoo—of course. Auralee had targeted us because of my tattoo. I'd taken her for some kind of highway thief, but no—she'd mistaken *us* for Las Oscuras. I wanted more than anything to see Paz's face. Should I try to explain? Should I say anything at all?

"I . . . I dunno what you're talking about," I said, failing miserably at mimicking the cadence of Lower City speech. "Las Oscuras captured us. Back in Paraíso. They captured me and . . . tatted my face. They would'a killed me—I'm sure of it—if Paz . . . Well, I guess there's no use keeping our names a secret anymore. I'm Rumi, and this here is Paz. I'd be dead if it weren't for her."

Auralee stood and walked around me to face Paz. "Is that so?" she said. "What, then, is this?" I could tell she was pointing to something, but try as I might, I couldn't turn my head far enough to see what it was.

"I can't . . . I can't see what you're—"

"Shut up, idiota," she said. "You think I'm talking to you?" Her voice turned quiet as she repeated herself to Paz. "What is *this*?"

I felt Paz flinch behind me as Auralee reached out and touched her. But Auralee didn't remove the cloth from Paz's mouth to let her speak. Both girls were silent. I imagined them once again going through the ritual I'd witnessed earlier that afternoon: a hand on the other's chest, eyes fixed. Only this time, it would be a one-sided gesture—Auralee reading the thoughts hidden in Paz's heartbeat.

"I see . . . ," Auralee said after a long silence. "I see, I see, I see . . ." She stood, scuffing her feet as she walked around to me and squatted to meet my eyes.

"Tell me more, boy. *Rumi*. Why on heaven an' earth would Las Oscuras waste their time roughing up two straggly little half bits as yourselves—this one with a sinner's arm, and you . . ." She looked at me with disgust, almost at a loss for words. "You with no talents to speak of? Las Oscuras recruits only the swift an' the cunning to do their work. The bravest revolutionaries . . ." She trailed off, and her gaze turned inward for a moment. When her eyes focused again on mine, she looked as though she might cry. "What the hell would they want with *you*?"

"My specs . . . ," I said quietly. I felt Paz stiffen behind me and take my hand, like she was trying to tell me, *No—not that, any-thing but that*. But the truth was the only way. I could try for hours to convince Auralee that we weren't working for Las Oscuras, but she might gut us anyway just to be sure. There was only one way to prove to her beyond any doubt that we were on the run from those tattooed savages. The greatest enemy of Las Oscuras was Upper City, I thought. And Auralee's enemy, it was becoming clear, was Las Oscuras. Perhaps the enemy of her enemy would be her friend. It was our only chance.

"What was that, boy?" Auralee asked.

"My pack. Look inside the small pocket at the front of my pack. There's something in there you need to see."

Auralee hesitated, torn between curiosity and distrust. But curiosity won. She grabbed my pack from where I'd dropped it and pulled from the front pocket a smooth silver case containing my DigiCloth and specs. "Ancho," she called. "Ven, Ancho. Come here." The quiet boy came to her side and stared at the case, his face full of questions. Auralee looked up at me. "What is it?"

"Touch that button to open the case. Those things that look like glasses—first, open the frames . . . Yeah, just like that. Then put them behind your ears." She unfolded the specs and placed them on the bridge of her nose. The lenses lit with their familiar sparkle.

"Eyeglasses," Auralee said. "Like they used to have in the Old World. For seeing far away. You greedy pungas got them from stealing someone's treasures, huh?" Ancho grabbed at the specs, but Auralee slapped away his hand. "Don't touch."

"No. They're mine. And they're much more than just eye-glasses," I said.

Paz squeezed my hand again, and I squeezed back as if to say, *I know. I have to.*

"Take that piece of cloth out of the case and smooth out the wrinkles." She did as I said. "If you'll permit me . . . I need one of my hands for this next step. You can keep the other arm tied." Suspicion hardened her face, but I could see behind it a growing curiosity.

"Go ahead, Ancho," she said. "Do as he says."

With one hand free, I held the upper-left corner of the DigiCloth. "Now you hold right there," I said. Auralee pinched the corner diagonal to the one I held. I pulled my corner taut, and the cloth went rigid with electric current—paper-thin, smooth as glass. Auralee let go of her corner and stepped back. The Digi fell to the floor.

"Witchcraft," she whispered.

"Now put the glasses on my face, okay? I need to see the screen for a minute."

Auralee seemed hypnotized. In a daze, she placed the specs onto my face. With my specs on, I could see a familiar orange holographic spiral swirling above the screen. The first passcode. I picked the Digi off the ground and waited until the spiral turned from orange to red to purple. When it turned purple, I touched my finger to its center and pulled down. A series of similar codes followed, and I unlocked each one. When I entered the last code, the main screen opened to a photograph. A picture of Father, Baba, and me.

I took off the specs. Without the lenses on, the screen glowed a soft, blank gray.

I handed the specs and DigiCloth to Auralee, and she put on the frames and gasped. "That's you!" She pointed. "You!"

"That's me," I said. "And that's my family."

"Madre Purísima." She took a step back, specs over her eyes, DigiCloth in her hands. "You . . . You're not . . . ? Upper City?"

"I am," I said.

"Nuestra Señora."

She sank slowly to sit against the wall and pulled her legs toward her chest. The light from the cloth in her hands lit her spectacled face as she moved her fingers across the screen.

I imagined the images dancing in three dimensions under the pull of her touch. At one point, music started playing—one of Baba's pre-Breach recordings. The haunting lilt of a sitar echoed behind a man's voice, singing in a language that no one on Earth spoke any longer. I closed my eyes as the melody swelled and imagined Baba's face, his expression caught somewhere between joy and sorrow. What swirling world of colors and smells did he remember when he listened to these strange scales? A world cracked and struggling, but still whole?

Auralee shook the cloth, sniffed it, knocked on it with her fist. Then she turned to Ancho, and they stared at each other, mystified.

"This changes things, Ancho," she said. "This changes things mightily."

24

PAZ

'll give you my spoon for all those pebbles," one of the older kids said.

"All?" said another.

"It's a real nice spoon."

"You got any of those mirror discs?"

"Not for trade," said the first kid.

"Not even for that bell I found down creekside?"

"Nu-uh."

"How about this button for two of your sling bullets?"

"No way!"

I was still bound. Still gagged. Night deepened.

The air in the room had long since gone cold. The stove sent out an arm's-length circle of warmth, and five kids huddled around it, not saying much. Three more children came in from outside. So many of them, por Dios. The smallest kid, a girl with tangled black hair and a sweet, open face, uncurled her palm to drop a handful of pebbles and a pair of human teeth on the concrete floor. Molars.

One of the older boys looked back at her, impressed. "How 'bout you change them teeth for this here rabbit ear I got?"

The girl nodded and smiled and took the tawny ear in both her hands.

The kids didn't seem to notice Auralee and Ancho in a corner of the room playing with Rumi's spectacles and magic cloth, whispering things I couldn't quite hear. More than once, I caught Auralee glancing at me. The glow of the cloth lit their faces like the light of the moon.

Auralee's little prisoner trick—gagging my mouth and tying us up so Rumi couldn't see me—had worked out for her splendid. It gave her all the knowledge she needed. From the moment she tore open my shirt, she knew I was Las Oscuras. But by tying us up like that she'd also figured out that Rumi didn't know a thing about my tat or my allegiances. She saw how Rumi trusted me like a pup trusts its master. Now she seemed to be buying time, sorting out the best way to use what she knew.

Auralee handed the glowing cloth to Ancho. Then she walked over to me and untied the rag from around my face. I spat the taste of mildew and iron from my mouth, glaring at her. At the dirty curls framing her hard, dark face. At her eyes weighing risk and reward.

She made no move to untie my hands.

"I hope you'll forgive me that bit of violence earlier," she said. She dabbed the cuts on my throat with a damp rag and gave me a look—a look Rumi couldn't see—as she dragged the rag down my throat to the middle of my chest and traced the circle tatted there. She wanted me to know she hadn't lost sight of my loyalties. She wanted me to feel her power.

And I couldn't say a goddam thing. Una mierda.

"Can't be too careful, you know. Not in my circumstance." She pocketed the rag and went back to sit with Ancho. "I'm a wanted soul, me an' these kids. And as I'm sure you're both mighty aware, Las Oscuras never tires on a hunt."

"We know that all too well," Rumi piped up behind me. "Don't we, Paz?" His fingertips found mine and squeezed them.

I didn't squeeze back, but I didn't pull away. "Sí, poh," I said. "We do."

"Las Oscuras is after you, too?" Rumi asked. "Why?"

Auralee looked to the ceiling, like she was trying to decide whether or not to trust us with her story. Or maybe she was just being a sly little zorra. I couldn't tell which.

"Why're they after me?" She pulled up one leg of her jumpsuit to show a melted scar the size of a fist on the inside of her thigh. Silvery ink swirled inside it, plain as day. "This is why."

I drew in a sharp breath. I'd seen scars like that on ex-rebels who'd come crawling back to Paraíso, begging forgiveness. They'd tried to burn off their marks or tear off their skin. But it never mattered. They were sentenced to the Lighthouse just the same.

So Auralee was one of them. One of *us*. Of course. A girl with no history, hiding out in the ruins. A girl who could wield a knife as natural as a fish breathing water, who could quiet her heartbeat under my touch and fill her eyes with mysteries . . .

"I tried to burn it off," Auralee said. "But wasn't any use. I'd have to cut off the whole leg to be rid of it." She ran her fingers gentle across the scar. "Once you join 'em, there's just one way out. You're in till you're dead."

I tried to guess what Rumi was thinking. Was he remembering the sound of his own screams as Las Oscuras plunged their needles into his skin? If Auralee told Rumi who I worked for, I'd be dead. Plain and simple. One way or another, dead—by her hand or burned up in the Lighthouse once Rumi told Cienfuegos who I was. My hand closed around Rumi's fingertips.

Bendito sea Dios, I thought. Bendito sea su santo nombre. Santo . . . Santo . . .

"You're one of *them*?" Rumi asked.

I stiffened. For a moment I thought he was talking to me.

"Sí, poh," Auralee said, looking me straight in the face. "Least, I was." Her look was unflinching. Unflinching but muddy. I couldn't tell what hid behind it. Revenge? Greed? What did she want? Why hadn't she killed me from the start?

I didn't notice the kid crying at first. I was too lost in Auralee's stare to hear much of anything. It wasn't till Auralee broke her gaze that I heard the noise, shrill and piercing, filling the room.

Auralee walked over to him. "Tranquilo, Blanco," she said. "Tranquilo . . ."

But the boy kept squealing, blubbering things I couldn't quite hear.

"Who?" Auralee asked. She touched his head. "Who dealt you crooked?"

The boy pointed, teary-eyed, to a squirrelly girl in the corner.

"Violeta," Auralee said to the girl. "Lo juro por Dios—if you can't deal fair with the little ones, you're gonna be the next kid tending the dogs. ¿Me oyes?"

The girl turned pink in the face and looked to the floor.

"Violeta!" Auralee repeated. "You hear me?"

"Sí, Mamita. I hear," she said. Then she held out her arms for a hug. As soon as Auralee picked her up off the ground, the girl started crying.

"Ay, mi niña," Auralee said, soft and tender. "Sh, sh, sh. No llores, niña. Don't cry . . ."

The girl tucked her head into Auralee's shoulder. "Please don't make me tend the dogs," the girl said, tears in her eyelashes. "Porfa', Mamita. Tengo tanto miedo de los perros."

Auralee smiled and brushed her hand against the girl's knotty hair. "Then don't deal the babies crooked, little girl! You know better than all that." The girl curled against Auralee's chest, working up another cry, but Auralee stopped her. "All right, niña. No more of that." She set the girl on the floor. "You know what to do now. Yes?"

"Yes, Mami."

The girl held out her hand to the little boy she'd cheated. Inside her hand was a key on a greasy chain. The boy snatched it from her and clutched it to his chest, glaring at her. Violeta wiped a tear from her cheek and sniffled.

"Lo siento," she said to the boy. The boy looked to Auralee. Auralee nodded, and the boy opened his arms to the girl for a hug.

What in holy hell was all this? I thought. Who was this person, all calm and sweet, training her kids in love and forgiveness? A terrorist, a traitor, and . . . a loving mother? It made no sense, but it gave me hope. If she was just a mama wolf defending her cubs with teeth bared, then licking them clean when the danger was past, could she have some mercy inside her after all?

Rumi's voice from behind me gave me a start. I'd almost forgotten he was there. "I've got a question for you," he said. "How is it that you went from working for terrorists to guarding a bunch of kids and dogs?"

Auralee scratched her hands through her hair till it frizzed into a bramble around her face. "That's a long story," she said, shaking her head. "Too long."

But I was eager to hear it too. "We got time," I said.

"Bueno." She took a bone from her dinner bowl and stuck it

in her mouth. "Where to begin? I was thirteen years old or so when I started 'prenticing with my father. He was a smart man. He used some Old World hospital healings, but mostly he worked with herbs and plants that he learned about from machis and curanderos. I could've learned so much if I'd stayed with him.

"But I was young and angry back then. Why should Papi run all over creation, I used to think to myself, trying to save folks who'd been poisoned by chems, folks who were dying from dirty water, when there were walled-in castles where people had clean water and all the food and medicine they could want? *More* than they could want! Why did the people of Upper City get to stand on our backs and live a life of dreams when we were out here, wasting away?"

I felt Rumi shift behind me. I wondered what he was thinking.

"Folks in my town didn't talk much about the walled cities. But we knew the history. We knew about the Hot Wars, about the virus that people used to kill each other. About how Upper City built walls to keep the rest of us out. We knew that Upper City copters still flew through our lands. The town leaders swore up and down that those copters had nothing to do with the poisons in our water an' our soil. But I thought different. It seemed to me the copters came around to be sure that we stayed in our place. That we never got strong enough to fight.

"Then one day, my little brother got into some bad water while he was out playing. Chem-poisoned. Papi was two towns over, called away for an outbreak of Zabrán, and I was home all alone." She stared up at the hole in the roof, her face unreadable. "I still remember the look on my brother's face—all twisted and confused as he pushed through our front door flap, holding his belly, big tears falling down his face.

"I tried everything I knew to fix him—all the stuff Papi taught me. When none of that worked, I carried him into the hills to our town's curandero. The healer gave him sacred herbs and whispered prayers. He sprinkled my brother with holy water, blessed him with holy songs. Then there was nothing left to do but hold him while he shook in my arms. I can still remember the moment his shaking went still. I don't suppose I'll ever forget that feeling."

She looked down at her open, empty hands. And in that moment, I lost my will to mistrust her. Her sadness was my sadness, her helplessness my own.

"Next day," Auralee continued, "a man came across me in the forest burying my brother. He had a tat on his neck—a viper, ready to strike. The man didn't need to say a thing. I knew what he wanted the moment I saw him.

"'I'll join,' I told him, just like that. 'What do I need to do?'

"So I left Papi's house and started my work for Las Oscuras." She took the bone from her teeth and turned it in her fingers. "I stole for them. Spied for them. Roughed up their prisoners and healed their wounded. I couriered secrets from one cell to another—secret plans to derail intercity trains, plans to worm into Upper City with our operatives, plans to infect their officials and ambassadors with new strains of old diseases. Don't think I'm proud of the things I did for them. I'm not. There just didn't seem to be another way."

The fire cracked with wood sap.

Auralee took a deep breath. "I still remember the first time I killed a man. I remember his name, even. Jaime Luis de Las Oscuras. He had this giant vulture tatted across his shoulder blades, its wings outspread and talons bared. Jaime Luis had botched his mission, and I was supposed to make an example of him. One night while he was sleeping, I took a scythe to his neck. Watched his blood seep into the dirt." Auralee tossed the bone she'd been sucking into a corner of the room. One of the kids ran to fetch it, dried it with his shirt, and added it to his pile.

"Like I said, I'm not proud of these things. But I don't deny them either." She looked at me with accusation as she said this. "I'm not hiding my secrets, dressing up my stories to cover the fact that I got plenty of blood on my hands. These hands've done their share of dirty work."

"What made you leave?" Rumi asked. "If you did all those things working for Las Oscuras, why'd you risk your life by deserting them?"

A slice of moon came into view through the plastic hole in the ceiling. Auralee's face looked stony in the play of fire and moonlight. She waited a long while before answering.

"One day they told me to kill a child," she said. "A little kid. Seven years old."

"A child from Lower City?" Rumi said. "That doesn't make sense."

She laughed. "That's 'cause you don't understand all the battles being fought," she said. "Battles between Las Oscuras and Upper City. Battles between Las Oscuras and the Lower City folks who want nothing to do with their violence. Battles between factions inside Las Oscuras themselves. I was supposed to kill the son of a village elder who wouldn't grant Las Oscuras access to his village's river port. I was supposed to kill this kid and . . ." She glanced at the cluster of children sitting near the fire, listening with eyes wide. "I was supposed to kill him and leave *evidence* of my act on his father's doorstep."

My breath caught in my throat. I knew Las Oscuras was

vicious. I knew they spilled Lower City blood for the greater good of their cause. But this? A seven-year-old child?

"I couldn't do it," Auralee continued. "I just couldn't. So I told the kid's father about the plan, and his father asked me to take the boy into hiding. Begged me, all tears an' sobbing. What could I do?"

Auralee looked with a mother's softness to the corner where Ancho sat with Rumi's lit-up cloth still in his hands. "He's a good-looking kid, no?" she said.

"Who, Ancho?" Rumi asked. "Ancho was the kid who . . . ?"

Ancho bowed his head, bashful to have so many eyes on him.

"Since that day, I been in hiding. I make rounds through the region, setting up camp outside of town, sneaking in to heal folks at night. That's how I make my bread, mostly. Folks barter for my medicines. They give me things I need—like the dogs. This knife, too." She took the hunting blade from the loop at her hip and held it to the light of the fire.

"I bring folks my healing," she said. "In return, they don't ask about my history. Some of them—the ones scared to death of Las Oscuras—even ask me to take charge of their own kids. Just till the danger passes, they say." She gave a sad smile and sheathed her knife. "But we all know the danger's not gonna pass. Don't we, Ancho?"

Ancho stood at the sound of his name and handed Rumi's spectacles and cloth to Auralee, who gave them back to Rumi. "Ancho, whyn't you untie Upper City here an' take him out back to see the new litter? Let him choose one of the pups to take on his journey tomorrow. The brown one'll make a fine guard dog when she grows into her paws. She understands words like you wouldn't believe. Whole sentences. Smart little perra."

I thought of our yellow dog, the way he'd screamed, and a knot formed in my throat.

Ancho left me bound but untied Rumi, who turned right away to face me. The tattoo on his neck shimmered in the light of the fire. It was the first time our eyes had met since he'd come running from outside to find Auralee's knife at my neck. He rubbed his tender wrists but didn't take his eyes from mine. His face filled with joy just to be looking at me. It struck me senseless to realize I felt the same way. Then his look changed to a question, asking whether it was wise to split up again. I nodded at him to go. I wanted a moment alone with Auralee. I had questions that needed answering.

Rumi and Ancho left the room, and Auralee set about rekindling the fire. She hauled an armful of logs from the wood-pile outside, then squatted to split it into kindling. I waited and watched her. She didn't say a word.

"So," I said after a long stretch of silence. "You gonna tell the cuico about me?"

"I'm not gonna tell him a thing," Auralee said. She didn't look up from her work. Her bare toes gripped the floor like fingers.

"I got to ask, why not? Why spare me, with all you know?"

She built a little fortress of kindling atop the coals, then blew underneath it. The coals buzzed orange with her breath. "You wouldn't believe me if I told you."

"Try me," I said. "I gotta know why I shouldn't send someone to find you once we're gone."

She smiled a heavy, weary smile.

"I'm done with violence, ¿me oyes?" she said. "Done with all that enemies-and-allies hogshit. My only enemy now is the one who comes attacking me. I defend these kids. They're my kin now. My dogs hunted you down in the forest 'cause I thought you were trackers for Las Oscuras. But when the boy told his story, I pieced it all together. The boy's clueless about your tat. He's loyal as hell to you. I figure you must'a done him a kindness bigger than anyone else has ever done him in all his life. And—pardon my saying so but as far as I can tell, you got yourself into a mission that's bigger than you can handle. Seems clear to me that you really did come out here for my help, not my blood."

I lowered my voice. "Cut the shit, all right? You can't tell me that seeing this Upper City swank with his high-tech gadgets didn't get you riled. After what happened to your brother?"

Auralee looked at me straight on. "See, that's where you're wrong. Upper City swanks like your boy-cargo out there—they aren't my enemy. You're not my enemy either, Paz. Hell, Víctor and Pascua and the rest of those tatted puta madres—I don't even think of them as my enemies anymore. Not 'less they come at me with a shiv." She prodded the fire, nurturing it, feeding it air. "I've seen too much blood. I've had enough killing. I've turned my hands to healing instead."

I rolled my eyes. "Well, don't you sound like a regular Jesucristo," I said. "You think that if you bind enough wounds, then all your misdeeds'll be washed clean and kindness will fill your heart and you'll walk blameless into the Kingdom of God?"

Auralee shook her head. "It's not like that. I still got a lot of hate. Some days, there's no way past the hate." She scraped crusted fox blood from the sides of the kettle into a bowl and handed the bowl to Violeta. The little girl closed her eyes as she licked the rust-brown flakes.

"But I've seen the other side of things too. I've seen what all the hate brewing inside Las Oscuras can do. How's what your tatted brothers do to their own people any different from what

Upper City does from far away? The way I see it, it's the head and the tail of the same fish."

It's not the same, I thought.

I tried to remember how the comandante had explained it that first day, in the stash house in the Wastes. But I couldn't quite hold his reasonings in my head. How could the comandante's logic justify the murder of children?

Auralee rose and untied my bindings without another word. I stood and stretched out the stiffness in my arms.

"That kid out there," Auralee said. "You think he's your chance at vengeance, is that it?"

"Something like that." But standing in that room full of mother-less children, the words sounded thin. If violence always followed violence, where would it end?

"It'd be a justice," Auralee said. "Nobody could say it wouldn't be a justice."

Rumi came through the back door with a matted, bloody mess of yellow fur in his arms. As soon as he stepped in the room, the pup wriggled from him and darted toward me, his tail whirl-ing in circles. It was our little stray, all cut up and limping. But his golden eyes still shined with sweetness.

"¡Ay, por Dios, Vio! You made it, cariño." I gathered him into my arms and let him lick the cuts on my neck. "Por Dios, you made it. . . ."

"That mongrel's yours, is he?" Auralee asked. "You're free to take one of our pups and leave that pile of bones here with us."

I scratched the pup's head and looked into his wide, eager eyes. "Thanks, but this perrito's been through a lot with us. I feel bound to see him back home safe."

"Suit yourself. Where did you say you two were coming from,

and where're you headed? I know these parts well. I could be of assistance."

Before I could catch his eye, Rumi told her—he spoke Cienfuegos's name and the healer Yesenia's, said we'd come from Paraíso and were headed north to Serena. I tried to tell myself that this was no big thing, that Auralee could be trusted. But something still felt wrong.

"Yesenia . . . ," Auralee repeated. "I remember my father speaking of her. A strange woman with more secrets than most. Last I heard, she was living at the edge of the trash hills—a real dangerous place. You know, I got this friend near Las Termas who owes me a favor. He runs an old hotel just off Ruta 45 that's direct along your way. If you hitch yourselves a ride up to his place, I bet he could find you a river ferry to Serena along old Ruta 5 Norte."

I thought this over. We were a full day behind schedule and off course already. This ferry route would get us to the healer much quicker than if we made our way on foot. And besides, Rumi's wound would make it near impossible to keep a quick pace over land.

Auralee watched me sorting out whether I should trust her. "My friend's name is Beto. You can tell him Auralee sent you. He won't ask nothing about Rumi's tat if you give him my name. He knows I wouldn't send trouble his way."

Rumi looked up. "Won't he want me dead?" he asked. "For being Upper City?"

Auralee smiled. "Not everybody picks the scabs off old wounds. Some of us're just trying to live as best we can." Ancho stretched and yawned, and Auralee laid her hand on his shoulder. "We'd best be sleeping now. Ancho will show you where you'll sleep, out in the pen."

"The pen?" Rumi asked.

"A person can never be too careful," Auralee said.

I picked up my satchel, and Ancho led us at knifepoint into the night. The dogs in their pen went wild with barking when they caught our scent, but Ancho hollered them quiet and motioned us inside. At the center of the pen was a tiny hut, barely wide enough to lie down in. A jail cell. The animals snarled at us and our pup as we stepped through their pen, but they didn't attack. Ancho opened the door to the cell.

"Don't try and escape, or the dogs'll rip you up," Ancho said. The words sounded strange in the sweet lilt of his voice as he locked the door behind us.

I looked around the tiny hut lit by shards of moonlight. Rumi sat on the cold dirt floor and scratched the bandage on his leg where maggots ate away at his wound. The pup sniffed at the bandage and then set about licking his own bloodied fur.

"We did good in there, I think," Rumi said. "We make a good team."

I smiled. "You bet, flaquito," I said.

I took a deep breath and tried to convince myself that Auralee wasn't going to cause any trouble. It wasn't my habit to trust—trust got you killed. But I was running out of choices. If I didn't get Rumi safely to the curandera, and soon, then I'd have failed my mission, proving what the Library claimed all along, proving my secret fear that I was nothing more than a weakling with a sinner's arm. A weakling who couldn't even transport an Upper City swank from one place to the next. A weakling whose rage was losing its heat . . .

In the darkness, I lay down on the ground and closed my eyes. The pup curled himself at my feet, and Rumi lay down behind me.

I could feel his breath on my neck. I could feel the weight of my heart shifting.

His hand rested for a moment on my shoulder, unsure. And I knew I shouldn't, but I let myself rest back against him, let myself feel his heartbeat pounding behind me as he wrapped his arm around my waist and held my hand in his.

"Buenas noches," he said with a thick accent.

The sweetness in his voice was too much. I pulled his hand to my chest and pressed it against the circle that marked the moment I'd betrayed him before I even knew him.

What the hell had I gotten myself into?

PART IV
THE CURE

Old Man of Tomorrow, Old Woman of the Dawn!
Young Woman of the Unknowable, Young Man of
*   Splintering Possibility!*
Look down on me and hear my stories.
Slice open my stories with your unerring blade.
Let me say something true, let me say something true!

O h, children. There once was a time when I believed you would know nothing if I didn't tell you. What lives would you lead, I thought to myself, if you didn't hear the stories that pull like thread through my bones? But it isn't true, children. It isn't true.

If I tell you that the Earth is as gentle as a mother, then its cruelty will lash you tenfold. If I tell you the Earth is a thing to be feared, you will come home with the dragon's head in your hands. Whatever I say, you will prove me wrong.

Still, what can I do, I who have lived my life? I have lived my life, and it has brought me here, together with you, met by your eager questions. And I am a teller of stories.

Tonight I have for you a tale of love and wildness and forbidden things, a story about the charming call of that which we cannot have. For this story, we must travel to the shining City of the Sky, a magical city that beats to the steady rhythm of progress, of numbers and light.

In this city, there lived a girl with a mind sharp as steel and a wit that could slice the air in two. Bathed in the light of her dazzling future, her face had a heavenly glow. But in one respect she was as ignorant as a newborn child: she knew nothing of the world beyond her city. Her mouth spoke one language only—the language of numbers and lights and progress.

Then one day, she met a boy who took refuge in the shadows behind the lights. This boy told her of a world outside the charmed clouds of her city. In dim, forgotten corners, he taught her new words, a whole language rich with sensations—the smell of the forest and the feeling of nightfall, the taste of fish and the color blue. These words had meaning, he said, in a world far from theirs, beyond their city gates.

The girl listened to the boy but did not believe him. His words were too wild and strange.

Time passed. The boy and girl grew older, tangled in each other's company like two birds, holding between them a hidden bond that only they shared. Together they'd sit in the shady grass and whisper words like "ocean" and "forest" and "love," "dignity" and "truth" and "lies." What was true, they asked each other? What was right and wrong when the Sky and Sea had split in two?

And so it happened one day, when she was not looking, that the girl found a well.

It was an ancient well in the center of the city, made of cold, mossy stone. But to her surprise, no one else seemed to see it. The girl stood by the well and waved her arms and shouted to those passing by. But no one stopped. The well, you see, came from another place—a place that spoke a language different from the language of progress and numbers and light. Because they did not speak its language, to the people of her city the well was invisible.

But the girl could now see it, for she had new words. She had words for things like "stone" and "water" and "dark." And though she did not yet have a word for "well," she could see the thing for what it was. A tunnel. A passage to some unknown place.

And so she went to find the boy.

"I've found something," she said to him. "Will you help me give it a name?"

But to her surprise, she found the boy too busy to care. He could barely hear her question over the crowd gathered around him beneath the shadowy trees. He was too busy teaching other girls words like "ocean" and "forest," words like "love" and "truth" and "lies."

"Come back later," he said to the brilliant girl. "Come back some other time."

We will never know what made the girl dive into the well. Did she dive into its mystery with her broken heart pulling her down? Did she dive for escape, for pity, or for show?

I don't think that she did.

If you ask me, I'd say she dove with her heart full of questions. What would it feel like to plunge into this mysterious passage-way? And what would meet her on the other side? Perhaps, on the other side of the well, she'd at last learn for herself things like love and dignity, right and wrong, the cool of the forest and the blue of the sea.

It's my belief, dear children, that she dove in to better know the world.

2 5

R U M I

Not twenty minutes passed before a wooden cart came rattling over the swell of the road that would take us north. Paz stood facing the road, our yellow dog beside her. I sat with my back to the pavement, hiding my tattoos beneath my scarf.

Paz and I hadn't said much after leaving Auralee's that morning. But it was clear that something had shifted between us in that prison hut the night before. Whatever was forming between Paz and me was different from what I'd felt with Laksmi. When Laksmi rested her head against me, I'd felt like a child pulled tight with wanting. But I didn't feel like a child next to Paz. Next to Paz I felt grown.

The cart cresting the road was stacked high with bales of hay. A young boy stood at the front and slowed his pair of oxen with a steady pull on the reins. Behind him sat an old man. Hay and road dust billowed behind them. As they drew near, I could see the old man was blind.

I dipped my chin into Cienfuegos's scarf as the cart slowed. Paz greeted the man and the boy warmly in Spanish. After she finished speaking, the boy nudged the old man and whispered a few words, glaring at me as he spoke. I looked down.

Please, I thought. Please don't let me be the reason we get into trouble again.

After a few more words from Paz, the old man grunted something to the boy, and the boy sat down obediently. Whatever she said had worked. They had agreed to take us north.

At the back of the cart, Paz shifted the hay bales to form a small cubby for us, enclosed on three sides and open to the sky. I helped the dog onto the cart and then took Paz's hand to climb onto its wooden bed. Her touch shot through me.

"What'd you tell them?" I whispered.

"Oh, I told the truth mostly—that we're headed north to the old hotel. They're campesinos on a long alfalfa haul. Said it's on their way."

"What'd you say about me?"

She squinted. "The boy seemed to suspect something. But the old guy is one of those trust-your-neighbor sorts. Didn't take much to convince him we'd not bring any trouble."

The boy at the reins snapped his whip, and the cart lurched into motion, pitching us both forward. I scooped the little dog into my lap to steady him, but he wriggled free and curled against the hay bales, his nose sniffing the air. Paz braced herself against the bales too, studying her maps. The cuts on her neck had crusted into deep-red scabs, but she hardly seemed to notice them. She never once mentioned her own discomfort. I wondered how she must perceive Upper City—where comforts were piled on top of comforts, as though the greatest achievement in life were to be extremely comfortable.

"Looks like we're somewhere around here," she said, pointing to a section of highway. I noticed the blood dried beneath her fingernails. Her blood and mine. "The hotel should be in the canyons just north of this town—Las Termas, it's called." She folded the maps and returned them to her pack and touched her cool hand to my forehead. "How's the leg?"

I shrugged. "Well, for starters, it's crawling with maggots. . . ." She smiled.

The warm, golden light seemed to cradle us both. I couldn't help but smile back.

The soft colors of morning hardened into a flat, unyielding blue as we rode in silence. I tried to catch the exact moment when the sky turned from one color to the next, but its shifts were too slow. My mind moved too quickly to sense such changes—the arc of the sun across the sky, the erosion of stone by water, the turning of a heart from fear to tenderness. A single cloud drifted across the blue expanse. How often had I lain in St. Iago in the park, staring at the clouds and imagining the distant lands they'd crossed? And now I was crossing these lands, together with the clouds. Would rain from this cloud fall on the roofs of my city? Would Laksmi suck its drops from her lips as she walked to class? Would it fall on my house as Baba sat in the kitchen with the windows open, listening? Would it fall on Auralee huddled next to a fire, struggling to keep dry?

As the day wore on, the air turned stagnant. Its heat seemed to reverberate across the stark and sandy mountains that rose on all sides, their bare faces opaque and unreadable. For the thousandth time, I began counting the number of days I'd been away from home. I'd been on the road with Paz for four days now, although these days had begun to feel outside of time—like I'd always been on the road with her, and the rest of my memories were only dreams.

By my tally, it had been eleven days since Father was infected.

The disease surely had moved to his lungs by now. His breathing would be short and ragged, dark purple sacs swelling under his eyes. Soon he'd lose the ability to speak. I had four days at most to get back to St. Iago. After that, even with viable medicine, there was little hope he'd recover. But without my heliocycle to power me across the desert, my return to St. Iago could take weeks. Assuming I survived the journey at all.

I curled onto my side and bit my fist with my teeth. Panic would get me nowhere, I knew. But I had this growing sensation that everything was my fault—Father's illness and Baba's disappointment and Paz's twisted arm and Auralee's starving children—all of it, the plight of the whole world. When I let myself sink into that feeling, I could hardly breathe. . . .

I felt her hand first. Her hand, then her shoulder resting against my ribs as she lay down beside me. The warmth of her, the steady pulse of her presence, made me shiver. She placed one hand on my arm and squeezed it gently.

Yes, I thought. Paz was still here. The one steady thing in a world spinning out of control. I closed my eyes, filled with the warmth of her hand on my arm, and my breath fell into her rhythm. My heartbeat slowed. And without realizing it, I fell asleep.

I didn't even notice that the cart had stopped until Paz nudged me, and I opened my eyes.

"Enough napping, flaquito," she said. "We're here."

I sat upright. It took me a minute to remember where "here" was. The cart. The hotel. Auralee's friend. Right. I adjusted the scarf to hide my neck and, with some difficulty, pushed myself to standing.

A vast desert riven with canyons stretched as far as I could see, glowing warm and red in the setting sun. The air was dry, but a cool wind cut through the day's heat, carrying on it the smell of water. I looked across the burnt-orange canyons and dull pink sky, and my hand reached instinctively for my specs. None of this seemed real. I wanted to pull back this layer of reality—just as I'd pulled off my specs that night in the square—to see the machinery at work underneath. But there was no underneath.

Paz nodded a thank-you to the boy in the cart, and the boy nodded back, unsmiling. The old man beside him stared straight ahead, his eyes clouded, as the boy cracked his whip. With a sharp "*hee-yah!*" the oxen trudged forward.

"C'mon," Paz said. "This way."

I followed her from the broken highway onto desert sand. The yellow dog trotted behind us. There were a few shanty homes huddled in clusters across the desert landscape. They looked empty, though. Long deserted. Only one pre-Breach structure was visible in the distance, a modest building just a few stories tall.

"That's where we're going?"

Paz checked the markings Auralee had made on her map. "That's it," she said. "Chuta, flaco, I've never stayed at a hotel before. Looks fancy!" I squinted at the crumbling balconies, the broken windows, and the flaking plaster walls, and assumed she was making a joke.

Behind the hotel, a nearly full moon rose in the pink sky. "How can you tell if the moon's growing or shrinking?" I asked.

"What, is that another riddle?"

"No. I'm just curious. I never know how to tell."

She looked up at the rising sphere. "Well," she said. "If the smooth edge of the moon cups in this hand, that means the moon's growing. The other way round means it's getting smaller." She took my hand in hers and cupped it into the shape of a letter C.

"See? It's growing now. Should be full tomorrow."

As we neared the hotel, the cool glow of the moon lit the building's facade, giving it a ghostly softness. The hotel must have been elegant at one time, but now the cracked white plaster clung to a structure on the brink of collapse. The entire east wing was wind-worn down to a skeletal frame. At the front entrance, four massive columns supported a sagging balcony. A single window on the balcony flickered with candlelight. If not for this sign of life, I'd have thought the hotel to be abandoned completely.

Paz and I warily approached the steps leading to the front entrance. But as we came near, a pack of dogs penned somewhere inside the lower level began to bark wildly. I jumped back. Our little dog cowered between Paz's legs, and she patted his neck to calm him. If she was unsettled too, she didn't show it.

Over the snarls of the dogs, Paz called up to the candlelit window.

"¿Disculpe?"

Silence.

"¿Disculpe, señor?"

A thud on the balcony above was followed by the thin sound of shattering crystal and a string of curses in Spanish and English. I looked at Paz over my scarf, and she raised an eyebrow.

"Hello?" she called.

The balcony's double doors swung open, and the barking downstairs went quiet. Light poured from inside. A few seconds later, a man—mostly bald, with a gray beard creeping up his cheeks—teetered out onto the balcony wearing a crimson smoking jacket and a single unlaced boot. Using the balcony railing for support, he inspected the sole of his shoeless foot.

"Buenas tardes, señor," Paz called up to him.

The man peered down at us with a look of surprise—as though he'd forgotten the voice that had called him onto the balcony. He nodded to us brusquely, then returned to inspecting his foot.

Paz turned to me and shrugged.

"Curse this cursed crystal," the man said in English, leaning against the shoddy railing.

"¡Cuidado!" Paz shouted. "Look out, señor! You're close to the edge. Awful close . . ."

The man looked over the edge and gasped, stumbling back. "So I am! Why, thank you, dear child!" With a thump, he sat on the balcony floor and returned to the work of his foot.

"Sir," Paz said, trying again. "If you don't mind, we'd like to inquire about a room. Have you got any space for the night?"

The man was silent for a long while. Then he abruptly cried out, holding a shard of bloody glass over his head in victory. "Great God!" he said. "The sweetness of such moments is beyond compare, wouldn't you say?" His voice had an eloquence to it that I associated with my teachers at school. But behind his articulate manner lurked something else. Something disheveled and feral.

"Uh, yes, sir," Paz said. "I guess I would."

The man stood and squinted down at us through the growing dimness.

"Say," he said, nodding at me. "What's with the brooding fellow? He's taken a vow of silence or something? Don't misunderstand me, I have the greatest respect for those on the spiritual path. I fancy myself a man of deep conviction! In fact, when I heard your call, I was just sitting down to reread my favorite account of the trials of St. Jerome in the deserts of Chal—"

Paz cleared her throat. "If you'll permit me, sir. A request?" she interrupted. "Could we maybe continue this talk in your quarters? Night's coming closer, and we need to know if a room'll be available tonight or if we should journey on."

Her question seemed to snap the man back into the present. "Of course, dear girl!" he said. "Of course! Plenty of room. Though, there *is* the matter of the fee. . . ."

Paz and I exchanged glances. "I'm sorry, señor, but we don't have anything as far as payment goes. You should know that a girl by the name of Auralee sent us to you, though. She said we should mention her name. . . ."

"Auralee—¿la peregrina?" He clutched his hands to his chest with a wide smile. "Ah, I'm forever in the debt of that blessed girl. What an occasion. Fees be damned! I'll uncork a bottle of pisco and we can swap tales!"

We sat outside on the old man's balcony as the hills and canyons darkened from pink to red to purple and the moon rose high overhead. Light from an oil lamp poured onto the balcony from open doors that led into the hotel's second-story parlor room.

A maze of dark corridors lay just beyond.

The old man's name was Beto. On the rusty table between us, he served plate after plate of food retrieved from somewhere deep in the hotel—a crispy pancake called sopaipilla fried with goat cheese and butter, candied plums stewed with barley, olives swimming in brine, slices of ripe papaya drizzled with sweet cream. Paz glanced at me, her face full of questions, as he placed the food in front of us. All of it he served with his own home-made version of something he called licor de chirimoya. The old man urged us to eat more, drink more, all the while sneaking our yellow dog fingerfuls of goat cheese under the table.

When we finished the fruity, homemade liqueur, Beto went

back inside and returned with a bottle of pisco. "Is this not the most magnificent sight your eyes have ever seen?" he asked, leaning back in a plastic lawn chair, his face to the darkening sky. "As the good woman Señora Mistral says, here we're all royalty, graced with such treasures—*ceñido de cien montañas o de más* . . . These skies are among the clearest in the entire world, you know! On moonless nights, you can see into the center of la Vía Láctea, our mother galaxy. A magical place, this is. Truly magical . . ."

Beneath the light of the moon, I could see that Beto's face was deeply cut with wrinkles, and when he smiled, his hard, shrewd eyes seemed to disappear into the folds of his skin. This gave his face an unsettling mixture of kindness and ill will—cold, calculating eyes hiding themselves beneath a warm, hearty smile. I couldn't decide whether or not to trust him.

"And you, my lovelies," Beto said, turning back to us. "What brings you to this Valley of Enchantments?"

Paz took an olive from the bowl on the table and spit the pit into the darkness beyond the balcony rail. "We're headed north from Paraíso, señor. To find a healer in Serena."

Beto sat back in his chair, impressed. "Two young ones such as yourselves traveling distances so vast? Whatever could lead you to undertake such a perilous journey?"

"Love," Paz said frankly, and I nearly fell from my chair. "The stupid, foolish love this kid has for his father. You want to tell him?" she asked me. "Or should I?"

I nodded, deferring to her. I still wasn't sure what to make of this man. I didn't want to be the one who divulged too much.

And so, with a full glass of pisco in her hand, Paz told Beto our story: how I'd snuck out of Upper City to save my sick father;

how she and I had been captured separately by Las Oscuras in the Wastes outside of Paraíso; how, against her better judgment, she'd chosen to save me. She told him how one of Paraíso's elders had commissioned her with the task of guiding me north to find the healer Yesenia, but that we'd been captured by Auralee when she mistook us for members of Las Oscuras. I was shocked by Paz's honesty. She'd been so careful with Auralee, so withholding, but now she was telling this man everything there was to tell.

Hours passed out on the balcony. Our glasses emptied and Beto refilled them, every sip a small fire in my throat going down. Paz asked where all these riches had come from, and with a crooked smile, Beto told us that he was a merchant who traded with powerful people on all sides. Such status had earned certain protections, he said. It also inspired a certain amount of fear.

After three pours of the heady golden liquor, the constellations above lost their sharpness. The little dog sleeping in the corner turned into a blur. I declined the next round, but Paz matched Beto glass for glass. "Auralee said that you know of a river ferry that can take us north," she said, tossing back another mouthful and setting her glass on the table.

"Yes," Beto said. "Yes, of course." But he seemed distracted, like he wanted to talk about something else. He settled deeper into his lawn chair, studying the thin line of pisco at the base of his glass. Then he looked up at me. "You say your name is Rumi?"

I nodded.

Beto downed the liquor in one gulp and set his glass on the rusty table. "Well, Rumi from St. Iago—I don't suppose you've ever heard the tale of the Upper City philosopher?"

I glanced across the table at Paz. She looked back, uncertain.

"No, sir," I said. "I don't believe I have."

"Oh, it's a good one!" He poured himself another glass and topped off Paz's. "So, there's this Upper City philosopher," he said, fighting back a smile. "He's sitting in his house, drinking his tea. Reading his Plato, you know. Reading his Hume. When all of a sudden, from the still of the night, there comes this howling—this terrible blood-cry of a scream. A sound so unspeakable that it sends chills to his very soul.

"Well. The philosopher stands from his desk and walks over to the window, teacup in hand. The screaming continues. It sounds like a man being torn limb from limb." Beto glanced eagerly between Paz's face and mine, shifting in his seat like a child, barely able to contain himself. "So the philosopher, he listens for a moment more, and he ponders the horrific tortures that the man must be enduring. He ponders this man's suffering— meditates on the nature of pain and violence and injustice. Then he takes a sip of tea and double-checks the locks on his doors, walks back to his table, and sits down with his books.

"'Thank god,' he whispers to himself. 'Thank god that I'm inside and safe!'"

With that, Beto downed the rest of his pisco and slammed his glass onto the table, unable to control his laughter. "HA! Thank god I'm inside and safe! And that the electricity is on!"

I smiled nervously at Paz.

Paz glared at Beto with a mix of intoxication and disgust. "I don't see how that's funny."

"It isn't," Beto said, wiping tears from his eyes. "It isn't funny at all!" His belly trembled with the aftershocks of laughter as he clapped me on the shoulder. "Oh, don't worry, son. I bear you and your nation of cities no ill will. But you must admit that what you people do up there—barricading yourselves from the likes of us, pretending we don't exist—it takes some advanced psychological gymnastics, no?"

I stared down at my glass. It was true that what we'd done to the people of Lower City—to the lands they lived on, the waters they drank, the babies they birthed—was unthinkable. Inhuman. But I didn't have a say in any of those decisions. I did what anyone in my position would do, didn't I? I went to school. I did my homework. I kissed my grandfather's cheek before I went to sleep. . . .

Before I could say anything, Paz cut in. "Seems to me like maybe they don't think about it," she said, dragging her finger slowly along the rim of her glass. "Those great big walls make it so they don't have to see us or hear us at all. Maybe if Upper City folks heard us crying every day and every night, like your philosopher, they'd find it in themselves to come out and help."

"Rumi, my boy!" Beto said. "You'd better hope this girl is the one by your side when you run into trouble. She's more gracious than most out here!" He lifted the bottle of pisco and poured another round. Paz sank back in her chair, her legs curled beneath her. She looked almost ashamed to have defended me. Her shame pierced through me, and I forced down the liquid in my glass. It burned my nose and eyes, muddying my thoughts. But something was brewing behind the haziness in my mind. Something I wanted Paz to hear.

"When I was little," I said. I tried not to slur my words. "A Governance official came to our school to teach us about the Breach. He told us that before the Breach, the world was weighed down with people. The weather had become deadly. There wasn't enough food or clean water. And so when Zabrán started raging all over the world, people got desperate. Humanity had survived earlier pandemics, but this one was different—the world was different. The man showed us footage of pre-Breach cities clogged with abandoned cars, protestors blowing themselves apart in front of petrol stations, victims of bioterror left to die in abandoned hospitals. When the footage was over, he explained that our founders had formed the Union of Upper Cities to protect us from that world. He explained the Deservingness Quotient, and why certain individuals had been admitted to Upper City instead of others. He said that the heights humanity had reached—our inventions and discoveries and religions and art—all of it would've been lost if the founders hadn't acted as they did. But all that stuff doesn't seem quite right anymore." I slumped in my chair and scratched at my tattooed jaw. "The truth seems more like what you said, Paz—that the founders built the walls so we wouldn't have to hear the voices outside, the screaming. So we wouldn't have to ask ourselves why we weren't helping."

Across from me, Paz gazed into the night. I wondered if she was even listening. She seemed so distant. So hopelessly beyond my reach.

Beto burst out laughing. "Is that what you've gleaned from your little Lower City adventure? I'm glad we poor folk could teach you something, Rumi!" He reached across the table and patted Paz's shoulder in mock solidarity. "Always nice to feel useful, no?"

Paz glared at him, unsmiling.

Hot-faced, I clicked my fingernail against my empty glass. He was mocking me, and I wanted to object. But there was truth to what he said. "I guess it makes sense to call it 'the Breach,'" I said. "The Breach formed this gulf between us, this distance we don't know how to span."

Beto lifted his glass into the air. "Here's to the Breach!" he cried out. "A breach of our trust in one another—a rupture in our shared humanity. Here's to a bunch of very high walls!"

Vio nudged my knee with his wet nose, and I scooped him into my lap. I glanced at Paz, her legs still curled beneath her. She seemed to be sinking even deeper into herself, unwilling to talk of Upper and Lower City—as though she were afraid of what she might say.

"Come now, children," Beto said at last. "I don't mean to be a bully. We're just engaging in some ideological banter! It's not often I have the privilege of entertaining such esteemed guests as yourselves." He tipped the bottle of pisco into his glass. When nothing came out, he tossed the bottle off the balcony into the night. It shattered in the darkness below. "I do wonder, though," he said with a mischievous glint in his eye. "What good are your well-intentioned words if there's no *action* behind them? Is it up to us Lower City folks to act? Perhaps those of us down here should all become revolutionaries, hm? Take up arms and storm the walls of your Bastille?" He winked across the table at Paz, but Paz only looked away with a quick, tense smile. "Maybe there really are too many of you, hm?" Beto continued. "Maybe we should start picking a few of you off!"

Abruptly, Paz uncurled her legs and walked into the parlor. Vio trotted at her heels. She paused beside the parlor's mantel-piece, her back to us, and began picking at the paint with her fingernail. Beto sat with his hands behind his head, looking smug and self-satisfied. But his accusations nagged at me. Why *did* people like me and my family—good people—live as though *this* were not the reality of the world? Why didn't we do anything to change it? The question itched like the maggots chewing my leg, eating toward some meaty center.

"It's true . . . ," I mumbled at last. "There *are* too many of us. But the problem isn't overpopulation or a shortage of water or petrol. The problem is that nobody feels like they can *do* anything. Not when you come down to it. We all feel like we've been swept up by some force that's outside our control. Like we're drops of water in the sea being tossed by waves. But what can one drop do to stop the wave?"

Beto's mouth curled into a smile. "I take it you've not heard of San Pedro?"

From inside the parlor, Paz turned her head slightly at this question.

"No," I said. "I haven't. What is it?"

Beto's eyes sparkled. "There's a colony in the heart of the desert, far north of Serena, where Upper and Lower City people live together. They claim they're trying to pull the Old World up by the roots, to grow something new in its place. Or, to extend your metaphor, to create their own wave. I've never been there myself. I'm too old to make the journey—desert travel is for the young, the strong, and the stupid! But I know of others who set off in hopes of finding a new way of life. In fact, our little peregrina Auralee has hopes to journey there herself, when Ancho and the children are grown."

Paz returned to the balcony with these words, her face flushed. "Las Oscuras wouldn't pursue her?"

Beto shook his head. "Once you set foot in the Northern Desert, they figure you're good as dead. Which, of course, you are." He yawned, rubbing his hand over his face. "Send me a postcard if you go there, eh? A postcard . . . Ha!" He leaned back in his chair, one arm over his face, and his voice trailed off. Soon his breathing rattled with phlegm and his head fell back, open-mouthed in sleep.

I glanced at Paz. She snapped her fingers, and Vio perked his ears, scurrying over to her. I stood from my chair to join her inside, when, all of a sudden, Beto sat upright, eyes wide.

"Hush now! *Hush!* Do you hear that?" he whispered. "That '*tué-tué, tué-tué*' out in the darkness? It's el Chonchón, the spirit of the night! El brujo que anuncia la muerte . . ."

Paz caught my eye, trying to gauge how much of this I understood.

Beto stood and crossed himself. "La muerte," he repeated as he stumbled into the parlor. "La muerte, por Dios . . ."

"C'mon," Paz said as he disappeared down one of the dark corridors. "Let's find a room." She took one of the lamps lighting the parlor off the wall. The lamp cast a gentle light on the corridor's walls and on Paz's body as we followed the hallway up the stairs. Road dust smudged her legs from the tops of her boots to the frayed edges of her shorts. The nape of her neck was too precious for words. I imagined the smell of her skin. The thought made me dizzy.

I listened for the sound of the creature, the Chonchón. And there it was, somewhere off in the night, crying in a voice both birdlike and human. *Tué-tué-tué, tué-tué-tué.*

La muerte, I knew, meant *death.*

At the top of the stairs, Paz chose a room. I followed her inside.

2 6

PAZ

Three floors up, I found a room with a fireplace and a nice stash of wood and high walls plastered with flowers. The room was empty save for a mermaid carved into a broken wooden bedpost and a metal safe, open and rifled through. The only thing left inside was paper money.

Rumi swept broken plaster onto the balcony with his foot. The pup followed him for a while, then lay down by the door as I tore up the bright-colored bills for tinder. Orange and yellow danced soft heat on my shins and forearms as the kindling caught fire. I closed my eyes. My head drummed with pisco, with things I wanted to forget.

The comandante. Las Oscuras.

My mission.

I rested my head on my knees, but the drumming wouldn't stop.

Rumi sat next to me and took off his boots. His shoulder rested against mine. "How about that guy Beto?" he said. "Makes you wonder if there's liquor left anywhere else in Lower City!" The fire sparked little gulps of sap. "I mean . . . You know what I mean."

I raised my head from my knees and tried a smile. Outside, the wind sang low and mournful.

"Are you thinking about that place?" he started again. "What was it . . . San Pedro?"

I shook my head. "Not really."

The drums in my head kept pounding. This was my life and these were my choices, and now el Chonchón—the spirit of death—was calling from outside the window. I laid myself back on the wood-plank floor, my arms folded across my stomach, and shivered.

Rumi lay next to me, so close I could feel the warmth of him. "What are you thinking about, then?"

"You really want to know?"

"I really do," he said.

"I was thinking about this old storeroom in Paraíso, down by the shoreline," I said. "During high tide, the whole thing fills with water, and when the tide goes out, it turns into this giant pool. Fish get trapped in there sometimes, or stingrays. One time a pair of porpoises got stuck for half a day. That was legendary stuff, the porpoise day. . . ."

We both were quiet for a long while. The high, white ceiling rippled over our heads in the light of the fire. "What made you think of that?" Rumi asked.

I bit my lip to stop its trembling. The world was pushing so heavy against me. I could feel myself sinking. All I wanted was for somebody to help me carry its weight.

"One day this kid challenged me to a race, a swim across the storeroom," I said. "Chuta—I must've been seven years old. 'First person to make it across without taking a breath wins,' he said. It was hot that day, and lots of kids were down there watching us, cheering. The race was close, right up to the end, but at the very last I pulled ahead and beat him.

"You should've seen this kid, flaco. He was so mad. Beat by a girl with a *sinner's arm*! So he started calling me names. Pendeja. Hija de puta. Zorra. Nothing I hadn't heard before. But then he said something that made me freeze. 'At least my mama knows who my daddy was,' he said. I remember his words exactly. 'I bet your puta of a mother shacked up with a fish just so she'd have someplace to sleep.' The other kids joined in, started calling me pez—*fish*—instead of Paz. They said I deserved my sinner's arm 'cause my mother was a dirty sinner. One of them pushed me down and pretended to have a go with me—said it was never too early to start. That was the first time I saw my mother through their eyes. I'd always fancied her nothing less than an angel who'd died giving me life. But to them she was a whore. And I was her bastard child, deformed by her sins."

The fire cracked, and the ceiling rippled as we stared at it, side by side. For a long while, I'd believed those kids were right. It wasn't till I learned about Las Oscuras that I realized they were full of shit. That it wasn't me and my mother and my sinner's arm who were evil. No, the evil lived in Upper City and its walls, and the only thing to do was fight. This anger had given me the courage to let the mark of Las Oscuras color my skin. But now I wanted to run from the weight of it. From Víctor, Las Oscuras, my mission. I felt dizzy. Trapped.

I turned to my side and let my sinner's arm rest on Rumi's chest, searching for gravity. His heart beat fast and heavy as he closed his hand around my twisted fingers. I tried to remember how I'd felt, prisoned in that cellar room, when I'd looked at Rumi and seen nothing but Upper City. That night, I'd been blind to who he was—a boy who'd left everything to save his father; who could speak only English, but who kept Old World poetry tucked in his memories; whose hands were soft but strong; whose eyes were dark and honest as they searched mine with questions I didn't know how to answer. I tried to remember my anger. Anger had gotten me into this, and anger was the only thing that could see me through. If I could just keep hating him—if he wasn't a boy with thoughts and memories and a family, with a smile and hands and a wounded leg. If he was just a mission I had to complete.

But those trustful eyes, that speeding heartbeat. He wasn't just an Upper City cuico anymore. He was Rumi.

"I've never met anyone as strong as you," Rumi said. "Not as strong, not as brave, not as selfless. I can't understand how someone could see you as anything less."

He looked at me, his eyes full of questions, and I stared back, lost inside a feeling I couldn't control. And as we lay there, the tatted lines on his neck and chest seemed to shift, to form themselves into a web. But it wasn't the web the comandante had spoke of, where each string was tied to power, and cutting one string would dissolve everything into beautiful chaos. No. The web I saw on Rumi's skin was knotted and thick: the web of the world. In it, I saw how the thread of his life tugged against the thread of mine. How, through him, I touched his father's thread and the thread of his people. How, through me, Rumi tugged on Javi's thread, and Auralee's, and the comandante's. And on and on.

And there, in the light of the fire, his lips met mine. His arms circled me. My whole self trembled against him. I pulled him close, and we pressed into each other like two souls caught in a storm. His kiss seemed like the only warmth left in the world.

But then his hand slipped under my shirt, and everything in me froze. The mark on my chest. The mark that made me his enemy. He couldn't see it. I couldn't let him see it. Right?

A dangerous thought came into my mind.

What if I told him—told him everything? About my mission, about the comandante. What would he do? Would he hand me over to the Library to be burned as a traitor? Or would he help me escape? His look was so tender. His kiss was so soft. Maybe he'd understand.

My heart pounded in my ribs. The silver circle on my chest burned as hot as the day the comandante had needled it into my skin.

"I've got to tell you something," I said, my voice trembling.

"It's okay," he said. He sat up and straightened his shirt. "I didn't mean to . . ."

My head felt light as I searched for the right words. *I've been lying to you all this time, Rumi. But I'm not going to complete my mission. That's why I'm telling you.*

The silence swelled bigger and bigger as I searched for words I never thought I'd say. *I'm telling you to save you. . . .*

But Rumi spoke before I could.

"You know, my mother died when I was just a kid too." He cleared his throat and turned away from me, looking out the balcony window into the dark. "It was Las Oscuras."

The room shifted underneath me.

"I don't have many memories of her. I remember that her hair was long and black. And I remember the smell of peppermint and coconut when she hugged me. She worked at a Governance lab making pharmaceuticals that were supposed to keep us all from going crazy inside our walls. Once a month, she had to travel to other Upper Cities for work. One morning, she took a BulletRail train outside our city and . . . well, she never came home."

My sight went narrow. I was just a kid when the BulletRail

attacks happened. In those days, Upper City's routine raids came so often that we lived in constant fear—of soldiers, of bombs dropped from planes. We never knew what to expect or when. Las Oscuras had grown strong during this time—which was before the Library's prisonings and burnings—and folks who'd been orphaned or widowed in the Upper City raids had jumped at the chance to join their revolution. Las Oscuras set up strongholds in the Wastes and linked themselves with other revolutionaries in distant lands, laying plans for their biggest attack yet—a world-wide mission to derail Upper City trains.

If I'd been old enough at that time, I'd have joined too.

"It's funny," Rumi continued. "I remember the night my mother didn't come home better than I remember any night I actually spent with her. I was sitting at the kitchen table. My grandfather was making dinner—lentils and rice. But he only prepared two bowls. Father stood by the window, looking into the dark. And I kept saying, 'Come eat, Father.' It seemed like everything would be okay if he'd just sit down and eat. So I waited, not touching my food, watching Father through the steam from my bowl." Rumi gazed out the window, like he was watching his father watch the darkness. "When I learned that the same terrorists who killed my mother had infected Father, I . . . I—" His voice broke. "There's only so much you can take, you know?"

The pisco stabbed sharp and sudden in my stomach, and I stumbled out the doors to the room's small balcony and dropped to my knees. The stars fell toward me in waves. With my head between the railing, I bared my guts to the night. My belly lurched again and again, desperate to be rid of everything—my past, my present, my future. There's no mercy in the world, I thought. No grace. The world was all vengeance. If this Upper City boy found out my allegiances, he'd drink up the ocean—like the boy in the Storyteller's tale—just to see me dead.

No mercy. No grace. No way out. Por mi culpa, por mi culpa, por mi gran culpa . . .

I curled on my side and clutched my hands to my face. Rumi sat next to me.

"It's okay," he said, his voice so gentle. "It's okay." He pulled me close against him. My tears soaked through his shirt till they touched his skin.

2 7

R U M I

I lay on my back on sun-warmed boards as the silty green river floated us toward Serena. Canyon walls rose on either side of us, guiding us through passageways of concrete rubble and stone. Paz sat beside me, one hand on our little dog's back, watching the sky.

That morning before dawn, she'd nudged me awake. Beto had already marked her map with the way to Serena, and by sunrise, we were floating downstream on a scrap-wood raft manned by a barefoot girl who couldn't have been more than ten years old.

All the while, Paz had barely met my gaze.

My head pulsed with a dull ache. I'd had more to drink the night before than in the rest of my life combined, but the canyon's slanting light and gentle sounds kept me suspended in the sweetness of the night before. I dangled my feet in the cool water and replayed each moment. How wide and bright Paz's eyes had looked in the light of the fire. How rare and honest it had felt to close my fingers around her hand. How I'd held her against me and kissed her. The words were so bold, I could hardly think them: I kissed her.

But then she'd pulled away. Recoiled, even. I had to think

around the edges of the memory. The just-before. The just-after. The moment itself was too much. Was it my city that had pushed her away, or was it me? Was I so repulsive? So weak?

Then another thought came to mind. Maybe she thought I was using her, that I was trying to take what I could get from her before returning home. The thought made my stomach turn. But in a way, it was true. Today, we'd reach Serena. If all went well, I'd return to St. Iago immediately. I'd leave Paz behind and go home. I closed my eyes and let myself imagine the feeling of standing on my front step, of opening the door and stepping inside to the smells of Baba's sabz chai. I imagined Baba descending the stairs, his face streaked with tears of joy, as though he were standing face-to-face with a ghost. I paused in that moment—before I said anything, before I saw how the disease had ravaged Father— when it was all just a feeling. The feeling of coming home.

"You thinking something nice, flaquito?" Paz asked. It was the most she'd said to me all day.

"Just thinking of home," I said. I stopped myself from saying more. Why would she want to hear of a place that had brought her nothing but suffering?

She turned onto her stomach and trailed her hand in the water. "What was it Beto said last night . . . ? Send me a postcard when you get there."

I wanted more than anything to take her hand. To feel the warmth of her skin. "Of course," I said. She almost smiled.

I closed my eyes again, and the sun blazed red behind my eyelids. Gradually I reconstructed the scene: the front step, the spiced tea, Baba's face. But slowly, I let the dream shift. I still stood on my front doorstep, but this time Paz stood beside me, nervously looking around. I imagined taking her hand, telling her it was okay. We were safe. My hand on the door felt different with her beside me. Next to her, my past became new. . . .

We continued down the river in silence. The canyon walls on either side of us rose in smooth curves that looked more like muscle than rock—the bodies of giants worn away by water and time. I could make out rippled layers of color—rust red and burnt orange, pale green. So thin, each layer, but together they towered above us. To think that there'd been a time when I couldn't imagine anything larger than my city's walls. To think I'd assumed that the great truths of the world were all contained inside.

It was early afternoon when the barefoot girl moored our raft onto the riverbank. Paz hopped from the raft, the yellow dog alongside her, and then steadied the raft for me. Icy water soaked through my bandage and pricked the tender wound underneath as I waded, boots in hand, through the reeds. The barefoot girl said nothing as she pushed off the riverbank with her stick, continuing downriver without looking back. Her long, tattered T-shirt rippled in the breeze.

On the sandy bank, I removed the wet bandage and crossed my calf over my knee to examine the wound. What two days before had been an oozing, stinking gash was now bright pink and clean. Most of the maggots had dropped off already, with no infected tissue left to eat.

"Hey!" I called to Paz. "I think it's healing!"

"That's real good, flaco," she said. She wasn't looking at me. She was scoping out the cliffs, shading her eyes with her hand. Our little dog lifted his nose in the air, sniffing for things she couldn't see. Meanwhile, I poured clean water over my calf, repacked the wound with gauze, and wrapped a new bandage around my leg.

"What do you think?" I called to Paz as I laced up my boots.

"Are we getting close?" But this time she didn't answer. When I looked up, her expression had changed. I followed her gaze upriver to a wooden boat that had just rounded the bend, manned by four bearded men. All were visibly tattooed. All had machetes strapped to their backs.

"C'mon," she said. "Let's get moving."

I shoved my first aid valise into my pack and followed her through the tall grass along the bank. My heart pounded in my ears. Vio ran ahead of us, glancing back every few seconds, urging us to go faster. I shadowed Paz as closely as I could through the tall grass and around the next sharp bend in the river. When at last we reached a clearing, she broke into an all-out run. The river widened, and the canyon walls opened before us onto a panorama of rolling dunes whipped with wind. I ran behind her at full stride, thinking nothing of my wounded calf, nothing but the need to keep up.

When it became clear that the men weren't following us, Paz eased her pace. My racing pulse began to slow. "Those men . . . ," she said, breathing hard.

I nodded, hands on my head, chest heaving. "Do you think they were Las Oscuras?"

Paz stared into the distance. "I don't think they . . ." But her words trailed off.

"Paz?"

She blinked. "I don't know. We should be careful, though." She took her map from her pack and crouched, pinning it against her thigh to shield it from the wind. "Let's see," she said. "This is us, I think. . . ." With her finger, she followed the thin blue line that Beto had drawn for her that morning. The line snaked north, from his hotel in Las Termas all the way to Serena.

She shaded her eyes and looked west over the dunes to gauge the remaining daylight. The dog sniffed the wind and whimpered softly. "I think we should cross the trash hills here," she said, indicating a spot on her map. "Looks like the narrowest part. All the Upper Cities around here dump their waste just south of Serena. That's why they call it the trash hills. Beto said we've got no choice but to go through them to get to Serena, but that we should move as quick as possible. Like Auralee said, it's a dangerous place." Paz spoke these words so solemnly, so knowingly, that I had a feeling "dangerous" was an understatement.

Without another word, we started walking. The dunes turned to hills dotted with gray, thirsty grass. The sun's heat evaporated my sweat, leaving my skin to bake dry. At one point my nose started bleeding, but I made a point not to complain. I just held my sleeve against my nose until the blood stopped.

After a while, a footpath became clear. Mounds of gutted clamshells and bundles of kelp littered either side of the path. As we continued, the trash multiplied. Plastic bottles and rusted cans, shards of glass, the skeleton of a bird. I nudged the remains of a refrigerator with my shoe.

"These are the trash hills?" I asked. "They don't seem so bad. . . ."

The wind picked up with these words, carrying on it a caustic smell that burned my throat. It reminded me of the stink of Paraíso but harsher, less biological.

"Mierda," Paz said. "They're extracting metals, I bet. Here, hold still."

With her knife, she sliced two strips of cloth from the bottom of her shirt and handed one to me. I followed her lead and tied it over my nose and mouth, ruffling Cienfuegos's scarf over the top of it. Just then a gust of wind blew the scarf from my neck, bathing my tattoos in the afternoon sun. Quickly, I pulled up the scarf to hide them, but as I did this, an idea flashed across Paz's face. She unwound the scarf, took a step back from me, and cocked her head to one side.

"That tat could be real useful, flaco. Only . . . you've got to look a whole lot rougher."

I shook my head, uncertain. "Wait. You want me to pretend I'm actually *one of them*?"

"A tat like yours is nothing to mess with. It means you'd kill a man just as soon as wipe the sweat from your face. Honest folks wouldn't trust us, that's for sure, but maybe the bad ones won't mess with us either if they think we're a pair of killers."

I crossed my arms and stuck out my chest, and Paz burst out laughing.

"What?" I smiled. "Not vicious enough?"

She shook her head. "We'll work with what we got, I guess. Give me that knife of yours." I rooted through my pack and handed Paz the knife I'd taken from my kitchen. She turned it over in her hands, frowned, then knelt to scrape the knife against a rock.

"Hey! What gives?" I shouted.

"You think Las Oscuras would have a knife with so much shine on it?"

"No," I said. "I guess not."

She went back to work with the knife. I couldn't help but notice her short black hair forming sweaty curls at the base of her neck, or the muscles in her back tensing and releasing. Suddenly, I was overcome with the memory of how it had felt, holding her in my arms.

"There," she said. She stood and feinted a jab at me with the knife. "Much better." The blade, once mirror-shiny, was now nicked and jagged. It looked murderous, I had to admit.

I stuck the knife into my belt, tucking my shirt behind its hilt so the blade was unmistakably visible. Paz took a step back and looked me over—my tattooed neck, the frayed cloth over my nose and mouth, the knife in my belt, the bloody bandage on my calf. A smile spread across her face.

"Oye," she said. "If I didn't know better, I'd be scared to look at you crooked!"

"So . . . it's good?" I asked.

A cold expression swept over her, as though she'd just remembered something.

"Real good, flaco."

She turned away from me and strapped her pack across her chest, and together we continued toward the crest of the hill. But at the top we stopped, dumbstruck. A vast expanse of hills spread before us. Nothing green grew on them. Instead, they glinted with lifeless specks of white and orange and yellow, pink and brown and gray. A haze of black smoke hovered over everything like a strangling fog. And across these rolling mounds of trash, small figures crawled.

"My god," I whispered.

Paz nodded, silent.

The hills held me by the throat as we walked wordlessly into them. Swollen mounds of waste rose all around us. Vio hung close to Paz's side, ears back, head down. The sharp smell of metal and burning plastic seeped through my cloth mask. I watched in horror as the figures in the distance began to transform. They weren't animals scouring the hills for food. They weren't bearded men scavenging for treasures. They were children. Barefoot, unsmiling children. Children with slingshots and knives hanging from wire twisted around their waists, children with shimmering circles tattooed on their chests.

Paz nudged me as we approached the first of them. "Act like we're here for scavenge, just like them," she whispered, gaze fixed on the ground.

I obeyed by nudging at trash with my boot—a sliced-open mattress, its foamy guts spilling out; a circuit board; a shredded tire; the severed head of a porcelain horse whose pastel mane was blowing in some ancient wind; a picture book; a beach ball . . . I touched the knife at my hip and felt absurd. This is me, I thought, a knife in my belt, crossing hills of trash, the sun beating down. This is me, breathing fumes through a rag, sweat burning my eyes. This is me, falling for a Lower City girl who despises me. This is the world. This is me.

I spotted a thin silver square, its glossy screen cracked and dark, and recognized the object immediately. An old-model DigiTablet. I picked it up and stared, incredulous, at the tiny gadget. It was a glimmer from another world, a tear in the fabric of reality. This shiny, discarded thing bridged the gap between my world and this one like a magical link. A talisman. I closed my fingers around it and held it to my chest.

Just then I heard a voice from behind me. A child's voice.

"Suéltalo," the voice said. "Suéltalo ahora."

Paz touched my arm. "Drop it, Rumi. Drop it now."

I turned. A little girl with soot-smeared cheeks and a rope tied around her distended belly pointed a slingshot at my face. Her chest was thin and her lips were cracked, but her eyes burned with wordless defiance that dared me to take what was rightfully hers. Instantly, I dropped the Digi and put my hands over my head. The girl didn't move. Her nostrils flared. Paz motioned for me to step back, and I stepped back. With animal speed, the girl snatched the Digi from the ground and darted down the hill.

"Jesus, flaco," Paz whispered. "I said to *act* like we're scavenging!"

"I thought you said they'd be scared of my tattoo."

"Maybe she's too young to understand what a face tat means," Paz said, watching the girl sprint away over the waves of garbage. "Or maybe she's too desperate to care."

Paz continued in the direction of Serena, and I followed behind her, shaking. I was so close to Yesenia, to a cure for Father, so close to leaving the horrors of Lower City. And that little girl could have split open my skull.

We passed more figures scouring the hills, more children with vacant eyes. I kept my eyes to the ground and indiscriminately scanned the trash under my feet. A soiled white dress. A pair of lens-less eyeglasses. An empty bottle of wine. To our left, a giant pit plumed with billows of thick black smoke. My throat tightened in its haze. As we drew closer, I peered over the edge of the pit. Down below, a group of kids tended small patches of fire, tossing DigiTablets and specs and pre-Breach computers into the flames and flipping the burning electronics with bare, sooty hands. They shifted around the pit unspeaking, like prisoners. Like the damned. A young boy crouched over a bucket, vomiting. A toddler squatted, relieved himself, then ran to the side of a teenaged girl who was prodding at plastic remains with her foot. The girl picked up the child and kissed his cheek. Then she looked up at me from below. Her eyes flashed in the flames.

Paz tugged at my sleeve, but I couldn't look away.

And that's when I saw them. At the far edge of the pit, I saw the sheets laid out in rows. On each sheet, a person. Some rocked back and forth. Some lay completely still. I could see their swollen feet, their clenching hands. I could see they were children, like the children working these hills. And the world dropped out from under me.

Who did this? I thought. I wanted it to be someone's fault. But who was to blame? It was my fault—mine and my city's—yet at the same time it wasn't my fault at all. How could a drop be held responsible for the swell of the wave? I tried to hold the whole thing in my mind—Paz and these kids, my mother and father and mountains of trash, the tattoo on my skin, the walls of my city. But it was all too big, too complex.

Together, Paz and I had crossed a wasteland. We'd fought off a pack of dogs, withstood sun and thirst and exhaustion. But soon I would return to my city, and Paz would remain here in this poisoned world. The thought made my chest ache with a conviction more powerful than fear. I had to protect her. To save her from the life she'd been born into, from the luckless lottery ticket she'd drawn by no fault of her own.

"Let's get moving," Paz said, tugging at my arm.

"Wait," I said. Paz glared at me impatiently, but I didn't move. "I have to ask you something. What if there were a way to leave all of this behind? To—"

She cut me off. "What the hell are you talking about, flaco? We've gotta keep moving."

"No. Just listen." I held her arm firmly. Her light eyes met mine and softened, just as they had in the old hotel room beside the fire.

But then, abruptly, her focus shifted to something behind me, and her face went pale.

"No . . . ," she whispered.

I followed her gaze across the pit. Not fifty meters from us stood the group of men from the riverbank, tattoos covering their arms, machetes strapped to their backs.

"Bendito sea Dios," Paz whispered. "Bendito sea Dios, y su santo nombre . . ."

The men moved swiftly toward us along the edge of the pit. The kids in the pit below stopped moving, heads bowed. Not one of them dared look up.

"Who are those men, Paz?" I asked as they came closer. But she said nothing. She just stood there, frozen. The men drew closer, their footfalls heavy and unfaltering. Their tattoos came into focus beneath their straggly beards. I could see the leather straps that secured their machetes to their backs. I could see their scars.

Cold terror washed over me. It trickled down my neck and into my legs and arms. "Who are those men?" I demanded, panic in my voice. "Damn it, Paz!"

But she was still as a stone.

Just then a man with shark eyes tattooed on his temples pulled ahead of the other three. The creases at the corners of his mouth were threaded with silver. A long purple scar ran the length of his cheek and neck. I buckled with the memory of that terrible room full of silks and weapons, of the man with a face shimmering with ink. . . . Had these men been searching for me since the day Paz helped me escape?

I held my breath, bracing myself for the first blow. But no more than an arm's length from us, the men stopped. The shark-man scanned my face, then Paz's.

"¿Quién vive?" he said in a voice like rusted metal.

Did he not recognize us? I wondered. Was it just a coincidence that they were here? I stared ahead, trying my best to seem unafraid, praying that Paz had some kind of plan. At my feet, the pup whimpered.

"Tú sabes quién soy," Paz said. "Yo busco a Víctor."

I didn't understand a word.

"No, no, no," the man said, smiling. He extended his thick, tattooed arm and grasped Paz by her shirt, staring fiercely into her eyes. "No, cabrita. El comandante te busca a tí."

Paz shoved his hand from her chest, shouting at him in English this time. "You don't want to cross us, cabrón," she said. "This kid may look small, but you haven't seen him with a knife. How'd you think he got that silver beauty tatted 'cross his neck?"

The man just smiled at her, then gestured to his men. One by one, each of them looked me in the face, spat on the ground, and walked away. The shark-man stared at Paz for another long moment. Then, in one swift motion, he stepped forward and kicked our little dog as hard as he could. Poor Vio yelped and crumpled to the ground.

"El comandante te busca," the man repeated. And then, just as suddenly as they'd come, the men disappeared into the haze on the other side of the pit.

Paz crouched and wrapped little Vio in her arms as he tried and failed to stand, wheezing. And in this helpless creature, I remembered my own body, collapsed on the floor after too many pills, that night alone in my room. How little I'd considered my life to be worth back then. I felt so much older now. How precious everything seemed.

"Is he okay?" I asked.

Paz held the pup in her arms, petting his face as he licked her hand. "He'll be fine," she said. "Lower City makes you tough, weón."

I nodded, looking across the pit. "I was sure they were going to recognize us. But whatever you said, seems like they bought it."

Paz stood, and the dog wagged his tail weakly beside her. "You bet, flaco," she said. Her face was a bloodless gray.

We continued away from the pit in silence until eventually sapling trees began to push through the trash. At the crest of one final hill, I squinted to see the jumbled roofs of a large town in the distance. To the west of the town spread the gleaming expanse of the ocean.

Serena.

28

PAZ

erena. Clocktower. Moonrise.

The note said these words only, the letter *V* scrawled at the bottom like the point of a dagger. The shark-faced man had slipped it into my shirt when he grabbed me.

V for Víctor. The comandante was out there waiting. Watching.

He must have lost track of us when we'd run off course, chased by Auralee's dogs. But now he'd found me. He held me once again in the iron grip of his gaze. How long would it take for him to sense the change in my heartbeat, to see the softness in my eyes? To realize that the rage that had made me a desirable recruit was fading? Or, not fading so much as changing.

I wanted to scream, but I couldn't. I wanted to run, but I couldn't run. How could a person make a choice like this? It wasn't fair.

I kicked a tin can lying in the path and yelled a string of curses at the sky.

The can spat brown water back in my face.

Rumi took a clean shirt from his pack and held it out to me like a kid who knows his mama's mad but can't tell if she's mad at him. But I ignored it and wiped my face with my sleeve.

"Everything okay?" he asked.

I snapped my fingers, and Vio limped to catch up to me. "Everything's fine. Just try and keep up, all right?"

Rumi tucked the shirt into his pack. "Sure," he said. I could hear the hurt in his voice.

No other way, I thought. All that shit last night was just a pretty dream.

We entered Serena from the south through the ruined port of Coquimbo, a maze of empty high-rises long ago abandoned to earthquakes and tsunamis and the grip of Las Oscuras. The ruins of Coquimbo reminded me of the Wastes outside Paraíso. They made me wonder if every city the whole world over had a dirty, broken sister city at its doorstep, a sister who'd made all the wrong choices and was paying for it with her life.

The ruins of Coquimbo came to an end at a makeshift wall that surrounded the heart of the city of Serena. This wall looked almost like a barricade, sheets of rusted steel and half-rotted beams topped with hoops of barbed wire. And standing on a platform overlooking the wall stood a pair of sentries, armed and watching.

We came closer. One of the sentries disappeared from his post and then by some magic reappeared on our side of the wall on horseback, riding toward us. He had a hard look about him—his cheeks red with wind, a crossbow strapped to his back.

"Buenas tardes," he said, no welcome in his voice.

"Buenas," I said.

"You've come from the trash hills," he said. It wasn't a question.

"Sí. The trash hills. But not for scavenging. We come to see the healer Yesenia."

The sentry tipped his chin toward Rumi, whose tattoos were still uncovered. "And him?"

I sifted through my satchel for the letter stamped with the Library's seal. The sentry took it and held it against the sky—scanning for powdered poisons, I guessed. But as he read Cienfuegos's words, his face flushed. He glanced between the letter and Rumi, piecing together our story. Then he folded the parchment and passed it back to me.

"You must see the señora at once," he said. "Come."

He opened a gate in the makeshift wall, and we followed him inside.

The city on the other side looked like something from out of a dream. An old stone church stood at one end of a sunlit plaza; a burbling fountain stood at the other. Little kids kicked a ball around a dusty patch of grass. Laundry lines hung heavy with clothes. The late sun's blindingness was cut by the cool of trees.

I scanned the shadows for the comandante, but of course he wasn't there.

The sentry got down from his horse and roped it to a post. "The healer lives on the easternmost edge of town," he said. "We'll go on foot from here."

We followed him east past earthen buildings with huge wooden doors and grape leaves breaking bud on trellised vines. Stray dogs raised their heads and sniffed as we passed, then flopped back down onto the warm cobblestones. In some shady upper room, heavy fingers strummed an uneven tonada on the guitar. And the quiet deepened as we walked farther from the center of the city, every sound whole and lonesome, footsteps on waterless soil.

Evening fell as we reached the eastern edge of the city's

haphazard wall. The wall was shorter in that part of the city, and I could see over the top of it easy to the other side, to a forest of tall algarrobo trees and brambled wild rose. And that's when I saw it. The tall stone tower.

"What's that on the other side of the wall?" I asked the sentry.

"That's the old clocktower," he said. "It no longer tells the time, but what do we need with that kind of time anyhow?"

Clocktower. Moonrise. I shuddered.

Soon we came to a tangled herb garden and a step-stone path that led to an old laurel tree with a ladder of boards nailed to its trunk. A thatch-roof hut was perched in the tree's canopy, and a bright-red cloth hung across the tree hut's door.

The sentry smiled. "She's home."

"The healer lives up *there*?" Rumi asked.

The sentry nodded. "We're always trying to convince her to move someplace safer, someplace easier. But she refuses. 'Ease is for the Old World,' she says. 'For those who fancy themselves gods. But we're monkeys, señores! And where do monkeys live? In trees!'"

I stared into the laurel leaves. Who was this healer anyway, living in a tree at the edge of lands overrun with Las Oscuras?

The sentry whistled up a greeting. "Oye, Yesenia," he called. "There are travelers here to see you." A dove cried in the forest outside the wall, but no answer came from the hut.

"Well?" he asked. "Should I send them up or no?"

"You're waiting for trumpets to sound, I suppose?" called the voice of an old woman.

The sentry smiled. "Of course not, señora," he called. Then he turned back to us. "I must return to my post now. Apologies for my coldness earlier, but it behooves us to be suspicious." He nodded at Rumi's tattoo. "Will we see you tonight, for the performance?"

"Performance?" I asked.

The sentry's eyes lit up. "Each full moon, one of our theater troupes puts on a play at the old city hall. The whole town comes out for it. It's an honor to be chosen to perform. A real honor." He slid off his hat and scratched the back of his head. "As it happens, my troupe was chosen to perform tonight. I'd be obliged if esteemed travelers like yourselves were to attend."

Moonrise, I thought.

An evening performance with the whole town in attendance would be the perfect chance for me to sneak away, nobody the wiser, for my meeting with the comandante.

"We'll do our best to be there," I said. "Our very best."

The sun dipped behind the wall, and the air turned cool.

"Ah, maravilloso," the sentry said. "¡Hasta pronto!"

"A performance sounds fun," Rumi said as the sentry disappeared through the garden and back into the city. His voice was all hopeful, like he was testing my good graces.

Stop trying so hard, flaquito, I wanted to say. *Don't you see we live in different worlds?*

But I swallowed these words.

"Sure thing," I said.

The pup waited in the tangled garden as we climbed up the ladder to the tree hut. At the top of the ladder, I gave a little knock on the doorframe.

"¿Señora?" I called.

No answer. So I peeked inside.

The room was round with wooden walls. Clutches of herbs hung from the ceiling. The hut was bigger than it looked from the outside. An oil lamp cast soft light on shelves of books and jars of colorful powders. A faded rug covered the scrap-wood floor. The old woman sat with her back to the door, her thick gray hair pulled into a wavy bun at the top of her head. She had a fullness about her. Something sturdy and warm.

"¿Señora?" I said again.

The healer spoke but didn't turn. "What is it you need?" she said in perfect English. English like Rumi's. "I was just about to ready myself for the play tonight."

"We apologize for intruding," I said. "For keeping you from your duties. We wouldn't have come unless it was urgent. And it is. Most, most urgent."

The old woman stood up slow, bracing her back, and turned to face us.

"You mistake me, child," she said, smiling. Her arched black eyebrows and bird-beak nose gave her face a kind of mischief. "I don't really care for these local productions. Aurelio—the sentry who brought you here—says tonight they're adapting the tale of the jaguar, a powerful tale that I fear our actors cannot do justice. He says I'll *love* it . . . but, between you and me, I wouldn't mind an excuse to stay home."

She sounded like no curandera I'd ever met. Most healers I knew spoke no English at all. Some refused even to speak Spanish, just the language of their people—Mapuzungun or Quechua or Aymara. Who was this woman anyway?

She slicked down the gray hairs that wisped around her face. "Now, what brings two young creatures like yourselves to my home on this lovely evening? And why on earth, child, are you wearing that ridiculous shawl?"

Rumi blushed.

I handed her Cienfuegos's letter. "This should explain," I said.

She studied the seal and lowered herself into her chair to read. I sat cross-legged on the floor at her feet. Rumi sat next to me. His breathing was shallow and anxious.

"You're from St. Iago?" she said, glancing at Rumi over the edge of the parchment.

Rumi nodded.

"Please. Take off that shawl and let me see you."

Rumi unwound his scarf, and the healer studied him—tattoos and all—without any expression. "Well," she said. "You haven't journeyed all this way to talk pleasantries, have you? Come. Show me the bloodwork."

Rumi took his magic cloth and eyeglasses from his backpack and passed them both to the old woman. She touched the metal frames lovingly, like she was stroking a baby. "Such fine things . . . ," she said. "And you left all this behind—perhaps never to see it again—in hopes of saving your father's life?"

"There wasn't any choice, ma'am," he said. His voice was shaky and dry.

The healer placed the fancy spectacles over her eyes. Rumi pressed his hands to his lips as she read from the screen. I'd been so caught up in my own mess that I'd thought scarce at all about Rumi's hopes and fears. But now I found myself wanting this healer to have a cure for his father, so that he'd have something joyful to go home to. This thought—of wanting to see him safe and happy—came so easy it startled me.

The healer shook her head. "Your father's strain is identical to what I've found in my patients here. I fear that the attack on your father was not an isolated incident. I fear it was an initial attempt at an infiltration of Upper City."

My heart raced as I thought back to the comandante's words that night by the fire, vials of ink lined up on the mildewed sheet. That Las Oscuras was trying to turn the Upper City people's bodies against them, to make them remember that we're all human beings.

"How long since he was infected?" the healer asked Rumi.

"Thirteen days," Rumi said.

Yesenia nodded. She took off the specs and folded them in her lap. "I must be honest. We've been tracking this new strain closely. I've seen people disintegrate in no more than a week. Now, of course, we don't have the same technology that you have in St. Iago. But your father can't have much time left. You must get back as soon as possible."

Rumi stared at her, unblinking. "So it's true. You have a cure."

The healer nodded. "I've successfully treated this new strain, yes. Las Oscuras uses human hosts to keep the virus alive. Sometimes they choose a host from among their ranks, but more often, they infect the children they've abducted who now work for them in the trash hills. The medicine I've developed is in scarce supply—its active component must travel from deep in the forests of Amazonia." The old woman furrowed her dark eyebrows. "Still," she said. "If I were to withhold this medicine from you now and Las Oscuras were to strike again, if Upper City had no access to treatment . . ."

A quiet fell over the room. So my mission was tied to those children I'd seen, laid out on sheets in the trash hills. In their quest to infect Upper City with Zabrán, Las Oscuras was keeping the virus alive by infecting those children. On purpose. I couldn't escape the horror of it.

"How do you keep it safe?" I asked, trying not to sound too

curious. "The cure, I mean. How come Las Oscuras doesn't come in here and steal it?"

Yesenia smiled. "All the components are here in my hut, it's true. But good luck to the person trying to guess what they are! I keep my formulas locked in here," she said, tapping her forehead. "I'd sooner die than write down such knowledge. But your question is a good one. Las Oscuras would do anything to get their hands on this medicine. And believe me, they've tried. The only way to keep the strain alive is by providing it a host. Many in their ranks have contracted the virus and died. Las Oscuras calls these deaths an honor, but they know they'd be stronger were they to have an effective treatment."

Yesenia sat forward in her chair and took Rumi's hands in hers. "That's why we must be so careful. Once I make this medicine, you must keep it safe until you reach Upper City."

"Of course," Rumi said. "I'll guard it with my life."

I pulled my legs close and circled the mark on my chest with my thumb. The comandante's plan was finally coming clear. It wasn't just about preventing Upper City from getting the healer's medicine. Las Oscuras wanted to keep the medicine for themselves. In that moment, I felt the urge to tell this healer about my allegiances, my tat, my mission. But after all she'd seen Las Oscuras do in her town, in the trash hills, how could she see me as anything but a monster?

Rumi shifted next to me and broke the silence.

"Is it true what they say?" he asked. "That you have connections to Upper City?"

I turned to Rumi, startled but curious. It was true that this healer was like no other I'd known. But could she be from Upper City? And who would've told this to Rumi?

The old woman cocked her head to one side and leaned back in her chair. "Yes, it's true," she said. "I'm from Upper City Boston originally, but I was in Quito studying medicine when I defected."

"Quito," Rumi said. "That's where my mom went to school."

"Your mom must be a smart gal," Yesenia said.

"Yes, she was," Rumi said. "Very smart."

Yesenia took this in. "It's just you and your father, then?"

Rumi nodded. "And my grandfather."

"I see." She passed Rumi his spectacles and cloth, and Rumi folded them into their case. "If I can arrange it, you'll leave here tomorrow at first light."

Rumi bowed his head and cleared his throat. "I'm sorry, ma'am, but there's one more thing. I came to Lower City on my heliocycle, but it's been destroyed. I thought, perhaps, I could purchase a mule and some supplies for my return. Some water, food . . .".

Yesenia burst out laughing. "A mule? Don't be absurd! No, no. Tonight, when we go into town for the play, I'll introduce you to Kai. He should be able to smuggle you by freight copter."

I tried to hide my bewilderment, but it was all too much. This woman was a healer, a defector, and a smuggler. An Upper City doctor living in a tree who would help Rumi find his way home. And I was caught up in the balance.

"A freight copter?" Rumi said. "But won't St. Iago's officials find me and think I'm some kind of terrorist?"

"Kai knows which operators to trust," she said. "He'll get you onto the right copter."

"But what if he's wrong?"

Yesenia crossed her arms and arched her thick black eyebrows. "I don't mean to sound harsh, Rumi—I know you've been through a lot. But honestly, what choice do you have?"

+ + + +

Night had fallen full by the time we left Señora Yesenia's tree hut and cut a path back toward the central plaza, our yellow pup limping alongside. The moon was waiting for me, just below the horizon. Its glow crept from behind the hills to the east, threatening.

Our walk was silent, and I was glad for the quiet. There was much to consider. How to break away for my meeting with the comandante at the clocktower. How to steal the healer's cure. But Rumi's question echoed the loudest.

What if there were a way to leave all of this behind?

What did he mean? I wondered. What was he asking?

2 9

RUMI

Torches lit the stage at Serena's old city hall. In the grassy park, children chased fireflies. Men and women sat on blankets, their babies playing nearby in the sand. Even though the sun had set, the air was warm and welcoming, and I could feel the weight of everything falling away from me like layers of clothing—the fear and alertness, the questions over how I would get back to Father. I stood in the balmy air of the plaza, unguarded for the first time since I'd set foot outside the walls of my city.

Paz lagged behind Yesenia and me, and the question I'd tried to ask her hung between us like a cloud swollen with rain. I needed to explain what I'd meant—that I wanted her to join me, to come *home* with me. I just needed to find the right words.

Yesenia pointed across the square to a man standing apart from the crowd.

"That's Kai," she said. "Upper Cities in this region pay him to dispose of their waste into the trash hills."

I looked closely at the man. His gray hair draped limply over his shoulders. "Is he from Upper City too?"

Yesenia smiled. "Not at all. He was born in the shanties near the trash hills."

"But he helps Upper City get rid of its trash?" I said, confused. "Why would he do that?"

"The citizens of Serena complain about his work to no end. They argue that the trash hills harbor terrorists, that the fumes cause chronic illness—all of which is true. But the trash hills also ensure a modicum of protection. We provide a valuable service to Upper City, and Upper City repays us with peace. Serena hasn't seen a bomb since before the Breach."

I turned to ask Paz if she'd heard about deals like this between Upper and Lower City. But a group of musicians had begun to play on the stage, and all around me people were standing to dance.

"Did you see where Paz went?" I asked Yesenia over the swell of the music.

Yesenia glanced around and then shrugged. "I'm sure she's just been asked to dance," she said. Then, sensing my nervousness, she smiled and patted my shoulder. "Don't worry. She knows how to look after herself. Come, let me introduce you to Kai."

The introduction was quick and formal. Kai wanted to know as little as possible. He didn't ask why I'd come to Serena; he didn't ask about my tattoo. Yesenia had vouched for me—that was enough.

"Can you be ready tonight, around midnight?" he asked.

I shot Yesenia a glance. She'd said the earliest transport would be the next morning.

"He can be ready," Yesenia said.

"Fine," said Kai. "You'll hear the copters come in. Takes about an hour, all told, to unload the freight. If you're not at the loading docks by takeoff, you're out of luck. Next transport to St. Iago won't be for another two days."

"He'll be there," Yesenia said.

Hearing these words felt like waking from a dream. I was leaving *tonight*. By tomorrow, I'd be back in St. Iago with Baba, giving Yesenia's medicine to Father.

And if I didn't speak with Paz tonight, I'd never see her again.

Yesenia made a move to rejoin the crowd, but I hung back with Kai. "Is there any way two people could fit into one of those shipping containers?" I asked him.

Kai tucked a greasy strand of hair behind his ears and leaned against the mudbrick building behind him. "Like I said. I don't wanna know a thing about the cargo."

"Right," I said. "But hypothetically. How many people could fit inside?"

He picked something from between his teeth and spat. "I hear they've fit whole families before," he said. "This shit's commoner than you think, kid."

I turned back toward the dancing crowd and imagined the scene: bringing Paz into my house, introducing her to Baba, telling Father how she'd saved me. There were so many things she'd never experienced before—hot showers, heliocycles, ice cream. I imagined introducing her to Wen and Laksmi, all the questions they'd have for her. Once Father was healed, Paz and I could travel abroad to some Upper City where no one knew my name. Wen could forge papers for her, I was sure of it. I could enroll in university. We could start a new life. . . .

Yesenia took my arm and smiled. "Room for two?"

"I just . . ." My voice faltered. "I can't—"

Her hand rested on my shoulder. "I understand. Logic has no place in the face of such feelings." She found a seat on the stump of a tree, wincing slightly and stretching out her right knee. "But you must keep in mind, the girl has lived a life very different from yours. Don't deceive yourself into thinking you understand what it means to be from Lower City. I've lived here nearly fifty years and still I know I'm not from here."

"But how is that possible?" I asked. "You've made your whole life here."

"The difference is in the choice. You and I both chose to leave Upper City and come here. Paz had no such choice."

I sat on the grass beside Yesenia. She took two pieces of candied ginger from a pouch around her neck and offered one to me. It tasted delicious—spicy but sweet.

"You know, I left Upper City when I was about your age. You are what, seventeen?"

"Sixteen," I said.

"I was nineteen when I decided to join those planning defection. Silly as it sounds, I joined because I was heartbroken over some boy. . . ." She laughed. "Such tragedies we create with our lives! If things had been different, I may have stayed in Upper City. Love is a force so strangely strong. . . ."

She chewed the candied root and sighed.

I considered this for a moment. If she was nineteen when she left, that would make her almost seventy now.

"How many of you are out here?" I asked. "Exiles, I mean?"

"I know of a handful," she said. "Most of us went our separate ways. But there most certainly are more. The elders in Paraíso know about some of us—and sometimes they ask for favors in return for protection from Las Oscuras, who have targeted our kind in the past. But I prefer to avoid the Library and its leaders altogether. Their bloodlust makes me suspect that they're not entirely what they seem."

A cool wind caught the hairs at the back of my neck. I turned from the healer and looked over the trash hills, then farther east to the snow-covered mountains in the distance. The full moon hadn't yet breached the horizon, but its glow was so brilliant that it looked like some bright metropolis was blazing into the sky just beyond the peaks.

"They teach us about you guys in school," I said. "The defectors of the fifties. They call it a mass suicide. There's this horrible footage. Bodies blown to pieces. Beheadings . . ."

Yesenia shook her head. "It makes sense that they'd tell it that way. They want you to believe there's no alternative, no way out. If more people knew, then perhaps . . ." She looked toward the mountains, and her voice trailed off.

"Have you heard about a commune north of Serena? I can't remember the name exactly. San . . . San . . ."

Yesenia looked at me, surprised. "Where did you hear of San Pedro?"

"San Pedro—that's it. A man in Las Termas mentioned it to us, but I wasn't sure I could believe him."

"I know of it," Yesenia said. "A new hope out in the desert. The journey is almost certain death—rogue land mines, nomadic thieves, lands drenched with chemical waste. Still, I pray that their community will thrive. I don't have the strength to make the journey, but I think often of those who've risked everything to try to make the world anew."

The musicians finished their song and exited the stage, and a hush came over the crowd. The play was about to begin. All around me, people took their seats. I waited for Paz to sit on the grass beside me. But she was nowhere to be seen.

3 0

PAZ

Moonglow pushed hard against the peaks of the Cordillera as I walked through the empty streets of Serena, Vio at my side. The music coming from the town square had stopped, which meant the play would be starting soon. Rumi would be wondering where I was. Maybe I'd tell him I got caught up dancing, that I found a seat someplace else. It didn't matter what I said, really. He wouldn't suspect anything as awful as the truth.

The air swelled with the hum of insects and the trill of frogs. My ears picked out the light tap and scratch of an animal in a nearby tree. I closed my eyes and pictured the creature—a degú, I guessed, or maybe a colocolo. I imagined him struck dead by my stone.

Vio whimpered beside me, like he knew what was coming. I knelt down and scratched behind his ears. "You can't come where I'm going, regalón," I said. "But there's lots of kind people here in Serena. I'm sure you'll find your way."

That's when I heard the crying, somewhere outside Serena's wall.

Tué-tué, tué-tué-tué.

El Chonchón. El brujo que anuncia la muerte.

Uphill ahead of me, the path forked in two. To the left was Yesenia's tree hut. To the right was the clocktower. Life and death. Vengeance and mercy. *World without end.*

Clutching my sling and stones, I scaled the wall and walked toward the clocktower.

31

RUMI

Thick marble columns at the front of the stage held up a roof overgrown with moss. A blue curtain strung between the columns hid the stage from view. The curtain was patched and torn in places, but it looked majestic as it rippled in the evening wind.

I called to Vio when I saw him weaving through the crowd, and he came toward me. But Paz had vanished—just like that horrible night at the Lighthouse in Paraíso. With a sinking feeling, I wondered if, now that her mission was complete, she'd decided to head home without saying goodbye.

The crowd fell silent. From behind the patched curtain, a man stepped out wearing a tasseled cap. It took me a moment to recognize him as Aurelio, the sentry who'd guided us to Yesenia's hut earlier that evening. In Spanish, he began to introduce the play and its players, and Yesenia leaned toward me to translate.

"*Tonight's play tells the story of how Man stole fire from Jaguar,*" she said. "*This is an ancient myth of the Kayapó people, who live in the distant rainforests on the other side of the mountains. Tonight, our troupe will interpret this tale.*"

With a flourish, the sentry pulled open the curtain and exited the stage.

At the center of the stage, a small fire burned. A large pot cooked on top of the fire.

Other than that, the stage was empty.

In the audience, everyone—even the children—waited, transfixed.

Just then a beautiful girl in a long, spotted dress entered the stage. The girl's eyes were painted dark, like a cat's. Her long black hair was pulled together into a tail. She was tall and lithe, and with every step, her weight sank pendulously into her hips. She sat on her knees near the steaming pot and, with a gentle hand, began to caress the skin of her arms—as though she were cleaning her fur.

The jaguar girl continued like this—cleaning her fur, tending the fire, stirring the pot—when a young boy stumbled onto the stage, a filthy swatch of cloth his only clothing. He looked half-starved as he stumbled, peering under rocks and scooping imaginary insects into his mouth. All the while, the jaguar blew on steaming spoonfuls of stew from the pot and licked them daintily into her mouth.

Eventually, the jaguar and the boy lay down to sleep at opposite ends of the stage. When they woke, the jaguar stretched herself and yawned, looking relaxed and rested. But the boy looked around furtively, as though he feared that everything in the forest was out to kill him. He darted across the stage, crouching and listening.

The jaguar watched him for a while and then smiled, shaking her head. Finally, she called out to him. "Ser humano," she said.

The boy froze in a terrified crouch.

"Ven aquí, ser humano."

The boy approached her cautiously on hands and knees.

"¿Tienes hambre, pobrecito?"

The boy nodded and clutched his empty belly.

"¿Tienes frío, pobrecito?"

The boy nodded again and clutched his arms, shivering.

"Quiero enseñarte, ser humano. Quiero enseñarte a vivir como yo."

Yesenia leaned in to translate. "The jaguar says she wants to teach the boy. She wants to teach him fire and hunting—how to live as a predator, not as prey."

Up on the stage, the jaguar girl showed the boy how to make a fire. She showed him how to string a bow and arrow and how to gut his prey. With gentle hands, she cleaned the smudges of dirt and filth from his skin. Day after day, the jaguar showed the boy new skills. And each night, they shared pots of stew made from the catch of their hunt.

It seemed a happy if unusual friendship, though the title of the play—*How Man Stole Fire from Jaguar*—made it clear that the friendship wouldn't last. I thought back on all the times Paz had warned me of jaguars prowling the roadways at night, though in our entire journey we'd never once seen one. And I remembered how desperately I'd begged Father to see the jaguars at the wildlife park in Sucre as a child, how in the adverts the jaguar had been touted as the fiercest, most cunning creature ever to have lived. And it made me wonder. As Upper City told it, the story of the jaguar was a tale of wild nature subdued; as Paz told it, it was a tale of wildness untamed. Either way, the jaguar was a symbol intended to plant seeds of fear, to make me trust the tellers of the story because I was helpless without them.

But this play, was it trying to show me something different?

On the stage in front of me, I watched morning break. The boy woke first and secretly hid a knife beneath his tattered clothes.

When the jaguar girl woke up, the pair went together into the forest to hunt. But while she lay in wait for her prey, the boy crept behind her and thrust his knife beneath her dress, skinning her of her beautiful spots.

The jaguar screamed in agony as the boy wrapped her spotted skin around his own shoulders like a cape. Then the boy took a flaming stick from the fire, held it over his head like a trophy, and poured water on the jaguar's flame. Whooping and howling, the boy ran from the stage with his flame held high and his spotted cape flowing behind him.

It felt so real, I could hardly breathe.

The jaguar girl, bleeding and nearly naked, crawled toward the fire pit. She touched the wet coals and wept, and the torches on the stage went dark.

When the lights came up again, the stage was filled with the boy and his friends laughing and playing. Each wore a cap made from the jaguar's spots. They hunted for their dinner. They lit a campfire and cooked a meal and ate their fill.

But all the while in the darkness behind them, the jaguar stalked them. When the boys went into the forest to hunt, she was there. When the boys played swords or danced around the fire, she was there.

That night, as the boys slept, the jaguar crept into their camp, her movements silent and unfaltering. She was coming for the kill. She crouched over the boy with the spotted cape as he slept beside the fire, and her jaws opened impossibly wide—wide enough to swallow the boy's skull whole. But just before she closed her jaws, she looked out across the audience, meeting our gazes. The light from the torch flames flashed like a knife against her yellow eyes and long white fangs. And the stage went dark.

3 2

PAZ

The face of the clocktower floated above the trees like a second, terrible moon.

There was a tree growing out of the base of the tower, and it seemed to be eating the tower bit by bit, swallowing the old stones into its tangled guts. I ran my hands across the stone and then reached out to touch the tree, felt the rivers of sap and water flowing up and down the trunk, into its heart and back out again, like my own blood. But I didn't feel like a tree. No, I felt more like the stony tower—like something useless being eaten, not something new getting strong.

On the wind I caught the sweet hint of tobacco, and I turned to see the comandante standing, shimmering, in the darkness. The hot orange tip of his cigarette threw embers into the leaves.

"Buenas," he said.

His voice was just as I remembered—a viper ready to strike. But as he came closer, I saw that he looked sick. His forehead dripped with sweat. Red veins webbed the whites of his eyes.

I backed myself against the roots of the tree behind me.

"Don't be frightened, mija," he said. "I'm not angry with you. You missed the checkpoint at Isla de Lobos, but I understand. You did what you had to do." He blew a stream of smoke across my face and smiled. "None of that matters now. Our moment has finally come."

He took the cigarette from his lips and twisted its burning tip into the tree's trunk, then he flicked the dead stub into the dark. I could smell the tangy char of his breath.

He took a step toward me, and I stepped back, pressing against the tree behind me.

"Such a tiny thing . . . ," the comandante said. His silvery face drew toward mine, and he rested his hand firm on my hip. His thumb circled the ridge of my hip bone as his hands gripped my waist. Strong hands. Hands that had killed and would kill again.

I wriggled from between his body and the tree, and he let me go.

"I'm doing my job, aren't I?" I said. I tried to sound bold, but I was shaking. "I guided the kid up here safe and sound. I took him to Yesenia, just like you said."

"You've done very well, Paz," he said. "Very well. We're all proud of you. I'm proud of you. You've proven yourself to be a revolutionary of the highest order."

He pulled a vial the size of a clamshell from his pocket and clutched it in his sinner's arm. It looked much like the little jars I'd seen on the shelves in Yesenia's tree hut. But inside the comandante's vial, a bloodred liquid swashed against the glass.

"The boy will return to Upper City soon," the comandante said. "Is this true?"

I nodded.

"And he still trusts you deeply, does he not?"

I couldn't tell what he was getting at. "Deep as a person can trust, I'd say."

The comandante coughed and spat phlegm on the ground. "Very good," he said, stepping closer to me. "The final piece is about to move into place, Paz. You are the pin that binds."

I backed away, edging toward the open forest. But just then two hands gripped my arms from behind, and I screamed. The shark-faced man breathed down my neck, lips curled in a rotten-toothed snarl.

"Now, now, mija. What's this?" the comandante said. "Are you no longer loyal to the cause?"

"I'm loyal, señor. I'm loyal," I said. But I was stumbling over my words. "I've done all the things you asked. I just don't appreciate being tugged around. Like you said, I kept good on my promise so far. Just one more thing and it's done. Right?"

The shark-faced man loosed his grip, but he didn't let go.

"You've done beautifully, Paz. Better, even, than we could have hoped. It's clear to us now that the boy doesn't just trust you. It's clear that he's coming to love you."

I blinked. "To love me?"

"I know you're not so unobservant, mija. Have you not seen how he looks at you? How he speaks to you? How he wants nothing more than to win your favor?"

I shrugged, my cheeks hot. "I guess I never took notice."

The comandante smiled and held the bloodred vial up to the light of the moon. "Here is the final piece of the puzzle," he said, tapping the glass with his fingernail.

"What is it?" I asked.

"This, mija, is what I lovingly call the Trickster. It looks just like the medicine the healer will give to the Upper City boy tonight. The same vial, the same scarlet liquid. You'll swap this vial with the remedy the healer gives to the boy, and you'll give the healer's remedy to us." He placed the vial in a small leather pouch and passed the pouch to me.

I breathed relief. I just needed to keep up the act a little longer. Then Rumi could return to his shining city with medicine for his father, and I could flee. North, perhaps. To San Pedro.

I remembered Rumi's question, then—*What if there were a way to leave all of this behind?* A thought came to me, and my heart fluttered. What if I asked Rumi to join me? To bring the healer's cure back to his father in St. Iago and then to join me in search of San Pedro, the one place trying to grow something new? I could start the journey ahead of him, hide out in the foothills. By the time the comandante came looking for me, I'd have disappeared. . . .

"My pleasure, Señor Comandante," I said. I forced a smile as I shoved the pouch into my pocket. "It's a first-rate plan, swapping out the medicines, getting the swank-ass kid to trust me and all—real clever."

The comandante said nothing.

I took a step toward the path, but the shark-man's grip tightened around my arms.

"Not so fast, mija," the comandante said. An awful reptile grin spread across his face. He waved off his man and pushed me up against the tree. His body pressed against me, his sinner's hand on my hip, his other hand at my throat. His eyes clawed at mine.

"I must apologize, Paz," he said. "I haven't been entirely truthful with you. . . ."

My heart raced. There was something vicious in the way he was looking at me, touching me. "What do you mean?" I asked.

He cupped my face with his palm, running his thumb across my cheek. Then his hand on my face went rigid. He gripped both sides of my jaw and locked it open. My eyes welled up. I tried to speak, but with his hand gripping my jaw, all I could do was groan as he pulled me against him and pressed his mouth onto mine. The stubble of his skin burned my lips. His tongue wormed into my mouth. I wanted to cry out, to bite off his tongue, to spit in his face, but he held my jaw firm. His hot saliva swirled with mine.

I couldn't do a thing.

My mind was blank when his tongue at last slid from my mouth. He wiped his lips with the back of his sinner's hand. "There you have it," he said. "The choice is yours now."

I spat on the ground and willed myself not to cry.

"What do you mean?" I asked. "What choice?"

He smiled. "I gifted you something with my kiss, mija. The beautiful virus—Zabrán, our savior. The same miracle eating away at the boy's father as we speak is now within you."

His hands clasped my hips again. This time I didn't fight.

"You mean you—?"

"That's right. I too have taken on the blessing of this sickness," he said. "Remember: our bodies are our only weapons, the one thing that brings us within striking distance of those Upper City swine. But our bodies can be turned against us too.

"I feared I wouldn't be able to trust you—such a young girl, and a new recruit!—to carry out our plan. How, after all, could I be certain that you'd willingly send this boy you'd come to care for to his death? You see, giving you this gift was the only way, mija."

"His death?" I asked.

The comandante coughed into his hand. I could see now that his sweaty skin and deep-sunk eyes were the early signs of the virus. "That little vial in your pocket is very, very important," he said. "The vial itself is coated with the virus—little miracles just waiting to spring into action. The moment the boy touches it, he'll be contaminated without realizing. He'll return to his city unaware, and the virus will spread like wildfire. It will jump cities. It will be the beginning of the end! Switch that vial for the one the healer gives to the boy, and you can keep the healer's cure for yourself.

"If you choose not to swap the healer's vial with our own, you will die. Do you understand? You'll die slowly and horribly. If you choose to be a fool and spare the boy, he'll return to his city without ever knowing that you sacrificed your life to save his. And everything will go on as it always has, with Upper City continuing their ascent at the expense of our suffering. . . .

"Back in the Wastes of Paraíso, I saw a spark in you," the comandante continued. "The spark of a true revolutionary. Now is your chance to end the cycle—to reset the scales that have always tipped in their favor! Don't allow your feelings to stand in the way of the greater good. Don't forget all of those who have died, praying this day would come. . . ."

"And if I switch your vial with the real one," I said, numb, dazed, "I get to keep the real one for myself?"

"That's right, mija," the comandante said. "The choice is yours. Choose well, and I'll meet you here at the clocktower at dawn to celebrate the coming of a new era. Choose poorly, and your bones will rot, unburied, gnawed upon by dogs. And your name will ring forever as the traitorous puta who betrayed our cause."

The comandante took a step away, and I fell back against the tree, stunned and hollow.

"I suggest you hurry, though, child," he said. "The town's performance is coming to a close, and the boy will be leaving for his city soon thereafter."

With that, the comandante motioned to the shark-faced man, and the two of them readied to leave. My chest heaved as I watched them walk back into the forest. No, I thought. Not like this. There had to be something I could say—something I could do. I just needed more time. . . .

"Wait!" I called out. Both men stopped. "How do I know you won't steal the cure for yourself?"

The comandante turned. On his face was a strange, knowing smile.

"That is a very good question," he said. "A question I suspected you might ask."

I stood up bold and tall as the comandante walked back toward me, smiling his joyless smile. This time I stared straight into his shimmering face.

"Gustavo," the comandante said, snapping his fingers. At once the shark-faced man unsheathed his knife and came up behind the comandante, holding the knife to his neck.

"Here is how you know, mija," the comandante said.

And with one swift pull, the knife sliced the comandante's throat.

I screamed and stumbled back against the tangle of roots behind me. The comandante's body jerked and shuddered to the ground. He held my stare as blood flowed thick down his neck.

The shark-man cradled the comandante's head in his hands as his body went limp and still. Then Gustavo crossed himself and hoisted the blood-soaked body over his shoulder.

"Now you see the depths of your leader's loyalty," he said. "May you one day prove worthy of such noble blood."

I sank to my knees and fell to the ground as the man carried the limp body into the forest. My whole self trembled. I gasped for breath and closed my eyes. I tried hard as I could to remember Rumi's kiss—how soft and gentle it had been, the way his lips had moved along with mine. But the taste in my mouth now was bitter as blood. There was no sweetness left in all the world. This world had choked my mother lifeless. It had damned the kids in the trash hills to a life of fire and smoke. It had spat into me the vengeance of a million souls. In a world so dark and bitter, there was no room for sweetness and light. There was no room for love or hope or soft, tender touch.

And from this world, there was no way out.

3 3

R U M I

The curtain closed on the stage. A giant golden moon rose over the mountains, bathing the audience in unearthly light as they stood and cheered for the players taking their bows.

But I stayed seated. The eyes of the jaguar had seared into my mind. They were the eyes of an ancient anger left to seethe in the dark. The threat of the jaguar had stalked me my entire journey, yet the jaguar herself had never appeared. I'd seen traces of her anger—in Auralee, in Beto, even in Paz. Was she out there somewhere, waiting to come in for the kill?

Yesenia rose with a groan from her stump, and I helped her to her feet.

"I have to hand it to Aurelio," she said. "I enjoyed that more than I expected. I suppose some stories are too timeless to botch, even for our ragtag theater troupes." She looked down then at the yellow pup wagging his tail at her feet. "And who is this little friend?"

"This is our dog, Vio," I said, then quickly corrected myself. "Paz's dog."

She patted his head and peered up at the moon.

"Well, Rumi," she said. "It's getting late. We'll go to my hut now to titrate the medicine for your father, and then it should nearly be time to meet Kai at the loading docks."

I looked one last time over the crowd. Still no Paz.

I tried to think rationally. She'd probably gone back to the tree hut for some rest. There would still be time to talk to her while Yesenia prepared the medicine, time to explain what I'd meant by my question in the trash hills. Where besides the healer's hut could she be?

Yesenia took my arm, reading the worry in my eyes as I scanned the faces around me. "Remember, Rumi. The girl has her own feelings. You cannot expect to understand."

I felt like I might start crying. "But I'm running out of time," I said.

A cold wind blew down from the mountains. Yesenia's torch cast a small circle of light on the three of us—the healer, the dog, and I—as we walked back to her hut in silence. As we approached Yesenia's garden, the dog raised his nose to the air, sniffing and whimpering in the direction of the forest on the other side of the wall. But the hut itself was empty.

So it's true, I thought. She left without saying goodbye. I was an assignment, nothing more. The thought made my body go numb.

Paz was gone.

Yesenia rekindled the stove and then sat at her desk. From the pouch around her neck, she produced a key that unlocked the small metal drawer beneath her microscope. Inside the drawer was a vial filled halfway with clear, viscous liquid.

"This vial represents a single dose of treatment," she said. "Your father will likely need multiple doses, since he's been sick for so long, but with Upper City's molecular sequencing capabilities, the Governance labs should be able to replicate the medicine easily enough."

Using needle-nosed forceps, she took two pinches of powder, each from a different clay bowl, and carefully weighed the amount. Then she poured these powders into the vial. The liquid inside turned instantly red—a chemical reaction the color of blood. She held the vial in front of her and turned it slowly in her fingertips.

"You remember the clocktower, yes?" she said. "Go down the path that leads through the garden and scale the wall—it's shorter on this side of the city and easy enough to climb. On the other side, you'll find a forking trail. Left leads to the clocktower; right leads to the loading docks, which are located near an Old World airport just north of the trash hills. This is the safest route, since it passes through the forest. You don't want to be caught out in the open near the trash hills. Remember: you won't have much time once you hear the freight copters overhead. Since Paz is gone, you must do this on your own. I would go with you if I could."

I nodded.

"It's been such a pleasure to meet you, Rumi," Yesenia said, locking the drawer and turning again to face me. "I can't even remember when I last spoke to a citizen of Upper City. I almost forgot what it was like. . . ." She seemed suddenly very old.

"Does it make you wish you could go back?" I asked.

"No. I don't regret my decision. But there are things I miss." She smiled and closed her eyes. "I miss cinnamon, for instance. I miss long drives at night on empty streets. I miss toothpaste and acetaminophen. And the music . . . My god, I miss having music at my fingertips."

I pictured the black disc spinning in the space behind the

screen. Tonight, I'd return to that world—a world of light and sound and abundance. A world of magic . . .

"Please," I said. "Do you have any idea where she might be?"

Yesenia opened her eyes. "If I were her," she said, handing me the vial, "and the boy I loved were about to leave my life forever . . . I'd probably want to be alone."

I looked at the vial in my hand and felt its weight. The weight of my journey. It seemed like a lifetime ago that I'd sat at the dinner table with Father and Baba. How different the world had seemed to me then. How changed I felt now.

"You have goodness in you, Rumi. I'm grateful to know that there are still those like you being born inside those walls." She kissed the tips of her fingers, crossed herself, and touched her fingers to my forehead. "Vaya con Dios, my child."

I stepped from the warmth of the hut and into the chilly night air with nothing but my pack and Yesenia's medicine gripped tightly in my hand. The trees above creaked in the wind. Once the copter flew over my head, Kai said I had an hour at most to get to the loading docks. That didn't give me much time to find her—and I didn't even know where to look.

So I started running.

I sprinted to the center of town calling Paz's name, not caring who heard me. The yellow dog ran silently alongside me. "Paz!" I cried out into the empty space. The pup's anxious eyes searched the square with mine. "Paz, where are you?" But my voice fell dead on the dusty streets. The patchwork curtain rippled silently over the stage, lit by the full moon.

I couldn't believe it. She really was gone.

Clutching Yesenia's vial in my hand, I walked back the way I'd come. By the time I reached Yesenia's hut, the lamps inside had gone dark. My eyes filled with hot, helpless tears.

"You've got to stay here, pup," I said to the dog. "I can't take you where I'm going."

He stared up at me, tail wagging.

"Listen. Paz is the one who left you, not me. She's the one you should blame."

He sniffed the air and shifted slightly on his haunches.

I sighed. "Fine. Follow me if you want. But you're just prolonging the inevitable. . . ."

I hoisted the dog over the wall, which on this side of the city was just a mound of rubble that I couldn't imagine offered much, if any, protection. In the forest on the other side, I followed the footpath until I came to the fork Yesenia mentioned.

Left to the clocktower, right to the loading docks.

The trees groaned in the wind.

But beneath that sound, I heard something else. A small whimpering in the direction of the clocktower. *If I were her,* Yesenia had said, *I'd want to be alone.*

Vio barked once at the sound and took off running in that direction.

I took one step, then another, down the path to the clocktower.

"Hello?" I called. "Is somebody there?"

The crying stopped.

Against my better judgment, I moved closer. The silver clock face seemed to glow through the trees. "I don't mean to bother you," I said. "I'm just looking for . . . my friend."

There was a sniffle and then a shifting sound as someone stood from the ground. I peered into the mottled darkness to see a small figure standing alone in a green shirt and frayed jean shorts, wiping her eyes. The dog wagged his tail at her side.

"Paz?" I said.

She blinked back at me and tried to smile. "Hey, flaquito," she said. There were tears in her eyelashes.

I set my pack on the ground and rushed toward her.

"What are you doing out here?" I asked.

She didn't answer, just took a step toward me and rested her head on my chest. Not understanding, not asking why, I held her in my arms. My pulse flew. I felt cold all over. I wanted nothing in the world more than this. To be with her.

This was my chance.

"Paz," I said, trying to remember the words I'd practiced. "There's something I've been wanting to ask you, but I didn't know how. So I'm just going to say it. I want you to come with me. I want you to come to Upper City."

Paz stepped back. She looked almost feverish. The only color in her face was the green of her eyes. "Don't be stupid, weón," she said. "That's not how the world works."

"Just listen," I said, my voice stern. "You can leave all of this behind you. We can go together. I'll protect you. I'll make sure you—"

But she cut me off before I could say any more. "Is that Yesenia's medicine?" she asked.

I nodded.

Paz opened her palm, and I passed her the vial. She turned it over in her hand, gazing into it as though it held the secret of the universe.

Just then I heard a low, distant rumble. The freight copter. Slowly the rumble chopped into a roar. With a surge of wind and a flash of light, the copter passed over our heads, flying toward the trash hills. The trees above swirled violently in its storm. I held Paz close as the wind whipped pine needles from the ground and hurtled them against our skin.

Then everything went silent.

But Paz kept clinging to me. I wrapped my arms around her. She was so small, but I could feel the strength in the curves of her muscles as she pressed herself against me.

"My god, Paz," I whispered. "I'm so glad I found you. I don't know what I would've done if I had to leave you behind. . . ."

She lifted her head from my chest and looked into my eyes. With one hand, I traced the delicate curve of her jaw. But when I pulled her close to meet her lips in a kiss, her eyes flared with fear. The wild fear of a cornered animal.

"No," she said, pushing me away.

"I don't understand," I said. "Paz, you have no idea what it's like in Upper City. I want to take you away from all of this. I want to *be with you.*"

She shook her head. There were tears in her eyes. "I'm Lower City, flaco. You're Upper City. And there's not a goddam thing we can do about it. Can't you understand that? It's never going to change. There's too many strings holding it all in place."

"But . . . there's a way." I touched her cheek with my thumb, aching to hold her. To kiss her. "There has to be a way. It isn't fair. It isn't fair."

I was crying uncontrollably now. I tried to pull her to me, but she shoved me away with all her strength, as though I had some kind of plague.

I took a step back, stunned. Yesenia was right. I didn't understand the person standing across from me at all. I could never understand her. She might as well have been a stranger.

I wiped my eyes with my sleeve. "Okay, then," I said. "I have to go."

There was nothing else to say.

Paz passed Yesenia's vial back to me. She wiped her nose with the back of her hand.

"Vaya con Dios, Rumi," she said.

With the sound of her voice ringing in my ears, I turned from her and ran down the path toward the loading docks. Vio barked once and then went silent as I ran from the clocktower, my cheeks streaked with tears. My heart pounding her name.

PART V
FLOOD
AND FIRE

3 4

RUMI

She wouldn't let me kiss her goodbye. Why wouldn't she let me kiss her goodbye?

I knocked my head against my knees in the hollow darkness and replayed the moment. What I'd said. What she'd said. The wild look in her eyes as she pushed me away.

The shipping container lurched in the bowels of the freight copter, and I instinctively felt for Yesenia's vial to make sure it was safe. This tiny vial meant that soon the world would return to normal and everything outside the walls would fizzle into news clips and dreams. In a few hours, I'd take tea with Baba and sleep under the sheets of my own bed. I'd get my tattoo removed and return to school and sneak behind the screen with Laksmi and Wen. Soon I'd forget the smell of old urine and rotting fish, forget the color of the ocean, forget Paz.

Soon.

The copter dipped once, then again, until finally it landed on solid ground and the engine shuddered off. In total darkness I waited, listening.

The hatch unlocked with a whir and a mechanized clank, and the heavy thuds of the operator's boots grew faint as he walked away. When his footsteps were gone, I pulled a lever and lifted the hatch open, just as Kai had instructed. The dim gray of early morning met my eyes. The familiar quiet of St. Iago at dawn.

I crawled from the hatch and climbed down the side of the copter onto the landing pad, heart pounding. A crew would come soon to unload the cargo. If someone saw me, I didn't want to imagine what would happen. I sprinted across the landing pad to a service ladder and descended it two rungs at a time. A meter from the ground, I jumped, stumbled, and crouched to get my bearings. To my surprise, I was on a side street I recognized. The avenue to my left led to Turing Square, while the alley to my right headed west toward home.

I turned right and ran as fast as I'd run in all my life.

I shot glances behind me as I ran, but no one seemed to be following. Gradually I slowed to a jog, then to a walk. My footsteps on the granite sidewalk made tidy, rhythmic sounds, and a wave of calm swept over me. I was safe. I was home.

I reached into my pack for my specs and put them on. In an instant, the streets lit up with scrolling colors, spiraling images, dancing rays of light. Glittering girls smiled at me in fiercely short dresses as ads traced the shapes of their bodies. The cafés had yet to open, but the holograms in their windows shimmered with plates of sticky buns and madeleines, steaming bowls of hot cereal, and cups of milky tea.

Dozens of missed message notifications dropped into my view, but I blinked them all away. I wasn't ready for that. Not yet. In the window of one café, I caught sight of myself. My hair was matted, my tattoo crusted with grime. The bandage wrapped around my calf was brown with old blood.

This is what Lower City looks like, I thought. I never have to feel this again.

Within an hour, I reached my neighborhood. Sprinklers watered my neighbors' lawns. Streetlights lit the pavement. The trees along the road were silent, free of birdsong. When at last I reached the front gate of my house, I paused. This was the moment I'd imagined since leaving St. Iago, the moment I'd dreamed of and hoped for and feared would never happen. Outside the front door, I slipped off my boots, crusted with Lower City filth, and set them aside.

I wrapped my hand around the doorknob and twisted it open.

The house was dark. The air smelled sour, like dirty laundry. A tray with two cups of tea sat untouched on the coffee table, molding. I imagined Baba brewing this tea, waiting for me to come home. Waiting. Waiting.

"Baba?" I called.

I flipped on the light in the kitchen. Baba's plants—the violet and jade, the orchids and bromeliads—were brown and wilted. The soil in their pots was dry.

"Baba?" I said, unlatching my specs. "It's me. It's Rumi."

The stale air followed me as I climbed the stairs to Father's empty bedroom. I pulled down the ladder and climbed into the annex, not sure what to expect. But at the top of the ladder, my knees buckled. Father's bed was empty. Father was gone.

3 5

PAZ

A cold wind sang through the hollows of the clocktower. Vio sniffed the ground, wet with the comandante's blood, but he turned up his nose at it and came to lick my face instead.

Our bodies are our only weapons, the comandante had said. But how awful it was to have a body in this world. I felt the weight of the vial in my pocket and threw curses down at the dark, bitter earth. I had no place. I had no people. I'd betrayed everyone I'd ever known.

Except for Rumi, who will never know, I thought, rubbing out the aches in my sinner's arm. Rumi, who must think I hate him.

Just then I heard footsteps crunching down the path.

In the morning's thin light, I could see Yesenia, bundles of herbs strapped to her back. "Hello?" she called. "Is someone there?"

I curled into a ball at the base of the clocktower and tried to disappear. But the pup barked, and Yesenia came closer. "Paz, my child," she said. "Have you been here all night?"

"Sí, señora," I said.

"The Upper City boy, did he find you before he left?"

Somewhere in the forest, a dove called his daybreak song.

"Sí, señora."

She drew back her hair and looked at me closer. "Do you wish to be left alone, child?"

"Sí, señora . . . ," I said. But the words caught in my throat, and I shivered.

Yesenia crouched in the pine needles beside me and wrapped me in her arms. "Come, child," she said. "Let's get you warm."

Inside her tree hut, the old woman brewed spiced tea and wrapped me in a wool blanket beside the woodstove. At her touch, my body shook into sobs. They poured out of me like a rising tide, like my tears could flood the world. I still had anger—so much anger—but there wasn't anywhere to point it now. At Rumi and his city? At the comandante? At this old healer with kindness and wisdom in her eyes?

I pulled back from her and wiped the tears from my face. I had nothing left to lose.

"I'm sorry, señora," I said. "It's just that I've got no place to go. . . ."

And so I told the healer my story—my whole story. I even showed her the tat on my chest, a snake swallowing its own tail. Yesenia listened without saying a thing.

"Last night, when the comandante put Zabrán inside me," I said at last, "he told me I could give your cure to Rumi or I could keep it for myself. He told me to switch it with this one, which he'd infected." I took out the leather pouch containing the vial the comandante had given me. Yesenia used a scrap of cloth to take the vial from the pouch, holding it up to the glow of the woodstove. Inside, the liquid looked thick as blood.

"I could have taken your cure from Rumi," I said. "It's not like I'm ever gonna see him again. But I—I just . . ."

Yesenia tossed the vial, the cloth, and the leather pouch into the woodstove and then turned to me with a smile. "Oh, child," she said. "You mustn't carry the whole world on those skinny shoulders of yours. You'll snap like a twig under its weight!"

Without another word, she walked to her microscope and unlocked the drawer beneath it. My heart fluttered. She hadn't called me a traitor. She hadn't torn open my shirt and bared my chest so the world could see my mark. When she came back, she handed me a tiny cup of the same medicine she'd given to Rumi.

"Drink it down," she said, and I did. It was bitter and heady as skunkroot.

She touched a cool hand to my cheek, and I softened into her. This must be how it feels to have a mother, I thought. Somebody tender and patient who wants only for her child to feel safe.

"Now, tell me," she said. "What do you mean that you have nowhere to go?"

I set the cup on the floor beside me and pulled my knees to my chest. "I can't go home to Paraíso," I said. I could feel the tears coming back. "Not with my mark. The Library burns traitors like me without a trial or anything. And if I stay here, the comandante's men will find me. They have eyes everywhere. They'll know I didn't send Rumi home with the virus. They'll figure it out somehow. And I'll live in fear till the day a knife slits open my throat."

"Shh . . . Shh . . ." She placed her hand on my knee. "The light of hope here is dim, I'll admit that much. But it's still there. You just need to look more closely! Just yesterday the Upper City boy asked me about a place. A commune north of here."

I sniffed. "He asked about San Pedro?"

Yesenia nodded. "So you know it too. The journey through the desert would be difficult, there's no mistaking that. But who knows? It might just be a great adventure."

I pulled the blanket around my shoulders. San Pedro. The only place on Earth where I wouldn't be met with fire or sword. "And you know how to get there?" I asked.

She smiled, soft and warm. "Here's what we'll do. I'm going into town to deliver some herbs, and I'll leave word that a brave young soul wishes to make the journey. Perhaps we can find you a fellow pilgrim." She stood and strapped the large bundle of herbs to her back. "For now, just try to get some rest. Sleep will help to quicken the effects of the medicine. I'll be home in a few hours. And whatever you do, don't leave this hut."

I lay on my side in front of the woodstove and listened to her heavy steps creak down the ladder. The chill inside me melted with the warm tenderness all around. Maybe the world wasn't just violence and vengeance after all. Maybe there were other ways to beat Leviathan than by drinking up the sea.

That's when I heard the noise.

I sat up straight and listened.

On the ground below, Vio barked once, then went quiet. Then came the sound of someone climbing the ladder to the tree hut. But it wasn't Yesenia. This climber was quick and strong. My chest pounded. Were the comandante's men coming after me already? I hid in the corner beneath the thick wool blanket and waited for a tatted face to appear in the doorway.

The door flap pulled open. A voice called my name.

"Paz?"

The voice was familiar. A girl's voice.

"Paz? Where you at, chica?"

I peeked from beneath the blanket. "Auralee?" I said.

She smiled bright. "¡Oye, weona!" She carried nothing—not even a knife.

"What the hell're you doing here?" I said, standing to greet her.

"I came to find you guys," she said, peering under the table and behind Yesenia's cabinets and bookshelves. "I see you still got that puny mutt. But where's the kid?"

"Rumi? He's gone. Back to Upper City."

"You let him go?" Her words seemed friendly, but her movements were fidgety. Distracted. "What about your mission for Las Oscuras? Your vengeance?"

"They had plans," I said. "I didn't follow along."

"You turned soft on 'em, weón? Good for you, good for you!"

I remembered something then. Hadn't Beto said that Auralee hoped to make the trek north to San Pedro? With her dogs and her strength, and with my knowledge of maps and the land, we'd have a good chance at surviving the journey.

"Listen," I said. "I'm in trouble. Serious trouble. Las Oscuras is gonna come after me once they realize what I did. I've got to get out of here quick. Your friend Beto told us you've got plans to get to San Pedro. If you're looking for a hunting hand, I thought maybe we could—"

But a sound on the ledge outside the tree hut cut my words short. The door flap pulled open again, and the shadows of two men filled the room. Two Library elders.

My stomach dropped.

"I'm sorry, mija," Cienfuegos said. "But you've chosen your allegiances poorly." He turned to Auralee. "Bind her arms."

Auralee's sweetness disappeared in an instant. Before I could run, she wrenched my arms behind my back with hands firm as iron. I bucked and kicked, but her grip was too strong. Cienfuegos unsheathed his knife, slipped it under my shirt, and sliced the cloth with a firm yank—like gutting a kill.

"See?" Auralee said to Cienfuegos and the other elder who stood silent beside him. "Just like I told you. Initiation tat. That's her only one, far as I know. Just a newbie."

Cienfuegos ran the cold blade of his knife down my bare skin, and my guts felt hollow. Then he rammed his knee into my stomach. Once. Twice. I groaned and doubled forward with a gasp, drowning and floating all at the same time. Then came a blow to my head. My sight went splotched and gray. Darkness swept over me, and I slumped into nothingness.

I opened my eyes from the floor of the tree hut. Dirt on my lips, blood in my mouth. Dusk outside. Voices spoke in low tones. "She saved the boy, Solomon," Yesenia's voice begged. "She *betrayed* them. That has to count for something."

"She cared for the boy. So what?" Cienfuegos's voice was cold as metal. "She gets what she deserves. A traitor's fate."

Auralee's voice came then from the corner of the room. "What's the plan, then? I come back to Paraíso with you? You pardon me, all official-like? I don't mean to push things along too much, but I got my kids to get back to."

Silence.

"I'm sorry, child," Cienfuegos said at last. "But there are no pardons for traitors. The law is without exception." There was a scuffle. Shouting. A squirming body thrown next to mine. Auralee's body. Cienfuegos stuffed a cloth in her mouth to silence her screams.

I closed my eyes. Sank back into darkness.

And I dreamed.

Of Upper City.

Of a place full of sunshine.

The air shimmered with light. Rows of glass towers poured music from open windows. The streets shone sapphire blue, like the ocean in springtime. There wasn't a speck of trash. Even my twisted arm had changed into a healthy one, the ache of it gone. In the fluttering trees, a kiskadee bird sang. "Ugly bug!" he sang in English. "Look, what an ugly bug!"

On this dream street, I came to a wooden door, old and worn smooth. It seemed out of place in such a sparkling city. The door opened and behind it, a white stairway rose as far as I could see. But as I climbed, the stairway turned dark and dirty. The paint peeled off in thick flakes that fell at my feet like scabs.

And all of a sudden, I realized where I was.

In total dark, I crawled through the rubble till I found the door to the yellow apartment. But when I tried to step inside, I couldn't. The apartment was full—crowded with people breathing heavy breaths. I pushed through sweaty bodies to the back bedroom and shut myself inside. Huddled in that room, all together on the bed, was the family from the photographs—the mother and father and boy my age, the gap-toothed girl, the baby making a fuss of the bow on her head. All of them stared with desperate eyes at the door I'd just entered through.

The mother scribbled a few frantic words in her journal and then held it out. "Bernardo threw the microwave off the balcony yesterday," she said out loud as she held the notebook in front of her. "I don't know what to do. . . ."

And I woke.

There was a jostling motion. Vio barked somewhere nearby, but the sound was moving away from me. I opened my eyes. I was in the back of a prison carriage. A stranger at the front of the cart drove a pair of oxen.

Inside the carriage with me was Auralee.

36

RUMI

The fluorescent bulb in the annex buzzed.

The plastic around Father's cot had been thrown to the floor, and Baba sat slumped in a chair beside the empty bed, a cup of tea on the table beside him. His cheeks were sunken, his lips cracked, his eyes half-lidded and glassy.

"Baba?" I said.

He blinked and turned toward the sound of my voice.

"Who is there?" he asked.

I knelt down in front of him. "Baba. It's me."

He clutched my hand and pulled me toward him. "I have searched the house. I have searched everywhere!"

"It's me, Baba," I said. "It's Rumi."

He held my hand in his, touching each of my fingers. His eyes passed over my face without seeing before the light of recognition flashed through him.

"Rumi," he said at last.

I smiled, wanting to cry. "Yes, Baba."

He touched the tattoo creeping out of my shirt, his eyes still clouded. "What has happened to you?"

I squeezed his hand. "Let me make you some tea, Baba. Please."

"I have tea here. I made tea just this morning." He reached beside him for a cup of liquid blooming with splotches of mold. I took the cup before he could drink from it.

"I'll make you a fresh batch, Baba. I'll make enough for us both."

I forced back tears in the quiet morning light of the kitchen as I poured the moldy tea down the sink and set the kettle to boil. My hands ran across the smooth stone countertop as I waited, the neat rows of teacups, the clean glass window. All of it new and unbroken.

With a steaming pot of tea, I returned to the annex, where Baba waited, expectant like a child. He blew gently on his tea and took a sip. "It is not safe here, Rumi," he said, glancing at the ladder. "They come and wait by the door. I hear them knocking, and I hold my breath. They come and they wait."

I held my mug in my hands and sat on the floor by his feet. "Who comes?"

A spark flared in his eyes. "You have never been dense, child. You know who comes."

"Governance agents," I said.

"They first came two days after your father arrived with the sickness. They asked if your father had returned from his mission, and I said he had not. They asked where you'd gone, and I said you were abroad visiting universities. This is what your friend Wendell told me to say."

"But you knew where I really was," I said.

Baba nodded solemnly. "The men were certain your absence and your father's were connected. Then one day, they burst through our front door just as I was pulling open the entrance to this annex. They took him away." Baba set his teacup on the side table and folded his hands in his lap. "And now it is now, and you are here."

I blinked. "Where did they take him?"

Baba's face hung slack. "What does it matter? They took him to study the sickness. They have no treatment. They are only waiting for him to die."

I slid my hand into my pack and pulled out Yesenia's vial.

"I brought something back with me," I said, passing him the vial. He held it close to his face, squinting. The red liquid inside seemed to glow. "It's a cure for Father."

Baba covered his mouth with his hand. "Oh, child . . . ," he said.

His face flushed with color then, as though he'd just woken from a dream. He fumbled in his shirt pocket, pulled out a slip of paper, and handed it to me.

"They told me if you returned that I was to give this to you right away."

I unfolded the paper carefully. On it was a set of handwritten coordinates.

"Baba, is this where I think it is?"

But Baba stared transfixed at the cot where Father had spent his last days in this house. "I never thought . . . ," he muttered. "In all my life, I never thought I'd see the day. . . ."

Downstairs in the bathroom, I scrubbed the dirt from my face and examined myself in the mirror. I touched the silver ink on my neck and chest. The violence of it. The strange beauty. Then I opened the medicine cabinet. Hydrocortisone. Antihistamines. Butterfly bandages. Health. Life. Comfort. I closed the cabinet and pulled on a hoodie.

I didn't know what the Governance would do to me. But they

had Father. I had to get the medicine to them before it was too late.

Father's vintage cycle, the one he hardly ever used, was parked in its usual spot in the garage. I loaded the coordinates from Baba's note into my specs and keyed open the garage door. A wave of sunlight washed over me as I mounted the cycle. With the soft whir of the engine beneath me, I pressed down the pedal and sped into the warmth of the day.

Baba's coordinates, as I'd thought, took me to the East Stacks, a district at the outer limits of St. Iago. I'd never been there before. Wen once told me that a group of kids had disappeared into the Stacks years ago. He said the mirror-smooth columns had sucked them in, and that if you walked among the columns at dusk, you could still see their reflections pounding on the glass, begging to be released. My face tensed into a smile at the thought of Wen trying to scare me with urban legends. The Stacks were nothing compared to the streets of Paraíso. Nothing compared to the Wastes or the trash hills.

Still, the hairs on my neck stood as I rode east on the speedway, the sun glaring behind me. On either side of the highway, mirrored towers rose like a digital forest. Faceless server columns the size of skyscrapers extended in every direction.

Traffic on the speedway thinned until finally I reached my exit and descended into the Stacks. I drove slowly through the maze of buildings, following the directions in my specs, until at last my specs blinked silver. I had arrived at my destination. I stopped and powered off my cycle. The wind blew dust against the buildings' blue-glass faces. All around me hummed the low drone of massive serverplex fans.

"Hello?" I called hesitantly. "I'm . . . I'm here."

Above my head, the speedway rumbled.

Why would they call me here? I wondered. And what was I supposed to do now? There were no Governance officials waiting, no signs of life at all.

Still, I had the unmistakable feeling that I was being watched.

In my specs, I glimpsed something blinking on the face of a server column across the street. Warily, I walked over to it. There didn't appear to be any doors or windows on the entire building— or on any of the buildings, for that matter. Had there even been a blinking light at all?

An image of myself, warped and tinted, stared back at me from the building's mirror-smooth face. I reached out and touched my steely blue reflection, staring at the spot where I thought I'd seen the light, but nothing happened.

A wave of terror swept over me then. Maybe the Governance had lured me to the middle of nowhere so they could "remove" me. Maybe they'd done the same thing to Father. I shot a glance over my shoulder, half expecting to see a blue-suited Governance official standing behind me with a pistol aimed between my eyes.

But no one was there.

I turned back to the server column. My distorted reflection stared at me from inside the glass, helpless and confused.

Just then the light flared again—a small square glowing on the surface of the building. It seemed to be some kind of sense pad. A scanner. I touched my finger to it and waited.

The blue square flashed three times and disappeared.

Instantly, my specs displayed a digital grid overlaid on the space around me. Embedded within the grid was a single, fluid line. A guide. A map.

I followed the line deep into the maze of server columns. My heart raced as I rounded corner after corner—each one identical to the last—until I'd completely lost my bearings. At every turn, my reflection stared back at me, disoriented and afraid. Ready to turn back and run as fast as I could from that place, I rounded one final corner. And there it was. At the base of an otherwise unmarked server column: a single, handle-less door.

I could barely breathe.

As I walked toward it, the door slid open to reveal a white staircase on the other side. The staircase curled in a rectilinear spiral, seemingly infinite, above my head. There were no sounds. No signs. No adverts dancing in my specs. Just a thin line directing me upward.

I followed the line seven stories up. Another unmarked door opened as I approached it, leading me into an empty hallway. The line in my specs continued down this corridor a few meters more and ended at a door. As I approached, the grid in my specs disappeared and the door opened onto a dimly lit room, empty save for a single lab desk. From behind the desk, a woman rose to her feet.

"Rumi Sabzwari," the woman said. She wore a medical mask and a blue lab coat, like the one my mother used to wear to work. A Governance doctor. Behind her specs, her eyes were young and weary.

I stepped into the room, and the door slid closed behind me.

The doctor motioned for me to follow her to the back of the room to what looked like a tall mirror. But when she pressed three fingertips to the mirror's sense pad, a light illuminated a chamber on the other side of the glass. Through the glass, I could see a plastic quarantine cell hooked up to tubes and monitors. Inside, asleep on a plain white cot, was Father.

"He's alive . . . ," I whispered. His skin was gray. Yellow secretions crusted his nose and mouth. Swollen purple skin puffed below his eyes.

"For the time being," the doctor said. Then she held out her gloved hand. "I believe you have something for me, Mr. Sabzwari?"

I dug into my pocket for Yesenia's vial. "How did you know I . . . ," I began to say.

But she shook her head resolutely. She wasn't going to tell me anything.

I passed her the vial, and without hesitation, she carried it back to her desk and carefully unscrewed the cap. She drew a small dose of the deep red liquid into a pipette, emptied this dosage into a tube, and secured the tube inside a small case. Then she closed the vial, still over half-full, and placed it in a freezer drawer inside her desk.

"What does this mean?" I asked. "What now?"

"Now we test its viability," she said, removing her gloves and placing them into a biohazard chute. "In the meantime, you must undergo the same chem baths and heavy-course antibiotics that field officers undergo after returning from Lower City. You must pass the same tests. . . ." Her voice trailed off as she keyed something into the DigiCloth mounted to her desk.

"But—" I looked over my shoulder at Father. "How much time does he have?"

She pushed her specs up the bridge of her nose and toggled a switch on her desk. "That's not our primary concern," she said.

The door behind me opened, and a man in full hazmat gear appeared. "Follow Dr. Massoud," she instructed me. "He will show you the facilities."

+ + + +

For the next two days, I passed through more scanners than I knew existed. I took a handful of pills at every meal, not knowing what they were. A team of nurses put me under anesthesia, and when I woke, my tattoo was gone. The skin on my chest and neck was pink and sore. The nurses gave me a cream to put on it.

No one offered any explanation. The doctors focused on their charts. Few looked me in the eye. I repeatedly asked after Father but was given no answer.

Then, on the third day, I woke to a fresh set of street clothes folded on my bedside table. I dressed quickly and hurried into the hallway, where the weary-eyed young doctor who'd taken the vial waited for me.

"You can thank your lucky stars, Mr. Sabzwari," she said. "The substance you brought back from Lower City has proven an effective virucide against your father's strain. We're not quite clear yet on the mechanism of its efficacy. But the important thing is that it works."

My heart pushed into my throat, and I let out a faint, involuntary sigh. "So, you're not going to *remove* him?"

She smiled slightly. "Come. Follow me."

I walked with her back to the dimly lit room where Father lay sleeping. The plastic quarantine cell around his cot was gone. The color in his skin had brightened. His fingers twitched lightly in his sleep. The doctor drew a small dose of red liquid into a syringe and shot it into Father's drip chamber. The bloodred medicine swirled in the bag. It was the third dose in as many days, she said.

"You've done Upper City an unprecedented service, Rumi. Now, of course, this will all be kept confidential. No civilians will know. But let me be the first to thank you." She extended her hand and gave me a firm handshake. "In the lab, we're calling the virucide RUMI-437. In your honor."

I forced a smile. "That's really not necessary."

"Of course it is," the doctor said. She placed her hand lightly on my shoulder. "Who knows how many lives you've saved by smuggling that little vial into St. Iago?"

"Please," I said. My face felt hot. "Can you call it something different?"

"If you'd like . . . ," she said, not looking up as she recorded the dosage and time into her chart. "You may sit with him now. He's no longer contagious."

I walked to the cot where Father lay sleeping and placed my hand over his. At my touch, Father blinked open his eyes and looked around the room—at the doctor, at the tubes in his arms and the bag of fluid. Then he looked at me, and his face softened.

"Rumi," he said. "You came back."

The doctor removed her gloves and placed them in the biohazard chute. "I'll leave you two alone," she said, and left the room.

For the next few hours, Father was full of questions. How long had he been asleep? How had I found a cure? What had happened to my face? I told him how Las Oscuras had captured and tattooed me. I told him about Cienfuegos and the Library and the Lighthouse. I told him how Auralee and her children lived off blood stew and how Beto had a cellar full of pisco. I did my best to describe the taste of roasted vizcacha, the symphony of the forest at dusk, the sharp stink of Paraíso. But it all sounded flat as it came from my mouth.

Father just shook his head.

"Those bastards . . . ," he said. "You never should have gone,

Rumi. How could I . . . How could your grandfather have gone on living if you hadn't made it home safely?"

I bowed my head. "Yes, Father."

"Still," he said with a slight smile. "You braved the wilds of Lower City and lived to tell the tale. How many citizens of Upper City can say the same?" There was a note of respect in his voice. He was talking to me like a man, not a boy. "And to think—you made this journey alone!"

I looked up. "I wasn't alone, Father. There was a girl." My voice faltered. To speak of Paz—to speak even her name—was nearly impossible. "A Lower City girl. She saved my life."

Father frowned. "You didn't tell her anything, did you?" His tone of respect disappeared. I was once again his disobeying child.

"I told her what I needed to tell her," I said. "To save your life."

Father shook his head. "You shouldn't have done that. You don't understand all the pieces at play." He scratched at the stubble growing thick on his jaw and neck. "You simply don't know who you can trust out there."

I sat back in my chair and crossed my arms. My fists clenched involuntarily. "I could trust her, Father."

He waved his hand dismissively.

My face flushed with heat. "No," I said. "It's not like that. She's the reason you're alive. I know what you think of Lower City. But you're wrong about Paz."

He pushed himself upright in his cot. "So, the girl has a name! And after spending a week in the company of this girl, you think you understand more about Lower City than I do? I find it difficult to believe that a son of mine could be so naïve."

A heavy silence hung between us. Father coughed into his

palm. Even weakened by the virus, he had the face of a man who never backed down. That must be why the Governance placed such confidence in him. Part of me wanted to drop the topic entirely. To treasure this moment that I'd risked my life to bring about. But another part of me couldn't let it go. I knew what I'd seen. The world simply wasn't as Father wanted me to believe it to be.

"There's something I need to know," I said, looking him square in the face. "What were you doing in Lower City the night of the attack?"

Father smiled and shook his head. "Now, Rumi. You know I can't talk about that."

But I was not about to back down. "I risked my life to save yours," I said. "I already know far more than any civilian should. I'm going to search for answers, one way or another. And my curiosity could get me in a lot of trouble." My pulse was racing. "I need to know. What business does the Governance have in Paraíso?"

Father rubbed the stubble on his face. Then he motioned for me to come closer. His voice dropped to a whisper. "You really want to know?"

I nodded.

Father squinted through the glass door behind me to be sure the doctor had left. "I was there to discuss our newest development. Soon St. Iago will acquire new lands."

"Lands?" I whispered. "What lands?"

He ignored my question. "That man you met—Solomon Cienfuegos—he's been on the Governance payroll for years. He and the Library elders serve as our eyes and ears in the region. They relay information. And when things get too heated, they serve as our fists. They stifle rebellion. Acts of terror have decreased dramatically since we formed an alliance with those men. In fact—"

Just then the door to the outer room slid open, and a lab tech stepped in. He exchanged the case in his hand for an identical one in the freezer drawer and then silently left the room.

Father waited a moment more before turning back to me. "I shouldn't be telling you any of this, Rumi. It's highly classified information. . . ."

"Please," I said. "I need to know."

Father looked at me. He seemed to be weighing his words carefully. "Let's just say that some good may come of the attack on me. You know the saying 'a good tragedy should never go to waste'?"

I shook my head.

"Look at it this way. The Governance can acquire land far more quickly through force than through diplomacy. After such a blatant, potentially devastating attack by Las Oscuras, the Security Council will easily approve new military action in the region."

My jaw tightened. "But what if these 'new lands' are people's homes?"

Father looked at me, incredulous. "What's this, Rumi? Has my son become a *sympathizer*? Those lands belong to whoever can use them best. You *know* this. Slums crawling with terrorists are by no means the best use for land with such potential."

I shook my head again. "I just don't understand. Why do we have to keep fighting? We won, didn't we? We have the petrol. We control the lithium flats. We have everything we need."

Father sighed. "That's where you're wrong. Across the globe, oil fields have become increasingly volatile. Upper Cities every-where are reaching their energy capacity. We have no choice but to expand." He crossed his arms over his chest and leaned back against his cot. "The invisible hand of the market doesn't negoti-ate, Rumi. Its demands must be met."

My skin tingled. A slow burn welled in my throat. "The Governance will never get away with it," I said, my voice rising. "I'll go public with what I saw. I'll tell everyone about the people living on those lands. They're *real people*, Father. They deserve—"

The door to the outer room opened again, and a short doctor in a blue lab coat peeked inside. "Is everything all right in here, sir?" the doctor asked.

"Yes, yes. No trouble," Father called back pleasantly. "It's just an emotional reunion."

The doctor nodded and continued down the corridor. The door slid closed.

Father turned back to me and sighed again. He seemed exhausted to have to explain to me such a simple truth. "Listen, Rumi," he said. "There's a fundamental aspect of humankind that you must understand if you want to succeed in life. People can justify any action that results in something they truly want." His voice was calm, almost resigned. "Sure, the citizens of St. Iago could prevent a military campaign. But the truth is *they don't want to*. People like to be safe, Rumi. To be free from hardship. We like our heliocycles and year-round strawberries." His face softened. "And there's nothing wrong with this! People will sacri-fice many things of their own volition—their liberties, their time, even their dignity—if it's for a cause they believe in. But they will never sacrifice their comfort."

Hot tears welled in my eyes. "You didn't answer me," I said.

"Which lands is St. Iago going to seize—Paraíso? Serena? The salt flats in the North? I bet all of these places are exactly the same to you."

But before Father could answer, the door slid open one last time, and the young doctor stepped into Father's quarters. "You may go now, Rumi," she said. It wasn't a request. "We'll keep your father for a few more days to monitor his recovery. You may visit, if you like."

"I know it sounds cruel, Rumi," Father said as I stood to leave. "But these are the realities of a civilized world. Sacrifices must be made in pursuit of greatness, of progress."

Father's words echoed in my head as I walked past dozens of unmarked doors—each with some secret behind it—and followed the white staircase down into the dusty sunshine. Father's cycle waited for me there. Cloud-seed aircraft circled overhead as I sped back home, releasing chemical compounds into the sky. Soon we'd have rain. I thought of the bumpy ride to Las Termas in the back of that ox-drawn cart. How the clouds had gathered slowly above my head as Paz rested against me. How we'd stayed that way for hours, watching the sky grow dim.

The invisible hand doesn't negotiate, Father had said. *Its demands must be met.*

I imagined a hand—hazy, like a ghost—floating over the trash hills. Beneath it, kids were sweating and coughing, searching for scraps. But the hand wasn't flesh and blood. It couldn't be scorched or poisoned. It didn't cough. It didn't hunger. It couldn't be held responsible. Just weeks earlier, Father's illness had seemed like the worst tragedy imaginable. How long ago that now seemed. How different the world had become.

My jaw clenched. You're wrong, Father, I thought.

I had no choice but to tell the people of St. Iago what I'd seen in Lower City—tell them about the military campaign, the expansion, the new lands. I didn't want to imagine what the Governance would do to the people who called those lands home.

Together, the people of St. Iago could fight this. We had to.

Old Man of Fear, Old Woman of Fear!
Young Woman of the Future,
 Young Man of Uncertainty!
You have tied my throat in knots;
You have crushed my fingers into clubs.
How I wish I could throw you from my back,
Loose your hold on my flesh and
 learn again to speak!
To say something true to these children,
 these people.
To say something true!

Oh, children. I am a coward. Perhaps you sense it. Perhaps you knew from the beginning. I am a coward, and you are my witnesses, you dwellers of the future. You wish to know more of the earth. You wish to know more because your minds were meant for wonder.

The gods gave me a story to tell you long ago, but I did not listen. I was afraid to tell it. And yet I see before me the deep, black circle of a mysterious well, and I realize there is nothing to fear. Who could fear the common horrors of men when the unknown stands before me, beckoning? What wonders await on the other side of my fear? Tonight, I shall tell you the story.

There once was a boy with bright-blue eyes who bore the

ancient name of a king. I remember him well. I remember his joyless laugh, and the way he cursed the stones when he stumbled in the street. How his voice made other children fall silent. But even though his voice was strong, the wall that rose between the Sea and the Sky made him shrink with fear. He feared his city's waters; he feared the darkness that would come. How would the sun shine on the fields, he wondered, once the waters rose? How would the wind blow through the trees?

Then one day his father told him a secret. Their family had been given a key to the shining city, an invitation to live on the other side of the wall. The boy listened, and his sharp eyes filled with hope. Here was their chance to escape their dying city, to flee their watery world.

But no. His mother and father agreed—to throw the key to this magical door into the ocean was the right thing to do. The only thing. The wall of stones was immoral, they said. Abominable. Inhuman.

When the boy heard these words, his eyes lost their brightness and turned brittle as ice. And he made a promise to himself that night. Someday, he swore, someday he'd earn his own key into the shining city. Someday, somehow . . .

The boy's father died not long after, and the boy refused to bless the body. It was his father's own fault, the boy thought. His stupidity had brought this death upon him. If only he'd taken the key to the city, if only he'd listened to reason. Soon after his father's death, the boy devised his plan. He knew now that there were doors in the wall. If only he could find a way to make himself invaluable, irreplaceable, then he could earn his rightful place in the kingdom of the heavens—a place his father so carelessly threw away.

And so he met the floods of his watery world with burnings.

Like the burning you will witness tonight.

But I'll tell you this. An enemy is only an enemy so long as they remain unclouded by contradiction. You see, the boy with the name of a king never understood this simple truth: that there are four powers in this world—the power to fear, the power to hate, the power to love, and the power to forgive.

Each of these you have known, dear children. And which is the greatest?

3 7

PAZ

In the east wing of Paraíso's Library, there's a door that locks without a key. Behind the door, a skinny flight of stairs leads deep underground to a room without daylight, where stacks of Old World paintings lean against the walls, rotting. Where damp eats into the pores of your skin.

This was the room where I was prisoned, together with my betrayer.

At first we didn't speak. Auralee would pace the room, searching for a chink in the walls, spitting curses at the cold gray stone. Sometimes she'd shoot me a glance that felt like a question. But I wouldn't even look her in the eye. Because of Auralee, I'd burn in front of everyone who knew me. And my ashes would mix with hers.

Sometimes a man with a smooth-shaved face came to fill our water. Other than that, we were alone. I chewed my fingernails raw while my belly crept toward my spine. My sleep wasn't sleep. My waking wasn't waking. Sometimes I dreamed of the world above. Sometimes I dreamed of Javi. Maybe this afternoon, at the peak heat of day, Javi would head down to the port and dive for clams. Maybe he'd sit on a sunny rock by the water and pry them open and suck out the meat and then fall asleep to the waves. How helpless he'd feel when he saw my name posted on the Lighthouse door. How ashamed. If only I could explain my side of the story.

"Oye, chica," I heard Auralee say. Her voice seemed to come from nowhere. It was the first either of us had spoke since we'd been down there.

I opened my eyes. She was standing with her back to me, eyeing one of the paintings in the room. Her gray jumpsuit hung off her skinny body like a sheet.

"Have you looked at these yet?" she asked.

I didn't answer.

In the painting, a group of pale armored men stood on a rocky hillside, the Cordillera in the background. In front of them crouched another man, bare-chested and brown-skinned, pointing at the earth, hot rebellion in his face.

Auralee pushed the painting aside to see the one behind it— a peaceful village, yellow with sunlight. A field in the background bloomed with wildflowers.

My jaw clenched. "I thought you said I wasn't your enemy," I muttered. Bitterness made my voice hard and cold.

"That's right," Auralee said, her back still to me. "You're not my enemy."

"Then why?"

She stood for a long while staring into the painting, bathing herself in the heatless warmth of its yellow sky. "I guess I was trying for a better life. For Ancho an' Violeta an' the babies." She turned to face me. Her cheeks sunk into the hollows of her skull, but her dark eyes still glinted sharp. "I just wanted a bit of rest. I was tired. I'm so tired. . . ." I remembered the ashen faces of Auralee's kids, the kettle of fox blood stew. How must it have felt with kids in her charge, on the run from Las Oscuras? I couldn't imagine.

She turned back to the sunlit village, and I felt the tightness in my chest soften. I rose to stand beside her, and she pushed the painted village aside. Behind it, a little boy in a worn hat and coat looked out from the canvas, his eyes pleading things words didn't know how to say.

"Where are they now, your kids?"

"I left 'em with Beto on my way to Serena," she said. "He'll do right by them till Ancho can care for them himself." Behind the painting of the boy, a ship on the ocean blew smoke into the sky. Auralee ran her fingertips over the brown, smoky curls.

"You know," she said. "If I could decide which things got kept and which things got thrown out—I think I'd hang on to these paintings."

"Like, if you got to plan out the world?"

She sucked at the skin beneath her thumbnail. "Yeah."

I looked back at the ship filling the sky with brown smoke.

"I know the first thing I'd throw out too," she said. "I'd throw out that goddam Lighthouse. Good riddance!"

I smiled a little, but deep down the thought made me sick. It was too much to think of myself inside. To imagine the roar of the crowd, the flames . . .

I changed the subject.

"I once rigged up a music player in an Old World apartment," I said. "The songs it played—a man singing with his guitar . . . It was one of the prettiest things I ever heard." Auralee pushed aside the painted ship. Behind it, a girl with braided hair had a vine growing out of her chest. The hole it grew from was ocean green.

"If it was up to me and I could plan out the world," I continued,

"I'd throw out all the other fancy Old World machines and furnishings. But I'd keep that music player."

Auralee looked back at me. "What about *that* place?" she asked, pointing up.

"What, Upper City?"

"Yeah," she said.

I thought for a minute. "I don't know," I said. "I'd tear down their walls, sure. And I'd throw out their chems and copters. But maybe the people deserve another chance."

Auralee shot me a glance and laughed. "Oye, weona, you're crazy! Those Upper City cuicos? They're *born* thinking they got a right to whatever they want. You think I don't want a warm coat on a rainy day? You think I don't want a roof that doesn't leak and medicine to keep my babies well? But that's the difference between us an' them. When they want something, they steal it and call it theirs. I'd give anything to light the first torch and throw it behind those walls."

Auralee pushed aside the strange girl's portrait to show a painting of a ghost-white woman lying naked across a bed of pillows. Her eyes looked sad and tired.

"What about all that stuff you said about being done with violence?" I asked.

Auralee spat on the floor, took a step back, and kicked a hole in the naked woman's belly. "I guess I changed my mind," she said.

The door opened then, and the man with the clean-shaved face came in to fill our water. He held his nose against the stink of us and hurried out the door again. My body tingled with its own emptiness. I leaned back against the stone wall and sank down to the floor.

"So Beto told you about San Pedro, huh?" Auralee asked.

"He told me a little," I said.

Auralee sat next to me and scratched at the scar inside her thigh. "Who knows? Maybe someday Ancho will take the kids up there, when he's older and strong. . . ." But her voice sounded flat, like a light inside her had gone dark.

"It's funny to think about it now," I said, "but I almost asked Rumi to go there with me. I had this crazy thought that, after he went home and saved his dad, maybe he'd come back to Paraíso to join me for the journey."

Auralee sat up straight, smirking. "No me jodas, weón," she said. "There's no way he'd come back here! I mean, I'm sure you two had something real special and all. But he's got a soft bed up there and water that doesn't make his mouth numb. There's no packs of wild dogs chasing him around, no tatted terrorists hiding in the shadows. Chuta, I bet right now he's kissing on some pretty Upper City girl, forgetting all about you."

I didn't say anything.

Auralee sighed. "Listen. I'm just telling it to you straight. I don't care how much he fancied those big green eyes of yours. There's just no getting around the power of living safe an' easy. It makes a person forget a lot of things."

I circled the tat on my chest with my thumb. "You're right," I said to Auralee. "I know. You're right."

Again, the door opened behind us, but this time I didn't turn. I assumed it was the baby-faced man again, checking to make sure we were still alive.

But then I heard his voice.

"Buen día, mija," Cienfuegos said. "I see you've made a friend."

Cienfuegos closed the door behind him. His cloak filled the doorframe.

With all my strength, I crawled across the stone floor and clung to the hem of his cloak.

"Señor," I said, kneeling at his feet. "Thank you for coming to hear what I—what we've got to say." I motioned behind me to Auralee, her arms wrapped around her skinny belly. "Me and Auralee, we talked it through, and if you let us go now, we'll disappear. We'll go north to the desert. Please, señor. Ten piedad. Have mercy on—"

But the old man didn't let me finish. He kicked me from his hem and stomped the heel of his boot onto my sinner's hand. "Mercy, mija?" he hissed. The bones in my hand crunched under his weight. "Your mission could have destroyed the lives of millions of people. *Millions*—do you understand this?"

I cried out and my eyes begged mercy, but he twisted his heel harder before lifting his boot. The release swept me with nausea. Hot tears filled my eyes.

"Thank God that the lands of Paraíso are so valuable." He dabbed at his forehead with the sleeve of his cloak. "Upper City has indicated that they'll uphold their contract."

Auralee glared at Cienfuegos. "What the hell are you talking about, old man?"

Cienfuegos got a strange look about him, almost a smile. "Soon, a mighty dam will be erected on these lands. Upper City engineers will build massive walls between the cerros—walls like nothing you've ever seen—and the heart of Paraíso will be transformed into a reservoir that will bring prosperity to our people. In fact, Paz, you and your fellow scouts have been instrumental in this project, gathering information about the valley. We couldn't have done it without your help. And for that, we thank you . . ."

At first I didn't understand what he was saying. His words—a dam, a reservoir—were hollow sounds. But soon the meaning turned clear. Upper City would build a new set of walls with a new purpose: to drown my home. The old Mercado, the forests where my mother had gathered her medicines, the plaza, the sacred grove, the paintings in the depths of the Library—Would all of these drown under a surge of water, as though they had never existed?

Cienfuegos knelt on the floor beside me.

"Come now, hija," he said, touching my chin with his wrinkled hand. "This can't have come as a surprise, can it? You must've known deep down that Paraíso's fate has always been in the hands of Upper City."

The comandante had told me that a system of strings held the world in place. He said that if you cut one string, the whole thing would fall into tangles.

But it wasn't so. It just wasn't so. There were some strings that could never be cut.

And with that, Cienfuegos stood and left the room, bolting the door behind him.

3 8

R U M I

The brightness of the city whirred past me as I sped home from the Stacks. Father had it wrong, I was certain. People would care what was happening in Lower City—people like Baba, like Laksmi and Wen. They'd be outraged. They'd join me in helping to stop it.

At home, I found Baba in the kitchen. He turned to me and smiled.

"Ah, Rumi. Sit, sit!" He took the kettle from the stove and poured hot water over a pot of sabz chai. The smells of my child-hood filled the kitchen.

Outside, a soft rain began to fall.

"He's going to get better," I said. "They said he's going to recover."

Baba took a seat across from me at the table.

"Yes," he said, nodding. "Just this morning, a man stopped by to tell me this very thing! He said you and your father would return home very soon." Baba looked so happy as he said this, so different from the man I'd found in the annex, staring blankly at his moldy tea. "Of course, the man also said that we are to say nothing about the incident. Always, we are to say nothing. What a quiet government we have, no?"

I tried to smile at this, but my conversation with Father still weighed on my mind.

Baba set his teacup on the table. "Something is troubling you, my child."

I shook my head. "I'm just tired, Baba. I've had a long couple of days, is all. . . ."

But Baba wouldn't accept this answer. He reached across the table and placed his hand on my arm. "Tell me, Rumi. What is it?"

I took a sip of tea. "Father is planning something . . . ," I said, and explained what Father had told me—about the alliance between the Library and the Governance, about the plans to acquire Lower City lands through military force.

When I finished speaking, Baba simply shook his head. He didn't seem shocked or angered. He didn't even seem surprised.

"Your father loves you fiercely," he said. "Such fierce love can make good men blind."

"But I've seen the people out there. They're my friends. . . ." The word sounded wrong the moment I said it. Yesenia and Auralee, Ancho and Beto, even Paz—could I really call them my friends? The word "friend" felt false, somehow. They were at once more and less than friends. They'd risked so much to help me, but I hardly knew them at all. "Lower City isn't full of devils and terrorists," I continued. "They're good people, Baba."

He smiled. "I have seen many years inside these walls, my child. Many, many years. My eyes have gone dull without a horizon to gaze upon. I have forgotten the brilliance of stars in an open field. And, until a few days ago, I had forgotten how it felt to burn with hope."

I bowed my head, ashamed. "I know," I said. "I should never have left like that."

But he shook his head. For a long moment he just watched me, his expression shifting subtly. "If you could see the light in your eyes, my child," he said at last. "If you could see how your face glows with all the things you have seen . . ."

We finished our tea in silence. Dusk turned to night with the rain still falling, and Baba rose to move to his chair in the living room. With a groan he sat and leaned back, and I covered his legs with a blanket.

"I died as an Animal and became Human," he said.

"Why should I fear?" I replied, squeezing his hand. *"When was I less by dying?"*

Baba closed his eyes, and I sat with him in the softly lit room as his breathing slowly roughened into snores.

But I couldn't sit still for long. My limbs were restless for motion. My chest ached with all the things I knew. I couldn't keep them to myself a moment longer. I grabbed my specs from the privacy antechamber and sent a message for Wen to meet me at Borlaug Square—that I was back and had something to tell him, something important.

On Father's vintage cycle, I flew through the city's empty streets. The night was cool from that day's rain. Streetlamps and manicured houses blurred past me. A dreampunk soundscape thundered in my ears.

Father's cycle, I thought. Father's cure. Father's protection. Father's city.

My specs whirled with ads for the latest SimPlay gaming system, ads for an excursion to the walled-in wilds of Omega-2, for a new line of body-form cycling jackets. Breaking news of

a thwarted bioterror attack on an unnamed Governance official scrolled across the bottom of my vision. The images of five
counterterrorism experts hovered in my periphery like mosqui-
toes, discussing the implications of a new military campaign.

A new campaign. So Father's plan was already in motion.

At Borlaug Square, I parked my cycle beneath the ladder. Wen
was late, as usual, and it surprised me to note how relieved this
made me. I thought that I'd want to tell him every detail about
Lower City, but now that I was here, I found myself growing
defensive of my memories. Had Wen been tattooed? Had his leg
been shredded by dogs or packed with maggots? Had he floated
downriver on a raft manned by a half-starved child?

At the base of the ladder, I leaned my head against a steel
beam, waiting, aching for something I couldn't name. I pictured
Paz—her wide smile, her filthy boots, her head on my chest in
that run-down hotel. I pictured the ocean. I pictured that night
on the beach around the bonfire. The music and dancing and
mountains of food. How Paz had sat beside me, her face glowing.
This was the world we lost, I thought. Wild forests and jade-green
rivers. The dazzling blue of the ocean, the flat blue of the sky. The
trust of one person in another. Openness, danger, possibility. This
world had always existed deep in my memory, in the salt of my
blood and the marrow of my bones.

Just then the sound of laughter came from across the square,
and I opened my eyes to see Wen and Laksmi walking toward me,
hand in hand. So they were together now. A couple. It surprised
me to realize how little I cared.

"How long have you been back, you wank?" Wen said, slapping my arm. "Why didn't you message me sooner?"

I had to work to form a smile. "Long story," I said.

"I bet it's a long story," Wen said. "I was ready to send, like, ten search platoons after you!" He handed me a marble to attach to my specs, and together we climbed the ladder to the door behind the screen. Laksmi lit a candle and sat across from me, twirling her long black hair into a bun at the back of her head, smiling in that way that used to leave me a stuttering puddle of desire.

Wen sat beside her. He flicked his hair from his eyes and examined my face. "What happened? Did shanty terrorists dump chems on you or something?"

I shook my head. "It was a tattoo. I had it removed."

"No shit, man! A tattoo on your face—that's *so badass!*"

"Yeah," I said. "But I don't think my father would have liked it much."

"Daddy's boy! I should've guessed. How's the old pops doing anyway? He wasn't at your house when I stopped by the other day—the day you left town."

"He's the same as always." I looked down. An ache swelled in my throat. This was my chance. To start spreading word of the Governance's plan. To stop the violence that my city was about to undertake. "Listen," I said. My voice hovered just above a whisper. "If I tell you guys something, something secret, would you promise not to tell anyone else until I say so?"

Wen and Laksmi nodded and leaned in close.

"My father's been working on this mission in Lower City—meeting people, forming alliances. He's been doing it for years." I looked back and forth between their faces, their eyes wide with anticipation. "Father was recently attacked by Las Oscuras. He nearly died. But here's the thing—the Governance is planning to use this attack to start another military campaign. I just saw it today on the news. They're going to use the attack as an excuse to steal Lower City land—land they've been trying to acquire for years."

Wen and Laksmi looked at each other. Then Wen sat back and let out a little laugh. "Jesus, Rumi! I thought you were gonna, like, reveal some big Governance secret or something."

I blinked. "But that's what I'm saying. It *is* a big secret, and we've got to do something about it. We've got to stop them. Those Lower City people—I've seen them. I've talked with them." I searched in vain for words that would help them see what I'd seen. "Our military campaigns have already poisoned their lands. And now we're going to take what little they have left. It's . . . it's savagery."

"You're calling *us* savages?" Laksmi said. "Did those shanty terrorists brainwash you or something?"

Wen rested one hand on my shoulder and one on Laksmi's. "Okay, okay. Everybody relax for just a second," he said. "Let's all make nice."

Laksmi shrugged his hand off her shoulder, but in a familiar, flirty way.

"I mean, I'll hand it to you, Rumi," Wen continued. "That's some pretty wicked, conspiracy-level shit if it's true. But you've got to admit that it's not *that* surprising. The Governance has never been—how shall I say—an altogether *charitable* organization. But everybody knows that. So. How about we set aside that political crap and you regale us with your harrowing tales of adventure!"

I stared down at my hands. My heartbeat echoed in my ears. It felt as though I were speaking to Wen and Laksmi from across a great chasm. The feelings I'd voiced in that derelict hotel—that

I was just one drop, that one drop could do nothing to stop the wave—came back to me, but they felt somehow hollow now, like an excuse for inaction.

I died as an Animal and became Human. What was Human, anyway? Humans built walls to block out what they feared. Humans rained down deadly chemicals to protect their own kind. Humans tattooed their faces so all would fear them.

Why should I fear? When was I less by dying?

I knew then what I had to do. I cleared my throat and looked up at my friends.

"I'm thinking of going back," I said quietly.

Laksmi lit a cigarette and glared at me in that contemptuous way that made me remember why I'd wanted her so badly. "You can't be serious," she said.

"There's this place I heard about. It's in the North—in the desert. Upper and Lower City exiles live there together. As equals. You guys could come with me, if you wanted."

I realized how ridiculous my words must've sounded. To Laksmi and Wen, Lower City was full of savages. Its people had no faces or names. How could a civilized person like me hope to live in peace with a faceless horde? Two weeks ago, it wouldn't have made sense to me either.

"What, and live like *them*?" Laksmi said. "No petrol. No citizen pills. Dirty water. Bands of terrorists. You've got to be fucking kidding me."

I shook my head. "It's not that I want to live like that. It's just . . . I don't think I can come back to living like *this*."

Wen smiled and draped his arm over Laksmi's shoulder.

"I dunno, mon ami," he said. "Leave St. Iago for good? Like, I get it. It'd be an adventure! But without a glorious return to the city of your birth, the sparkle's gone from it, you know? If you don't get to come home again, what's the point?"

Laksmi took a long drag from her cigarette and passed it to Wen. "I know you think you'd be righting the world's wrongs by leaving Upper City," she said, "but that's just not how things work."

I nodded and bowed my head. "I know," I said. But I also knew that my city was changed for me now. It wasn't my home anymore.

Wen stamped out the cigarette and stood. "We're about to head to Tique's for some SimPlay immersion. *Plague VI: Cairo Edition* came online yesterday. You should totally come."

"No, thanks," I said. "Not tonight." I was distracted, already working through a plan. Maybe the BulletRail to New Kingsport had been repaired by now, I thought. Maybe the Governance would be surveilling me more closely.

I had to be careful, I knew. But I also knew I had to find a way.

"Don't get me wrong, man," Wen said. "It's noble and all, what you want to do. But to be honest, it's just about the dumbest thing I've ever heard. Think about it for, like, five minutes and I bet you'll change your mind." He took Laksmi's hand and opened the door. "See you Monday."

As Wen's cycle whirred into the night, I set a record on the turntable. A man's voice sang in Spanish over the sad pluck of a guitar. Maybe I would never understand what Paz had been thinking that night by the clocktower beneath the full moon. Maybe I'd never understand why she'd pushed me away. But I knew I couldn't forget her. She had changed me for good. I couldn't go back to the way I was before.

I closed my eyes once more and leaned my head against the steel beam.

Paz the fleet-footed, I thought. Paz, the girl whose name means *peace*. The girl who knows no hunger. Whose hair smells like the earth. Whose hands are cool to the touch.

Whose hands, in mine, slowly begin to warm . . .

3 9

PAZ

Hunger broke Auralee before it broke me, and for days all she could do was cry. She'd been starving even before our prisoning, and now she had nothing left. So I started telling her stories—stories from the Old World journal, stories from Beto and Yesenia. A story is a powerful thing. You lose yourself between its beginning and its end. You forget.

It was the stories, I think, that conjured you.

It happened on the day Auralee stopped crying, the day she sat silent in open-eyed sleep, and I was left all alone in that stone-gray prison. In you walked, a miracle.

"I've come to collect your stories, oh children," you said in a voice like an angel.

It was a dream. It had to be a dream, didn't it? But I spoke to you anyway.

The Storyteller had come to see *me*.

"Señora, contadora," I said. "How can it be that you are here?"

You waved away my question with your hand. "I've come to collect your stories," you said again. "To hold them up like a lantern in the dark for the generations to come."

I looked at Auralee, but she said nothing. Her eyes were fixed on the air.

Your face was bright and round, your shoulders wide and sturdy. You looked so real. I could even smell the woodsmoke on your clothes.

"What stories?" I asked.

"The stories that give your breath its warmth, my child. The stories of your life!"

"What do you want to hear my stories for? So you can tell kids how not to be like me?"

You smiled. "I wish to collect them so that others might better know the world." You bent to sit on the stones between Auralee and me, and you nodded for me to begin.

"Tell me, child. What have you seen?"

So that others might better know the world.

A benediction.

"You know, they're gonna drown this place," I said.

"I know, child," you said. "I know."

"So why do you want to hear what I got to say? It's not like it matters anyway."

"Because stories create the world, my child. Our stories create the world. . . ."

Your face breathed tenderness into me. Your eyes softened mine.

They say you can change the meaning of a story just by the telling. When you tell a story, you get to decide who's the dragon and who's the hero and all that. You can spin light out of darkness and water out of sand. Maybe one way you tell it and everybody loves it, and you end up happy, but another way you tell it and you end up dead.

They're tricky things, stories.

As I looked at you, I knew I had to make sure I told this one true.

"To begin," I said, "I am Paz Valenzuela-Valenzuela de Paraíso. Daughter of no man, daughter of the jaguar. There's fire in my blood and the sea in my eyes. And this is my story. . . ."

The old woman listens to me, quiet as a ghost. When I've told my story from beginning to end, she dips her head and smiles. "My child," she says in a voice of whispered light. "There are four powers in this world: the power to fear, the power to hate, the power to love, and the power to forgive. Each of these you have known. And which is the greatest?"

And then, like an angel, she is gone.

When the door opens for the last time, it's Cienfuegos. His steps boom toward me. I don't struggle as the guard lifts me from the floor, don't even push against him.

But I turn my head to look at Cienfuegos as the guard carries me up the stairs. I want him to see me. To know that I am Paz de Paraíso, daughter of no man. That I am still here.

her hair was the same tangled mess of jet-black curls. But her arms—arms that had once been strong enough to bind Paz into submission—looked too weak to even lift herself from the ground.

I tried to come up with an explanation but found only questions. Auralee had been on the run for years. This wasn't even her home. How had the Library elders found her?

Cienfuegos kicked Auralee in the stomach, and the crowd cheered as she curled her head to her knees. But when Cienfuegos held up his hands, everyone fell silent. The darkness beyond the Lighthouse sucked and hissed with breaking waves. The air felt charged, like the moment just before lightning strikes.

Then Cienfuegos spoke again.

"Paz de Paraíso," he said.

I lost my breath.

Somewhere in the crowd, a woman started sobbing. The group of teenagers clung to each other, turning their heads from the Lighthouse tower. But I couldn't look away. The door opened, and the men came out carrying her. They threw her in the dust beside Auralee.

And the ocean crashed. And the wind swirled.

Her head hung limp. I couldn't see her face.

I thought I might vomit or faint. I shouted her name into the night, but my cries were lost among the roar of the crowd. A mistake, I thought. A horrible mistake. Without thinking, I started shoving my way through the crowd, trying to reach her, to take her in my arms and flee with her into the forest. But the spectators were packed too tightly. I couldn't find a path forward. In desperation, I pushed to the edge of the crowd and sprinted through ankle-deep water toward the Lighthouse. The loose rocks of the jetty slid away beneath the slap of my boots.

40

RUMI

It was dusk when I arrived back in Paraíso, but somehow I managed to find the gulch north of the city. In a nearby thicket, I stashed Father's vintage cycle, which I'd stocked full of dehydrated meats, respirators, backup solar fuel cells, extra boots.

The unmistakable reek of Paraíso stung my nose as I crept downhill over downed power lines and puddles of filth. I thought of the last time I'd walked this path, when Paz and I left Paraíso at dawn that first morning. It almost hurt to think how close I was to finding her. I wondered if she'd made it back yet from the North, or if she was still on her journey. The easiest way to find out would be to ask Cienfuegos. But after the things Father had said, I didn't know if I could trust Cienfuegos anymore—or if he would trust me.

As I walked, I came across a line hung with clothes. Without a second thought, I stripped down to my underwear, stuffed my cycling jacket into my pack, and hung the rest of my clothes on the line. My shirt and pants looked so bright against the Lower City clothes beside them. I switched out my clothes for a pair of pants and a faded shirt from the line, and then I draped a woolen poncho over my shoulders to hide my pack beneath it. The fabric smelled of woodsmoke. I smiled to think what Paz would say when she saw me like this.

The streets were silent save for the distant draw of the sea. Strange, I thought, that no one would be around. A hint of daylight remained in the western sky. Where was everyone?

Just then a creaky door opened ahead of me and a woman and three young children stepped into the street. Behind them, a bearded man carrying an oil lamp came through the door. The man lifted the smallest child onto his shoulders, then glanced up the street, meeting my eyes.

My skin went cold. My hand flew instinctively to my jaw, where my tattoo used to be. Then I remembered that it was gone—replaced by smooth, pink skin. With a sinking feeling, I realized that this disfigurement probably helped me better fit in.

The man nodded and I nodded back, and the family began their walk downhill. I followed behind at a distance, watching the oldest girl pick up pieces of trash from the road and throw them at windows as she passed.

It wasn't until the family turned south at the port that I realized where they were headed.

The Lighthouse, I thought. Tonight must be another burning.

Memories of the last burning made me shudder—the sunken cheeks and cracked lips of a woman who could barely hold up her head. But as intolerable as these memories were, I knew that such a gathering would likely make it easier to find Paz.

A low murmur hummed in the air as I neared the coastline, and I rounded one last corner to see thousands of people standing, torchlit, around the Lighthouse, its white and red stripes twirling skyward, its glassed-in top charred with greasy residue.

I made my way down the pier through the crowd, searching for

Paz. On a rocky outcrop where the land met the ocean, a group of teenagers huddled together, away from the larger crowd. I edged toward them. Perhaps Paz would be among them, or maybe she'd be joining them soon. As I came closer, I noticed several were crying. Others looked angry. Under their breath, they swore the same bitter curses I'd heard Paz use so many times.

"Conchadesumadre," one whispered.

"Una mierda," another said.

I swallowed hard, wishing Paz were there. She had laid the footing on which I could stand in this world. Without her, Lower City seemed to shift like waves.

Just then an uneasy silence fell over the crowd, and I turned to see the door at the base of the Lighthouse open. Five robed elders with long beards emerged, and one looming figure stepped forward to speak. Solomon Cienfuegos. Though I couldn't understand his words, the boom of his voice was full of a deep sense of danger. It was the same authoritative voice used by Governance officials on the news, railing against terrorism.

Those who seek to destroy our freedoms have grown stronger than ever, I imagined him saying. *They wish to make us weak with fear. But our city stands united against them. The threat is ever present, and so we must be vigilant! We will prevail over evil!*

I shuddered as the crowd around me roared approval. But the group of teenagers, separate from the rest, just shook their heads.

That's when Cienfuegos spoke three words that I understood perfectly.

"... Auralee del Campo ...," he said.

The door opened, and two men dragged Auralee between them, tossing her into the dirt at Cienfuegos's feet. She wore the same frayed jumpsuit from her hideout in the mountains, a

Cienfuegos unsheathed his knife. No, I thought. No, no, no! I was so close to her. So close, I could see the dirt on her cheeks and the vapor from her breath. I ran faster, gasping the cold, salty air, not knowing what I'd do when I reached her. But I didn't make it in time. Stumbling helplessly over the jetty's rocks, I watched as Cienfuegos sliced open her shirt.

That's when I saw it—the thin circle at the center of her chest. Unmistakable. I stopped cold. I couldn't catch my breath. His knife seemed to pierce my own breastbone.

One of *them*. It couldn't be.

Shouts of anger flew from the crowd as Cienfuegos displayed the mark. A man at the front of the crowd spat in Paz's face. A sound welled up in me then—a moan in the vague form of words.

"Oh god," it said. "Oh god, no."

At this sound, a single face at the edge of the crowd turned to look at me. His face was angular, pulled taut by a long ponytail. His eyes seemed to both ask and tell me something. I looked back at him, helpless.

Cienfuegos continued to speak, but I had stopped listening. All I could think of was the bloodlust in his ice-blue eyes as I'd stood by his side weeks earlier, watching the Lighthouse dance with flames. And I remembered his words.

When you return to Upper City, he'd said to me, *you can tell your father that this is how we deal with terrorists.*

Maybe it was some kind of trap, I thought. Maybe Paz had been set up by the elders, by Cienfuegos. My fingers tingled with the urge to shout at the top of my lungs and reveal who Cienfuegos really was—a double-dealing, self-seeking traitor who, year by year, was selling off these people's homeland for his own gain.

But a nagging question kept me silent. Why would Cienfuegos

frame Paz as a terrorist? He had nothing to gain from such an act. And how did Auralee fit into all of this? I tried to piece together the facts, but they just wouldn't fit. Then I remembered the fear in Paz's eyes at the base of Serena's clocktower. I remembered the rip in her shirt as Auralee had held a knife to her neck. I remembered the hate in her voice the night before she'd saved me from Las Oscuras and told me to follow her. Had she been working for them all along? I had wanted to trust her so badly that I hadn't bothered to ask her how she'd escaped that day or why she'd chosen to save me. I'd stuffed such questions beneath my own gratitude and never taken them out to examine them.

Cienfuegos motioned for the guards, who lifted Paz and Auralee from the dirt. Paz's head was bowed, but Auralee met Cienfuegos's eyes. She tried to spit, but her mouth was dry. The crowd shouted her down with curses and jeers. Then Paz looked up, and the crowd fell silent. She said nothing, but her stare blazed with indomitable wildness.

Cienfuegos nodded, and the guards turned, carrying the girls between them. Paz's bare feet dragged in the dirt as they took her through the Lighthouse door.

That was the last thing I saw of her: the dirty soles of her feet.

She was gone.

41

RUMI

The fire burned for over an hour, swelling from faint orange flickers to a hellish blaze. No one spoke. I covered my nose with my sleeve and willed myself not to think of the flames scorching her hair, kissing her lips, devouring her sea-green eyes. I tried not to think at all.

Eventually the flames dwindled and the crowd dispersed. They walked toward the city, to their homes. But I went the opposite direction, climbing over slick rocks to sit beside the ocean. The moon cast a cold sparkle onto the waves. I cupped it in my hand. A waning moon.

All along. She'd been working for them all along.

What was her plan? And why had she let me go? I'd never know the answers, and the questions exhausted me. I looked out at the water, overwhelmed with a feeling that wasn't quite sadness. It felt like a hole, like a tear in the fabric of myself. As though a breeze were blowing through me, hollowing me out. I felt dizzy and lost. Fragmented.

Paz was gone. And I was here.

Just then I heard a sound from behind me. A figure with a long, dark ponytail climbed the rocks toward me. As he came closer, I recognized him as the person who'd turned and stared at me in the crowd. He crouched beside me.

"You are from Upper City?" he said quietly in English.

I nodded, taken aback by the question.

He took a cigarette from a tin in his pocket, lit it with the one already between his teeth, and handed it to me. I took it from him, and he sat down.

He smiled slightly. "I heard about you." With his cigarette, he gestured at my face. "What happened to your ink?"

"I'm sorry," I said, confused. "Who are you?"

"I'm Javi." He extended his hand, and I took it.

"How'd you know who I was?"

"Are you kidding me?" he said. "You've got Upper City written all over you." He took a long drag on his cigarette and leaned back against the rock.

"I came back here for her," I said. The words caught in my throat. My eyes turned glassy.

Javi nodded. "So you didn't know."

"I didn't know."

We sat in silence. The crowd had gone. Only the elders remained, standing in a cluster at the base of the Lighthouse. Javi took another long drag from his cigarette and then flicked it into the ocean.

"I have no idea what I'm going to do," I said. "I had this absurd idea that I'd leave Paraíso with Paz and go north. But without Paz, I just—"

I couldn't finish.

Javi sniffed and spat on the rocks below. "That's kind of what I came to ask you about." He took another cigarette from his tin, lit it with mine, and handed mine back to me. I held the burning thing between my fingers, watching the dried tobacco turn to ash.

"The other girl who died here today—Auralee del Campo— she's the one who turned Paz over to the elders, thinking she'd earn herself a pardon. A few days ago, this old drunk from the North brings all these kids to Paraíso, looking for her, saying Auralee was supposed to meet him and pick up the kids. But she never came."

"Beto?"

Javi nodded. "Anyway, he mentioned you. He said he wouldn't trust a soul but you to care for the kids. I told him I didn't know you and didn't think I ever would. But he thought differently. So when I saw you in the crowd, I thought, hey—the old borracho was right!"

I stared out at the waves. It was Auralee's fault that Paz was dead. And now Beto wanted me to look after her kids? I shook my head. "No way," I said. "Why would I help the person who . . . who . . . ?"

Javi looked at me and nodded, then he turned to face the sea. He took another drag from his cigarette and exhaled slowly. "They're just kids," he said. "When does the vengeance end?"

I thought of Ancho and Violeta and the rest of the kids in that rotting house. Was it their fault Auralee had loved them so fiercely that she'd sacrificed Paz's life to save theirs?

"I'm hiding Beto and the kids in a safe place," Javi continued. "They're sweet kids. But they can't stay in Paraíso—not after Auralee's been branded a terrorist."

I took a single drag on the cigarette. The smoke scorched my lungs, and my stomach turned. The flames, the smoke. I flicked the red-hot stub into the darkness and thought of all I'd left behind. My friends, my family, my city, my memories. Everything familiar and easy and safe. And what for? To continue seeking revenge?

"Can you take me there?" I asked.

Javi smiled a wide, bright smile, and in it I saw Paz.

Peace.

42

PAZ

uralee and me sit back-to-back on a pile of wood, our hands bound. Auralee's voice is so hoarse I can hardly hear it. Our death is upon us, clotting our ears.

"Tell me another one of your stories, will you?" she says. Her voice sounds small inside the thick glass walls, black with rancid soot.

So I close my eyes.

The words come all at once from somewhere outside of myself. They float up from the city like ghosts. They rise like mist from the sea.

"The pain is a black and bitter ocean, and we've got to make it clean," I say in a voice that isn't quite mine. *"When the drop left its ocean home and returned—it became a pearl. It couldn't go back to the way it was before."*

I swallow each word, making it mine. Nothing—not Cienfuegos, not even the flames—can take these words from me. And all of a sudden, I'm floating on top of the cool green ocean, the Old World buildings drowned underneath me, the gray-white clouds up above, threatening rain.

One drop in the ocean became a pearl. Could one drop somehow change the wave?

"Where's that come from?" Auralee asks me.

I open my eyes. "I don't know," I say. "I can't remember."

Outside the Lighthouse, the crowd begins to roar.

Everyone is out there. Everyone I know.

"¡Listos!" I hear Cienfuegos shout.

If only I could've told the others about the Library's dealings with Upper City. Javi, Beto, Mami, Yesenia—anybody. If only they knew. What could they have done?

"¡Apunten!" Cienfuegos shouts.

Auralee takes my hand. The hot stench of Paraíso swirls together with the salty spray of the sea. My city. My home. Memories built atop a million memories.

World without end . . .

"¡Fuego!"

The flames catch the tinder and lick at my feet. *From the top of my head to the bottom of my foot, all I am is tongue. What am I?*

Fire, I think. Fire, fire, fire.

And then there she is. The old woman, the spirit, the Storyteller. Perhaps she is the death angel. Perhaps my stories to Auralee conjured her again. Perhaps she is here because on Festival nights, the world is pierced. And as dark comes on, a kind of magic spills over from some other place—the magic of dreams and nightmares and other miracles that have no name.

On Festival nights, anything is possible.

Here she is, her face shining, untying our wrists. She's showing us a ladder. She's beckoning with weather-worn hands, saying something I can't quite hear.

But I know the words without hearing a sound.

Run, she's saying. *Oh, my children, run.*

Old Man of Creation, Young Man of Creation,
Old Woman of Stories, Young Woman of Truths,
Though my throat is tied in knots,
Though my fingers are crushed into clubs,
I have thrown the beast of fear from my back.
I have loosed its hold on my flesh and walked
　　　　into the fire
To say something true. To say something true.

O h, children. What can I do, I who have lived my life? I have lived my life, and it has left me here, together with you, as ashes rain down all around us. I am a teller of stories, and I am a coward. But even a coward finds courage sometimes.

Do you remember the story of the Sky and the Sea—how the Sea's dark waters heaved and surged? How the Sky was afraid, so he gathered up stones? This story is true, children—but as you well know, in this world some stories hold more truth than others. For what is right and wrong in a world such as ours, when we do not know how this story shall end?

I'll leave you now with one final story. Listen carefully, and heed it well:

Two girls run barefoot through the forest. Their hair is singed, but they are unharmed. They run swiftly, with purpose, but they do not run with fear—for they have stared death in the face, and they know that fear is his only weapon. If you see these girls running barefoot, give them your bread and your water. Wish them blessings on their journey. Give them your bread and water, for they are tired and thirsty, and they have a long way yet to go. . . .

R U M I

And now I'm walking. Ancho hikes alongside me with a long stick to help him keep up with my stride. Javi walks behind, pulling the young ones in a wagon. The littlest ones take turns riding on my shoulders. We follow Old World highways, mostly. The highways are less direct, but there are many of us, and the mountains are steep.

I traded Beto my heliocycle in exchange for maps, a loaded gun, and a list of trusted contacts along our route. He threw in some food and a bottle of pisco for free. We're heading to Serena first to find Yesenia. I'm bringing her the information I have of the Library's dealings with St. Iago. Yesenia will know best what to do—if there's anything that can be done.

After Serena, I don't know. I hope one day we'll make it to San Pedro. Though on more difficult days, I wonder if San Pedro is just a myth. A place made of dreams.

I still fall asleep to questions. I wonder what my life would be like if I hadn't left. Would I fall back into the normal rhythm of school and SimPlay, tea with Baba and applications for uni? Would Father be proud of me? But mostly I find myself wondering when it was that Paz changed her mind and decided to sacrifice her own life to save mine. When did she decide to help me instead of doing whatever it was Las Oscuras had wanted her to do? In my dreams, I hear her speak my name and I cling to her arms as dogs try to drag me down.

"Rumi," she says. "Listen to me. Don't let go, Rumi."

Sometimes I dream of a record player sending messages across a vast canyon, and it makes me feel so small—like one drop in an ocean wave. But in the morning, I feel the weight of Violeta on my shoulders, I sense the rhythms of Ancho matching his steps to mine, and the chasm of the Breach seems to close ever so slightly.

One day we passed through a graveyard, and Javi asked Ancho to translate the headstones so he could practice his English. Ancho obeyed enthusiastically.

"*I will trust, and I won't be afraid,*" he translated, then ran ahead to find another.

"*It's not the whole of life to live,*" he said. "*And not the whole of death to die.*"

But at a smooth granite headstone overgrown with grass, he paused. "I don't know about this one," he said. "The words say that . . . there's *something*—it doesn't say what—something that's all tangled up, like vines growing on a wall. And that this *something*, whatever it is, is pushing itself free, like moss growing out of a stone." He turned to Javi. "But that doesn't make sense."

I stared at the words, disbelieving. Paz had translated the same epitaph on the first day of our journey. On that hot afternoon, I had asked her what "it" was. *What* was tangled? *What* was breaking free? But now I understood. It was life. Life tangled us all together like vines weaving, inextricable, one from the other, tender young things new with possibility, bright-green moss sprouting from a stone. We had the power to encircle the rigid, brutal structures of the world, not by becoming rigid and brutal ourselves, but by becoming more lush and green and vibrantly alive. Who knew where this life would take us next?

I understood this because of Paz.

Then I got an idea.

"Hey, Ancho," I said. He peeked at me over the granite slab. "I run and run and never walk, sometimes whisper, never talk. I have a bed, but I don't sleep. I have a mouth, but I don't eat. What am I?"

Ancho stared back at me, confused.

"I think it's a riddle," Javi said.

"Yep," I said. "It's a riddle. So? What am I?"

Ancho scratched his cheek and looked at the sky. I waited, letting him think it through, and looked out over the cemetery. Blanco and Joaquín tumbled about in the grass. Violeta sat beneath a tree, weaving a garland of wildflowers for her hair.

I looked back at Ancho. He was still thinking, biting his lip at the corner of his mouth. Trying to reason through a problem that seemed to have no solution.

"Well?" I said at last. "Give up?"

AUTHOR'S NOTE

When I first set foot in Chile in 2008 on a gig for a small travel guidebook, I had no idea it would one day be the setting for this novel. Twenty-three years old, traveling alone internationally for the first time in my life, I stepped off the plane in Santiago and asked for directions to the bus I needed to catch. That's when my stomach dropped. Although I'd lived abroad in a Spanish-speaking country before, and although half of my family is Cuban, I could hardly understand a word of Chilean Spanish.

But over the next several months, I fell in love with Chile. As I traveled, the Chileans I met along the way taught me about their country—about its politics and history, its food and language, its music. I still remember one windy evening, sitting outside a cabaña in Guanaqueros, when my host played for me Violeta Parra's exquisite song "Volver a los diecisiete." *You've never heard Chilean music before?* he asked, incredulous. *You poor thing!* He proceeded to share his whole collection of Chilean music—traditional cueca and Nueva Canción and the haunting melodies of Víctor Jara, a Chilean musician and activist who was tortured and executed during the brutal US-backed coup of dictator Augusto Pinochet.

Language in Chile was deeply connected to poetry, that much was clear, and Chilean poetry was connected to the land. But land was also connected to music, and music to history.

I had so much to learn.

In the years following that first travel-writing gig, my enchantment with Chile never left me, and I began piecing together a story set in a future version of Valparaíso. But it wasn't until I returned to Chile years later that the story started to take the shape of the novel you hold in your hands. In 2015 I once again boarded a plane, this time with a rough map of Paz and Rumi's journey and a whole host of questions and curiosities. I was eager to learn more about this country that had given birth to musicians like Violeta Parra and poets like Gabriela Mistral, a country whose people had such an uncommon spark of wonder, such a dedication to place, such a spirit of defiance. On this second trip, I learned about the ceaseless battles that everyday Chileans fought to protect their wild rivers and lands from megadams and multinational corporations, about the many ways that distant countries had wielded power and destruction over a place where they'd never set foot—all of which had been taking place for decades, for my entire life, with me none the wiser. It made me think of a book called *Slow Violence and the Environmentalism of the Poor*, in which Rob Nixon defines slow violence as the "violence that occurs gradually and out of sight, a violence of delayed destruction that is dispersed across time and space . . . that is typically not viewed as violence at all." In this book, Nixon asks readers: How do we tell stories of violence when they happen across vast distances of space and time, when it's so hard to show how one action is connected to another?

In other words: How do we make visible the web of the world?

The colonization of the Mapuche people, the largest indigenous population in Chile, is one such story of slow violence. I knew very little about the Mapuche before coming to Chile this second time, but bit by bit I learned of their history. Like so many indigenous populations across the Americas, theirs is a story of resistance that has unfolded over centuries and continues to this day.

Before the Spanish arrived in the sixteenth century, the Mapuche called a huge region in the south of present-day Chile their home—from the foothills of the Andes to the Pacific Ocean, and from the Mapocho River to the island of Chiloé. The Spanish, insatiable in their quest for gold, arrived in this vast Mapuche territory intent on forcing the Mapuche people to work as slaves. But the Mapuche—led by legendary fighters like Lautaro, Pelantaro, and Caupolicán—defended themselves fiercely. For centuries, their warriors fought back against colonization, first against the Spanish and later against the Chilean state. However, after hundreds of years of resistance, the Mapuche suffered a series of massive defeats against the Chilean army, and the Chilean state began to sell off the most fertile Mapuche lands to private farmers and forestry companies, forcing the Mapuche onto degraded territories that represented a fraction of their ancestral home.

In recent decades, after the fall of the Pinochet dictatorship, the Chilean government claimed it would begin returning some of these ancestral lands to the Mapuche people, who today represent roughly 10 percent of the Chilean population. But this has mostly been an empty promise. Some Mapuche groups have started to take matters into their own hands, attacking forestry trucks and carrying out other violent acts of protest in the region. These groups have demanded that the Chilean government return the lands that were stolen from their ancestors. As of this writing, they have vowed to continue to fight until their demands are met.

In *Under This Forgetful Sky*, I chose to imagine a future in which this present-day conflict leads to Mapuche autonomy and the reclamation of their ancestral lands. In this imagined future, people from the sovereign Mapuche Nation have earned widespread respect throughout Lower City due to the success of their resistance. But their sovereignty has come at a price: Upper City elites control the surrounding area's resources, and since the Mapuche Nation has refused to have anything to do with Upper City, their daily lives are fraught with danger.

In this imagined future, as in the past, the cycle of power and resistance continues. It's a system of strings. A web of interconnection. A slow violence that extends backward and forward for centuries. But this web of connection doesn't lead only to violence. It can also lead to understanding, to solidarity, to hope. The Storyteller, a Mapuche shaman who at first tells her stories out of fear, finds in her connection to Paz the courage to rebel. Paz and Rumi find similar courage in each other. Their connections to each other give them strength, help them imagine new possibilities in the world around them.

I hope you find courage in their story too. The world we share is full of violent systems that are so much bigger than us—climate change, refugee crises, resource wars. It's easy to feel like we're just one drop in the ocean, powerless to change the waves of history. This novel imagines the story of one possible future. But in reality, the story of our time is far from written. As writer Margaret Atwood says, there is no inevitable future. The real story is unfolding between us all the time. It's a living thing we create together, green and new—like vines encircling a wall, like moss springing up through stone.

ACKNOWLEDGMENTS

Many, many strings pulled on mine as I wrote and revised this novel.

Thank you to everyone in Chile who opened their homes and shared their stories with me—to Pablo, who showed me the ins and outs of Valparaíso on multiple hours-long walks through the city; to Patricio in Guanaqueros, who shared his entire music collection and, over a feast of grilled mariscos and homemade goat cheese, told me the legend of La Lechuza; to Lolo in La Serena, whose family helped me learn the names and uses of the region's medicinal plants; to Rosario, Juan, Mariante, and Wenewen, who shared over many meals the story of their family's spiritual journey in the heart of Mapuche ancestral lands; to Roberto and Alejandra in Vicuña, who offered me homemade licor de chirimoya and volumes of Gabriela Mistral's poetry under some of the clearest skies in the world; to Juanfe, who speculated about the histories and futures of the small fishing villages in the fjords of northern Patagonia as we drove through tunnels of giant nalca leaves; and to Gabriel in Cochrane, who recounted the incredible story of activism by a group of small-town sheep farmers who successfully prevented a multinational corporation from building a megadam in their community. For the generosity and warmheartedness of everyone whose path crossed mine, for the gift of an unqualified welcome, for all of this—and for the impossible blues and greens of its waters—I am forever grateful to the country of Chile and its people.

Thank you also to my writing mentors and teachers at every stage—especially to Chris Coake, who guided me through early versions of this manuscript, and to Deborah Achtenberg, Jane Detweiler, and Vicki Lane for their insights at various moments in the drafting process. And thank you to those teachers who helped me understand the kind of writer I wanted to be in the first place—to Alan Michael Parker, Douglas Glover, Brenda Flanagan, and Luke Butler. Your words of praise and critique have stayed with me for many years, little guides and cheerleaders when I needed them most.

Thank you to my agent, Andrea Somberg, for believing in this story, even as a pandemic was beginning to sweep the world. And thank you to everyone at Atheneum Books for Young Readers—to Justin Chanda; Reka Simonsen; Jeannie Ng; Tatyana Rosalia; Michael McCartney; and Stephanie Evans Biggins; but especially to my editor, Sophia Jimenez—your care and attention to these words and characters continue to amaze me.

Thank you to Ana Mariella Bacigalupo, whose anthropological work with Mapuche shamans greatly informed the character of the Storyteller, and to Rob Nixon, whose concept of "slow violence" forever changed how I see the world.

Thank you to everyone who read and offered feedback on this book over the years—especially to Jorge Inzunza for insights into everything from Chilenismos to Chilean fauna—¡un montón de gracias!—and to Holli Flannagan and Sarosh Arif, for helping me see the blind spots in my own experience. Thank you also to Ali McGhee, Josey Dixon, Alicia Araya, Andy Kifer, Bellamy Crawford, Lyra Butler-Denman, and my Appalachian State critique pals.

To the many coffee shops where I wrote for hours on nothing but espresso—Albina Press in Portland, Oregon; Bibo and Homage in Reno, Nevada; Battlecat in Asheville, North Carolina; and Zuma in Marshall, North Carolina—bless you.

To my family, especially my parents—your continued support in so many ways has meant everything to me.

And lastly, overwhelmingly, to Alex. Thank you. This book would still be in a drawer if it weren't for you.